Gripping Novels of
Crime and Detection

SIGNET
DOUBLE
MYSTERIES:

COP OUT

and

THE LAST WOMAN
IN HIS LIFE

SIGNET Mysteries You'll Enjoy

COP OUT

AND

THE LAST WOMAN IN HIS LIFE

by

Ellery Queen

A SIGNET BOOK

NEW AMERICAN LIBRARY

TIMES MIRROR

PUBLISHER'S NOTE

These novels are works of fiction. Names, characters, places, and incidents are either the product of the author's imagination or are used fictitiously, and any resemblance to actual persons, living or dead, events, or locales is entirely coincidental.

NAL BOOKS ARE AVAILABLE AT QUANTITY DISCOUNTS WHEN USED TO PROMOTE PRODUCTS OR SERVICES. FOR INFORMATION PLEASE WRITE TO PREMIUM MARKETING DIVISION, THE NEW AMERICAN LIBRARY, INC., 1633 BROADWAY, NEW YORK, NEW YORK 10019.

 SIGNET TRADEMARK REG. U.S. PAT. OFF. AND FOREIGN COUNTRIES
REGISTERED TRADEMARK—MARCA REGISTRADA
HECHO EN CHICAGO, U.S.A.

SIGNET, SIGNET CLASSICS, MENTOR, PLUME, MERIDIAN AND NAL BOOKS are published by The New American Library, Inc., 1633 Broadway, New York, New York 10019

First Printing (Double Ellery Queen Edition), June, 1982

1 2 3 4 5 6 7 8 9

PRINTED IN THE UNITED STATES OF AMERICA

COP OUT

We dedicate this
our fortieth anniversary novel
TO OUR READERS,
here and abroad,
who have so loyally followed our adventures in print.

No man is an island, entire of itself.

—*Donne, 1624*

CHAPTERS

Wednesday

The Bag

It had been a good Indian summer and there were still
leaves on the tiring maples behind the plant. It was the
evergreens that looked expectant, under the moon they
stood like girls waiting to be asked by the tall dark
handsome sky.

Howland turned away from the window, unadmiring.
He hated November. November meant December, and
December meant Christmas bills. He had no feeling for
nature or religion or almost anything else but money. It
seemed to him that for all his fifty-seven years he had
been reaching out for money that would stick to his
fingers. The irony was that so much of it had passed
through them.

He compared his watch with the steel hands over the
Manila driftwood door, lettered in computer-type characters CURTIS PICKNEY, *General Manager*.

Almost ten.

Howland went back to his desk. He studied the payroll.

So near and yet so far is the story of my life.

It had started with his first job out of the commercial
course at New Bradford High. Old man Louie Wocjzewski

had taken him on to tend register in the sandwich shop across the blacktop from Compo Copper and Brass. It had seemed to him then that there could not be so much cash in the world. They were working six-day shifts in those days and eight to nine hundred dollars a week had gone through the register. What he had got from it was twelve greasy singles, counted out in cautious cadence by old Wojy every Saturday night.

It had been worse at The Taugus County National Bank during his cage days when he had handled thousands belonging to everyone in town but Teller Howland. He had not even been able to afford a checking account at first because he had just married Sherrie-Ann and she had stupidly got herself pregnant and sick and then aborted in a mess of hospital and doctor and drug bills, she was still that way throwing their lousy few dollars around like he was a millionaire, my personal dollar drain, Howland's Sewer I ought to call her. Why I didn't ditch her long ago I'll never know, she even makes rotten chowder.

He sat down at his desk before the greenbacks.

He had felt the tiny kick of hope when Curtis Pickney hired him for the new New Bradford branch of Aztec Paper Products. Pickney had spoken rapidly of company expansion, opportunities for advancement (to what?), fringe benefits (and no union), salary to start $103 (take-home $86.75, but you know those g.d. do-gooders in Washington, Mr. Howland), and after nine years he was all the way up to $112.90 take-home and he was still the bookkeeper of the New Bradford branch of Aztec Paper Products. And he would remain its bookkeeper at Pickney's pleasure or until he was hauled out feet first or he made a stink, in which case he'd be still breathing but out on his canister. And where would a man fifty-seven get a decent job in New Bradford? Or anywhere else?

What in hell is keeping them?

As he thought it he heard the triple knock at the back door of the plant.

Howland jumped.

One, two-three.

But he stood there.

The payroll was in undistributed sheafs of rubberbanded bills beside the canvas bag as he had brought it from the bank in the afternoon accompanied in their every-Wednesday waltz by Officer Wesley Malone, the town cop with the eyes that always seemed to be scouting for Indian sign or something.

I wonder what Wes would think of this, probably stalk me like he did the bobcat that showed up from Canada or someplace and played hob at Hurley's chicken farm. And put a bullet between its eyes.

The thought turned about and it strengthened him. Still, as Howland hurried to the back door through the dark plant his lungs labored and his heart punched away at his Adam's apple.

But his head held trueblue to his plans. They did not include Sherrie-Ann. They did not even include Marie Griggs, the twitch-britches night countergirl at Elwood's Diner.

He was not sure what they did include.

Except $6,000.

A year's pay practically, tax-free.

Howland unlocked the door.

Hinch was at the wheel. My wheelman, Furia called him. Hinch drove into the empty parking lot behind the plant and stopped the car on the tarmacadam ten feet from the rear entrance. It was a Chrysler New Yorker with a powerful purr, like Hinch. Black satin under the dust and not a dent. Furia had picked it out personally on the main drag in Newton Center, Mass. in broad daylight. They had switched plates on a back road near Lexington and Hinch crowed. It was a sweet bus, the neatest they had ever copped. It even had a police band on the radio. Furia was sitting up front with Hinch. Goldie was in the back seat flipping one of her Lady Vere de Vere cigarets, goldtipped what else.

Furia got out.

He had a stiff's skin, tight and yellow, and Mickey Mouse ears. Goldie, who was gone on *Star Trek* and Leonard Nimoy, had once called him Mr. Spock for a gag, but only once. Furia wore an executive three-button Brooks, a no-iron white shirt, a bleak gray silk tie, a two-inch Knox, black gloves, built-up heels, and amber goggles, the latest type, that made him look like a frogman. His London Fog he had left on the front seat.

He stood there like a spinning top, motionless to the eye. He looked around.

"No." He had a spinning sort of voice, too, so hard and tight it practically sang.

12

Goldie stopped in the act of stepping out of the car. Hinch did not move.

"Why not?" she asked.

"Because I'm giving you the word."

"Bitch," Hinch chortled.

Furia looked at him. Hinch gave him a rather embarrassed spread of the hand.

"I gave you the word, Goldie."

Goldie shrugged and stepped back into the Chrysler banging the door. When Goldie shrugged her long gold hair shrugged with her. She had borrowed the effect from the TV commercials. She was all gold and scarlet, a girl of bottles and pastes. Her miniskirt came eight inches under her crotch. She was wearing gold fishnets and tall gilt boots.

Her eyes sat on purple cushions, not eye shadow.

"Looks okay," Hinch said.

"Don't kill the engine just in case."

"Don't worry, Fure."

Furia stepped up to the plant door. He walked on the balls of his feet like an actor playing a thief. As he walked he felt for his shoulder holster the way other men feel for their zippers.

He knocked three times. One, two-three.

The pair in the car sat very still. Hinch was looking into the rearview mirror. Goldie was looking into Furia.

"He's taking his sonofabitch time," Furia said.

"He chickened out maybe," Hinch said.

Goldie said nothing.

The lock turned over and Howland stood in the moonlight like a ghost in shirtsleeves.

"Took your sonofabitch time," Furia said. "Where's the gelt?"

"The what?"

"The moo. The payroll."

"Oh." Howland yawned suddenly. "On my desk. Make it snappy." His teeth clicked like telegraph keys. He kept sneaking looks at the deserted lot.

Furia nodded at the Chrysler and Hinch got out in one move: he was behind the wheel, he was on the macadam. Goldie stirred but when Furia gave her the look she sat back.

"Has he got the rope?" Howland asked.

"Come on." Furia jabbed at Howland's groin playfully.

13

The bookkeeper backed off and Hinch laughed. "What's the stall? Let's see that bread."

Howland led the way, hurrying. His steps echoed, Furia's and Hinch's did not. Hinch was wearing gloves now, too. He was carrying a black flight bag.

Howland's desk was in a corner of the outer office near the window. There was a greenshade light over the desk.

"Here it is." He yawned again. "What am I yawning for?" he said. "Where is the rope?"

Hinch pushed him aside. "Hey, man," he said. "That's a mess of bread."

"Twenty-four thousand. You don't have to count it. It's all there."

"Sure," Furia said. "We trust you. Start packing, Hinch."

Hinch opened the flight bag and began stuffing the bundles of bills in. Howland watched nervously. Into his nervousness crept alarm.

"Hey, you're taking too much," Howland protested. "We had a deal. Where's mine?"

"Here," Furia said, and shot him three times, one-and-two-three in a syncopated series. The third bullet went into Howland no more than two inches above the first two as the bookkeeper's knees collapsed. The light over the desk bounced off his bald spot. His nose made a pulpy noise when it hit the vinyl floor.

Furia blew on his gun the way the bad guy did it in Westerns. It was a Walther PPK, eight-shot, which he had picked up in a pawnshop heist in Jersey City. It had a double-action hammer and Furia was wild about it. "It's better than a woman," he had said to Goldie. "It's better than you." He picked up the three ejected cases with his left hand and dropped them into his pocket. The automatic he kept in his right.

"You cooled him pretty," Hinch said, looking down at Howland. Blood was beginning to worm out on the vinyl from under the bookkeeper. "Well, let's go, Fure." He had all the money in the bag, even the rolls of coins, and the bag zipped.

"I say when we go," Furia said. He was looking around as if they had all the time in the world. "Okay, that's it."

He walked out. Hinch lingered. All of a sudden he was reluctant to leave Howland.

"Where's the rope, he says." When Hinch grinned his mouth showed a hole where two front teeth had been. He

14

was wearing a black leather windbreaker, black chinos, and blue Keds. He had rusty hair which he wore long at the neck and a nose that had been broken during his wrestling days. His eyes were small and of a light, almost nonexistent, pink-gray. "We forgot the gag, too, pidge," he said to Howland.

"Hinch."

"Okay, Fure, okay," Hinch said. He catfooted after Furia, looking pleased.

"I knew it," Goldie said. Hinch was backing the Chrysler around.

"You knew what?" Furia had the flight bag on his lap like a child.

"The shots. You killed him."

"So I killed him."

"Stupid."

Furia turned half around and his left hand swished across her face.

"I don't dig a broad with lip neither," Hinch said approvingly. He drove across the lot on the bias, without lights. When he got to the turnout he braked. "Where to, Fure?"

"Over the bridge to the cloverleaf."

Hinch swung left and switched on the riding lights. There was no traffic on the outlying road. He drove at a humble thirty.

"You asked for it," Furia said.

There was a trickle of blood at the corner of Goldie's pug nose. She was dabbing at it with a Kleenex.

"The thing is I don't take names from nobody," Furia said. "You got to watch the mouth with me, Goldie. You ought to know that by this time."

Hinch nodded happily.

"What did you have to shoot him for?" Goldie said. In his own way Furia had apologized, they both understood that if Hinch did not. "I didn't set this up for a killing, Fure. Why go for the big one?"

"Who's to know?" Furia argued. "Howland sure as hell didn't sound about our deal. Hinch and me wore gloves and I'll ditch the heater soon as we grab off another one. So they'll never hook those three slugs onto us, Goldie. I even picked up the cases. You got nothing to worry about."

15

"It's still the big one."

"You button your trap, bitch," Hinch said.

"You button yours," Furia said in a flash. "This is between me and Goldie. And don't call her no more names, Hinch, hear?"

Hinch drove.

"Why I plugged him," Furia said. "And you had a year college, Goldie." He sounded like a kindly teacher. "A three-way split is better than four, I make it, and I never even graduated public school. That shlep just bought us an extra six grand."

Goldie said fretfully, "You sure he's dead?"

Furia laughed. They were rattling over the bridge spanning the Tonekeneke River that led out of town; beyond lay the cloverleaf interchange and the through road Goldie called The Pike, with its string of dark gas stations. The only light came from an allnight diner with a big neon sign at the other side of the cloverleaf. The neon sign said ELWOOD'S DINER. It smeared the aluminum siding a dimestore violet.

"Stop in there, Hinch, I'm hungry."

"Fure," Goldie said. "My folks still live here. Suppose somebody spots me?"

"How many years you cut out of this jerk burg? Six?"

"Seven. But—"

"And you used to have like dark brown hair, right? And go around like one of them Girl Scouts? Relax, Goldie. Nobody's going to make you. I'm starved."

Goldie licked the scarlet lip under the smudge on her nostril. Furia was always starved after a job. At such times it was as if he had been weaned hungry and had never made up for it. Even Hinch looked doubtful.

"I told you, Hinch, didn't I? Pull in."

Hinch skirted the concrete island and drove off the cloverleaf. Neither he nor Goldie said anything more. Goldie's face screwed smaller. She had a funny feeling about the caper. Fure was flying. It never works out the way I plan it. He always queers it some way, he's a natural-born loser.

Hinch swung the Chrysler into a slot. A dozen others were occupied by cars and trucks. He turned off the ignition and started to get out.

"Hold it." Furia turned to examine Goldie in the violet haze. "You got blood on your nose. Wipe it off."

"I thought I wiped it off."

He ripped the tissue from the box over the dash, spat on it, and handed it to her. "The left side."

She examined her nose in her compact mirror, scrubbed the smudge off, used the puff.

"Do I look all right for Local Yokel?"

Furia laughed again. That's twice in three minutes. He's real turned on. He'll try to be a man-mountain in bed tonight.

"We don't sit together," Furia said to Hinch. "You park at the counter. Goldie and me we'll find a booth or somewheres."

"That's using your tank, Fure."

"Goldie don't think so. Do you, Goldie?"

He was sounding amused. Goldie risked it. "Does it matter what I think?"

"Not a goddam bit," Furia said cheerfully. He got out with the black bag and made for the diner steps without looking back.

That's what I love about you, you're such a little gentleman.

The diner was busy, not crowded. Furia went in first and snagged a booth from four teenagers who had been nursing cheeseburgers and malts. Goldie managed to join him at the cost of a few stares. She saw no one she recognized. She slipped behind the partition and hid her miniskirt under the fake marble top. I told Fure I ought to wear slacks tonight but no he's got to show off my legs like we're on the town, these studs will remember me.

She was angrier with Furia than when he had struck her.

Hinch slouched in a minute later and settled his bulk on a stool a few feet away. He became immediately enchanted with one of the girls behind the counter, who had just come out of the kitchen. The girl had sprayshine black hair done up in exaggerated bouffant and a rear end that jerked from side to side as she moved.

"You'd better watch the pig," Goldie said. "He's already got his piggy eyes on a girl."

"Don't worry about Hinch," Furia said. "What'll it be, doll? Steak and fries? Live it up."

"I'm not hungry. Just coffee."

Furia shrugged. He had stripped off his gloves and he began to drum on the table with his neat little nails. His

17

Mediterranean eyes were glazed. In the glare of the fluorescents his skin had a greenish shine.

The diner was jumping with soul music, orders, dishes, talk. There was a lively smell of frying onions and meat. Furia drank it in. The overcast in his eyes was from pride at his achievement and regret that these squares could not know his power. Goldie had seen it before, a recklessness that would later rush to relieve itself. She had her own needs, which involved perpetual thought. His violence kept her squirming.

"Hey, you," Furia said. The girl with the versatile rump was delivering a trayful of grinders to the next booth. "We ain't got all year."

Goldie shut her eyes. When she opened them the girl was clearing the dirty dishes from their table. She was leaning far over, her left breast over Furia's hands.

"I'll be right back, folks." She flicked a rag over the table and seesawed away.

"That chick is stacked what I mean," Furia said. "As good as you, Goldie."

"I think she recognized me," Goldie said.

"You think. You're always thinking."

"I'm not sure. She could have. She was starting high school when I left New Bradford. Her name is Griggs, Marie Griggs. Let's split, Fure."

"You make me throw up. And she did? It's a free country, ain't it? Two people having a bite?"

"Why take chances?"

"Who's taking chances?"

"You are. With that bag between your legs. And packing the gun."

"We'll take off when I've ate my steak." His lips were thinning down. "Now knock it off, she's coming back. Steak medium-well, side order fries, two black. And don't take all night."

The waitress wrote it down. "You're not having anything but coffee, Miss?"

"I just told you, didn't I?" Furia said with a stare.

She left fast. His stare warmed as he watched her behind. "No wonder Hinch got his tongue hanging out. I could go for a piece of that myself."

Flying all right.

"Fure—"

"She didn't know you from her old lady's mustache."

18

His tone said that the subject was closed. Goldie shut her eyes again.

When his steak came it was too rare. Another time he would have turned nasty and fired it back. As it was he ate it, grousing. Steaks were a problem with him. Cooks always thought the waitress had heard wrong. He hated bloody meat. I ain't no goddam dog, he would say.

He hacked off massive chunks, including the fat, and bolted them. The fork never left his fist. Goldie sipped carefully. Her skin was one big itch. Psycho-something, a doctor had told her. He had sounded like some shrink and she had never gone back. It had been worse recently.

Hinch was working away on the girl behind the counter, and she was beginning to look sore.

One of these days I'm going to ditch these creeps.

At eleven o'clock, as Furia was stabbing his last slice of potato, the shortorder man turned on the radio. Goldie, on her feet, sat down again.

"Now what?"

"That's the station of Tonekeneke Falls, WRUD, with the late news."

"So?"

"Fure, I have this feeling."

"You and your feels," Furia said. "You're goosier than an old broad tonight. Let's hit it."

"Will it hurt to listen a minute?"

He sat back comfortably and began to pick his teeth with the edge of a matchpacket cover. "First you can't wait to blow the dump—"

He stopped. The announcer was saying: "—this bulletin. Thomas F. Howland, bookkeeper of the Aztec Paper Products company branch in New Bradford, was found in his office a few minutes ago shot to death. Mr. Howland was alone at the plant, preparing the payroll for tomorrow, when he was apparently surprised by robbers, who killed him and escaped with over twenty-four thousand dollars in cash, according to Curtis Pickney, the general manager, who found the slain bookkeeper's body. Mr. Pickney was driving by on his way home from a late Zoning Board meeting, saw lights in the plant, and investigated. He notified the New Bradford police and Chief John Secco has taken charge of the case. The Resident State Trooper in New Bradford is also on the scene. A search is being organized for Edward Taylor, the night security guard, who has disappeared. Police fear that

19

Taylor may also have been the victim of foul play. We will bring you further bulletins as they come in. In Washington today the President announced . . ."

"No," Furia said. "Stay put." He nodded at Hinch, who had turned their way. Hinch was blinking his pink eyes. At Furia's signal he tossed a bill on the counter and ran out with two truckdrivers who had jumped up and left their hamburgers uneaten.

"I told you, Fure!"

"Say, Miss America, how's about two more coffees?"

The waitress took their empty cups. "I can't believe it," she said. "That nice old guy."

"Who?"

"That Tom Howland."

"The one they say got shot? You knew him?"

"He ate in here all the time. Used to bend my ear by the hour. I can't believe it."

"You never know," Furia said, shaking his head. "Step on those coffees, huh, doll?"

She went away.

"Some day you'll learn to listen to me," Goldie muttered. "I told you to just tie him up. No, you've got to go and shoot him."

"Goddam it, Goldie, you bug the living hell out of me sometimes, you know that?"

They drank their second cups in silence. There was no music in the diner now. The cook had turned the radio off, too. People were arguing about the robbery and murder. Furia said, "Now," and rose. Goldie slid from the booth and made her way safely to the door. Furia, carrying the black bag, strolled up to the counter and said to the waitress, "How much for the lousy steak and javas?"

Goldie slipped out.

Hinch had the motor running when Furia got in beside him. "Turn on the police band."

Hinch turned it on. The air was full of directives and acknowledgments. The state police were setting up roadblocks throughout the area.

"Now what?" Goldie had her arms folded over her breasts. "Big shot?"

"You want I should shove your teeth down your throat, is that what you want?" Furia said. "I ought to let Hinch work you over."

"Any time, pal," Hinch said.

"Who asked you? I got to think."

"What's to think?" Hinch said. "We hole up in the hideout till the heat goes away, like we said. No sweat. Let's drag, Fure."

"If you had a brain you'd be a dope." Furia had a roadmap of the area spread on his lap under the maplight. "To get there from here we got to cross this intersection. There's no other road in. That'll be one of their main checkpoints. We can't make it tonight. We got to think of something else."

"You'd better get rid of the gun," Goldie said remotely. She was burrowed as far as she could get into the corner of the rear seat.

"Not till I get me another one."

"You going to kill somebody else for one?"

"I told you!"

"Why didn't you take the watchman's gun?"

"Because it landed in some bushes when we jumped him. We couldn't hang around looking for it in the dark. I'll get one, don't worry."

"It's a wonder you didn't shoot him, too."

"You're asking for a rap in that big moosh of yours, Goldie. I'm telling you! When Howland sent this Taylor into town for coffee and we hit him on the road, he put up a fight and we had to cool him with a knock across the ear. We tied him up and threw him in some bushes. How many times I got to tell you?"

Hinch said, "We parking here all night?"

"Let me think!"

Goldie let him think. When she thought the time was ripe she said, "Maybe if we think out loud."

Furia immediately said, "So?"

"The watchman can't finger you, you hit him in the dark. Nobody saw us at the plant except Howland, and he's dead."

"That's why I hit him. That and the extra cut. But you got to make out like I'm a dumdum."

"If we'd worked it the way I said," Goldie said, "he'd have cut his throat before he fingered you, Fure. But I'm not going to argue with you, Fure. The big thing went sour was the manager driving past the plant. So now we're hung up here. For a while they're going to stop every car trying to leave New Bradford."

"I know," Hinch said brightly. "We bury it."

"And have the paper rot or be chewed up? Or somebody find it?" Goldie said.

21

"We sure as a bitch ain't throwing it away," Hinch growled.

"Who said anything about throwing it away? It's got to be put somewhere safe till they stop searching cars. The shack would be good, but we're cut off from there till they get fed up and figure we made it out before they set up the blocks. Meantime—the way I see it, Fure—we need help."

"The way she sees it," Hinch said. "Who's fixing this match, Fure, you or her?"

But Furia said, "What help, Goldie?"

"Somebody to keep it for us."

"That's a great idea that is," Furia said. "Who you going to ask, the fuzz?"

Goldie said, "Yes."

Hinch jiggled his bowling-ball head. "I tell you, Fure, this broad is bad news. Some joke."

"No joke," Goldie said. "I mean it."

"She means it," Hinch said with disgust.

Furia picked a sliver of steak out of his teeth. "With a farout idea like that there's got to be something in it. What's on your mind, Goldie?"

"Look," Goldie said. "I've been keeping in touch with my family off and on through my kid sister Nanette—"

"That is absolutely out," Furia said. "I ain't stashing no twenty-four grand with a bunch of rubes."

"Are you kidding? They'd break a leg running to Chief Secco with it. Ma's the big wheel in her church, and my old man thinks having a bottle of beer in your car is a federal offense." Goldie laughed. "But Nanette's no square. She's looking to cut out one of these days, too. I know from her letters. She does a lot of baby-sitting nights and one of her steady jobs is for a couple named Malone, they have a kid Barbara. The Malones live in a one-family house on Old Bradford Road. It's one of the original streets of the town, never any traffic, and the neighbors pull their sidewalks in at nine o'clock. Well, Wesley Malone is a cop."

"There she goes again," Hinch said.

"On the New Bradford police force."

"What gives with this dame?" Hinch demanded of Taugus County. "Some idea! We should park our loot with the town cop!"

But Furia was heavily in thought. "How old did you say their kid is, Goldie?"

22

"Must be eight or nine by now."

"You got yourself a deal."

"But Fure," Hinch protested.

"That's the beauty part," Furia said. "A cop's got to know the facts of life, don't he? He ain't going to panic and try something stupid. Okay, Hinch, get going."

"Where to?" Hinch asked sullenly.

"This Old Bradford Road. Direct him, Goldie."

Goldie directed him. They went back into the cloverleaf and across the bridge, past three blocks of midtown, and sharply right into a steep road called Lovers Hill, Goldie said, because there was a parking strip on top where the town kids necked. Halfway up she said, "Next right turn," and Hinch turned in grudgingly. There were no street lights, and towering trees. It was a narrow street, almost a lane, lined with very old two-story frame houses in need of paint.

The road swooped and wound in an S. At the uppermost curve of the S Goldie said, "I think that's it. Yes. The one with the porch lit up."

It was the only house on the street that showed a light.

"Almost," Furia said, sucking his teeth, "like they got the welcome mat out."

Ellen began praising the film the moment the house lights went up.

"Not that I approve of all that violence," Ellen said as her husband held her cloth coat for her. "But you have to admit, Loney, it's a marvelous picture. Didn't you think so?"

"You asking me?" Malone said.

"Certainly I'm asking you."

"It's a fraud," Malone said.

"I suppose now you're a movie critic."

"You asked me, didn't you?"

"Hello, Wes," a man said. They were being nudged up the aisle by the crowd. "Good picture, I thought."

"Yeah, Lew," Malone said. "Very good."

"*Why* is it a fraud?" Ellen asked in a whisper.

"Because it is. It makes them out a couple of heroes. Like they were Dillinger or somebody. In fact, they used some stuff that actually happened to Dillinger. You felt sorry for them, didn't you?"

"I suppose. What's wrong with that?"

23

"Everything. Nobody felt sorry for those punks at the time it happened. Even the hoods were down on them. The truth is they were a couple of smalltime murderers who never gave their victims a chance. Clyde got his kicks out of killing. His favorite target was somebody's back. Hi, Arthur."

"Great picture, Wes!" Arthur said.

"Just great," Malone said.

"It got the nomination for Best Picture," Ellen sniffed. "You're such an expert."

"No expert. I just happened to read an article about them, that's all. Why kid the public?"

"Well, I don't care, I liked it," Ellen said. But she squeezed his arm.

The Malones came out of the New Bradford Theater and made for their car. Ellen walked slowly; she knew how tired he was. And how stubborn. Loney had insisted on following their Wednesday night ritual, which involved dinner at the Old Bradford Inn in midtown and the movies afterward, even though he had not slept eight hours in the past ninety-six. It was the only recreation she got, Loney had said, flattening out his chin, and she wasn't going to lose out just because the flu hit the department and he had to work double shift four days running. He could get a night's sleep tonight, Mert Peck was out of bed and Harry Rawlson was back on duty, too.

"How about a bite at Elwood's?" he said at the car. It was a beatup Saab he had picked up for $650 the year before, their old Plymouth had collapsed at 137,000 miles. The big Pontiac special he drove on duty belonged to the town.

"I don't think so," Ellen said. "I'm kind of worried about Bibby. Nanette had to leave at ten thirty, her mother's down sick, and I said it would be all right. But with Bibby home alone—"

"Sure." He was relieved, she knew every pore in his body. Then she saw him stiffen and turned to see why.

One of the New Bradford police cars had torn past the intersection of Grange Street and Main along the Green, siren howling. It was being chased by several civilian cars.

"I wonder what's up," Malone said. "Something's up."

"Let it. You're coming home with me, Loney. Get in, I'll drive."

Malone got in, and Ellen went round and took the wheel. He was looking back at Main Street and she saw him feel for the gun under his jacket. Ellen hated Chief Secco's rule about his men carrying their revolvers off duty.

"Lay off the artillery, bud," Ellen said grimly, starting the Saab. "You're going nowhere but beddy-bye."

"It's something big," Malone said. "Look, Ellen, drop me off at the stationhouse."

"Not a chance."

"I'll only be a couple minutes. I want to find out what gives."

"I'll drop you off and I won't see you till God knows when."

"Ellen, I promise. Drop me off and go on home to Bibby. I'll walk it up the Hill."

"You'll never make it, you're dead on your feet."

"That's what I like about you," he said, smiling. "You've got such confidence in me."

Grange Street was one-way below Main and the Green, and Ellen sighed and turned into Freight Street and past the dark brown unappetizing railroad station. She had to stop for the light at the corner near the R.R. crossing. Malone was squinting to their right, across the bridge and the Tonekeneke and the cloverleaf to The Pike. Two state police cruisers were balling south on The Pike, sirens all out. Ellen deliberately jumped the light and turned left.

She made another left turn east of the Green, drove the one block up to Grange again, and swung right. The Colonial redbrick town hall stood at the southeast corner of the Green and Grange Street, extending into Grange; the New Bradford Police Department was near the rear of the building, with a separate entrance. The entrance was a little windbreak vestibule. There were two green globes outside.

Ellen stopped the car. He was on the sidewalk before she could put on her emergency.

"Remember, Loney, you promised. I'll be hopping mad if you doublecross me."

"I'll be right home."

He hurried inside and Ellen peeled off, taking her worry out on the Saab.

To Malone's surprise no one was in the station but Sam Buchard, the night desk man, and Chief Secco and a middle-aged woman. The chief was over in the corner at the steel desk normally used by the Resident State Trooper, and he was talking to the woman seated beside the

25

desk. Her makeup was smeared and her eyes looked worse than Malone's. She was smoking a cigaret rapidly. Buchard was making an entry in the case log. The LETS—the Law Enforcement Teletype System out of the state capital—was clacking away as usual in its cubicle behind the desk.

Malone walked around the glassed partition to the working area. Chief Secco looked up with a disapproving glance and went back to his interrogation. The woman did not turn around. The desk man said, "What are you doing here, Wes?"

"Sam, what's up?"

"Didn't you hear?"

"I was at the movies with Ellen."

"Murder and robbery over at Aztec."

"Murder?" The last homicide in New Bradford had been four years ago when two men and a woman from downstate had decided to try some illegal night fishing off the railroad trestle over the Tonekeneke. They had been tanked up and the men had got into a fight over the woman. One of the men had fallen off the trestle into thirty feet of water and drowned. Malone and Mert Peck and Trooper Miller had fished his body out the next morning fifty yards downstream. Malone could not recall a bona-fide Murder One in all his years on the New Bradford force. "Who was murdered, Sam?"

"Howland, the bookkeeper. Shot three times in the chest. The payroll was stolen."

Malone recognized her now. Sherrie-Ann Howland, the one the women called "the bloodsucker." She had never even given Tom Howland the excuse of being unfaithful to him. Townspeople rarely saw her, she was said to be a secret drinker. She was sober enough now. Malone knew nearly everyone in town, its population was only 16,000.

"Any leads, Sam?"

"Not a one. The state boys have set up roadblocks throughout the area. Curtis Pickney found him by a fluke, and they say Howland wasn't dead long. So maybe the killers didn't have a chance to get away. Anyway, that's the theory we're working on."

Malone knuckled his eyes. "Where was Ed Taylor?"

"We just found him."

"For God's sake, did Ed get it, too?"

"No, they slugged him, tied him up, and threw him in some bushes. Ed says there were two of them. No I.D., it was too dark. They took Ed to the hospital. He'll be all right. He's a lucky guy, Wes. They could have shot him, too."

Malone hung around. Secco was still questioning Mrs. Howland. He took the log and pretended to read it. The familiar form—B. & E. and Larceny, One-Car Accident, Etc., Obscene or Harassing Telephone Calls, Non-support, Driving under Influence, Stolen and Recovered Motor Vehicles, Resisting Arrest, Destruction of Private Property, Attempted Suicide—had ghosts in it like the TV sometimes. He dropped the log and wandered over to the cabinets. Each officer had a drawer for his personal property. He opened his and fingered its contents—summons book, warning book, his copy of the motor vehicle laws, tape measure, a torn-off brass button Ellen had replaced and then found in the lining of his leather duty-jacket, a crayon self-portrait Barbara signed BIBBY TO MY LOVING FATHER in multicolor curlicue capitals, a copy of a five-year-old income tax return. He shut his drawer and took a Hershey bar from the department commissary drawer, depositing a dime in the cashbox. He stripped off the paper, dropped it into the waste basket, and chewed the chocolate slowly. Chief Secco was still talking to the widow.

Ellen will have my hide ...

Malone took inventory. The E & J Emergikit on the counter—resuscitator, inhalator, aspirator. The two-watt, two-channel walkie-talkie. The case with the camera and flashbulbs. Nothing changes. Only for Sherrie-Ann Howland. I hope he left some insurance. It's a dead cinch Pickney didn't pay him enough to sock anything away. The whole town knew Pickney's and Aztec's way with a buck. And there was all that talk about Howland and Marie Briggs at Elwood's. How do you kill in cold blood? A man had a right to live out his life, even a life as sorry as Tom Howland's. A woman had a right to a husband, even a woman like Sherrie-Ann.

Secco rose. Mrs. Howland got up in a different way. As if her back ached. "You sure you don't want me to have one of the boys run you home, Mrs. Howland?"

"I parked my car in the town hall lot." There was nothing in the widow's voice.

"I could have it delivered to you in the morning."

"No." She walked out, past Sam Buchard, past Malone,

27

past the partition, through the vestibule. She walked stooped over like a soldier holding his guts in.

"Goddam," Sam Buchard said.

"Oh, Wes," Chief Secco said. "One thing. When you met Howland at the bank today and took him back to the plant with the payroll, how did he seem to you?"

Malone was puzzled. "I didn't notice specially."

"Did he act nervous?"

"Well, I don't know. He talked his head off."

"About what?"

"A lot of nothing. Now that I think of it, maybe he was nervous. Why?"

"All right, Wes," Chief Secco said. "Out."

"Chief," Malone began.

"Didn't you hear me?"

"John, you'll need all the help you can get."

"When you went off duty, Wes, what did I tell you?"

"You said take a couple days off—"

"Then do it. We're under control here. I'm not about to have you come down with exhaustion. I've told you— more than once—this isn't a one-man department. Believe it or not, I've got ten other men most as good as you."

"Four of them trainees."

"That's my problem. You leaving under your own steam, Wes, or do I have to run you out?" Secco looked as if he could do it. He was almost sixty but he had a steer's build and a tough face under the gray crewcut. He was home-grown New Bradford like most of the force. His father had been a dairy farmer and he had grown up tossing hay bales and stripping teats. He still had a knee-buckling grip.

"All right, John, but just one thing. How does it look to you?"

"An outside job, I make it. I didn't tell Mrs. Howland, but I think Howland was in on it and got crossed. That's why I asked you if he seemed nervous this afternoon. Now get out, will you?"

"You can't leave me hanging, John! What's the indication of that?"

"Ed Taylor says Howland all of a sudden sent him into town for coffee. Ed thought nothing of it at the time, but after he got slugged and came to it struck him funny. Howland never did that before. Looks to me like a setup: Howland got Ed out of the way so he could let the robbers into the plant. He'd probably dickered for a cut of the loot, and after making the deal they shot him down. Go home."

"Any hard evidence?"

"Not yet."

"Mrs. Howland have any ideas?"

"She can't see two inches past her own miseries. Go home."

"Who's at the plant?"

"Trooper Miller. He's waiting for the state lab men and the coroner. Go home, Wes!"

Malone left on dragging feet, not all from fatigue.

He walked east to the corner, turned right, did the one block past the Ford agency to Three Corners, and started up Lovers Hill.

How did a man get to the point of kicking his whole life away? Even a life as rotten as Howland's? Or maybe that was the answer. Howland's wife was a drag and a drain, his job was a lot of nothing, he was going nowhere, he was in his upper fifties, and he handled a lot of other people's money. It made some sort of cockeyed sense if you were in Howland's shoes. He had never seen a happy look on Howland's face, even at the times when he dropped into Elwood's for a coffee on a cold night and caught the guy playing up to Marie Briggs.

He wondered if the Briggs girl was involved. No, Marie was too smart. Besides, she had a thing going with Jimmy Wyckoff and it looked serious. Jimmy was a good-looking kid who pulled down a good salary as a machinist at Compo Copper and Brass. If there was anything between Marie and Howland it had all been in Howland's head.

Malone felt a rush of affection for his own girls.

Suppose I didn't have them? Suppose Ellen had turned out a nag and a spender like Sherrie-Ann? And as lousy in bed as she must be? Suppose Ellen had miscarried with Bibby, as she had done twice before and once since Bibby was born, when Dr. Levitt advised her not to get pregnant any more? There would be no little girl with copper curls and a valentine for a face and those big honey eyes full of love for the hero in her life. (And hadn't Ellen been floored when, at the age of six, Bibby had climbed into his lap and clutched him around the neck and looked deep into his eyes and asked, "Daddy, do you love mommy more than you love me?" He could still see the expression on Ellen's face.)

Malone turned up into Old Bradford Road.

No, life would be as big a zero as Howland's without his girls. Until he had met Ellen, with her snapping Irish eyes and tongue, he had never been serious about a girl. He had never had a girl. Only girls, and most of those had been the kind who drifted in and out of Rosie's over on Lower Freight, and they didn't count. He had never had any close friends of either sex before Ellen. It was Ellen, with her insight into people, who had quickly seen him for what he was and dubbed him The Malone Ranger, from which he became "Loney" to her and to her alone.

He found himself smiling as he trudged around the curves of the S. In bed sometimes he called her Tonto, just to get her mad. ("If you haven't found out the difference between Tonto and me yet, Wesley Malone, you need a course in sex education!")

He had always had to make out. His father, a cold and silent man, had worked on the roads for the state, and Malone's memories of him were colored by the black oil he could never seem to clean off his hands and face. He had died when Malone was thirteen, a stranger, leaving a bed-fond widow who chainsmoked and never combed her hair, and four younger children. They were girls, and he became the man of the house before he had to shave. It still made him mad when he thought of the monthly check from the town welfare fund. It provided just enough to keep them from starving, and an inexhaustible supply of ammunition for the town kids. He had hunted up work for after school, swearing to himself that the first time he could make enough to turn down the town handout he would kick somebody's teeth in. He did his studying at night—his mother insisted, with a stubbornness he now recognized as the source of his own, that he go through high school. During the summers he mowed lawns, bagged groceries at the supermarket, farmed out for the haying season, painted divider lines on the roads. Anything to earn a dollar. He turned it all over to his mother. Money meant little to him except as it kept her from complaining.

By the time she died of lung cancer in New Bradford Hospital, his sister Kathleen was old enough to cope with the household and the younger girls. He began bringing his earnings to Kathleen. He had supported his sisters through high school, he had seen them safely married, he had kissed them goodbye as one by one they left town with their husbands and kids, wondering whether he would ever see them again. Most of them he never had seen again, although he got a letter once in a blue moon, usually griping, they came by their complaining ways honestly. And his favorite, Kathleen, was living in San Diego on the base, her husband was career Navy, and he did not hear from her at all.

He had never played Little League ball, he had never joined 4-H or a club at high school, he had never prowled the town with a gang on Halloween, he had never gone dragging on The Pike with other teenagers when the car bug hit. Instead, when he had been able to slip off into the woods with his .22, a hand-me-down from his father which he had kept fiercely cleaned and oiled, he pretended to be a Marine—wriggling through the brush on his belly, drawing a bead on the snapping turtles that infested Balsam Lake (and never shooting except at the empty gin and whisky bottles with which the Lake woods abounded)— always by himself. Somewhere along the road he had lost or strangled the need for group enjoyment. By the time he was free and on his own, the boys he had grown up with avoided him and the girls laughed at him as a square. That was when he had spent so much time at Rosie's.

One of his recurring regrets was that he had been too young for Korea and too old for Vietnam. He had enlisted in the Marines instead of waiting to be drafted and spent two of his four years on sea duty in the Med, all drill and mock-landings and spit-and-polish and the whorehouses of Barcelona, Marseilles, Kavala, Istanbul; the rest of his hitch he sulked at Parris Island handing out fatigues and skivvies to frightened recruits. He was not, his C.O. told him, a good Marine, too much rugged individualism and not enough esprit de corps. He was a lance corporal twice and a corporal once; he wound up a Pfc. His only achievement of record was the Expert Medal he earned on the firing range. He formed no lasting friendships in the Corps, either.

It was John Secco who had talked him into joining the New Bradford force. He had always looked up to Chief Secco as a fair man, his standard of goodness. Secco had an understanding of boys. His policies had kept the juvenile delinquency rate in New Bradford among the lowest in the state.

"I won't kid you, Wes," Secco had said. "You'll never get fat being a town cop. You'll have to learn how to handle selectmen, sorehead taxpayers, bitching storekeep-

31

ers, Saturday night drunks, husband-and-wife fights, kids out to raise Cain, and all the rest. A good smalltown policeman has to be a politician, a squareshooter, a hard-nose, and a father confessor rolled into one. It's almost as tough as being a good bartender. And all for a starting pay of eighty-some bucks. I've had my eye on you for a long time, Wes. You're just the kind of man I want in my department. There's only one thing that bothers me."

"What's that?"

"Can you follow orders? Can you work with others? Can you discipline yourself? Your Marine record says you can't."

And he had said, "I don't know, Chief. I've done some growing up. I think so."

"All right, let's give it a try. Take your training at the state police school, and let's see how you make out on your six months' probation."

He had chalked up the best record of any recruit in the New Bradford department's history. But he thought that John Secco still had questions in his eye. John and Ellen. They sure hold a tight rein on me. And it's not so bad.

The porch light was on, which meant that Ellen was waiting up for him. Leave it to Irish. The Saab was in the driveway, too, not put away. She had probably left it handy in case he failed to show in what she considered a reasonable time and she decided to drive back down into town to haul him home by the ear.

As he turned into his gate Malone paused. There was a strange car across the street, a black dusty late-model Chrysler New Yorker sedan. No one on Old Bradford Road could afford a car like that. It was parked at the Tyrell house, but the house was dark, so the people couldn't be visiting. The Tyrells rarely had visitors, and never so late at night, they were an old couple who went to bed with their chickens. The people from the Chrysler might have been visiting the young Cunninghams next door, but the Cunningham house showed no lights, either. Maybe I ought to check it out. But then he remembered Ellen's look at the stationhouse and decided that discretion was the better part of whatever it was.

Malone trudged up the walk and onto his porch, reaching for his keys. He felt suddenly like dropping where he was, curling up on the mat and giving himself totally to sleep. He could not recall when he had felt so tired, even on maneuvers. I wonder what kind of hell I'd catch from that little old Irisher of mine if she opened the front door and fell over me.

He was still grinning when he unlocked the door and stepped into the dark hall and felt a cold something press into the skin behind his ear and heard a spinning sort of voice behind him say, "Freeze, cop."

It's got to be I'm dreaming. I did fall asleep out there. This can't be for real. Not my house, Ellen, Bibby.

"Don't do it," the spinning voice said. "I just as soon shoot the top of your head off." It turned in another direction. "See if he's heeled."

Malone heard someone say, "Where's my wife and daughter?"

"Just stand still, fuzz." The muzzle dug in.

Rough hands ran up his body. Another man, a strong one. The hand scraped his left nipple and found the butt of the revolver sticking out of his shoulder holster, the one he used off duty. The hand came out and he felt lighter, lost.

"I got it," a second voice said. This one was as rough as the hands, but muted, a gargly purr like a cougar's.

"Put the lights on," the first voice said. It sounded happy. "Let me have it, Hinch."

Hinch.

"Just a minute, Fure."

Fure?

The lights went up. The first thing Malone saw through the archway was Ellen in the parlor perched like a Sunday school kid on the edge of her mother's New England rocker. She still had her coat on. Her face was the color of milk with the butterfat skimmed off.

"Can I move my head?" Malone asked.

"Like a good little cop." The spinny one.

Malone moved his head and came to life. The two men were wearing masks. If they had meant to kill they would not have cared if he and Ellen saw their faces. He let his breath out.

The masks were ridiculous. They were fullface and skintight, brown bear faces. The bear face on the little man was too big for him; it was wrinkled up like something unwrapped after a thousand years. The big man's fitted. The little one was a fashion plate. The big one was strictly motorcycle mugg, a hard case.

33

They go to the trouble of wearing masks and then they say each other's names out loud. Don't ever take chances with the dumb ones, John said; they either panic like animals or they like it.

The man called Fure liked it. He was now holding two guns, his own and Malone's. His was a seven-inch automatic, a foreign handgun. At first Malone thought it was a Mauser. But then he saw that it was a Walther PPK, a gun popular with continental law officers. Must be stolen. There had been nothing European in either voice.

That's the gun they killed Tom Howland with. The gun the little guy killed Howland with. It would have to be the little guy. He digs guns.

Fure was digging Malone's gun. The eyes behind the bear mask were crazy with joy. He had the Walther in his left armpit now and he was turning Malone's revolver over and over in his gloved hands.

"A Colt Trooper, Hinch. Six-shot, .357 Magnum. You ought to feel the balance of this baby. You're a pal, fuzz. Here." He handed the Walther to the big man. "Where's the ammo belt goes with this?"

"I don't keep it in the house—" Malone stopped. Fure was laughing. He reached into the hall closet and straightened up dangling the ammunition belt. The holster was empty, the bullet holders were full. "Naughty, naughty. Okay, fuzz. Inside with wifie."

Malone went into the parlor, his own gun digging into his head.

"Not near her. On that sofa over there."

Ellen's eyes followed him each inch of the way, saying do something, don't do anything.

He's a shrewd bugger for all his dumbness. He figures that together we're strong, apart we're helpless. Malone felt the rage rising. He sat down on the sofa.

"Ellen. Where's Bibby?"

"Upstairs with the woman."

"Is she all right?"

"I don't know. I think. I found them here when I got home. They won't even let me see her."

The woman. Then there were three of them. Apparently Ed Taylor had not seen the woman. Making it tougher for John and the state boys. They're looking for just two males.

"Your kid's okay for now, Malone," Fure said. He was running his hand over the Colt as if it were alive. "You

34

want her to stay that way you jump up and roll over. Hinch. The bag."

Hinch reached behind the sofa and came up with the black bag. He handed it to the fashion plate. It seemed to Malone that he did it very slowly.

"It's yours." The bag landed in Malone's lap. Fure scraped Ellen's treasured antique crewel chair over to him, the one with the shaky legs, and dropped into it. He kept fondling the Colt. They had to turn their heads to face him.

"What do I do with this, Fure?" Malone asked.

"Mr. Furia to cops."

"Mr. Furia."

"Take a look inside."

Malone unzipped the bag. Bundles of greenbacks stared up at him.

The purr behind him said, "I still think—"

"Just don't, Hinch," Furia said. "Know where this loot comes from, cop?"

"I can guess." Malone said in a soft voice. "You don't know about this, Ellen. Tom Howland was killed tonight at the Aztec plant and the payroll stolen. That's what all the excitement was about. This is the Aztec payroll. Right, Furia?"

"*Mister* Furia."

"Mr. Furia."

"Right."

He thought Ellen was going to topple over.

"Can I go to my wife, please? She looks sick."

"No."

Ellen's eyes were begging him. They made a quick upward roll toward where little Barbara was. "I'm all right, Loney."

Malone said, "What did you mean, this is mine?"

"You'll never have so much bread in your hands your whole life. Enjoy it."

"What did you mean?"

"Like for the time being."

"I don't get it."

"No? You're putting me on."

"I don't get any of this."

"You want I should spell it out? What you do, cop, is you hold this for us. Like you're a bank."

Malone tried to look stupid.

35

"You still don't get it," Furia said. "We drew a real dumb one, Hinch, a dummy town cop."

Hinch heehawed.

"Okay, dummy, listen good," Furia said. "With the bread on us we can't get through the roadblocks. Without it we can. They'll have no reason to handle us different from anybody else. Specially seeing there's going to be four of us in the car."

"Four of you," Malone said. His mouth was sticky. "I thought there were three."

"Four," Furia said. "Me, Hinch, Goldie, and your kid. Only she'll be Goldie's. Her mama, like."

"No," Ellen said. "*No*."

"Yeah," Furia said. "Your kid's our receipt for the loot. All clear?"

"It's taking chances," Malone said carefully. "Suppose one of the officers recognizes her when you're stopped? This is a small town. Everybody knows everybody. That blows it."

"You better pray it don't. Can you pray?"

"Yes," Malone said. He wondered if it was true. He had not been inside a church since his confirmation. Ellen took Barbara every Sunday to the second mass, she's not going to grow up a heathen like you, Loney Baloney, you're a cross he has to bear Father Weil says.

"They tell me it helps," Furia said. One of the eyes in the bear mask winked. "All clear now?"

"All clear," Malone said.

"It better be. You try any cop stuff, dummy, or your missus there sets up a squawk, and the kid gets it through the head. Be a nice dummy and keep your old lady's yap shut and you get the kid back with her noggin in one piece. It's that simple."

Ellen's eyes were scurrying about and Malone said, "Ellen."

"I won't. They can't!"

"They can and you will. We have no choice, honey."

"You listen to your papa, honey," Furia said. "He's a smart dummy."

"How do we know they'll keep their word?" Ellen screamed. "You know what you've always said about kidnapers, Loney!"

"This isn't a kidnaping except technically. All they want is to hold Bibby as security till they can get the payroll back."

36

"We'll never see her again."

"They'll keep their word," Malone said. "Or they'll never see this money again. I'll make sure of that." He said to Furia, "All right, we have a deal. But now you listen to me and you listen good."

"Yeah?" Furia said.

"You hurt my daughter and I'll hunt you down and cut you to pieces. If it takes the rest of my life. You, and this goon, and that woman upstairs."

A growl behind him. "Fure, let me. Let me."

"You close your goddam mouth, Hinch!" Furia shouted. He jumped up and sprang forward, eyes in the wrinkled mask boiling. "I ought to knock you off right now, cop, you know that?"

"You need me," Malone said. He tried not to swallow.

"I ain't going to need you forever. Nobody talks to me like that. But nobody!"

"Remember what I said."

Their eyes locked. I could jump him now. And get a bullet in my back from the goon. And leave Ellen and Bibby to their mercy. Malone looked away.

"Goldie!" Furia yelled.

A woman's voice from upstairs said, "Yes, Fure."

"Wake the kid up and get her dressed!"

"Let me," Ellen whimpered. "Please? She'll be so scared."

"Let her," Malone said. "She's not going to try anything."

"She damn well better not." Furia waved the Colt. Ellen jumped to her feet and ran up the stairs.

Furia sat himself down on the rocker. The Colt was aimed at Malone's navel. He'd love to pull that trigger. He'd pull, not squeeze. He's kill-crazy. Malone looked down at his own hands. They were gripping the edge of the sofa so hard the knuckles resembled dead bone. He put his hands on the black bag.

They appeared at the top of the stairs, Ellen clutching Barbara's hand, the woman strolling behind them. The woman was wearing a mask, too. Through the mouth slit she was smoking a goldtipped cigaret. That was all Malone saw of her.

He said with a smile, "Baby. Come down here."

She was still sleepy. Ellen had dressed her in her best outfit, the red corduroy dress, the patent leather shoes, the blue wool coat and hat.

37

"Have you told her anything, Ellen?"

"What could I tell her?" Ellen said. "What?"

"Are we going someplace, daddy?" Bibby asked.

He set the black bag on the sofa and took her on his lap. "Bibby, are you all waked up?"

"Yes, daddy."

"Will you listen to me very, very hard?"

"Yes, daddy."

"These people are going to take you somewhere in a car. You're to go with them like a good girl."

"Aren't you and mommy going, too?"

"No, baby."

"Then why do I have to go?"

"I can't explain now. Let's say it's because I ask you to."

Her lips began to quiver. "I don't like them. Why are they wearing those masks? They're hor'ble."

"Oh, they're just pretending something."

"They have guns. They'll hurt me."

"I have a gun and I've never hurt you, have I?"

"No, daddy . . ."

"Come on," Furia said. "Time's up, like the screws say."

"Wait a minute, Fure," the woman said. "Let him explain it to his little girl."

"They won't hurt you, Bibby. I promise. Have I ever broken a promise to you?"

"No . . ."

"Remember, they won't hurt you. And you do whatever they tell you, Bibby. Whatever. You may even have to pretend, too, the way you did in the school play."

"Pretend what?" Barbara asked in an interested voice.

"Well, the chances are some policemen are going to stop the car. If they do you make believe you're sleeping in the lady's lap. If they wake you up and ask you questions, just say the lady is your mama and that's all."

"My mama? That lady?" She looked at her mother. Her mother looked at her.

"It's just pretend, baby. Do you understand?"

"I understand, but not *why*."

"Some day I'll explain the whole thing to you. But for now you've got to promise me you'll do whatever they say. Promise?"

"All right. When will they bring me back?"

"Oh, I don't know. A day, maybe two."

38

"Well," Barbara said. "I don't like to, but I guess I will. Goodbye, daddy." She held her face up to be kissed. Valentine face. He kissed it. She jumped off his lap and ran to her mother.

Ellen held on to her.

"Okay, okay," Furia said. Malone could have sworn he was grinning under the mask. "Let's get the show on the road, like they say."

"Ellen," Malone said.

The woman walked over and pulled Barbara from Ellen's clutch. Sexy figure, flashy getup, hard voice—maybe late twenties, though it was hard to tell without a face to go by. And brains, she's the brains. I know her from somewhere. I've heard that voice before. A long time ago.

"Come on, honey," the woman said. "We'll have just buckets of fun." She took Barbara's hand. "Fure. It won't hurt to buy insurance. With Barbara in the car, and you and her and me making like one happy family, it will look better if Hinch isn't with us. That getup of his doesn't go with the act."

"What, what?" Hinch said.

"Goldie's right," Furia said. "You hoof it, Hinch. You can cut off that main road into the woods somewheres and stand a good chance of not even being stopped. If they stop you, so what? One guy on the hitch. Stow your mask in the car. Also the heater—I'll drop it in the river before we get to the checkpoint. We'll meet you at the shack."

Hinch glanced at the Walther automatic in his hand. He's not used to guns. Malone tucked the observation away. "If you say so, Fure. Not because of her."

"I say so."

"Goldie and you and the kid'll meet me?"

"You worried about something?"

"Who, me? I ain't worried, Fure."

"Then do like I say. All right, Goldie."

The woman immediately said, "We'll be seeing you soon, mommy. Won't we, Bibs?" and they marched out through the archway and into the hall and out the front door and, incredibly, were gone.

Furia backed his way out. At the door he said, "Remember, cop, that's your kid we got. So don't be a hero."

And he was gone, too.

They were left alone with the black bag.

Standing at the window watching the Chrysler back

39

around and straighten out and head down Old Bradford Road toward Lovers Hill.

Standing at the window until the sound of the Chrysler died.

Then Ellen whirled and said in a voice full of hate, "You great big policeman you. You cowardly sonofabitch, you let them take my Bibby away. You *let* them!" and she was punching his chest and sobbing and he put his arms around her and said in a hoarseness of baffled rage, "Ellen, they won't hurt her, I'll kill them, they want that money more than anything, don't cry, Ellen, I'll get her back."

Thursday

The Child

Malone spent the first two hours trying to get Ellen to go to bed. She just sat in the rocker rocking. He kept at it like a gung ho D.I. because he could think of nothing else. Finally Ellen said, "How can I sleep when my baby is in the hands of those murderers?" and he gave up.

At one thirty Malone said, "Would you like some coffee?"

"I'll make some."

"No, I'll do it. You sit there."

"I don't want any."

"Watch the bag."

"What?"

"The bag. With the money."

She stared at it with loathing. It was on the coffee table before the sofa. "How much is in it?"

"I don't know. A week's payroll for Aztec."

"Count it," Ellen said. "I want to find out how much my child's life is worth."

"Ellen."

"It's like an insurance policy, isn't it?" Ellen said. "And

I've been after you for years to take one out for Bibby."
She laughed. "For her college education."

"Ellen, for God's sake."

"I know, we can't afford it. Can we afford it now? Oh, never mind. Go drink your coffee."

"I only thought—"

"All *right*. I'll have some, too."

He hurried into the kitchen and put the kettle on to boil. When he came back she was counting the money.

"Over twenty-four thousand dollars."

He looked at it.

"It's a lot of money," Malone said inanely.

Ellen grinned. "She's a lot of little girl."

He crammed the money back into the bag with trembling hands.

Neither took more than a few sips.

She kept rocking.

At three A.M. she suddenly said, "Is this all you're going to do, Loney? Sit here?"

"What else can I do? There's nothing I can do tonight."

"What kind of a man are you? I thought I knew you." Her eyes summed him up like an obituary.

"That little one, Furia," Malone explained to the floor. "He's gun-happy. I want them to get to wherever they're holing up without any trouble. It's the best protection Bibby can have. They'll have no excuse ... Look, why don't we talk in the morning? You're dead for sleep."

"Look who's talking."

"I'll go to bed in a while. Let me give you a pill."

"No."

"What good are you going to do Bibby sitting up all night? You'll need your strength."

"And you won't?"

"I'll go, too, I tell you. Come on, how about it?"

At a quarter of four she allowed him to give her one of the sleeping pills left over from Dr. Levitt's prescription, when she had had the last miscarriage. She undressed stiffly. She moved like Barbara's walking doll. He tucked her into bed and stooped to kiss her.

She turned her face away.

He dragged back down to the parlor.

He carried the coffee things into the kitchen, washed and dried them, put them away.

Then he went back upstairs.

The robe and slippers were on the gilt chair. Little

pajamas on the floor, the ones with the daisies she was ape over. He picked them up and folded them and hung them with care over the foot of her canopy bed. She loved her bed, with its lace-trimmed tester. It was a cheap one, everything they owned was cheap except a few of Ellen's mother's things, but Bibby was crazy about it. Her homework was on the worktable, in her hentrack handwriting. She always gets U-for-Unsatisfactory in Neatness. He picked up her plaid schoolbag and looked in. It was full of drawing papers, crayons of fun trees, happy cows, sunny houses, huge suns. E-for-Excellent in Art. Her drawings laughed, her teacher said.

Those killer skunks.

The sheet and blanket were flung back from when Ellen had awakened her. The pillow still showed the dent of her head.

He felt the bed, trying to feel his child.

But it was cold.

He eased the door to Barbara's room shut and looked in on his wife. Ellen was asleep. One arm was drawn across her face to shut the world out. She was making mewing sounds. Poor Ellen. Who else has she got to blame? She's got to get back at somebody.

He went downstairs again. He opened the black bag and counted out the money on the coffee table. $24,-358.25. It was like counting out Bibby. Is this all my kid is worth? Figure a life expectancy of seventy years. That makes her worth less than $350 a year.

Not enough. I'll kill them.

He fell asleep on the sofa, the black bag hugged to his belly.

He was driving the Pontiac along the river road through pearly fog at a hundred miles an hour leaving a sand wake like a launch and John Secco was sobbing, "Ease up, Wes, for God's sake take it slower, you'll kill us both, that's an order," but he kept his foot on the accelerator and he was grinning because the black Chrysler was right there up ahead. He could see its red lights through the fog and Bibby's face in the rear window frightened to death and the gold woman blowing cigaret smoke in her little white face. He stepped harder trying to push the pedal through the floor but no matter how hard he pushed the Chrysler kept the same distance ahead. Then it was rising in the air

44

in an arc like a flying fish heading for the Tonekeneke's black water and he tried to pull it back with both hands to keep it from falling into the river but he had no strength, it slipped through his fingers and the splash hit him like a stone wall and he found his voice Bibby *Bibby BIBBY* . . .

He opened his eyes.

Ellen was kneeling by the sofa with her arms around him.

"Loney, wake up. You're having a dream."

He sat up. His belly felt sore. It was the bag digging into him.

"Oh, Loney, I'm sorry."

"About what?" He was shaking.

"The way I acted last night." Ellen's arms tightened. "As if it's your fault. I'm a bitch."

"No, you're not." He kissed the top of her head.

"Forgive me?"

"What's to forgive?" He swung his legs to the floor and groaned. "I swear I'm tireder now than I was last night. No calls?"

"No, darling. She'll be all right. I know she will."

"Of course she will."

"Why didn't you get undressed and into bed? No wonder you're exhausted. This sofa is the original torture rack."

"I must have dropped off. I could use a couple gallons coffee, Mrs. Malone."

"It's all ready for you. You just sit here. I'll get it."

"No, I'll come into the kitchen. What time is it?"

"Seven thirty."

"I have to make a call."

She was instantly alarmed. "To where?"

"To the station."

"Loney, you promised—"

"Don't worry, Ellen."

They went into the kitchen. Ellen spooned out the coffee, watching him. He went to the wall phone and dialed.

"Wes Malone," Malone said. "Who's this?"

"Trooper Miller. Oh. Wes." The young Resident Trooper sounded groggy. "What can I do for you?"

"Chief Secco there?"

"He's gone home for some shuteye. Don't ask me why, but I volunteered to hold down the fort till the day man comes in. Where the hell is he? I haven't slept since night before last."

"What's doing? I mean about those killers."

"Not a thing. Looks like they slipped through before we set up the blocks. Anything I can do for you?"

"No. I was just wondering."

"Forget it. Somebody 'll pick 'em up somewhere. Chief says you're on a couple days' leave, Wes. Make love to your wife or something. No rest, but it's recreation."

Miller hung up, chuckling.

Malone hung up.

He turned to find Ellen standing over the cups with the kettle poised, a human question mark.

"They got through, Ellen. So Bibby's okay."

I hope.

"Thank God."

Ellen poured. A silence dropped between them. He sat down at the kitchen table and set the black bag on the floor between his feet, where he could feel it.

When Malone came down from his shower Ellen was just cradling the phone.

"Who was that?"

"I called Miss Spencer."

"Who's she?"

"The school nurse, for the umpty-eleventh time. We have to have some excuse why Bibby won't be in school today, Loney. I said I was afraid she might be coming down with the flu and that I'd probably keep her home over the weekend just in case."

He touched her black Irish hair. "What would I do without you?"

"I'll bet you say that to all your girls."

"Yep." He kissed her and felt the tension of her body through the terry robe. "I'm one hell of a cop. I never even thought of the school."

"Oh, Loney, I've got to do something!" His stomach contracted. She was jerking with sobs again. "My baby ... waking up this morning with those horrible people ..."

"A few minutes ago you were thanking God they got through all right."

She kept sobbing. He kept stroking her. He could find nothing else to say. He had always hated to see Ellen cry,

46

he was a complete coward about her tears. They made him furious, they brought back memories of his mother, who had cried her eyes out when his father was alive. The night after his mother-in-law's funeral Ellen had cried till dawn, and he had run up and down in their bedroom finding no words of comfort, only curses at his helplessness.

"I'm sorry," Ellen pushed away from him. "Bawling isn't going to help Bibby."

"You cry all you want."

"No, sir. That nonsense is *over*. Let me make you some breakfast."

"I'm not hungry."

"You've got to. You hardly touched your dinner at the Inn last night, you were so tired."

"I'd throw it right back at you," Malone said. "Look, hon. We've got to figure out where we stand."

"All right, Loney." She immediately sat down. They both avoided the empty third chair.

"There's got to be something we can do besides stay here like bumps on a log."

"Let's get settled first on what we *can't* do," Ellen said. "What we can't do is let Chief Secco or anybody know they were here last night and took Bibby. That's the one thing I won't let you do, Loney. We'd better have an understanding about that right off."

"What do you think I am, crazy?"

"Loney, look at me."

He looked at her.

"You're not a cop in this thing. You're Bibby's father."

"I told you," he said gruffly.

"Just remember," Ellen said. "Or I swear on my child's life I'll walk out on you and you'll never see me again."

"What do you want," he shouted, "my blood?"

"Loney. I had to say it. We have to have that clear."

"All right, so it's clear! She's my child, too, remember!"

"Don't be mad at me, Loney."

"All right." He reached down and brought up the black bag and set it on the table between them. He stared at it bitterly. "We don't even know what they look like. Those goddam masks."

"Yes," Ellen said. "Goldilocks and the Three Bears."

"Huh?"

"Didn't you notice?"

"Notice what?"

47

"The woman was wearing a Goldilocks mask. The little one—Furia—he was wearing the Papa Bear mask, and the big bruiser was wearing the Mama Bear one. It must be a set."

"Then there's a Baby Bear mask! For Bibby?"

"That's what I'm wondering."

He jumped up, sat down again, shook his head. "No, that wouldn't make sense. Why would they put a mask on her? It wouldn't serve any purpose."

"I just thought I'd mention it," Ellen said.

He sat thinking. She got up and refilled their cups. "We can do one of two things, Ellen. We can either sit here and wait—"

"I'd *die*."

"Or I can try to find their hideout and get Bibby back."

"Wouldn't that be terribly dangerous for Bibby?"

"Could be."

"Oh, God."

"Ellen. Why don't I try? I can size up the situation better if and when I find out where they're hiding. If I see it's too dangerous for Bibby I won't move a muscle. How does that sound to you?"

"If you're sure. How can you be sure?"

"Then, if I can get Bibby safely away, we can turn the payroll over to John and tell him the whole story."

"And have those three come after us in revenge?" Ellen said with a shudder. "Forget about John, Loney."

"This money belongs to Aztec. We can't just let them walk off with it. I mean of course first we get Bibby back—"

"That's what I was afraid of. You're being a cop again."

"I'm *not*."

"Let them have the money. As long as we get Bibby back. Maybe the best thing after all is to sit here and wait. They'll come back with Bibby and we'll hand over the bag and that will be that."

"And maybe that won't be that," Malone said. "I won't kid you, Ellen. We've got to face up to the facts. If we do what you say—wait for them to bring Bibby back and pick up the money—all three of us stand a good chance of getting shot. That Furia would get a kick out of it. Why should he leave us alive? Even if we didn't see their faces, we've heard their voices and we know their names. Hoods like that must have a record somewhere—I think Furia's

48

served time, he used the word 'screw,' which is a prison term for 'guard'—they can probably be identified through the FBI central file in a matter of hours. They can't be that dumb—I'm pretty sure the woman isn't. And they're already in the bag for one murder. No, we can't trust them, Ellen. We've got to take some kind of action. Try *something*."

Ellen's face had gone the color of skim milk again. "All right then, Loney, you find their hideout the way you said. If you can rescue Bibby we can go off somewhere, hide or something, till those monsters are caught."

Malone got up and went over to the kitchen sink to look out the window. But he was not seeing the dirt driveway. When he turned around his eyes had come back. "It might not be so tough at that, Ellen. Actually when you think about it we have quite a few leads to where they're holed up. Furia told Hinch to walk there, so how far can it be? And it's likely somewhere across The Pike on the way out of town or they'd have been able to get there without worrying about being stopped at a checkpoint. On top of everything, the little punk mentioned woods and a shack."

"Balsam Lake," Ellen breathed.

"That's how it figures to me. If it's a Lake cabin—"

"They must have broken into one of them."

He shook his head, fighting his way through the mush. "That would be leaving a lot to luck. This wasn't set up that way, Ellen. It's been planned well in advance. I didn't mention it, but John says Tom Howland must have been in on the robbery and they doublecrossed him at the last minute. That would mean previous contacts between the robbers and Howland. That means they've been in town before. Also, the woman sounded familiar to me. I know I've heard her voice, a long time ago, I think. I'm betting she comes from New Bradford. Which could be why they picked it for their robbery in the first place, because she knows the town. Anyway, it all adds up to preparation. If they prepared everything else, they'd prepare a hideout too. Maybe months ago."

"A rental?"

"Why not? They could have rented one of the cabins, even used it during the summer. So if the police come nosing around the cabin now, what have they got to be afraid of? Of course, they'd rather nobody knew, but if they can produce a lease—"

"But in November, Loney? Nobody's at the Lake in November."

"That's not so. A few people from downstate rent cabins by the year—use them for weekends after the summer season. We patrol that Lake road the year round."

Ellen was considering his argument stubbornly. "I don't know. It sounds too dumb to me. I mean robbing and killing and still planning to hide out for any length of time within walking distance of where they did it. It seems to me that's the last thing they'd do."

"And maybe that's just why they did it," Malone insisted. "Who'd think of looking for them practically on the scene of the crime? The more I think about it the more I'm sure we've got something. I'm going to find that cabin, Ellen. Do you feel up to staying here alone while I scout around? I don't think they'll try coming back before dark."

"Don't worry about me. Do you think you can locate it in one day, Loney? There's an awful lot of cabins around Balsam Lake."

"I'm not starting at the Lake. I'm starting in town."

"What do you mean?"

"If they rented a cabin, it had to be through a real estate agent."

"Loney, be careful! You'll get people suspicious asking questions."

"Not if I do it right. I wish to hell I knew how the real pros go about a thing like this."

"Just keep remembering Bibby. Please, Loney?"

She clung to him, begging with her whole body. He kissed her and pulled away. She remained in the kitchen doorway.

Malone went upstairs. As he was rummaging through the clothes closet in their bedroom he suddenly remembered his hunting rifle. He had not used it in years. Had they searched the upstairs before he got home last night and found it? Ellen might have forgotten to mention it.

It was still on the top shelf of the closet, wrapped in oil rags.

He took it down and unwrapped it. After all this time not a speck of rust. That was one thing the Marines had taught him, how to take care of a weapon. With the rifle in his hands the tiredness was rubbed out. He felt around

50

on the shelf and found the boxes of .22 long-rifle cartridges.

You pulled a boner, *Mister* Furia.

He could have shouted with joy.

But he stood there, weighing and sorting. As he weighed and sorted the tiredness came back.

Not with Bibby in their hands. And a .22 wasn't much. You could kill a rabbit or a fox with it, but a rabbit or a fox wasn't a man with a Colt Trooper and a Walther automatic. I wish I could have afforded that .303 at the discount store. But the shells for it came to five-six dollars a box. Or that M-1 carbine they had on sale.

"Loney, what are you doing up there?"

He rewrapped the rifle and stowed it along with the cartridges at the rear of the shelf and went out into the hall to the linen closet and got some bathmats and went back and covered the gun and ammunition.

He changed into sneakers and put on his oilstained green-and-black plaid hunting jacket and cap and went back downstairs. Ellen was still standing in the kitchen doorway.

"What were you doing up there?"

"Don't let that bag out of your sight," Malone said, and left.

Malone drove the Saab off The Pike a few hundred yards north of the cloverleaf into the gravel driveway past the gilded white sign T. W. HYATT & SON REAL ESTATE and pulled up before the one-story frame building. It was his fourth stop of the morning.

He went in.

"Hi, Edie."

"Well, if it isn't the lawman," Edie Golub said, looking up from her typewriter. There was a pencil stuck in her dead-black-dyed hair. "Don't shoot, Officer, I'll come quietly." She was one of the girls from high school who wouldn't give him the time of day. She had never married. "Don't you ever crack a smile, Wes?"

"I'm off duty, I guess I can risk it," Malone said, smiling. "Young Tru in?" Old Tru had retired the year before and taken his grouch and arthritis to St. Petersburg, Florida. The whole town had breathed out. He had always been the one who stood up in town meeting and threw a monkey wrench into the works.

"He's going through the mail." She got up and opened the door to the inner office. "It's Wes Malone, Mr. Hyatt. Can you see him?"

"Wes? Sure thing!" Young Tru sounded eager.

Here we go again.

Malone went in. Hyatt was waiting with his best sales smile. He was a tall thin man with a badly pockmarked face, dressed as always like an *Esquire* ad. He was one of New Bradford's ladies' men, big on church socials and parties, the last one home. He was supposed to have been sleeping with Edie Golub for years—he had an old black leather couch in his office—with her "Mr. Hyatts" in the presence of third parties as their coverup.

"Sit down, Wes, park it. How's the manhunt going?"

"Oh, they got away." It was the fourth time he had had to say it.

"I understand Tom Howland was in on it up to his fat ass."

"Where did you hear that?" It was impossible to keep a secret in New Bradford.

"It's all over town," Hyatt said. "I heard it in the bank a few minutes ago. Is it true, Wes?"

"I wouldn't know. I went off duty before the case broke. Tell you what I dropped in for, Tru—"

"I knew that outfit would get shlogged some day," Hyatt said. "Whoever heard of a company in this day and age still paying their help in cash? If they'd invest a few bucks in a modern bookkeeping system—with an honest bookkeeper, ha-ha!—put in one of those computers, pay off in checks ... But I guess they got a big inventory in pay envelopes."

"You're right, Tru, they asked for it all right," Malone said. "Oh, what I'm here for. We've been having a little trouble over at the Lake. Now that the season is over some kids have been going down there nights to booze it up and generally raise hell—they've broken into a few cabins—and we've had some complaints from people who lease by the year. I've been getting up a list of the year-round renters to make sure we don't miss any. You know how some people are, afraid to make a complaint. Did you place any one-year rentals at the Lake in, say, the past six-seven months, Tru?"

"I don't think so. Bob Doerr gets most of the Lake stuff. Did you try Bob?"

"I got a few names from him. Well, I won't keep you."

There was only one real estate office in town he had not covered. If I strike out at Taugus Realty . . .

"No, wait a minute," Hyatt said.

He sat still.

"Now that I think of it, I seem to recall there was one. Edie?"

She popped her hairdo in. "Yes, Mr. Hyatt?"

"Didn't we write a lease for one of the Lake cabins around May, June, somewhere around there?"

"I really don't remember."

"Well, look it up, will you?" Hyatt sat back. "Y'know, Wes, I can never figure you out."

Find it Edie.

"What have I done now, Tru?"

"Here you are off duty and you're working. What are you, bucking for John's job? Don't you ever relax?"

"I guess I'm not the relaxing type."

Find it Edie.

"That's the thing with you married suckers. You don't know how to live. Now you take me."

"The way I hear it," Malone said dutifully, "you've been taken by experts."

"Who, me? The hell you say! Who said that?"

"Here it is, Mr. Hyatt." Edie Golub had a lease in her hand. Malone watched it all the way across the rug. Hyatt took it from her, and she stood there. But when he stared up at her she left quickly, shutting the door with a bang.

"Yes, this is the one. Somebody named Pratt, William J. Pratt. Signed the lease May twenty-third. How's that for a memory? You want to see this, Wes?"

"If you don't mind." Malone took the lease as casually as he could manage. William J. Pratt typed in. The signature unreadable. Deliberately so, he was positive, a disguised handwriting. It had to be a phony!

For Hyatt's benefit he produced a list and added the name and location of the cabin to it. He could have found it with his eyes shut. He could taste it. He handed the lease back and rose. "Thanks a lot, Tru. I'll check this one out with the others."

Hyatt waved. "Think nothing of it."

The real estate man went back to his mail, still a little miffed. Malone jumped for the Saab.

The description on the lease placed the cabin at the southeast end of Balsam Lake where it narrowed to muddy shallows. It was the least desirable section of the Lake.

According to Malone's list, "Pratt's" rental was the only one in this scattered cabin area that extended beyond the summer season. Made to order for a post-season hideout.

He drove off the blacktop into a lane, little more than a dirt path, and cached the Saab behind a clump of diseased birch trees in a thicket of wild huckleberry bushes. The bushes were nearly bare, but they made a tall tangle and they camouflaged most of the car. He draped fallen evergreen branches over the parts that showed, and when he was satisfied that the Saab was effectively hidden he left on foot.

He was a mere three hundred yards from the cabin, but his approach took the better part of a half hour. After a few yards he got down on his belly. It was the Marine game of his boyhood over again, traveling on hips and elbows, never raising his head above the underbrush, avoiding dried-out branches, sticking where he could to the cushioning ground pine. He made so little noise that once he surprised a squirrel on the ground; he could have killed it with a stone.

At last Malone reached the clearing.

He did not enter it. The clearing had been hacked in a rough circle out of a thick stand of pine woods and along its perimeter wild azalea, laurel, and sumac had taken root in an almost continuous band of bush. Here Malone settled himself.

He had a good view of the cabin. There were some expensive handhewn log structures along the Lake, but most of the cottages were of cheap clapboard or shingle construction, labeled "cabins" by the Balsam Lake Properties Association, whose brochures leaned heavily toward fiction. The "Pratt" cabin was a slapped-together shack of green-painted shingle walls streaked with years of damp. It had a badly weathered shake roof and a midget open porch with two sagging steps. The power line that provided its electricity dropped in from above the woods and hooked onto a naked insulator attached to the outside of the house. A bluish haze seeped out of the tin chimney on the roof. Like all the Lake cottages it used propane gas for cooking; Malone could see the silvered tank at the side of the cabin.

The haze coming out of the tin vent told Malone what he wanted to know.

The cabin was occupied.

They were there.

Malone had been lying in the bushes for almost two hours—he had just looked at his watch, it was half-past noon—when the door of the cabin opened and a man stepped out. He was not wearing a mask but his face was in shadow and Malone could not make out the features. He was sorry now that he had not stopped in town to pick up a pair of binoculars or at least borrow a pair from Jerry Sampson at the drug store, well it was too late for that. The man was a very big man with very heavy shoulders and Malone knew he was the one the small man had called Hinch.

The man looked around and then he jumped off the porch and strolled toward the woods east of the cabin. Malone got a good look at him in the sun. He was wearing a black leather jacket and tight black pants and blue Keds, and he had red hair that bushed down over his bull's neck. He had a broken nose and a face that went with it, brutal and stupid.

Here's one guy I'd better stay out of his reach. He'd stomp me to death and not even breathe hard.

Malone stopped thinking and started tracking.

He slid back on his belly until he was protected by the trees and then he got up in a crouch and keeping to the ground pine made a rapid quarter circle to the east, traveling on his toes. He knew where Hinch was headed, the other dirt road that led to the cabin. They must have their car hidden there.

He was right. They had parked it off the road and made an attempt to hide it but it was clumsily done and Malone could see it from the bushes across the road. It was the black sedan, the Chrysler New Yorker, covered with dust.

Hinch was bulling around in the underbrush. He got to the trunk and unlocked it and dug in for something inside. When the hand reappeared it was holding a half gallon of whisky by the neck. The seal on the bottle looked intact. He closed the trunk lid and shambled back toward the clearing.

Malone backtracked. He was just in time to see Hinch step into the cabin and shut the door.

He settled himself in his original hiding place. It would be a long wait if they were starting on another bottle. He did not know exactly what he was waiting for. A chance. A break. Anything. They might not show at all. Or they might all get drunk and pass out. The whisky might do the trick. I'll have to see where I go from there.

I should have taken the rifle. Why did I chicken out? I could have shot this Hinch in the brush. From ten yards away even the measly .22 cartridge in the right spot would have taken him out for good.

Yes, and what would the other two do to Bibby when they heard a shot?

No. Wait them out.

If only they hadn't taken his revolver. There was always something reassuring about the Colt's weight on his hip, even though he had never fired it except on the state police pistol range during refreshers, and once at a marauding bobcat.

He could see Ellen's face. Waiting.

Ellen's face wavered, and Malone became aware of another, immediate danger.

His eyes insisted on drooping.

Those damned four days and nights on duty, and that heavy cold before that. The couple hours' sleep I got last night were an appetizer, worse than nothing. He began to fight the droop.

His eyes kept doing it.

He fought them desperately. He pushed them up with his fingers. But even holding them open did no good. The clearing shimmered, fogged over.

If they're drinking in there they're maybe frightening Bibby. Don't be scared, baby. Daddy's coming.

The sky began to swing like Bibby's swing in the backyard. Up . . . down . . .

If I maybe shut my eyes for just a few seconds.

Bibby I'm out here. It won't be long.

He was still talking to her when sleep washed everything out.

"No more," Furia said. He took the bottle from Hinch and screwed back the top. Hinch was left with a few drops in his glass.

"Aw, Fure," Hinch said.

"I said that's enough." Furia was not drinking. He never drank anything but soda pop, not even beer. You're scared to let go Goldie once told him, laughing.

"Okay, Fure, okay." Hinch upended the glass and let the drops trickle into his mouth. He tossed the glass into the sink. It hit some dirty dishes and shattered.

"Watch it," Furia said. "You'll wake up the kid. That's all we need is a bawling kid."

"She's out like a light," Goldie said. She was still nursing hers, her third; she knew there would not be a fourth, not with Fure around. "It's wonderful what a mouthful of booze will do to a nine-year-old. She's gone on a real long trip." She giggled. "Byebye Bibby."

"You could be sent up for feeding a kid the sauce," Hinch said with a grin. "You want to get sent up, Goldie?"

"Listen, buster, when I'm sent up it's going to be for something important," Goldie said. "Like for murder?"

"All right, all right," Furia said. "You better get going, Hinch."

"Yes, *sir*," Hinch said.

"And don't go getting smart, Hinch. Just do like I told you. You remember what you got to do?"

"What am I, a birdbrain? Sure I remember. Hang around town, keep my ears open. Right, Fure?"

"That's right. Nothing else. No more booze, no picking up a broad, no anything. Just listen. And don't call attention to yourself."

"The best place to hear the dirt is Freight Street," Goldie said. "That's the street that runs past the railroad station. The old town rummies hang out down there. Cash their social security checks and run to the liquor store. Buy a bottle of cheap port, Hinch, and pass it around. They'll tell you what's going on. They get the word before the Selectmen do. You can park the car in the railroad lot. Everybody uses it."

"Yes, *ma'am*," Hinch said, and started for the door.

"Wait a minute. I'm going with you. We can meet afterward at the lot."

"The hell you say." Furia banged on the table with the bottle. "You're going no place, Goldie!"

"Will you listen to me?" Goldie said wearily. "Before you blow your stack. I've got to get a few things."

"Like what?"

"Like Tampax, for one, if you must know. I fell off the roof this morning. Also I need hair dye, I'm starting to sprout green around the roots. And some deodorant for Hinch. I can't stand being around him any more. He stinks."

"I ain't heard no complaints from my broads," Hinch said hotly.

"Well, I'm not one of your broads. Why don't you

57

break down and take a bath once in a while? We need some groceries, too, Fure. Bread, and there's no milk for the kid."

Furia considered this.

Hinch spat into the sink. "I thought you were the one so scared to show your pussy around here."

"You're sore because I wouldn't put out for you," Goldie said, smiling.

Furia went up to Hinch and stuck his jaw out. The top of his head came to Hinch's chin. "You been making passes at Goldie?"

Hinch backed off. "Fure, I never! I swear to God. She's just trying to get me in trouble. She don't like me."

"And that's a fact," Goldie said, still smiling.

"You lay one finger on her, Hinch, and you know what? You're dead."

"I never," Hinch mumbled.

"Just remember I gave you the word. About going, Goldie, the answer is no. It's too risky."

"It might be if I went to a beauty parlor. But there's a drug store in town that didn't use to be here. And I noticed a supermarket last night that's new, too. I'll be careful, don't worry."

"The hell with the milk," Furia said. "Nobody ever bought me no milk. I was lucky to get a glass of water without no cockaroach in it."

"Whatever you say, Fure."

"Tell you what, Goldie. Long as you're going, bring me back some of that frozen pizza pie crap. I feel like a pizza. And some cherry-vanilla ice cream."

"You'll go to hell in a hand basket," Goldie said, laughing. "Okay, pizza and ice cream."

"And say. Does this wide place in the road have a newspaper?"

"Sure, a weekly. Comes out on Thursdays."

"That's today. Groovy. Pick me up one." Furia chuckled. "I want to read my reviews."

Goldie nodded. She was in slacks and tight turtleneck and pea jacket, she had her hair bound in a scarf. She picked up her purse. "Okay, Stinkfoot, let's go. I'll stick my nose out the window."

"I swear to Christ," Hinch gargled, "if it wasn't for Fure I'd tear that bitch tongue of yours out by the roots."

"Then what would he play with?" Goldie said, and sailed past him as if he weren't there.

Malone awoke to pain. Something that felt like a needle was scratching his face and his back was one burning ache. For a moment he did not know where he was.

Then he remembered and he brushed the branch out of his face. He sat up in the darkness.

Dark.

He had slept all afternoon and into the evening, well into it. The moon was high. He could not see the hands of his watch but he knew it must be late. He had slept ten hours or more.

He stared over at the cabin. It was lit up; the shades were only half drawn. A figure passed, another. A third. They were careless. He could not see above their waists, but they were all there.

What chances have I missed?

How in God's name could I have let myself fall asleep with Bibby in there?

He strained to see her.

Bibby Bibby.

There's no sense to this.

There's no sense to me.

Malone crouched in his bush for ten minutes arguing with the prosecution. While he argued he found himself working his muscles, beginning with his feet and going up. Isometric exercises got the aches and stiffness out. It was something he had learned to do during the cramped hours in the patrol car.

He worked at it with passion.

It was like a miracle. When he was altogether limbered up he had a plan readymade. He did not know where it came from. One moment he was blundering about in a mystery, the next it was all clear, solved, perfect.

He began to crawl about in the dark, feeling for dry twigs, brittle leaves, pine needles. He arranged them just outside the clearing on a line of sight with the cabin's front windows, making a little pile of tinder in the heart of the brush and laying down thicker pieces of branch like the spokes of a wheel over it, Boy Scout fashion. It should be enough to blaze up and start a smoky fire. The bushes would burn slowly, it had been a wet month, there was not much danger of setting the woods on fire. But I'll burn the whole damn county down if it means getting Bibby out of there.

They're bound to see the fire or at least smell the smoke. They can't afford to have half of New Bradford roaring into the woods to put it out. They'll have to leave the shack and put it out themselves. If the woman stays inside I'll break her neck.

He blocked the view from the cabin with his body and on hands and knees struck a paper match and very carefully touched the flame to the tinder.

It flared up.

Malone ducked into the woods and made his way rapidly around the perimeter of the clearing to a point at right angles to the porch. Here he stopped. He had both the fire and the front door in sight. The fire had grown taller and huskier, it was jumping. Then the bushes began to smoke. The smoke tumbled into the clearing like a surf, a shifting wall through which the flames licked and darted. The sharp sweetness of burning leaves and green wood rolled through the clearing and struck the cabin. Malone's eyes began to water.

Come *on.*

They came. One of them opened the door and Malone heard a startled yell, then something about blankets, and a moment later three figures dashed out of the shack and across the clearing and began slapping the fire and stamping on embers, shouting orders to one another. They ran around like hooched-up Indians in a Western.

But Malone was not there to applaud. Even before they were at the fire he was on his way around to the back door of the cabin and yanking at the knob. The door was locked. He ran at it and through it without feeling anything. He found Barbara immediately. She was lying on a cot in a tiny bedroom with a door open to the kitchen and he ran in and snatched a blanket and wrapped her in it and flung her over his shoulder fireman style and ran out and through the broken door and into the woods and made a great circle around to where he had hidden the Saab and then he was on the dirt road and a heartbeat after that on the blacktop speeding away from the Lake.

Only then did the smell from the sleeping child's mouth register on his brain and he knew what they had done to her to keep her quiet.

Through the rage he kept telling himself well it could have been worse a lot worse I hope Ellen sees it that way goddam their slimy souls.

It was like a movie. One shot he was in the shack bundling Bibby in a blanket the next he was in the Saab pushing it at its top speed and the next he was in his own parlor.

And there was Ellen, flying from the rocker, grabbing Bibby from him, sitting down with the child in her arms to rock her the way she used to when Bibby was an infant. And staring up at him with such fear in her eyes that he wondered if he wasn't dreaming.

"What is it, Ellen? What are you so scared about? Wake up, honey, I got Bibby back and she's okay, they gave her a shot of whisky to keep her quiet, that's why she's sleeping and smells like that but it won't hurt her, don't worry, maybe give her a headache tomorrow morning, that's all. Now you put her to bed while I call John to shoot some cars over to Balsam and pick those three hoods up," he could not seem to stop talking, something was terribly wrong, her eyes said so, and he didn't want to know, it was too much, he had had enough for one day, "and we'll give John the bag with the money—"

Ellen mouthed, "It isn't here any more."

Thursday—Friday

The Money

"What do you mean?" Malone said. "What do you mean it isn't here any more?"

"Somebody took it."

"Who? How? I told you not to let it out of your sight!"

"Don't yell at me, Loney. I don't think I can take any more."

"Will you answer me, for God's sake? How did it happen?"

Ellen got out of the rocker with Barbara. She pressed her lips to the child's defenseless neck. "After I've got this baby in bed."

He sank onto the sofa staring. Halfway up the stairs she turned. "Did you say whisky? They gave a nine-year-old *whisky?*"

He did not answer. She hissed something profane and vicious and ran the rest of the way.

Malone sat there listening to the small sounds from upstairs.

I got Bibby back. The money is gone. Now what?

His elbows dug into his dirt-soaked knees and he took his head in his hands and tried to think. But the thoughts were stuck, going round and round like a toy train.

When Ellen came down she was calmer. Give a woman her kid to tuck in and she doesn't give a damn about anything else. She took his cap off and got him out of his hunting jacket and smoothed his hair. "I'll get you some coffee."

Malone shook his head. "Now tell me what happened."

She sat down by his side and held on to her own hands.

"There's not an awful lot to tell, Loney. It happened so fast. I had to go to the bathroom this afternoon—"

"And you left the money in here?"

"What was I supposed to do, take the bag to the toilet with me? Why didn't you chain it to my wrist? How was I supposed to know—?"

"All *right*." He did a swiveling exercise with his head, making his neckbones creak. "I can't seem to get this tiredness out. I could be coming down with the flu."

"You're such an optimist. You could be fighting it off." She smiled at him, anxious to get away from the money. She didn't want to talk about it.

"You went to the toilet and you left the bag here in the parlor," Malone said. And he could think of nothing else. "You came out and it was gone?"

"No, he was still here."

"Who was still here?"

"The man—"

"What man? What did he look like?"

"I'll tell you if you'll only let me," Ellen said sullenly. "He must have heard me flush and realized I was coming out so he hid in the hall next to the bathroom door. I guess. Anyway, just as I stepped out something hit me on the head and I fell down."

"Hit you?" For the first time Malone saw the bruise. It was well up in her hair, a purple and yellow-green lump the size of a robin's egg. The hair around the lump was stiff with clotted blood. "Christ!"

He clutched her. She made a hard bundle in his arms.

"And I sounded off at you! We'd better get Dr. Levitt to look at your head right away."

"I don't need any doctor. It throbs like hell, that's all. The main thing, Loney, we've got Bibby back."

He cursed. He did not know whom or what he was cursing—the unknown thief, the punks, Tom Howland, himself, or fate. The main thing, yes, but it was not over, not by a long shot. Not with that money gone. They'd have real blood in their eyes this time.

65

"I don't get it," Malone said, trying to. "Who could it have been? Did you get a look at him, Ellen?"

"Barely, as I was falling. And then it was all in a blur, sort of. It's a wonder I saw anything at all. I don't even remember landing on the floor. I must have been out fifteen minutes."

"Can you give me a description? Did you see his face?"

"Not hardly. He was wearing something over his head."

He was startled. "One of those Three Bears masks?"

"No, it was a woman's stocking. You know, like they use in movie holdups. That they can see through, but you can't make out anything clear."

"Did you see what he hit you with?"

"No, but I found the pieces afterward," Ellen said grimly. "It was my St. Francis." Ellen's St. Francis had been given to her by her father's sister Sue, whose name became Sister Mary Innocent. It was a cheap ceramic, but Ellen prized it. "I tried to paste the pieces together with Epoxy glue, but there were too many little ones."

He knew what losing her St. Francis meant to her. Her aunt had died in a Bolivian mission, throat cut by a crazy bush Indian convert.

Crazy. This whole thing is crazy.

"Did you see anything else, Ellen? What about his clothes?"

"A jacket, pants."

"Anything else?"

She shook her head and he saw her wince. He clutched her tighter.

"How big was he?"

"I don't know. Not very big. I'm not sure of anything, Loney. It's like I saw it all in a dream."

"Did he say anything? Did you hear his voice?"

"No."

"It's one of those three."

It was Ellen's turn to be startled. She twisted in his arms.

"One of them doublecrossed the other two. It's got to be, Ellen, nothing else makes sense. I fell asleep in the bushes out there while I was spying on the cabin. I was so exhausted I slept the whole day. Any one of them could have gone into town and I wouldn't have seen. They could even have taken turns. It figures. Nobody else knew the money was here. And if he wasn't big, like you say, it couldn't have been that Hinch. So it looks like it was the gun-happy one, Furia. You didn't see or hear a car?"

"I told you, I was in the bathroom not paying attention. And afterward, by the time I came to, whoever it was was gone. I ran outside and there wasn't a soul on the street, no car, anything."

Malone was glaring at the carpet.

"What is it, Loney?"

"Listen, baby, I've got to tell you. We're in a worse spot than before."

"But we've got Bibby back," Ellen said, as if that wiped out everything. She pulled away and jumped up. "I think I'll go back up and see if she's all right."

He reached for her. "You don't understand—"

"I don't want to!" And that made a lot of sense, that did.

"You've got to. Will you please listen, honey? They'll be back for their blood money. They'll be mad as mad dogs because I got Bibby away from them, and when they find out the money's gone, too, our name is mud."

"But one of them took it! You said so yourself."

"You don't think he's going to admit it to the other two, do you? Ellen, you and Bibby are in terrible danger. I've got to get you both out of here fast. I'll phone John right now. You go on up and get Bibby awake and dressed—"

"You do and you're dead," said the spinning voice.

They filled the archway.

He had not heard them come in, they must move like cats after a nest, it was ridiculous, they didn't look dangerous, they looked like a corny act on TV, the little one in the neat suit, the bruiser in the leather jacket and sneakers, the blonde in slacks and pea jacket with a scarf of psychedelic colors hanging down her front, as freaky as some farout hippie combo and as unconvincing. Ridiculous.

But my revolver in Furia's mitt, that's not ridiculous, and the Walther automatic in Hinch's (so Gunslinger didn't throw it in the Tonekeneke after all, he couldn't bear to part with it), and the look behind the eyeslits in the girl's mask that's somehow worse than the guns—not ridiculous, no.

They were back in their masks again (why? was it for

making horrible faces like the kids make when they're feeling nasty, to get the upper hand through looking horrible, half in play, half serious?), but there was nothing playful about these three, Tom Howland found that out, so did Ed Taylor, and what game is little doublecrossing Furia going to play now?

I wish I could see his face.

Furia marched in and asserted himself from just outside Malone's reach. The Colt Trooper was doing a dance. Malone watched it, fascinated. The bobcat's tail had done that just before he shot it. I wish I had it now. Put a slug right between Papa Bear's eyes. And a lightning second shot at Mama Bear. He fought with his fantasy.

"There's one thing puts me uptight it's a wise-guy cop," Furia was saying. There was a thickness, a curdle, in his tight voice; Malone could almost taste the sludge. "You made a first-class monkey out of me, fuzz. Didn't you?"

"She's my kid," Malone said. "What would you do if it was your kid and she's in a spot like that?"

But Furia wasn't listening. "Look at my hands!"

The trim little hands were stippled with soot. The spidery black hairs on their narrow backs had been singed off by the brush fire.

"I'm sorry about that," Malone said. In that TV drama he had seen recently, where the escaped convicts took over a suburban household led by a kill-crazy nut, the father had defied the criminals and talked tough to them through the whole thing. He had thought the father nuttier than the convicts. You don't get tough with a desperate criminal holding a gun on you, not if you want you and yours to keep on living. "My wife has some ointment if you got a burn."

"Shove it! Where's the kid?"

Malone half rose. Ellen was standing there like a deer.

He saw her throat move as she swallowed. "What are you going to do to her?"

"That's for me to know and you to find out, missus! Give me the bag."

Malone got all the way up, taking it slow, as he had done approaching the bobcat. He had no idea what he was about. I'll have to do something, I can't just let him shoot us down without lifting a finger. My bare hands against two guns ... Ellen ... Bibby ... Maybe if I talk. The way I say it.

"Look, Mr. Furia," Malone said.

"The bag!"

"I'm trying to tell you. I got home with my daughter tonight to find my wife practically in hysterics. This afternoon, while she had to go to the bathroom, somebody got into the house and ran off with the money. No, I swear to God! We knew how sore you'd be, and we've been sitting here trying to figure out—"

An ammunition dump exploded. When the peace fell Malone found himself sitting on the floor with his back against the sofa seat holding his shattered head, Ellen moaning and batting his hand away and dabbing at the wound with a bloody handkerchief, Furia an arm's length away, the Colt in his fist shaking. Malone had not even seen the barrel coming.

He shook his head cautiously, trying to clear it.

"He's lying," the blonde woman said. "Don't you believe him, Fure."

"Heisting us," Hinch snarled. "Let me at the sonofabitch, Fure. I'll open him up."

"I'm handling this!" Furia shouted. He poised the pistol over Malone's head. "You want another clout, smart cop? Or I should put a bullet in your old lady's ear? Now you tell me and you tell it like it is. Where's that bag?"

Malone raised his arm defensively. There was a rising howl in his head that overrode argument and any sort of rational plan. All he could think of was I'm going to get my brains splashed over my own rug by my own gun in front of my own wife without a lousy prayer to help her or Bibby or myself and then they'll get it, too.

"He's telling you the truth, Mr. Furia," Ellen screeched. "It was stolen from me by some man with a stocking over his head. I came out of the bathroom and he hit me over the head with my St. Francis, the pieces are in the garbage pail if you don't believe me. Look at the lump on my head if you don't believe me."

Furia seized her by the hair and yanked her backward. Malone to his own surprise made a feeble attempt to get at him. Furia kicked him in the jaw. Everything stopped.

When it started again Furia was saying in a worried way, "I don't get it."

"So she's got a lump," the woman Goldie said. "How do we know she got it like she says?"

"Yeah," Hinch said. "She could of fell down or something."

"But you saw the pieces of that statue in the pail," Furia said.

"So what?" Goldie said. "She broke it herself to make it look good, Fure. That's the way I see it."

"The gall," Hinch said. "To heist us out of our own heist!"

"They're lying all right, Fure."

"You're lying!" Furia yelped.

"You know we're not," Malone heard Ellen cry. He wanted to stop whatever she was going to say, push Ellen to the wall and thinking is out. But he had no strength to do anything. I wonder if he broke my jaw. "You're putting on a great big act for your two friends!" Ellen cried. "You came here today and stole that bag so you could keep all the money for yourself."

"Me?" Furia screamed.

Malone thought Furia was going to throw a fit on the carpet. The prospect turned him on. The howling cut off, the dark began to turn gray. He pulled himself back to a sitting position. He could feel the restorative adrenaline shooting. He'll turn on Ellen now. Malone bunched himself.

But it was a funny thing how Furia calmed down. He did not throw a fit. He did not turn on Ellen. He made no further move toward Malone. Instead he backed off with the Colt half raised, and when he spoke it was to Hinch and the blonde, in a wary tone. Malone saw his trigger finger tighten the least bit.

"You fall for that, Hinch?"

Hinch was staring at him. "You could of, Fure," he said. "While me and Goldie was in town."

"I never left the shack!"

"Fure wouldn't do a thing like that," Goldie said to Hinch. "Not Fure. Aren't you the clever one?" she said to Ellen. "Trying to split us up."

"She's trying to split us up," Furia said. "Yeah. She figures she can get us in a three-way fight they might find a chance to cut out. You see that, Hinch?"

Hinch hesitated. "I guess," he said.

"You better believe it." He turned to the Malones, gesturing with the revolver. "Sit down!"

Malone pulled himself up to the sofa. Ellen fell down beside him.

"Now," Furia said. "Payup time, folks. Where's that twenty-four grand?"

"Do you think I'd pull a stunt like this and put my family in danger of getting shot?" Malone said. He sensed a hairline advantage, a sliver of crack in the doom. He tried to keep the thump and throb of his head and jaw out of his voice, you don't show weakness to an animal. "Just to get somebody's payroll back because I'm a cop? Or even to keep it for myself? You can beat up on us, torture us, kill us, we can't tell you what we don't know. We're telling the truth. Somebody sneaked in here today and half brained my wife and took the bag. She didn't even get a good look at him."

Furia pounced. "Then why'd she say it was me? Huh? Huh?"

"Because nobody knew the money was here except us and you three. We didn't take it, so we figured it had to be one of you. As my wife was falling she saw he wasn't a big man. If he wasn't a big man we didn't see how it could be anybody but you. Anyway, that's what we figured. Maybe we were wrong, Mr. Furia. Maybe it was some housebreaker who just happened to pick our place today to see what he could steal and hit the jackpot. But that's the way it happened. That's all we know."

The eyes in the mask blinked uncertainly.

"He's a real con, this cop," Goldie said. "A regular mouthpiece. You going to swallow this, Fure?"

"See?" Hinch said. "He says it couldn't of been me."

"No," Furia said. "No, I ain't, Goldie! It's a stall, all right. You and Hinch turn this dump upside down. After we find our dough I'll learn this smartmouth who he's dealing with."

The first search was slapdash. Malone saw half a dozen places in the parlor where the money could have been hidden that Hinch missed. And from the sounds of Goldie's hunt upstairs, the rapidity with which she went through the bedrooms told the same story. The Malones sat with clasped hands under Furia's gun, straining for the first whimper of Barbara overhead, but she slept through the noise.

At one point in the dream Ellen asked if she could go get ice for her husband's jaw and something for his head, but Furia sneered, "You're breaking my heart," and Malone had to lick the blood off his lips. It was still trickling down from his hair.

Hinch was crashing around in the cellar when Goldie

71

came downstairs lugging Malone's rifle and the boxes of ammunition.

"Look what I found, Fure."

She offered it to him like a mother with candy. He grabbed it with a snarl of pleasure. But he had regressed, it was not the sweet thing he wanted, and he flung it back at her.

"A lousy .22! No dough?"

"I couldn't find it."

Furia ran over to the landing under the stairs and yelled down, "Any sign of it, Hinch?" and when Hinch came clumping up shaking his head Furia ran back and jabbed Malone's throat with the Colt and squealed, "Where is it, you mother lover?" while Ellen, eyes starting from her head, tried to cover him with her body and to Malone's surprise the woman Goldie took hold of Furia's arm with her free hand and pulled him off.

"Shooting them now won't get us our money, Fure. Fure, you listening to me? What good are they dead?" which sounded true to Malone and left him feeling gratitude, that was the New England tradition talking, her good old Yankee horse sense. Bless you, Goldie Whoever-you-are.

Furia tore the mask from his face and for the first time Malone and his wife saw him in the flesh, a corpse-face with the shine of corruption and ears like the White Rabbit's in Barbara's tattered *Alice* and the sad dead expression of a younger version of the little comic on the Smothers Brothers show, Pat Paulsen, but without the humanity or discipline, one of life's rejects, as frightening as an incurable disease.

He seemed to need air.

"You okay, Fure?" Goldie asked. She sounded concerned.

Furia batted her hand away and dropped into the rocker breathing like a fish. He kept hugging the revolver. Hinch and the automatic were holding up the arch looking at Furia with anxiety and a little something extra. A doubt?

Malone shut his eyes.

When he opened them Goldie was saying, "Why not, Fure? We can hole in here for a day or even two and like really take the place apart. That money's here, it's got to be. Right?"

She had taken her mask off, too. Her hair was just-

72

polished brass. The mask had smeared her makeup, it gave her features a blurred look like the TV sometimes when it pulsed. Malone squinted, trying again to place her, but she kept just out of reach. She was younger and must have been fresher then, not runny around the edges, maybe that's why I can't put my finger on it.

He stopped trying because Ellen was leaning her head on his shoulder and her face was turned up, her eyes were faraway glass. Even if we get out of this she'll never be the same, she'll have nightmares the rest of her life, she'll make a nervous wreck out of Bibby, she won't let the kid out of her sight ... and never, never forgive me. Not because all this is my fault but because I somehow didn't rise to it like one of her heroes, Sean Connery, Peter O'Toole, Michael Caine, or her special favorite Spencer Tracy on the Late Late Show the two or three nights a month when the cramps keep her from sleeping. I'm the dropout of her dreams, a smalltown hick who can't make it even medium-sized. And the cop tag a big gas.

Malone hauled himself back to what was going on. Furia had recovered, he was the boss man again. "Didn't you hear what I said, fuzz? You pay attention when I speak!"

"I'm sorry," Malone said. "What did you say? My head aches."

"I said we're moving in on you till we find that bread. You got nosy neighbors?"

"No," Malone said.

"How about delivery men?"

"Just milk. He leaves it on the porch around eight A.M."

"The rube who delivers the mail."

"He drops it in our mailbox near the gate."

"That's all?"

Malone nodded with caution. His head felt like a bongo drum.

"Well, just in case. Anybody comes to the door and asks, we're relatives from out of town. How'd you like me for a relative, missus?"

Ellen almost said something.

"Not good enough for you, ha?"

"I didn't say that," Ellen said.

Furia laughed. "You got it, fuzz?"

"Yes," Malone said.

"You, too, missus?"

Ellen gulped something and finally nodded.

"And don't let me catch you trying to use the phone, I'll break your dainty ladyfingers one at a time or, hell, why not? I'll sick Hinch onto you. You like that, Hinch?"

"Mama mia," Hinch said. "What I could do with her."

Malone was hit by ice water. I never thought of that. I never thought of that danger to Ellen.

"Now Hinch," Furia said. "This is a nice lady. Don't go thinking none of your dirty thoughts about Mrs. Fuzz." Goodhumored now, the thing was settled for him by Goldie and he can act the big brass with the reverse of responsibility—ordering the tactics after the chain-of-command below works out the strategy, a hell of a way to run a war. But it was a cockeyed war. Malone kept his eyes on Hinch.

Hinch took off his bear mask, too. No doubt to give Ellen the benefit of his manly beauty. He was looking pleased. Malone's glimpse of that Neanderthal face in the clearing had hardly prepared him for the reality of the closeup. He could imagine how Ellen was feeling at her first look, especially with thoughts of rape trembling in her head. He felt her shudder and he wanted to tell her that gorillas were peaceable animals, it was the sort of thing he would have said to Barbara to hush a fear. But Ellen shuddered again and burrowed closer, a big smart girl who knew the difference between a fairy tale and seeing it like it is, baby. Malone found himself fumbling around with a prayer.

"That goes for both of you," Furia said. "If the phone rings you don't answer without me or Goldie listening in. And about the door, front or back. Anybody comes you don't open till I give you the nod. Got all that?"

Malone said they did. Ellen said nothing.

"Okay. Soon as we tear your bedroom apart I'll let the two of you go up there, I'm sick of looking at you. But you stay there and no tricks. Remember about that phone."

"There's no phone in their bedroom," Goldie said.

"Anywhere."

"My child," Ellen said. "Is it all right if we take my child in with us?" She added quickly, "In case she wakes up, Mr. Furia. I don't want her to be any trouble to you."

"After we search your room, okay." Her humility seemed to gentle him. Or maybe he's turned on. Can he be

74

high on junk or LSD? No, not him. He's got to have control.

"She can remind you the spot you're in, missus."

Malone saw suddenly that Furia's bag was fear.

"Thank you," Ellen said humbly.

Furia had done a job on their room all right. While Hinch held the Walther on them downstairs. Every once in a while making a face at Ellen. He seemed to enjoy watching her shrivel and blanch. Malone could see Hinch's lips, red and wet as fresh blood, and occasionally the gray tip of his tongue. Those lips on Ellen. The picture made him pull his legs up as if he had been kicked in the groin.

Everything in their bureau drawers had been tossed every which way. The clothes in their closet had been ripped apart garment by garment. The bedroom rug, a handhooked American Colonial that Ellen had wheedled out of her mother, had been slashed in three places—how could it have hidden anything?—and kicked aside. A loose board of the old chestnut floor Ellen kept in a perpetual gleam had been hacked with Malone's handax from the cellar and pried up; they could see in the cavity before Malone replaced it a fossilized rat's nest that had probably been there for generations. Their imitation maple double bed had been taken apart and two of the slats broken, sleep-on-that-damn-you they seemed to say in Furia's alto, Malone had had to put the bed together again before they could transfer Bibby from her room. The child's head was lying on his hunting jacket. Furia's switchblade had disemboweled their two pillows, goose feathers lay all over the room.

They sat on the floor at the foot of the bed in the wreckage listening to Barbara's heavy breathing. She had waked from her alcoholic sleep when Malone picked her up and begun to cry, complaining that her head hurt, and Ellen had had to get the boss man's permission to go for an aspirin in the upstairs bathroom. She finally got Bibby back to sleep. Malone was holding an icebag to his swollen jaw, and with the bandage on his bloody head that Ellen had applied he looked like a refugee from a defeated army.

Ellen said with a shiver, "Hold me, Loney."

He held her.

"I'm scared."

75

"We're still alive," Malone said.

The Irish in her stirred, and she showed the faintest dimple. "You call this living?"

He lowered the icebag to kiss her. "That's my girl."

"Loney, are we going to get out of this?"

"I think we're all right for the time being."

"And how long is that?"

He was silent.

"Couldn't you make a rope out of the bedclothes and climb out the window while they're tearing up the house?" She's back at the movies again. "You could make a call to Chief Secco from the Cunninghams' or the Rochelles' . . ."

"How long do you think you and Bibby would last if they found me gone? You've got to face it, Ellen. We're in this alone."

She was silent.

I'm in this alone.

A glass crashed downstairs and they heard Hinch laughing. He's found the bottle of scotch Don James gave me for finally catching that white kid who kept heaving trashcans through their front windows. He tried not to think of Hinch drunk and tightened his grip on Ellen.

After a while Malone said, "Our best chance is if we can get the money back or at least figure out who took it. I could maybe make a deal with Furia, the money for him letting us go."

"I thought you thought Furia stole it."

"I thought he did. Now I'm not sure. A punk like him could put on an act, I suppose, but I think I'd see through it, I can usually tell when they're lying. He sounded pretty convincing to me."

"But if it wasn't Furia who could it have been? Maybe it was Hinch after all, Loney. He could have been like in a crouch—"

"Can't you remember anything else about the man who hit you?"

She set her head back against the patchwork quilt. "I told you all I saw."

"Sometimes things can come back. We've got to try, baby. Ellen?"

"Yes?"

"I know you're fagged out, but don't go to sleep on me now. Think! His suit. What color was it?"

Ellen's head rolled a negative.

"Was it a suit? Or could it have been a sports outfit?

76

Did the pants and jacket match?"

"I don't know. I didn't notice."

"Or maybe a leather jacket?"

She shook her head again.

"Could he have been wearing a topcoat?"

"I just didn't see, Loney."

"A hat?"

"No," Ellen said this time. "No hat, or I'd remember. The stocking was drawn over his whole head."

"You can see *something* of the face through one of those sheer stockings. Do you remember anything about his face?"

"Just a mashed nose."

"Mashed? Like Hinch's?"

"A stocking would mash . . . anybody's . . . nose . . ."

"Ellen, you're falling asleep again." He shook her, and she opened her eyes.

"I'm sorry."

"Hair? Ears? Tie? Hands? Feet?"

She kept shaking her head. But then her eyes got big and she pushed away from the bed. "His feet, Loney! He was wearing galoshes. Or overshoes."

"Overshoes." Malone stared at her. "Today? It's been dry all day, not a cloud in the sky. You sure, Ellen?"

She nodded.

"That's a hot one. Overshoes . . . What's the matter?"

"I just remembered something else."

"What?"

"His hands. He was wearing gloves. I saw the hand coming down after I was hit. I didn't see flesh. It was a man's glove. Black leather."

"Gloves," Malone muttered. "That could figure. If he kept his face covered he might also be careful not to leave his fingerprints around . . . if he was, say, a house-breaker."

"In New Bradford?" Ellen actually smiled. "You're making like a detective again, Officer. Why would a sneakthief in this town worry about fingerprints?"

"I admit it's a lot likelier one of them, the way we've been figuring. But why gloves? All three of them came here tonight barehanded . . ."

Malone looked surprised at the destination of his train of thought. He set the icebag on the floor carefully and slipped off his shoes and put his fingers to his lips and got up, not like an exhausted man now. He went to the door

77

and listened. When he came back he got down on one knee and said in a whisper, "Ellen, you've kept telling me it was a man hit you. Why a man?"

"Huh?"

"Why've you been saying the one who hit you was a man?"

Ellen frowned. "I don't know. His jacket, the pants—"

"That doesn't make a man. Not these days. These days you can hardly tell some women and men apart. A woman can put on a pair of slacks and a man-style jacket and with her hair squashed down by that tight stocking you wouldn't be able to tell, not from the front and while you were falling from a hit on the head. But there's two things about a woman would be a dead giveaway if they weren't disguised some way and that's her hands and feet!

"That's why she wore the men's overshoes on a dry day and men's gloves. She was taking out insurance in case she was spotted. Remember Hinch saying downstairs he and this Goldie went into town today? Ellen, it's Goldie who's doublecrossing the other two. She must have given Hinch the slip in town and come here on her own.

"She's the one knocked you out. She lifted the bag, and it's a cinch she hid it somewhere before she went back to the cabin. It adds up, because she's been trying like mad to sell Furia that we stole it. Yes, sir. That's it!"

Malone was feeling the small triumph. He craved Ellen's adoration. He wanted her to say, You've redeemed yourself in my eyes, my darling, you're my very own hero, you sure can overcome, I feel safe again.

But all Ellen said was, "All right, Loney, she's got it. How does that help us?"

And of course she's right.

Malone got back up and began to pad about. "That's the problem. What else have we got to work on? Nothing. So we've got to make use of it some way. How?"

"That is the question," Ellen said. She did not sound anything but beat. Her head sank back against the end of the bed.

But Malone's second wind continued to blow. It was something. It was a light where everything before had been black as the inside of the old gravity well out back that hadn't been used in fifty years and was full of green slime, like Furia must be.

"Maybe if we accuse her of it in front of the other two," Ellen murmured.

"No, that wouldn't work. She's smart, she's got Furia around her little finger, he'll believe anything she says. She mustn't even suspect we suspect her, Ellen, or she might get Furia to knock us off. I wouldn't put it past her. Deep down she's worse than he is."

"Could we make a deal with her . . . ?"

"What have we got to offer? That we'll tell Furia? Even if it put a doubt in his mind we can't prove it to him, and she'd talk him out of it. Up to now, Ellen, she's held him back. She wouldn't hold him back any more." Malone looked down at her. "The way it shapes up, we'll have to somehow find out or figure out where she's hiding it."

"You do that."

"Ellen, we can't give up."

"Who's giving up?"

"You are!"

"What do you want me to do, Loney? I can't fight them with my bare hands." That was it. That was it. "All I know is, I've got my child's life to protect—"

"*We've* got!"

"Do you want them to hear us fighting?"

Malone cracked his knuckles and began padding again.

Ellen's eyelids came down.

"I'm not sleeping," she said. "The light hurts my eyes."

He flipped the switch savagely. But then he collapsed against the wall. This is no good. We're at each other's throats. What did I expect from her? Up against the first real spot in my life and I try to lean on her like I never leaned on even my own mother. She wants to lean on *me*. She's got a right, I'm her husband. It's one man one vote time. You go into the booth and you're all by yourself. The American way.

He buckled down to it like Robinson Crusoe.

"Ellen." Malone shook her gently.

It was much later.

"Loney?" She had fallen asleep. She sat up and groped for his hand. "Is something—did they—?"

"No, they're quiet, they've given up for the night." Malone squatted beside her in the dark. "I've got to talk to you."

"Oh."

"No, this is different. I've been going over the whole thing in my head. I think I'm onto something."

"Oh?"

"Ellen, wake up, this could be important. Then you can climb into bed with Bibby. Are you awake?"

"Yes."

"Something struck me funny. How come these creeps picked our house Wednesday night?"

She moved and the floor creaked. "They were running away. Maybe they saw our light on. I don't think anybody else on the block had their lights on when I got back from the movies."

"But why pick Old Bradford Road in the first place? There's a Dead End sign at the entrance off Lovers Hill. A blind man can see it. Robbers running away aren't going to box themselves in on a dead-end street. And another thing. Before I got home from the station Wednesday night, did you tell them I was a cop?"

"Of course not. I was afraid if they knew they might shoot you down as you came in the door."

"Right. But just the same they knew, didn't they? Furia called me a cop straight out. How did he know? I wasn't in uniform. How did he know, Ellen?"

"That is funny."

"I'll tell you how. They had advance information!"

"You mean they saw you on duty in town during the day?"

"Then why did Furia say, 'Freeze, cop,' as soon as I stepped into the house? He couldn't even see my face, they had all the lights out except on the porch, and my back was to that. No, Ellen, they knew without ever having seen me before."

"But how could they?"

"Nanette."

Ellen said, "My God. The girl I've trusted Bibby to all these years! Nanette's in on this, Loney?"

"I don't know. It wouldn't have to be. Remember how many times Nanette's mentioned her older sister, how their parents practically disowned her because she went bad? Ellen, this Goldie is Nanette's sister."

"That's just a guess."

"It's a fact. I knew right away I'd seen her before, years ago, I was sure she came from New Bradford, but I didn't place her till I started asking myself all these questions and then it came to me just like that. Nanette said herself they've kept up a correspondence on the sly since Goldie left home. My guess is Nanette mentioned her regular baby-sitting job for us, and Goldie remembered it when they were in a jam Wednesday night and talked Furia into coming here and taking Bibby as security for the money. So I've got to get to Nanette first thing in the morning—"

"They won't let you go."

"I've got an idea about that, too. Ellen, it's our only lead. I can't pass it up."

"Lead to what? How can it possibly help us?"

Malone got to his feet. "Maybe it can't. But it's better than sitting here like three chickens waiting to get our necks chopped off."

"Oh, Loney, if you only could!"

And that was better, lots better.

He stooped to kiss her. "Now you're getting into that bed, young lady."

"Not unless you do."

"I'll come to bed in a while."

He waited until Ellen's breathing told him she was asleep.

Then he felt around in the dark until he located the loose board. He split a fingernail prying it up and he stretched out on the floor in front of the door with the board in his arms.

I'll have to pull it off in the morning.

Some way.

Friday

The Bottom

His eyes opened to cloudy darkness. The sun rose at a little past six thirty this time of year and so it must be after six. Yes, there goes old man Tyrell's rooster. The cock was past his prime in everything but his doodledooing, he was worse than an alarm clock. The Tyrells were down to one ancient biddy still trying for fertile eggs. Somebody ought to tell the poor old slobs, all four of them, the facts of life.

Eggs.

How do you walk on them?

Malone sat up swallowing a groan and shivering, the house was cold and he had slept without a cover. He stretched and a minefield of muscles went off. When was the last time I sacked out on a bed?

On eggs. How do you walk on them?

He listened. Ellen and Barbara were breathing as if it were an ordinary day. There was a great quiet in the house. So the Three Bears were asleep, too.

He wondered where.

Malone went through his isometric exercises to get the circulation going and when he was satisfied he got to his feet with no noise, which was his objective for more reasons than Ellen and Barbara.

He felt around with his big toe and located the hole and slipped the floorboard back over the rat's nest, thanking the Lord he hadn't had to use it. Hinch must be sleeping off the one he tied on with Don's scotch.

I could get away from them now, maybe all three of us could.

The thought came to Malone with the unexpectedness of all good things, in a rush of warmth.

All we have to do is slip out of the house and down the Hill to the station and we're safe in John's hands and that's the end of the nightmare!

It could be that easy.

Or could it?

He took two minutes to open the bedroom door.

His eyes were used to the half dark now and in his stockinged feet he made his way inches at a time along the hall, hugging the wall so the floor would not creak.

When he came to Barbara's room he found the door shut. With care Malone grasped and turned the porcelain knob and with more care pushed. The door refused to give. *It can't be Furia or Hinch, it must be the woman. But why should she lock the door? If she'd jumped into the hay with Furia I'd have heard them through the wall. It must be Hinch, she doesn't trust Hinch.*

He tucked that thought away with the others he was accumulating.

The door to the spare bedroom across the hall was half open. *Were the two hoods bedded down there?* Malone was puzzled. *With his broken nose and a bellyful of scotch, Hinch ought to be sounding off like a freight train.*

Malone crossed the hall in a tiptoe stride and pulled up at the other side, holding his breath. He listened some more. Very carefully he looked in, he could see well enough by now. But the room was empty.

One of the cots was gone.

They're sleeping downstairs.

He catfooted to the landing and risked a look over the railing. He could see down into the parlor and he could see through the archway into the entrance hall. The sofa was gone from its place, they had dragged it into the hall and set it up against the front door. A small figure lay curled like a cat on the sofa, covered by Ellen's afghan.

The sight of Furia defenseless tightened Malone's hand

85

and the railing squealed. Furia woke up like a cat, too. The Colt Trooper looked enormous in his hand. Malone dodged back to the protection of the wall, holding his breath.

After a while he heard Furia settle back to sleep.

Hinch must be bedded down in the kitchen on the cot from the spare room, blocking the back door as Furia was blocking the front. Malone strained and heard snores. He's there, all right. Maybe he drank so much that I could ... But there was Furia, who slept like a cat and woke up like one.

Malone made his way back to Ellen and Barbara. In the bedroom he made a slight noise and Ellen shot up in bed.

"Loney?"

The terror in her voice touched him like a live wire. He went over to the bed and stroked her tumbled hair and whispered, "It's all right, honey. Go back to sleep now," and she sighed and did.

Later, at the window, he even considered Ellen's suggestion about a rope of bedclothes. But Ellen and Bibby couldn't climb out without lots of noise and then there'd be hell to pay.

I'll have to play it like it is.

Malone settled down, going over desperately what he had muddled through during the night. Does it stand up? Or is this another pipe dream?

Goldie wouldn't have hidden the payroll where there's any chance Furia might find it. So the cabin is out. Ditto the Chrysler. And she couldn't hide all those bills on her body.

Then where?

Had she set up a place in advance, the way they set up their hideout at Balsam Lake? But she couldn't have known they were going to be hung up in New Bradford because of Pickney finding Tom Howland's body so soon and the roadblocks being set up so fast. Or even if she figured on that, the thing just didn't smell of a planned doublecross before the murder and robbery. The stocking on her head, the men's overshoes and gloves, she must have bought them in town yesterday afternoon when she and Hinch came in, at some store where she could be sure she wasn't known, maybe the Army-Navy Store on Freight Street, Joe Barron was only in New Bradford two years, it all smacked of spur-of-the-moment.

If that was true, then her hiding place for the money must have been picked on the spur of the moment, too.

All right. She's got this loot. And she's smart. She has to choose a hiding place where Furia can't possibly put his hands on it even by accident. Even if he suspects her and tries to muscle it out of her. Even if he makes her tell him. That would be Goldie's style.

All right.

The way it worked out, nobody in town knows the Aztec job was pulled by a gang including a woman. Nobody but Ellen and Bibby and me, and we don't count. That's the way she'd figure. So she can come and go in town like she did yesterday, with just the small risk that she might run into somebody who'd recognize her from the old days. And even if they did, so what? She's back to visit her family. Nothing to tie her in to the crime.

Yes, one likely place. Just the hiding place a smart cookie like Goldie would hit on. I've got to check it out.

But the way things are, where do I go from there?

At this point Malone shut his mind down.

One thing at a time.

He waited with his ear against the door and heard the woman go downstairs and the whistle of the kettle in the kitchen and the spin of Furia's voice.

Ellen was explaining things to Barbara.

"I knew those people were bad," Barbara said in her grownup voice, the one she used when she disapproved of something. "Did Daddy get me back?"

"Yes, darling. How's your head?"

"It feels icky. You know what they did, Mommy? That lady made me drink some *liquor*. She said it would make me sleep. I didn't want to, it tasted awful, but she forced me."

"I know, baby. Don't think about it."

"Why did I sleep in your bed last night?"

"They're here in the house, Bibby," Malone said. "I want you and your mother to stay in this room. Be very quiet and do what Mommy says."

"Where are you going, Daddy?"

"I may have to go out for a while."

"I don't want you to."

"Now none of that," Malone said. He turned away.

"I'm *famished*." It was her latest favorite word.

"I'll get you some breakfast later," Ellen said.

"Ellen, I'm going down," Malone said.

"Loney, for God's sake."

"Don't worry. Just stay up here unless they call you. Do exactly what they say. Don't cross them."

"What are you going to do?"

"Try to get Furia to let me go into town."

"Do you think he will?"

"He's got you and Bibby."

"How long will you be gone?"

"I don't know. I'll be back as soon as I can."

Malone opened the door. He could hear Hinch grousing and Goldie's sarcastic laugh. He went over and kissed Barbara and then Ellen and left in a hurry so that he would not have to see their faces any more.

They were in the kitchen slurping coffee. The kitchen looked like a battlefield on the morning after. They had yanked out every drawer and emptied every cupboard. Dishes and cutlery and pots and bottles and boxes of cereal lay strewn about like the unburied dead. The door to the freezer compartment was open and Malone saw that half Ellen's supply of meat was gone.

"Well look who's here," Goldie said. It seemed to him her brightness was forced. She's walking on eggs, too.

"Who told you to come down, fuzz?" Hinch growled. He had a growth of red pig bristles and his eyes were shot with pig pink.

"Shut up, Hinch." Furia looked at Malone over his cup. "Going somewheres?" Malone had changed into his good civvy suit. He was wearing a tie.

"I'd like to talk to you."

"Now that's being a smart fuzz."

"I mean about—"

"I thought you're ready to talk."

"Sure," Malone said. "I'll tell you everything I can, Mr. Furia. But what I mean—"

"For openers, how about where you stashed my loot?"

"I told you, I didn't take it. For one thing I had no time."

He tried to keep his eyes off the revolver on the table beside Furia's cup. Hinch had the rifle and the automatic.

"Okay, you had no time. But your missus did. Where did she hide it?"

"She didn't take it either. I don't know what I can do, Mr. Furia, but keep telling you that. Ellen's not out of her mind, you had our daughter. Look, I know this town inside out. If some local Lightfinger Louie snatched that bag yesterday, which is what I think happened, I could maybe get a line on him. If you'll let me nose around. I want you to get the money and get out of here as bad as you do, Mr. Furia."

"It's a trick," Hinch complained. "Don't listen to him, Fure. I don't know why you won't let me bang it out of him."

"Because he just ain't the bang-out type," Furia said. "Drink your coffee, Hinch. You think it's a trick, too, Goldie?"

Goldie shrugged in a swirl of hair. She had not bothered to brush it and she looked like a witch. "I still say they took it. He's stalling for time."

"I don't know." Furia pulled on his longish nose. Then he drummed on the table. He had scrubbed the soot off his hands and they were clean and neat again. "Suppose they see you?"

"Who?" Malone said.

"The fuzz. Your buddies. I was going to tell you to call in sick."

"That isn't necessary," Malone said quickly. "The flu hit the department and I did double tricks for four days running. The Chief gave me a couple days off to rest up. So nobody'll think anything of it if I'm seen in town in civvies."

"He's telling the truth about that, anyways," Furia said. "I read in this New Bradford paper yesterday about how the flu hit the cops."

Goldie said, "I still don't like it."

"Who asked you?"

"You did."

"Well, I'm letting him go in. He ain't going to be a hero, not with his wife and kid with us. Wait a second, fuzz." Furia picked up the revolver. "Go upstairs, Goldie, and make sure those two are okay."

Goldie pushed away from the table and brushed past Malone without a glance. She's walking on eggs is right. He stood where he was respectfully.

"Okay," Goldie called down.

"Okay," Furia said. "Your story is this was an outside heist, Malone, you prove it. You got till one o'clock. You either bring me that bread or proof where it is or who's

89

got it. If you know what's good for the missus and kid upstairs. Oh, and one more thing."

"Yes?" Malone said.

"When you come back here you better not have nobody with you. And don't try any hairy stunts like coming back heeled. Put it out of your clyde. Because you do that and Hinch and me we're going to have to decorate your floor with your wife and kid's brains. Kapeesh?"

"I kapeesh."

The Vorsheks lived in the Hollow near a narrow bend in the Tonekeneke. It was a settlement of poor men's houses huddled in the companionship of misery, but with an impersonal beauty unknown to city slums. The usual dirty children played on the tincan landscape or on the lunar stones of the riverbed during droughts and there were always flapping lines of wash, but backyards in the spring showed unbuyable stands of very old magnolias in impossible bloom, and everywhere in the summer vegetable plots as green and true as Japanese gardens.

Peter Vorshek worked in the incubator rooms at Hurley's chicken farm. Mrs. Vorshek did handironing for the ladies of New Bradford to boost the family budget, her free time given passionately to her church. Their daughter Nanette ran a loom at the New Bradford Knitting Mill and baby-sat nights for a few favored clients. The Vorsheks were of Slovak or Czech stock, Malone had never known which. The old man, who carried around with him the smell of chickenshit, still spoke with an accent. He had the European peasant's awe of authority. He always called Malone "Mr. Poleetsman."

Malone pulled the Saab up at the front gate and got out. Nanette was perched in a rocker on the porch reading a movie magazine. She was wearing skintight slacks and a turtleneck.

They look a lot alike all right.

"Mr. Malone." Nanette jumped up. "Something wrong with Bibby? I had to leave early Wednesday night because my mother was sick—she still is, that's why I'm staying home from work—"

"I know, my wife told me," Malone said.

"Oh! What happened to your head and face?"

"A little accident. Mind if I sit down a minute, Nanette?"

"Mind? I should say not."

She sat down looking flattered. He took the other chair and made his onceover casual. She was a large girl, larger than Goldie in every department, with the heavy Vorshek features but plainer than Goldie's, the pug nose, the high bones, the straight brown hair her sister camouflaged. He had seen Nanette at least once a week since her high school days, but he had never absorbed more than an impression of a sort of homely niceness, Bibby worshiped her and she was reliable, which was all he cared about. From what he had heard she rarely went out on a date. The talk among the studs was that she couldn't be made, her old man and old lady kept her on too short a leash, the YPF type, they said, a hardnose churchgoer, as tough to crack as a nun. But Malone thought he saw a certain something in her hazel eyes.

She's wondering why I'm here. No sign of being scared or worried like she'd surely show if she was in on this with Goldie and the two hoods. My hunch was right, she probably doesn't even know her sister is in town.

"My father's working and my mother's in bed," Nanette said with a downward look. For some reason her face was red. "You want to see mom, Mr. Malone?"

"I'm here to see you," Malone said. "I took a chance you'd be home, knowing Mrs. Vorshek is down sick." He managed a smile.

"Mrs. Malone know you're here?" He could barely hear her.

"Yes. Why?"

"Oh, nothing."

By God, she's got a thing for me. All these years and I never knew. He had been racking his brains trying to work out an approach, and he had come up the walk still trying. This could be the break.

"Nanette."

She looked up.

"How long have you known me?"

She giggled. "That's a funny question, Mr. Malone. You know how long. Years."

"Have I ever made a pass at you?"

"You? Oh, no!"

"Ever catch me in a lie, or trying to take advantage of you?"

"I should say not."

91

"Do you trust me, Nanette?"

"I guess I do. I mean sure."

"I'm glad. Because I'm going to have to trust you, too. In a very important thing. Something I can't even tell you about. I need information."

"From *me*?"

"From Goldie's sister."

She went white. She whispered, "Wait a minute," and jumped up and ran into the house. When she came back she said, "It's okay, mom's sleeping," and pulled the rocker closer to Malone and sat down on the edge and clasped her big hands on her knees. "She's in trouble, isn't she?"

"Yes," Malone said. "But I can't tell you what trouble, Nanette, or anything about it. All I can do is ask you to help me."

Her lips came together. "You want me to do something against my own sister."

"The kind of trouble Goldie's in, Nanette, she can't get out of. Whatever you do or don't do, sooner or later she's going to have to pay for it. Nothing can make it worse for her. But by cooperating you can maybe help Bibby and Mrs. Malone and me. *We're* in trouble through no fault of our own. Bad trouble."

"Because of Goldie?"

He was silent. Then he said, "Will you help us?"

"I don't get it."

"I wish I could tell you, Nanette, I really do. But there are reasons why I can't. Will you help us?"

She banged back in the rocker and began to rock in little fast rocks, like an angry old lady, lips' fleshiness thinned, hairy brows drawn tight. Malone waited patiently.

"It'll hurt Goldie?"

"I told you, it can't hurt her more than she's already hurt herself. You'll just have to take my word for that, Nanette. You've got to make up your mind that your sister made the bed she's lying in. But you can help out people who've always treated you right and never did anything against you."

"She's in New Bradford, isn't she?"

"I didn't say that. I didn't say anything, and I'm not going to. Nanette, look at me."

She looked at him.

"I'm desperate. I mean it."

Whatever she saw in his eyes, it made her stop rocking. She looked out over the porch rail at the hills, seeing something he could not. "I guess I always knew Goldie would wind up bad. When I was a little girl I used to look up to her because she was so much prettier and smarter than me and the boys were all ape over her. And because she wasn't scared of my parents. She'd sass papa back to his face something awful and he'd smack her hard and she'd never even cry, I thought she was so brave ... What do you want, Mr. Malone?"

He let out his breath. "When is the last time you saw her?"

"Years ago."

"You didn't see her, say, this past summer?"

"This year? No."

"Does she ever write to you?"

"Once in a while. Not often, but regular, if you know what I mean. From all kinds of places. My father always goes to work before the mailman comes, but I get to the mailbox in the morning before my mother in case there's a letter from Goldie. Mom would tear it up on the spot if she got there first. My parents are still very Old Country, they never changed. Since Goldie ran away they won't even let me mention her name. Not that she uses it any more, the Vorshek, I mean. She calls herself Goldie Vanderbilt, I don't know why."

Malone heard her out. When she stopped he said casually, "Ever save any of her letters?"

Jesus let this be it.

"Oh, all of them," Nanette said. "I keep them hid in my old toy chest in the attic that mama hasn't touched for years."

"Could I please see her last letter?"

Nanette got up without a word and went into the house. Malone sat on the Vorshek porch looking out at the half-naked willows stooped over the river and the fading hump of hill beyond, seeing nothing but his predicament.

Even if my hunch proves out I'm a long way from home.

One step at a time is how you have to do it.

Then you figure out where you go from there.

Till one o'clock.

At this point Malone's mind got stuck again.

When Nanette came back she was in a hurry. Her red hands were clasped about an envelope, trying to hide it. Malone had never noticed before that her fingernails were bitten all the way down.

"Mama's getting restless," she whispered. "You better go, Mr. Malone, before she wakes up. I don't want to have to explain what you're doing here." She shoved the letter into his hand. "Put it away."

He put it into his pocket without looking at it.

"It isn't typewritten?"

"Goldie don't know how to type."

"Nanette, if I just knew how to thank you."

"Go on, Mr. Malone!"

A hundred yards shy of the turnoff from the Hollow road to The Pike, Malone pulled the Saab over and killed his engine.

The envelope was cheap supermarket stuff but the note-paper was heavy and had a gold *GV* monogram on it and a powerful perfume. The envelope was postmarked JERSEY CITY, N.J. 23 OCT, the return address at the upper left said "G. Vanderbilt, care P.O. General Delivery, Boston, Mass. 02100." The letter was less than a month old, just what the doctor ordered, a recent specimen, God knows I'm no expert, but this ought to do it.

From bitter compulsion he read the letter. It was full of news that couldn't be pinned down: her "job" (without specification—and what sort of job would it be that spanned Jersey City and Boston?—that wasn't very smart, Miss Vanderbilt), her "loaded boy friend" (no name), the glamorous nightspots, the marvelous clothes, the great times, and so on and on, no mention of a Furia or a Hinch or the grimy life the threesome must lead . . . all of it a fairy tale to impress the yokel kid sister (like the elegant stationery) and maybe get her to follow Goldie Vander-bilt's example and split from the old family homestead out of some vicious need to corrupt Nanette and break what was left of the Vorsheks' hearts.

The bitch.

The only good thing was that she wasn't fooling any-body but herself. Maybe Nanette once felt envious, swal-lowing the fairy tales, but not any more; she knew it was all made up. She probably looked forward to the per-fumed letters the way she did to a rerun of *Snow White* or a costume movie in bigger-than-life Panavision.

Malone put the letter carefully away, started the Saab, and drove on into town.

He waited on the three-seater leatherette bench outside the steel railing while Wally Bagshott turned down a nervous young couple for a personal loan. Wallace L. Bagshott was president of The Taugus County National Bank, founded by his great-grandfather in the days of the granite quarry and the hitching post. A Bagshott had settled New Bradford; the old Bagshott house, dated 1694, still overlooked the Green, a historic showplace opened to the public one day a year. The double statue on the Green of Zebediah and Zipporah Bagshott, known to the town as the Zizzes, was the favorite privy of the starlings.

"Wes, boy." Bagshott had ushered the young couple out and was smiling over at Malone. "You want to see me?"

Malone jumped up. The banker was tanned halfway up his scalp, a result of spending all his free time hacking divots out of the New Bradford golf course. His employees called him "Smiley" behind his back and his customers "Wally the Knife," on explosive occasions to his face.

"Hey, you look like you're in line for a couple of Purple Hearts. What happened to you?"

"Believe it or not, I fell down the stairs. Wally—"

"What are you doing out of uniform? John fire you I hope I hope? You know my standing offer—"

"I'm off duty," Malone said, going through the gate. "Wally, I have to talk to you."

"Squattee voo." The banker sat down, still smiling. "Though if it's about a personal loan, Wes, I've got to tell you right off—"

"It's not about a loan."

"That's a load off. The way things are we're having to tighten up. Well! Sit down, Wes." Malone sat down. "How's the better half? That's one damn fine piece you grabbed off. Every time Ellen comes in my tellers get all worked up. And not just my tellers if you know what I mean. Ha-ha."

"Look, Wally," Malone said.

"No offense, Wes, no offense. Share the wealth is my motto. Talking about that, terrible thing about Tom Howland, isn't it? They say he was in on it."

"I wouldn't know. Wally, I need a favor."

"Oh?" Bagshott immediately stopped smiling.

"I'd like to inspect your safe deposit records."

"What for?"

"I can't tell you anything about it. Except that it's important."

"Well, I don't know. You're out of uniform—"

"Let's say it's undercover work."

"No kid?" The banker leaned forward eagerly. "It's about this stickup, isn't it?"

Malone was quiet.

"Well, if you can't. Okay, Wes, I don't see why not, seeing you're an officer of the law."

"One thing, Wally. I've got to ask you to keep this absolutely to yourself."

"You know me, pal." Bagshott winked. "Tightest snatch in town."

He waved his Masonic ring and led the way to the rear of the bank. He dismissed the woman on duty in the Safe Deposit Department and unlocked a drawer.

"Here's the check-in card."

"The one they sign when they want to get into their box?"

"Isn't that what you want to see?"

"Yes. But I'm also interested in your latest applications for box rentals."

"How far back you want to go?"

"Yesterday."

The banker looked startled. "Yesterday?"

Malone nodded.

"You mean to say—?"

"I'm not meaning to say anything. Just let me have them, would you mind?"

Bagshott took out three cards. He was so conscious of the hot breath of crime that he broke his own rule about never allowing himself to look worried. "Three new boxes rented yesterday," he said with a careful look around. "They haven't even been put in the master file yet."

"I'd like to take these into one of the rooms."

"Good idea. Sure thing."

"Alone."

Bagshott frowned. Then he walked quickly away.

Malone went into the nearest unoccupied cubicle and shut the door. He sat down at the desk and pulled the light chain and spread the cards and took Goldie's letter from his pocket.

He spotted it at once. "Georgette Valencia, The Cascades, Southville." The Cascades was a twenty-year-old housing development straddling the town line, in an unincorporated village policed on contract by the New Bradford department. Malone knew every family in the Southville district. No one of that name lived there. So the "Georgette Valencia" was a phony.

For confirmation, the Gs and Vs in the signatures on the application and check-in cards were identically formed with those in Goldie's letter, the Gs with a squared-off bottom line instead of the usual curve, the Vs like hasty checkmarks. Even the small ts were the same, with the crossmarks tilted downward from right to left in a fancy swash.

No doubt about it, Georgette Valencia was Goldie Vorshek, alias Goldie Vanderbilt.

So I doped it right. Goldie hijacked the stolen payroll and stashed it in the one place where nobody else could get to it, a safe deposit box in the bank.

So now I've got the money back.

Well, not exactly got it back, but I know where I can lay my hands on it.

Not exactly lay my hands on it, unless . . .

Malone stowed the letter away, gathered up the cards, turned off the light and went out into the banking room. Bagshott was alone at his desk, talking on the phone. The moment he saw Malone he hung up. Malone laid the cards on the desk and said, "I'd like to get into one of your boxes."

The banker looked around. "Sure, Wes," he said. "Sit down, make it look natural. I mean sure, soon as you bring me the court order."

Malone lowered himself into the chair, holding onto the corner of Bagshott's desk. "You won't let me see it without the judge's authorization?"

"I can't, Wes. You know the law."

"Well, how about these cards? If I could just borrow them for a few hours—"

Bagshott stared. It was his banker's stare, the fish eye. "There's something funny about this. You trying to pull something, Wes? You know I can't let any official records out of the bank. What's going on?"

"I can't tell you."

"Which box is it?"

Malone got up and walked out.

He drove over to Elwood's and sank onto a stool. The breakfast rush was over and the diner was almost empty. He was grateful that no one had the juke box going. His head was kicking up a storm.

He was famished. He had not been conscious of his hunger until this moment. I haven't eaten in how long is it?

"Morning, morning, Wes," Elwood said, slapping his rag around. "Some excitement."

"I can live without it, Ave," Malone said. "Double o.j., wheats and sausage, stack of toast, coffee."

"You sound starved," the old man cracked. "Like it's your last meal."

Malone tried to appreciate the joke.

"And peaked, too. Damn shame how they run you boys ragged." Elwood went into his kitchen wagging his head.

Run ragged.

That's for sure, Ave.

What do I do now?

I can't go to the judge without telling him why I want the order, and if I do that I set Ellen and Bibby up for cemetery plots. Judge Trudeau is a stickler for the law books, people don't mean a goddam to him, he'd have the house surrounded by state police in ten minutes. So I can't get into the box. I can't produce the money for Furia.

I can't even take possession of the bank forms that along with Goldie's letter would show Furia she rented the safe deposit box. And without proof that she doublecrossed him he wouldn't believe me, it would be my word against hers, and I don't go to bed with him. He'd get so worked up about what he'd think was a stall he'd likely shoot the three of us on the spot.

So where do we go from here.

Nowhere.

End of the line.

There's just so much a man can do by himself.

It came to Malone suddenly that he had just thought a profound thought. It was the exact story of his life.

Ellen didn't start calling me The Malone Ranger just for laughs. She tagged me good from the start. Wes Malone against the world and to hell with you, neighbor. Malone the on-his-own-two-feet guy, he asks nothing from nobody. Not even from the only man in the world he respects and trusts. Too proud, that's Loney. Maybe too sore at the whole raw deal that began with the old man crawling into the sack every night giving nothing to anyone, not so much as a word or a look, and the mother cursing her life and taking with both tobacco-stained hands. So you grow up giving in spite of yourself.

Giving is giving out.

Taking is giving in.

Giving-out keeps you on top of the enemy.

Giving-in is crawling on your belly to the sonofabitch world.

Or is it? Is it being a loser to ask for a helping hand when you can't make it any more on your own? What the hell else is the Marine buddy system but I'm-right-here-brother?

That's why I was a lousy grunt.

That's why I'm a lousy cop and husband and father. That's why John and Ellen look at me the way they do sometimes, Bibby's too young to know better.

I've been kidding myself. And shortchanging them.

But there's the but.

Can I do it?

My whole life says no.

My whole life is my bag, that's been my hangup. Now I've got to. No choices left. My back to the wall and Ellen's and Bibby's, too.

Their whole lives are on the line.

That's what it comes down to.

Malone looked up at the diner clock.

Ten minutes past eleven.

Less than two hours to putup time.

He dropped a couple of one-dollar bills on the counter not bothering to wait for change I might chicken. And ran.

John Secco got up and took a few turns. He hated his private office and spent as little time as possible in it. It was down the hall from the three cells and it was not much bigger than they were, whitewashed brick walls and nothing on them, the only real difference was a door instead of bars. He looked tired, almost as tired as Malone.

Malone watched him.

After the third turn Malone said stiffly, "If you want my badge, John."

The chief stopped. He had black brows under the gray

thatch and they went up like windowshades. "What are you talking about?"

"I know I ought to have come to you right off. Any way I slice it I'm an officer of the law—"

"Any way you slice it you're Ellen's husband and Barbara's father. What kind of a man do you think I am? I'd have done the same thing." He dropped into the swivel chair and leaned back from the steel desk. "We've got to think this out, Wes. We can't afford a mistake."

"God, no," Malone said.

"The first problem is Ellen and Barbara. And you, if you go back."

"No if, John. I can't leave them there alone."

Secco nodded slowly. His face reflected his father's pastures, full of steel ruts and the patience of livestock. "The question is, Wes, how to capture those three without endangering the lives of you and your family."

"That isn't the question at all," Malone said. "I started out thinking that way, too. It can't be done."

The chief seemed about to argue. But he did not. "What do you mean it can't be done?"

"There's no way," Malone said. "Believe me, John. As long as they've got the guns and Ellen and Bibby there's no way. Any move we make they'll shoot them. Or threaten to unless we let them make a getaway, using Ellen and Bibby as shields. Either way they're goners. Furia's got nothing to lose. He's in for one murder, he may as well be in for three or four. You don't know this man, John. Any way this thing winds up, Furia's going to go out shooting. I doubt he can be taken alive."

Secco said quietly, "What do you suggest, Wes?"

"The money. Give him the money."

Secco looked away.

"Get it out of the safe deposit box. If you talk to him, maybe Judge Trudeau will play ball. He owes you, John, if not for you he'd never have made judge. So get Trudeau's order and get the money out of the box and offer Furia the twenty-four thousand in exchange for Ellen and Bibby. Give him a safe conduct and time for a getaway. The money is what he wants. It's the only deal he'll make."

Malone stopped, exhausted.

The chief said nothing.

"You won't buy it," Malone said.

"No, I won't, Wes. Do you know why?"

"Why?"

"Because it's not in my power to do what you want. That payroll belongs to Aztec."

"The hell with Aztec!"

"It's not that simple," Secco said. "I guess I'd feel the way you do if I were in your spot, Wes. But I have the legal responsibility. Even if I were willing to do it, it isn't my money to dispose of."

"Then put it up to Curtis Pickney! What the hell is twenty-four thousand dollars compared to two lives? Even Pickney ought to be able to see that!"

"It doesn't belong to Pickney, either. It belongs to his company. It really wouldn't be Aztec's decision, either. They're insured against robbery and theft, so it's the insurance company that's holding the bag. Can you see an insurance company authorizing a deal with a payroll robber at their own expense? Wes, you're dreaming. If you weren't so desperate you'd realize it."

"You've got to do this for me, John," Malone said hoarsely. "I don't care whose money it is. If I could borrow twenty-four thousand dollars from the bank or a personal finance company I'd do it in a shot, even if it meant going into hock for the rest of my life. But you know Wally Bagshott or nobody would lend a man with my salary and no collateral that kind of money. Even selling my house wouldn't do any good, I have less than six thousand dollars' equity in it. That Aztec payroll is all I've got to bargain with! John, for God's sake."

John Secco shook his head. His eyes were screwed up as if the sun were in them.

"You won't do it for me." Malone cracked his knuckles, not knowing he was doing it. "The first time I've ever asked you or anybody for a goddam thing and you won't do it!"

"I can't do it," Secco said. "I'm the police officer in charge of law enforcement in New Bradford, Wes, I've got a sworn duty. I can't take somebody else's money and make a dicker with a gang wanted for murder and robbery—I'd be open to indictment for conspiracy and grand larceny myself. And even if I did it, do you think this gang would trust a police chief to hold up his end of such a deal? They'd still take Ellen and Barbara as hostages for their getaway. No, there's got to be some other way—"

The telephone rang.

"Yes?" Secco said. His face turned to stone. "Yes, he's here, Ellen."

Malone gaped.

"Wes." Secco held out the phone.

"Ellen," Malone said in a whisper. "What is it?"

"I've been trying to reach you all over town." He did not recognize her voice, it was inhuman, something out of a machine. "They've left."

"Left."

"Furia got nervous. He decided he couldn't trust you. That woman worked on him. So they left. They took Bibby with them."

"Let me get this." Malone ran the back of his hand over his forehead. "They took Bibby . . ."

Now she was crying.

"Honey. Please. Did they say where to make contact with them? Did they go back to the cabin at the Lake?"

"I don't know, Loney, I don't know . . ."

"Ellen, you've got to stop crying a minute, I've got to know exactly what they said. They must have said something."

"Furia said you're to have the money by noon tomorrow here in the house and wait with it till they get in touch with us he didn't say when and no police he said or we'll never see Bibby again, not even her body, it's our last chance he said . . ."

"I'll be home as soon as I can."

Malone hung up.

"I heard it," Chief Secco muttered. "I'll give you all the time you want, Wes, I won't make a move or say a word to anybody about this without your permission and if there's any way I can help, I mean except . . ."

"Go to hell," Malone said, and walked out.

He made his approach with the old stealth knowing it was unnecessary and hoping it was necessary but they were gone except for a garbage can full of empty food tins and liquor bottles and some filthy dishes in the sink.

Malone searched the cabin for a clue, anything that might tell him where they had gone. There was nothing and for a time he went out of his mind, he did everything in a trance of fury, blundering through underbrush and kicking cabin doors in and racing up and down dirt roads along the Lake looking for a sign of life, a smudge against the sky, a car in the bushes, anything.

Afterward, in the dusk, he drove the Saab slowly back to town.

First I had the money but lost Bibby.
Then I got Bibby back but lost the money.
Now I've lost both.

Saturday, Sunday, Monday, Tuesday

The Weakness

The house was cold. Malone turned up the thermostat but nothing happened. He went down into the cellar and pressed the emergency button on the stack and the furnace boomed. Afterward he could not remember anything about the heat, the cellar, or the furnace.

It had been a night to forget. Ellen had spent the day cleaning up the mess and getting things put back, and after Malone got home she cooked a dinner from something the visitors had left in the fridge and Malone could not remember what he had put in his mouth. He had not wanted to go to bed, saying "Suppose . . ." but Ellen rapped his lips with her finger and stripped his shirt and pants off and his underwear and socks and got him into his pajamas as if he were a child. As if he were Bibby. She tucked him in and crept in beside him and for the first time Malone cried. He kept jerking as if under a whip and Ellen tightened her arms and legs about him and murmured mothering sounds until, like a child, he fell asleep.

When he fell asleep Ellen got out of bed and shuffled to Barbara's room. She spent the rest of the night sitting in Barbara's little rocker with Miss Twitchit in her lap. Once she sang the soft song she had made up before Bibby could even crawl, not the tune really, it was let's face it the Brahms *Lullaby*. I couldn't make up a tune Ellen used to say with a laugh I'm practically tone-deaf. But the words were her own, hush and baby and love, words that came from her womb.

She woke up in a nasty dawn and found that she was crying. When she was over it she put Miss Twitchit back in her doll cradle that Loney had made from a broken-down rocker of his mother's and only then did she go back to the big bedroom and stretch out beside her husband. She lay on the edge of the bed so as not to disturb him. When she heard him grunt and sit up she made sure to have her eyes shut.

Thank God she's getting a decent sleep.

At first Goldie was all for lighting out, even before they came back for the kid.

"It's getting more and more risky, Fure. I don't like this hanging around New Bradford."

"The payroll," Furia said.

"I know, but what's the sense being mules about it when we're hot for a murder rap? There are plenty other payrolls around. So we take our lumps on this one. I say let's scramble and lose ourselves in the scenery. We ought to get out of the state. Maybe hit for Kansas or Indiana, those farmers out there are sitting ducks."

"I ain't leaving here without the bread," Furia said, and from the way he said it Goldie knew that she had better clam up, her skin was starting to itch again.

She picked the emergency holeup after they got the kid back. The shack they had rented at Balsam Lake was out of the question, they agreed on that, but Furia wanted to bust into one of the other cabins, maybe at the other end of the Lake, he was in a rotten mood and it took special methods to work him out of it. Goldie worked him out of it on the bed in the shack they were abandoning after she did what he liked best, which Hinch had watched through a good crack in the door, it was his favorite. Hinch was supposed to be guarding the kid, Furia had told him to, but he enjoyed their wrestling holds when he could do a Peeping Tom without getting caught. Anyways the kid was too scared to try anything, she was right there with

107

him in the kitchen shivering on a chair, he could hear her teeth going clackety-clack without turning around.

"The Lake is the first place he'll look, Fure, believe me," Goldie said, "as soon as he gets the message we grabbed the kid again. He'll tear up these woods. So it figures like we get out of here fast and settle in where he can look all year long and he won't find us. We oughtn't to have come back to this shack at all. What's the sense having to cool him before you get the money back?"

"Okay, okay," Furia said dreamily, "I buy it."

Hinch was making faces at the kid for kicks when they came out of the bedroom.

They spotted the Saab with Malone at the wheel hell-bent for the Lake, he was hunched over blind, he passed the Chrysler without a look.

"What did I tell you?" Goldie said with a laugh. "Drive on, Stinkfoot."

The house she had picked was at the other side of town, near the town line of Tonekeneke Falls but well away from both centers, standing by itself on a back road a good hundred yards in and hidden by shade trees taller than the house. You could pass it a thousand times and never know it was here, Goldie said. Which is a fact, Furia said with satisfaction.

There was even a flagstoned patio out back and an outdoor pool with a heater attachment, but the pool was drained for the winter, too bad, Furia said, we could have had ourselves a dunk like the richbitches.

The place was owned by a New York family who used it for summers and long holiday weekends the rest of the year. Goldie knew about it because her sister Nanette had mentioned the Thatchers in her letters, she was their regular summer baby-sitter, they went out a lot. They had three impossible children but Nanette said they paid her twice the going rate so who's kicking. There was no chance of the Thatchers showing up all of a sudden because they had traipsed off to Europe till after the Christmas holidays, that's how the other half lives.

Furia approved. Aside from the money he was feeling great after Goldie's special treatment and when Hinch broke through the back door and Goldie locked Barbara in the downstairs maid's room he didn't even get mad at the furnace, it wouldn't go on, the tanks must need oil. Maybe they don't pay their bills, he cracked.

He went around admiring. The country furniture was

108

kingsize and handfinished, white pine treated with just lin-seed oil, all dowels, not a nail in them. The fieldstone fireplace in the living room was almost tall enough for Hinch to walk into and there were genuine oil paintings on the walls. Though Furia took a dim view of the paintings. They look like cripples did them a skillion years ago, he said, and look how they're all browned up and full of cracks. There was even a big-screen color TV set in a special white pine cabinet which right away Goldie turned on, but Furia said, "The hell with that, we got to listen to what's going on around here," and he turned off the TV and turned on the radio, a kingsize transistor, standing on the mantelpiece. He tuned in the station at Tonekeneke Falls, there was a rock combo on, and he left it on while he went exploring.

The country kitchen made him do a little dance like Hitler. It was all of pine and brick with a regular Rock-ette lineup of gleamy copper pots and skillets on wrought iron racks hanging from the beams, like a color spread in *House Beautiful* or something. "Would this 'a' bugged my old lady's eyes out! What she had to cook in shouldn't happen to a dog. When she had something to cook." The refrigerator was empty, but there was a twenty-cubic-foot freezer loaded with steaks and roasts and other great stuff and a for-real cooking fireplace with a black iron door at the back that opened into something Goldie said they called a Dutch oven big enough to do a whole lamb in and a black iron pot hanging on a black iron dohinky that swung out in the damnedest way. "Man, that pot's bigger than my old lady's washtub," Furia said, practically smiling, "you sure can pick 'em, Goldie."

He felt so good that when Hinch found a room lousy with books from floor to ceiling and a white pine bar full of bottles of the best stuff and poured himself a waterglass of Black Label, Furia let him. "Live it up, Hinch, have yourself a grin." But then he had to show what a big man he was, he said, "What the hell is the kid bawling for? I'll give her something to bawl," and he unlocked the door to the maid's room and slapped the little girl around some, not much, he pulled his punches, he had nothing against kids, but it only made her bawl louder. "What's with this little punk?" Furia said disgustedly. "You'd think being her old man is fuzz she'd be used to getting banged around, give her some booze, Goldie, and shut her up." So Goldie got a couple slugs of Jack Daniels into Barbara and after a while she stopped crying and fell asleep on the bed with her mouth open, snoring like a little lush. Furia got a charge out of that and when he locked her back in he was smiling again.

He kicked off his shoes and stretched out on the pine-and-cowhide sofa in the living room like the little king. "Think I'll have me a couple filly minyons for supper tonight, Goldie," Furia said. "Can you make 'em like the fat cats do, in that kitchen fireplace?"

"Don't see why not," Goldie said, "though I can't barbecue them, I don't see any charcoal."

"What the hell difference? Medium well, Goldie, can you do medium well in a fireplace?"

"Coming up," Goldie said, she was certainly anxious to please these days, "if Stinkfoot 'll get me a load of kindling and firewood. I saw a woodshed out back that's stacked."

But by this time Hinch had finished the fifth and thrown it through the mirror behind the bar.

"He shouldn't ought to done that," Furia said, "not a highclass dump like this. Hinch?"

"I heard her," Hinch said, coming in from the den. His face was white and his nose red, his eyes bugging. He looked steamy. "I ain't lugging no wood for her, I ain't her nigger."

"That shows how ignorant you are," Goldie said. "You have to say Negro or black."

"Nigger nigger nigger," Hinch said. "I ain't hauling no wood for nobody, special not for her."

"How about for me?" Furia asked.

"I don't feel so good," Hinch said, and sat down on the floor suddenly.

"You ain't used to fat cat booze is why," Furia said indulgently. "It's my fault for letting you. What the hell, Goldie, I'll get the wood," and to her surprise he sprang off the sofa and trotted out on his stockinged feet. She almost called after him it's a dirt floor out there but didn't, you never knew with Fure and things were going too good. She heard the back door open and stay open.

Goldie went into the downstairs bathroom which was all tiled in black and white real tiles and used the black porcelain john, it made her feel like a movie queen squatting there. Christ I'm going to live this way and no fooling, it's the only life. Soon as I shake Fure and that smelly Hinch.

She was primping her hair in the bathroom mirror which had the cutest little frosted bulbs set all around the frame à la Hollywood stars' dressing rooms when she jumped a foot. She had never heard such a scream except in the movies. It was like a police siren going off in her ear or a pig getting stuck, she remembered that from when she was a little girl and sneaked off to Hurley's chicken farm after her old man against orders just to watch what they did to the pigs. When the sound turned all bubbly she could practically see it choking on its blood.

She made it to the woodshed before Hinch, who had trouble getting off the floor.

Furia was backed off in a corner of the shed chucking firewood in every direction while his mouth opened and closed and nothing came out. The shed was full of furry things jumping and dodging. His eyes were dropping out of his head, the corners of his nose were blue. There was drool coming out of his mouth.

"Rats . . ."

Goldie couldn't believe her ears. She walked over to him and shook his arm hard.

"What are you talking about, Fure?" she said. "They're field mice."

"Rats," he panted. His tough little body felt like Jello under her hand.

"Fure, for Chrissake. I ought to know a field mouse when I see one. They used to run all over our kitchen in the Hollow. They won't hurt you."

"They went for me . . ."

"They couldn't do that. They're harmless."

"They bite . . ."

"Not people. They're grain eaters. Not like rats. See, they're all gone now." There was a hundred-pound sack stamped GOLDEN BULKY in the shed. The mice had gnawed holes in it, the dirt floor was honey brown where they had burrowed. "The Thatchers must keep a horse here summers. This is horse feed, Fure, that's what they were after, not you."

He didn't believe her. He kept shivering and hugging himself.

Hinch was spreadlegged in the entrance with a puzzle written on his face. He was looking from Furia to the dirt floor of the shed and back again. Furia's wild heaves had struck two mice. One was lying with its head flattened out

111

in an omelet of blood and brains. The other was still alive, scrabbling with its forelegs as if its back were broken.

"You scared of these bitty things?" Hinch asked in a wondering voice.

Furia swallowed convulsively.

Hinch walked over to the wounded mouse with a grin and kicked. It flew up and against the back wall of the shed and fell like a shot. He picked it up by the tail and went back and picked up the other one by the tail and went back again and dangled the two dead mice inches from Furia's nose. Furia screeched and tried to climb the wall. Then he was sick all over the dirt. Goldie had to jump back.

"Be goddam if he ain't scared shitless," Hinch said. He walked out and threw the mice all the way over into the empty pool. It was as if Hinch had just learned that babies didn't come out of their mothers' armpits.

Furia couldn't get down more than a couple of mouthfuls even though Goldie did the steaks exactly the way he liked them. She almost laughed in his face.

She found it a gas too the way he kept hanging on to the fireplace poker, a five-footer with three prongs at the business end. His eyes had grown as quick as the mice, darting about the floor, especially in corners. He drank three cups of black coffee without letting go of the poker.

Barbara woke up whimpering and Furia got ugly. "Shut that brat's yap or so help me Jeese I'll ram this thing down her goddam throat."

"All right, Fure, all right," Goldie said, and found some powdered milk in the cupboard and stirred up a glass. She brought the child the milk and a piece of cold steak. Barbara sipped some of the milk but turned away from the meat, her eyes were rolling up, I guess I gave her too much of a slug, well, better drunk than dead. She finally dropped back to sleep.

"She won't bother you now," Goldie said, coming out.

"Cool it, big man," Hinch said with a wink. "A couple of lousy mice."

That was when Furia swung the long fire tool and ripped Hinch's cheek. If Hinch hadn't been so quick the prongs would have gone through to his tonsils. He looked astounded. Goldie had to swab the wound with antiseptic she found in the medicine chest, she swabbed good and hard, and she slapped one of those three-inch Band-Aids over it.

112

Hinch kept looking at Furia with his eyebrows humped up like questions.

Saturday morning passed in jerks like a film jumping its sprockets. Malone wandered about the house picking things up and setting them down as if to satisfy himself that they were still there. The next thing he was taking in the milk. The milk brought Bibby into focus and he shut the refrigerator door as reverently as if it were the lid of a coffin. When Ellen set breakfast before him he simply sat and looked at it. He did not even drink the coffee. She finally took the dishes away.

Ellen had mourning under her eyes, bands of dark gray. Once she said, "Noon. What happens after noon, Loney?"

He turned away. He resents my reminding him. As if he needs reminding. What a thing to say, now of all times. Why am I so good to him at night and so bitchy daytimes?

But she's my child.

My lost, my frightened baby.

They sat in the parlor, he on the sofa, she on the rocker, watching the little cathedral clock on the mantel. When noon came they both sat up straight, as if at a call. When the clock stopped striking it was like a death.

Ellen began to cry again.

Malone jumped up and ran out into Old Bradford Road leaving the front door open. It was a mean day and the meanness slid into the house. He stood in the middle of the empty street staring in the direction of Lovers Hill. The Cunninghams' mongrel bitch came trotting up and licked his hand. Malone wiped his hand on his pants and went back into the house, shutting the door this time. Ellen was upstairs, he heard her moving about in one of the bedrooms.

Bibby's I'll bet.

He sank onto the sofa again and placed his hands uselessly on his knees, looking at the clock. When John Secco drove up it was twenty minutes of two and Malone was still sitting there.

Secco came in his own car, a three-year-old Ford wagon with no markings. He was in civvies.

"No sense getting your neighbors wondering," the chief said. He had more than midafternoon shadow and Malone

113

doubted he had shaved. For some reason it made him angry. "Ellen, I know how this has hit me, I can imagine what you're going through." Ellen said nothing. "Been a call? Letter, message?"

"Nothing," Malone said.

"Well, it's early. Could be they're putting some pressure on. Or giving you plenty of time to play ball."

"With what?" Ellen said. Secco was silent. "I knew that's what you'd do, Loney."

"Do what?" Malone said.

"Tell the whole thing to John. You promised you wouldn't. I told you I'd walk out on you if you did."

"Wes did the only thing," Secco said. "Do you suppose I'd put your little girl in danger, Ellen?"

"I don't know."

"I thought you considered me your friend."

"You're a policeman."

"I'm also a husband and a father. You ought to know me better than that."

"I don't know anything any more."

"Do you want me to leave?" the chief asked.

They waited a long time. Finally Ellen's mouth loosened and she said, "John, we don't know what to do, where to turn."

"That's why I'm here, Ellen. I want to help."

"Sure," Malone said. "Get me that money."

"Ask me something that's possible, Wes. Anyway, I think there's something we can do."

"Without the twenty-four thousand?" Malone laughed. "Furia thinks I've lifted it. You figured out a way to convince him I didn't?"

"I've been thinking over what you told me, I mean about what you did on your own." Secco seemed to be picking his way through the available words and choosing only the finest. "Maybe when they rented that cabin at the Lake last summer they at the same time rented a second cabin as a backup just in case. I thought it worth a try."

Malone raised his head. "I never thought of that."

"Only they didn't. I've spent the day so far doing another check of the real estate offices." He added quickly, "Don't worry. I didn't tip the hand."

Malone slumped back. Ellen just sat there.

"All the other possibilities were either vacated as of Labor Day or they're rented the year round by people who are known. So wherever they've dug in this time it's likely not at the Lake. It could be anywhere, out of the county even. It would take a hundred men—"

"You mustn't do that!" Ellen cried.

"Ellen, I told you. I wouldn't take chances with Barbara's safety."

"All I know is I want my baby back."

"Isn't that what we all want? Look. Wes, you listening?"

"I'm listening," Malone said.

"This woman who hijacked the payroll, Goldie. She could be working with Furia against the other man, Hinch, to squeeze Hinch out. They could be both putting on an act for Hinch's benefit."

"Damn," Malone said. "I never thought of that, either."

"But I doubt it. From what you told me about the way Furia acted when they were here in your house, it's likelier she's doublecrossing the two of them the way you doped it."

"Round and round we go," Malone said.

"No, listen." Chief Secco leaned forward in his effort to hold them, they slipped away so easily. "The way you described this Hinch, Wes, he seemed to be the weak sister of the three, a dumb character."

"He hasn't a brain in his head."

"The dumb ones of a gang are the ones to go after. In this case, from what you say, the groundwork with Hinch has already been laid."

"How do you mean?"

"You told me that the first time they came here—when they first took Barbara—Furia told Hinch to meet them at the cabin and Hinch was upset, you got the impression he was worried they might run out on him."

"So?"

"You also said that the second time they came, after you got Barbara back, when you told them the money'd been stolen from the house and Ellen accused Furia of having been the one, Hinch seemed half convinced it was true. That's what I mean by the groundwork being laid. He doesn't trust Furia. He's already got his doubts. Suppose we could convince him."

"That Furia took the money? But he didn't, John. Goldie Vorshek took it."

"We know that and the Vorshek woman knows it, but Hinch and Furia don't." There was nothing in the chief's voice or manner to suggest that he was about to sell

115

something, he was being very careful about that. "If we can get Hinch to believing that Furia is playing him for a sucker, even a bear of little brain like that is going to start thinking of his own hide. It's a cinch he's in this thing for his cut of the loot. If there's no cut for him he's going to want out. The only way Hinch could get out now is by making a deal with us, in his own interest and to get back at the partner taking him for a ride. He'll make contact. He'll tell us where they're hiding. He might even help us when we close in. That's the way I figure it."

"And that's the way my Bibby would get killed," Ellen said. "Absolutely no."

"Ellen," Secco said. "Would Barbara be in more danger than she is right now if they got to distrusting one another? She might even be in less, because if the plan worked out Hinch would have a personal interest in seeing she stays safe. He'd know what would happen to him if he let Furia hurt her." Secco took out his pipe and fiddled with it. He put it back in his pocket. "Look, I'm not saying this is guaranteed. There are a lot of ifs when you're dealing with dangerous morons like these. But as things stand, Furia won't give up Barbara without the money, if then—I have to be frank with you, Ellen—and we don't have the money to give them. You've got to accept how things are, not how you'd like them to be."

Ellen was giving her head little stubborn shakes.

"But, of course, you've got to make the decision. I don't have the right to make it for you. Even if I had, I wouldn't."

"The answer is no," Ellen said.

"Ellen." There was a hint of life in Malone's eyes. "Maybe John has something. God knows we don't. Maybe such a trick . . ."

"No."

"Wait. John, how would you get to Hinch? What do you have in mind?"

"Wherever they're hiding out it's a sure thing they've got a radio. So that's our channel of communication. Manufactured story, some cooked-up announcements on the air, I don't know, I haven't laid it out yet. But the point is, if we can get the right message through to him—"

"But Furia and this Goldie would hear it, too."

"Let them. It would make her more jittery than she already is, a doublecross inside the gang is the last thing

116

she wants the other two to start kicking around. And as far as Furia's concerned, it puts him on the defensive with Hinch and that could make them go for each other's throats. It's a tactic that's broken up a lot of gangs. But as I say, I can't make the decision for you people. She's your flesh and blood."

"It's up to you, Ellen," Malone said. "What do you say?"

"Oh, God."

Secco got up and went to the window. He took out his pipe again and sucked on it emptily. His back said he wasn't there.

"Loney, help me, help me," Ellen moaned.

"Do you want me to make the decision?"

"I don't know, I don't know."

"You've got to know. There's no time for this, Ellen. Do I decide for both of us, or do you, or what?"

"They'll murder her, Loney."

"They may murder her anyway."

She stiffened as if he had struck her.

Ellen, Ellen, how else do you prepare yourself?

"Well?"

He could just hear her. "Whatever you say."

"John," Malone said.

Secco turned around.

"We go for broke."

It turned out that the chief had Harvey Rudd waiting in the wagon. "I brought Harvey along in case you said yes," Secco said. "He'll have to be briefed, Wes. I told him nothing."

Harvey Rudd was The Voice of Taugus Valley. He was an ex-Marine news broadcaster who had passed up a top job with a New York network to start an independent radio station, WRUD, in Tonekeneke Falls. He owned it, programed it, edited its news, sometimes took its mike, and he had been known to sweep it out. He was a fortyish Down Easter with a long Yank nose and a short Yank tongue.

Ellen said one thing in Rudd's presence. She said it to Chief Secco. "Can this man be trusted?"

When the chief said, "Yes," Ellen nodded and went upstairs, not to be seen again during the afternoon.

Rudd didn't say anything, not even with his eyes, which

117

were northern ocean blue and looked as if they belonged in a four-master's crow's-nest. They did not even express anything at the sight of the plaster on Malone's hair and the welt on his jaw. He set his surprising Texas-style white Stetson on the sofa beside him and waited.

Malone told the story leaving out nothing. The radio man listened without a word. When Malone was finished Chief Stecco told about using WRUD to get to Hinch. "Will you do it, Harvey?"

For the first time Malone heard Rudd's voice.

"I have two children of my own." Malone had expected a voice like a cheap guitar, like fellow-officer Sherm Hamlin's, Sherm had been born in Boothbay Harbor and had served as a guard at the prison in Thomaston before following his married daughter down to New Bradford, he had never lost his whangy accent. But this voice was more like one of Lawrence Welk's baritone saxes. "What exactly did you have in mind, John?"

"Well, I got an idea while Wes was filling you in. You could put on the air a series of those now—what d'ye call 'em?—like trailers, teasers, of a, say, radio drama. You know, like you were working up advance interest in a show you were going to run next week or month, give pieces of the plot. Like that. What we'd do is use the actual facts of this case, except we'd make out like the head man of the gang was doublecrossing the other two. The idea is to get Hinch to worrying . . . No, Harvey?"

Rudd was shaking his head. "In the first place, John, WRUD doesn't run dramatic shows, they went out a long time ago on radio, so it would sound phony straight off to anybody who does any listening at all. Second, if this Hinch is as stupid as you say he is you're not going to get anything through his skull with subtlety. Third, from what Mr. Malone says, there's no time to prepare anything elaborate. Whatever's done has to be started right away— today, if possible."

"Then how would you handle it?"

"I'd do it on a straight news basis. It's something even a halfwit would understand and it would have the added advantage of sounding legitimate."

"You can't do that, Mr. Rudd," Malone said.

"Why not?"

"Because Furia would hear it, too. And he'd know that the only way such information could have gotten out was through me or my wife shooting our mouths off. That would spell curtains for my little girl. He warned us to keep quiet or else. He's dangerous, Mr. Rudd, maybe even psycho. He means it. At least I can't take the chance that he doesn't."

"We can handle it so you and Mrs. Malone are put absolutely in the clear."

"How?"

"You leave that to me."

Malone's chin flattened. There was a pulse beating in the bruise. "I don't know. I'd have to think about it."

"Will you let me work on it, Mr. Malone? I promise not a word will go out over the air without your okay. Have you got a typewriter here?"

"No."

"Then just some paper," Rudd said easily, "I can't type worth a damn, anyway."

Malone went hunting for paper while he listened for a sign of life from upstairs and heard it, the creak-creak of the rocker in Barbara's room.

The kid was acting up again and Furia said give the little puke some more juice but Goldie said any more and she might get poisoned you want her alive don't you. She came up with a bottle of Sleep-Tite tablets she found in one of the upstairs bathrooms, so that problem was solved.

Furia ordered a top sirloin roast for his Saturday night dinner and Goldie had it thawing all day. The Thatchers had obliged by installing an electric spit in the old kitchen fireplace and Goldie built just the right fire, a slow one, to do the roast over. Furia spent a good twenty minutes watching it go round and round. I picked me a real cool broad, he said, fondly pinching her behind, I ought to set you up in the chow business, Goldie, I'll have that banana ripple ice cream for dessert they got in the freezer. Then he went back to the living room where Hinch was nursing an Old Crow on the rocks like a grudge, Furia had put him on short rations after the broken mirror, Hinch wasn't taking it as well as usual. Furia turned on the radio, which was set at WRUD, and stretched out on the sofa while Hinch brooded over at him.

There was the national news, then the news from the state capital, and Furia said to the radio come on, come on. Finally the announcer, who had a voice like a sax-ophone, said: "And now for the Taugus Valley news.

"First Selectman Russ Fairhouse urged residents of New Bradford today to support the Jaycee cleanup campaign, Operation Civic Pride. 'Please join your neighbors,' Mr. Fairhouse pleaded, 'in picking up gum wrappers and such and ridding our town of unsightly junk like abandoned old cars and washing machines and any other thrown-out items that may be laying around your property causing eyesores. Your administration is doing its part repairing the highway signs defaced mostly by teenagers the past summer, please do yours and impress on your children that in the end the cost of such vandalism is borne by you, the taxpayer.'

"A two-car accident on The Pike one mile north of Tonekeneke Falls today took the life of nineteen-year-old Alison Springer of Southville and sent three other teenagers to the New Bradford Hospital with critical injuries. State police say that the cars were engaged in a drag race.

"There has been no progress in the statewide hunt for the two holdup men who shot Thomas F. Howland to death and stole the Aztec Paper Products Company's payroll Wednesday night, according to Colonel Doug Pearce of the state police. 'It's my belief,' Colonel Pearce told WRUD today, 'that they made it out of the state. An All Points went out to authorities in adjoining states yesterday.' "

"Aha," Furia said with a grin. "They sure freaked out. Hear that, Hinch?"

"So what," Hinch grumbled. "We ain't got the bread."

"And now for today's Lighter-Side-of-the-News item," the saxophone continued with a chuckle in it. "There's another mystery of sorts in New Bradford that for a while today had Police Chief John Secco and his department thinking they were in the middle of a crime wave.

"A twelve-year-old boy named Willie, who runs a paper route in the Lovers Hill section of New Bradford delivering the New Bradford *Times-Press,* came into police headquarters this morning to report a crime. Willie claimed that on Thursday afternoon, while he was delivering his papers on his bicycle at the upper end of Old Bradford Road, he witnessed—in Willie's own words—'a short skinny guy with like a stocking over his head' sneaking into one of the houses. According to Willie, he promptly hid behind a rhododendron bush across the road and watched.

'The man came scooting out after a while,' Willie said, 'and he was carrying a little black bag that he didn't have when he went in—' "

"What the hell." Hinch sat up.

"Shut up, let's hear this!" Furia hissed.

" '—and he took off the stocking and beat it down the road.' Willie alleges that he followed the mysterious man and saw him turn into Lovers Hill with the black bag and head for the center of town still on foot."

Hinch was looking at Furia with his mouth open. Furia was on his feet glaring at the radio.

"Willie, who wears thick glasses, could give no description of the man beyond his short height and skinniness. Chief Secco was doubtful about the story on the face of it, since no housebreaking was reported Thursday and Willie, it seems, has a reputation for an overactive imagination. Nevertheless, the chief sent Officer Harry Rawlson to Old Bradford Road with the boy, who pointed out the house he claimed the man had burgled. It turned out that Chief Secco's doubts were all too justified. It was the home of a member of the New Bradford force, Officer Wesley Malone. Officer Malone, who has been off duty for a few days, said that he and Mrs. Malone had had no visitors at all on Thursday, illegal or otherwise, and that in any. event nothing was missing. Mrs. Malone confirmed this, stating that they had never owned a little black bag. 'Willie either made a mistake about the house,' Officer Malone told his fellow-officer, 'or he's been reading too many mystery stories.' A check of the other houses on Old Bradford Road produced no confirmation of Willie's story, and he was sent home after a fatherly lecture by Chief Secco.

"Thus endeth New Bradford's latest excitement.

"Funeral services will be held tomorrow at two P.M. at Christ Church, Stonytown, for—"

Furia jabbed the radio off. When he turned around he saw Goldie standing in the doorway from the kitchen.

"What was that all about?" Goldie said.

"Nothing!" Furia said.

"Thursday afternoon," Hinch said slowly. "Small skinny guy. That fuzz and his old lady were telling the truth. I'll be goddam."

"Don't look at me!" Furia yelled. "It wasn't me! I was in the shack, damn it. I didn't even have the car, so how would I get into town?"

121

"Neither did the skinny guy," Hinch said. "He walked, this Willie said."

"So it was some local," Goldie said, "the way Malone said. There are lots of small skinny guys in this world. Looks to me, Fure, like this really ties it. Why don't we give it up as a bad job?"

"No," Furia said. "*No.*"

"How do you expect Malone to get the money back when he doesn't even know who took it?"

"That's his problem!"

"You could 'a' walked," Hinch said, "it ain't that far. I hoofed it easy the night we pulled the heist."

"Maybe it was you!"

"Small, skinny," Hinch said. "Do I look small and skinny? Anyways, Fure, I wouldn't do that."

"And I would?"

Hinch did not reply. He was looking into his empty glass and frowning.

"Well, at least Malone and his wife didn't blow the whistle, you scared 'em good," Goldie said brightly. She was scratching one hand with the other. After a while she said, "The roast won't be long now. No potatoes or I'd make you some French fries, Fure. What vedge do you want?"

Furia told her what she could do with her vedge.

"I still think it's taking useless chances to hang around here," Goldie said. "Specially now that we know somebody did hijack the payroll. What do you say we write it off, Fure? We could be somewhere opening a bank and like grabbing us a real pile, not some snotty twenty-four grand."

"What do you think, Hinch?" Furia asked suddenly.

Hinch looked up.

"You think we ought to cut out, like Goldie says?"

Hinch got to his feet. He seemed to go up and up indefinitely. Goldie took one look at the expression on his face and stepped back into the kitchen.

"I think," Hinch said deliberately, "I'm going to make myself another drinkee."

Fure was uptight all Saturday evening, brooding over at Hinch getting smashed in his corner.

Furia had his right hand stuck under his coat like Napoleon. But he wasn't dreaming of new worlds to

122

conquer, he wanted the Colt in his shoulder holster handy just in case, at least that was Goldie's analysis. This whole thing is a bust why did I ever tie in with these cockamamies? Better watch your step, girl, this could wind up with fireworks.

There was almost a fight over the TV. Furia wanted the TV on, Hinch wanted the radio on. The nine o'clock movie was a remake of *The Maltese Falcon,* I like that old fat guy, Furia said, he's real cool. Goldie said he's also been real dead for years it's somebody else in this version, why doesn't Hinch take the radio into the den then everybody's happy. Hinch said to hell with you bitch I like it right here. Furia said I want to see Humphrey Bogart and that's it and Goldie said he's dead too, Fure. Fure said according to you everybody's dead and Hinch said in a peculiar way so let that be a lesson to you. And he wasn't looking at Goldie when he said it. Goldie decided to go to the bathroom in case the argument heated up.

In the end Hinch took the radio into the den and Furia watched his movie. He kept complaining all through that it stank I liked the fat guy and Bogey better.

But Goldie noticed that he turned his chair so he could keep one eye on the den.

Come eleven o'clock there was Furia standing in the doorway of the den.

"What you listening to?" he asked Hinch.

"What do you think?" Hinch said. There were about three fingers left in the bottle of Smirnoff's.

"At the signal it will be exactly eleven o'clock," the announcer said. "This is Station WRUD, the Voice of Taugus Valley. Now for the news."

"What do you got to listen to the news for?" Furia said. "We heard it on the six o'clock."

"You don't want to hear it don't," Hinch said. "Me, I want to hear it."

"They didn't find us, if that's what you're worried about," Furia said. Hinch said nothing. "That's a joke, son."

Hinch said nothing.

Furia stayed where he was, looking at Hinch. He kept his hand under his coat.

Goldie turned the TV off in the living room so she could listen, too. From the living room.

National news. Statewide news. Then the saxophone voice said, "One of the three teenagers injured in today's

123

two-car accident at Tonekeneke Falls which took the life of nineteen-year-old Alison Springer of Southville died this evening at the New Bradford Hospital. He was Kelly Wilson, Junior, eighteen, of Haddison. The two surviving teenagers are still listed in critical condition.

"Review of the additional salary upgradings proposed for New Bradford town employees last week has been completed, First Selectman Russ Fairhouse announced today, and the revised salary schedule will be brought before a town meeting next Friday night at eight P.M. in the New Bradford High School cafeteria.

"A combined meeting of the Women's Auxiliaries of the fire department of Taugus Valley will be held Monday evening at eight o'clock at the home of Mrs. Jeanine Lukenberry of Stonytown to complete plans for the joint pre-Christmas rummage sale for the benefit of Better Fire Prevention."

"Aaaa, turn it off," Furia said. "Who's interested in that crap?"

"I am," Hinch said, not moving.

"—a footnote to the Lighter-Side-of-the-News item we broadcast on our six o'clock news," the baritone sax was playing.

"See what I mean?" Hinch said. "You got to wait for the good stuff. What's the matter, Fure, you nervous?"

"Listen here, you—"

"Shut up," Hinch said quietly, "I want to hear this."

Furia's ear-points began to turn red. But he shut up.

"—seems that Willie is a persistent little cuss," the voice chuckled. "When Chief John Secco sent him home this afternoon, Willie didn't go home. He went back to Old Bradford Road and, as he told WRUD's Lighter-Side-of-the-News reporter this evening, 'I scouted around, they don't believe me about the man with the stocking over his face I'll prove it to 'em, I seen him throw that stocking away.' To everyone's surprise but Willie's he did just that. He went back to New Bradford police headquarters with a woman's nylon stocking which he claimed he found under the privet hedge in front of Officer Wesley Malone's house, where the alleged housebreaking took place. Chief Secco sent an officer over to the Malone place with the stocking, and Mrs. Malone identified it as one of hers which she had had drying on her clothesline and which had disappeared days ago. 'It must have been Rags that did it, she's the Cunninghams' dog next door, she's always stealing things off my line," Mrs. Malone told the officer. Willie was sent home with a personal escort, Officer Mert Peck. Officer Peck advised Willie's father to take Willie on a tour of the woodshed, which Willie's father said he sure as heck was going to do. Please don't report any howling you may hear from that section of New Bradford. It's just Willie learning that free enterprise doesn't always pay.

"In one minute the music of the Taugus Rock Quarriers. But first, a message from—"

Hinch snapped the radio off. He turned about and began a leisurely survey of Furia. Furia's hand dug deeper under his coat.

"Hinch," Furia said. "I don't know from no stocking. That's the word."

"If you say so, Fure." Hinch held out the Smirnoff. "Need a little snort?"

Furia snarled, "That'll be the day," and backed out.

Furia looked up the Malones' number in the book and dialed.

Right away Malone's voice said hoarsely, "Yes?"

"It's me," Furia said. "Don't bother trying to trace this call, fuzz, it's a public booth a long ways from you. Well?"

"I haven't got it," Malone said. "For God's sake, I told you and told you. Look, there was a boy in town here who saw the thief sneak into my house Thursday and come out with the black bag—"

"I know, we heard it on the radio," Furia said. "You and your missus played it cool, that was smart, fuzz. But I don't care who took it. I want it back."

"I told you—! How is my little girl?"

"She's okay. So far. Did you think I was kidding, Malone? I want that bread or you never see your kid again."

"How am I supposed to do it? Why don't you get it through your head that you lost out on this deal through no fault of anybody and let Barbara go?"

"No dice," Furia said. "Look, it don't have to be the payroll. I ain't particular. Any twenty-four grand'll do. Work on it, Malone. I'll call you."

"Damn you, where would I get—?"

Furia hung up and stepped from the booth outside the railroad station. It was Sunday morning and Freight Street

125

looked like Gary Cooper's town at high noon. When he turned around there was Hinch.

"What are you doing here?" Furia snarled. "I thought I told you to stay in the house."

"Cabin fever," Hinch said.

Furia hesitated.

"I took the car, too," Hinch said. "You want to make something of it?"

Furia began to walk.

Hinch swung into step. The crease between his pink eyes had smoothed out.

"I'll give you a ride back," Hinch said. "If you say please?"

"I should never have listened to you," Malone stormed. "I should have told him Goldie had it and about the safe deposit box while I had him on the phone."

"That would have queered the whole setup, Wes," John Secco said. "You heard Furia. It's working. They've swallowed Rudd's bait hook and line. That means it's stewing around in Hinch's head. He can't possibly have missed it, dumb or not. Give him a chance. When he's finally made up his mind that Furia crossed him he'll call in for a deal."

"But Goldie—"

"You said yourself she'd talk Furia out of it if you accused her. Then the whole thing might be shot. Don't go complicating things now, Wes. Have a little patience."

"But I can prove it to him!"

"How?"

"I forgot about the keys. When you rent a safe deposit box you get your own key, even a duplicate. So she's got two keys to a Taugus National safe deposit box. All Furia has to do is search her and that's it for Goldie."

"Do you think a woman like that would be fool enough to keep them on her, Wes? She's hidden them somewhere. That was the first thing I thought of." Secco shook his head. "Go up to Ellen."

Malone went upstairs. Ellen was in bed with a slight fever. She had an icebag on her forehead and her eyes were closed.

He sat down and thought of Barbara. Everything else was boiling around.

Chief Secco sucked on his pipe downstairs beside the telephone.

Thank God I was raised the son of a farmer.

A farmer grew patience the way he grew grass.

The call came two hours before daylight on Tuesday morning. Secco was sleeping on the cot in the kitchen near the wall extension, Malone on the sofa in the parlor beside the phone. He had it off the cradle before it rang twice. Secco was a breath behind picking up the extension.

"Hello?" Malone said.

"This Malone?" It was the cougar voice, the cougar voice, pitched in a mutter.

"Yes? Yes?"

"This is Hinch. You know. Look, I can't talk long, I had to wait till they were corked off good before I could use the phone. I'll make a deal."

"Yes?"

"I want out. I'll turn state's evidence. Do I get a deal?"

"Yes," Malone said, "yes."

Secco came running in noiselessly. He put his lips to Malone's ear and whispered, "Ask him where they are."

"Yes," Malone said again. "Where is the house?"

"I don't know where, I mean the street. Some crummy back road. It ain't far."

"Telephone number," Secco whispered.

"What's the phone number there?"

"7420."

"7420."

Secco wrote it down.

"Can you get my girl out of there, Hinch?"

"Fure took all the artillery. Anyways, Goldie's got her sleeping in with her and she locked the door."

"Then don't try anything. Stay put. We'll be out there. If you see a chance after we show, make a break for it with Barbara. Anything happens to my daughter it's no deal, Hinch, you get the book thrown at you. You hear me?"

"Yeah," Hinch muttered. He hung up.

Malone hung up.

He sat back and looked at the chief. Secco said briskly, "Don't sit there, Wes. Hand me the phone."

Malone handed it to him.

Secco dialed 411. It took a long time for the local

127

information operator to answer. He waited patiently. When she answered he said, "This is John Secco. Who's this, Margaret?"

"Sally, Chief."

"Sally. This is an emergency. Who in town has the number 7420?"

He waited again.

"Thanks, Sally. Keep quiet about this." He hung up. "It's on Maccabee Road, the Thatcher place. They closed it up for the winter. Wes?"

"I'm listening, John," Malone said.

"Why don't you go up and tell Ellen about this? I've got a police department to round up."

"John."

Secco stopped in the act of picking up the phone again. "What, Wes?"

"Maybe one man could get in and cover Furia before he can wake up—"

"You mean you."

"Give me a gun."

Secco shook his head. "You said yourself Furia sleeps like a cat, so no one man's going to take him in bed. Anyway, Wes, you're too involved, you'd be sure to mess it up. This is going to be a delicate business even with a squad. Let me handle it regulation procedure. It's the right way. The only way."

"She's my child—"

"And you're one of my officers, Wes. One of them."

"All right," Malone said. "But, John, I swear to you, if anything goes wrong—"

"How well have you done by yourself?" John Secco asked.

They stared at each other.

"Loney? What's going on down there?"

Malone went upstairs running away.

128

Tuesday

The Deal

Malone went into action chewing on doom. I have no part or place in this, I'm the only one without a uniform or a gun, John doesn't trust me, I should never have gone to him, Ellen was right, it's not John's fault what else can he do it's his job, the fault is all mine I had no business becoming a cop. Being a cop is like being a Marine and what kind of Marine did I make. I should have handled this by myself all the way through. How could it have come out worse than this?

They were a force of twenty-two men, eight New Bradford officers besides Chief Secco and Malone, and a dozen troopers. They were packing shotguns and carbines and tear gas launcher attachments and gasmasks from the state police barracks and enough ammunition to face down a riot mob, no missing ingredient but the barricades.

And all for what. They don't begin to realize the kind of kill-crazy kook they're up against, a show of force like this is going to put his back up like a skunk and make him piss his stink, he'll see all the dreams he dreamed of hate and glory in whatever shit pile he was dragged up in come

130

true and he'll go out blazing away and taking Bibby with him and me too I'll be there I'll be there to go with her. And what Ellen gets out of the deal is two graves side by side in New Bradford Cemetery. Poor kid. You rate better.

Unless . . . unless Hinch wants to live more than he's scared of Furia. And wanting will find the brains he wasn't born with to figure out a way to get on top. Get the better of Furia before it's too late. You're my ace, Hinch. In this hole I'm in.

One man one vote. That's what it comes down to. Furia against Malone. Furia against Hinch. Not Furia against twenty-two law officers creeping up with funk in their mouths and guns in their hands.

"Don't worry, Wes," Chief Secco said. "It's going to be all right."

"Give me a written guarantee?"

"What you are and how you operate," Secco said. "That's the only guarantee there is, Wes."

There was no communication after that.

The cars were left a quarter mile from Maccabee Road and they made their professional approach in the predawn lugging their weapons and ammo and masks to the Thatcher place like a platoon of grunts on search-and-destroy, every man's face tight as a secret, every tongue tasting the death of somebody else. Can't John see that? They're disciplined and they're set to follow orders but let Furia draw blood and see what happens.

John John.

Bibby . . .

Come on Hinch.

Chief Secco's operational plan was an attack in force while the enemy's guard was down. Furia was not aware that his hideout was blown, he had no reason to post a lookout, they would have all the advantages of near darkness and a sleeping or sleepy foe, and overwhelming surprise would carry the day. A noiseless entry front and back, coordinated, the main group with rubbers over their shoes sneaking upstairs, Secco knew the old house well it was built in 1799 the chestnut floors were all creaked out and the stairs heavily carpeted . . . one burst into Furia's room, heave a couple of gas cans, and that would be it. The child was sleeping with the woman in another bedroom according to Hinch, an auxiliary force would handle that at the same time. The woman was too smart to try

131

anything foolish and Hinch was spoken for. If Furia elected or was able to shoot it out he would be blasted into a better world by a dozen guns before he could get his weapons up.

The sky was turning gray and there was just enough light to see by. Chief Secco had had the men synchronize their watches and every eye was on the second hand. There were eight men behind trees to the front of the house, eight men behind trees at the rear, and three men to each side hiding in shrubbery.

The men behind the house could see the back door broken half off its hinges where the gang had got in. The problem was the front door. It was shut and probably locked. They had debated whether to make entry in a body through the back door but decided to carry out the original plan. Sergeant Louis Lombard of the troopers had a picklock for tumbler locks and a can of 3-in-1 to oil the hinges as a precaution against squeaks. The men at the rear were to give him forty seconds to get the front door open before they made their move.

Six men were to remain on guard outside against the impossibility that the gunman might break away from the force inside.

How could it go wrong?

It did. At zero minus fifty seconds, Sergeant Lombard, allowing an extra ten seconds for his approach, ducked out from behind his tree. He was forty-three years old and he had a son fighting in Vietnam. He was a large man with large hands. In one he carried the oil can and the picklock, in the other his weapon. He ducked out from behind his tree and doubled over began to run on the balls of his feet across the lawn toward the front door. He was no more than a third of the way to the door when Furia shot him from a downstairs window, one-and-two-three. His favorite number. Because of the poor light the first shot missed Lombard's heart and smacked into the shoulder of the arm carrying the oil can and the picklock. The oil can and the picklock flew up and over his head. The second shot struck him in the business hand and the revolver went off from the convulsion of his trigger finger. The weapon dropped in a plumbline to the grass. The third shot zinged over his head and struck the tree behind which Malone was hiding. The sergeant became a crab, by instinct skittering on all fours away from his death, shattered right hand between body and grass holding his shattered left shoulder.

For two seconds there was nothing but the morning. Then, as one man, as by an order heard in the blood, Chief Secco's army opened fire front and rear. Every window on the ground floor was a black hole in a moment.

They kept firing.

Sergeant Lombard reached the trees, gave Sherm Hamlin a white grin as Hamlin hauled him to safety, and passed out.

"Stop firing, stay under cover!" Secco was yelling. "Harry, work your way around to the back and tell them to stop firing there, too!"

Soon they stopped. A truce settled over the unconscious trooper's moans. One trooper ran back in the direction of the cars, another began to drag the wounded man away.

"They could have killed Bibby," Malone was saying brokenly, "maybe they did, John."

"No, she's all right, I tell you, I know she is." The seams in Secco's cheeks seemed rubbed with dirt. He grabbed a bullhorn. "Furia! Can you hear me?"

"I hear you." The call, a saucy spin, came from behind a wide crack in the front door. "Anybody else shoots and I blow the kid's head off. I got her right in front of me. Want to see?"

The door opened wider. The light was better now and Malone saw a small white valentine face with blank eyes like her doll's. Behind her crouched Furia. The Colt was jammed against her head, just behind the ear.

She's alive she's still alive. Hinch why don't you jump him from behind? Now.

"Nobody's going to shoot any more if you don't." The enlargement of Chief Secco's voice by the bullhorn gave it an almighty quality, stern, patient, paternal. "Furia, the house is surrounded by twenty-two police officers. You can't get away. You wouldn't have a prayer. Send Barbara out unharmed and toss out your guns. If you do that without any further resistance or bloodshed the district attorney says he'll take it into account. You'll get the best break possible, I have the D.A.'s word on that. What do you say?"

Now Hinch while John does his thing.

The door banged open and Furia rose from his heels where he was squatting. He had Barbara about the waist

133

with his left arm, holding her up before him. As the gunman straightened Secco grunted in surprise. Furia's face was covered by the Papa Bear mask.

So now you know what you're dealing with, John.

"You think you can con me with that D.A. crap?" Furia shouted through the mask. His right hand flourished the Colt, the Walther automatic was stuck in his waistband. "No more than Hinch. Your stooge is a Mr. No-Brains, don't you know that? He couldn't keep nothing from me, I'm way ahead of him, always was. I worked him over and it wasn't ten minutes ago I got out of him about that call to the kid's old man. I know all about your deals. Here's the only deal Hinch rates. And it's not from you, fuzz, it's from me."

Hinch appeared. His arms were jammed behind his back, apparently lashed together. A handkerchief had been shoved into his mouth, his own belt was the gag that secured it, nothing-sounds were coming out. His pants were halfway to his knees, he was wriggling like a go-go dancer from the waist down in a comical effort to keep them up without hands. His hair had turned a brighter shade of red that had run down his face and dripped onto his shirt. The same shade of red was dribbling from his mouth. One eye was closed and swollen a funereal purple-black.

"Go, man, go," Furia gurgled. He set his foot in the small of Hinch's back and kicked. Hinch staggered forward and fell on his face. He was up in an incredible acrobatics and hobbling furiously toward the trees. Furia leveled the Colt and shot him one-and-two-three. He stuck the Colt in his belt and whipped out the Walther. The child shielding him showed no expression.

"You wanted my answer, fuzz, there it is," the little man in the Papa Bear mask said. "Malone?"

"Here I am," Malone said.

"Wes, for God's sake!"

Malone stepped out from behind his tree.

"Here I am," Malone said again.

"Your fuzz buddies think I'm putting on an act," Furia said. "They think that's ketchup on Hinch and we're playing like in the movies. Go over to Hinch and tell your fuzz buddies that's real blood and he's real dead."

"Wes, he'll shoot you, too . . ."

Malone walked over to the grass to Hinch. Hinch lay on his face with his knees drawn under him as if he were

134

praying to Mecca. All three of Furia's bullets had gone into the back of his head, most of which was not there.

Malone looked around and nodded.

"Come back, Wes!"

"Stay there, Malone, I'm talking." Malone remained over Hinch's body. "Okay? Got the message? Now here's the rest of my answer. You fuzz sonsabitches out there blow. You're going to let me and my woman and Malone's kid ride out of here and you ain't going to raise a hand to stop us. I give you five minutes to make up your mind. If you ain't gone in five minutes, every mother's fuzz out there, I'll throw the kid out on top of Hinch without a head."

He stepped back with Barbara. The door all but closed.

Malone walked back to the trees.

"He means it," Secco said thoughtfully.

"Aren't you going to do it, John?" Malone asked.

Secco was silent.

"You've got to. He told you what he'd do to Bibby if you don't."

"He killed Tom Howland. He's shot Sergeant Lombard. He murdered this Hinch in front of my eyes."

"So you want him to add my daughter to his list?"

"Let's not go for each other, Wes. Even if I were willing I have no authority to order the troopers away. With Sergeant Lombard out of commission I'd have to get in touch with the barracks—"

"There's no time for that. Five minutes, he said."

Secco touched Malone's arm. "We'll have to rush him. There's no other way now. We'll use the tear gas first so he won't be able to see Barbara to shoot her—"

Malone twitched and the hand fell away. "You'd gamble on that after what you just saw?"

"I have no choice."

"I have."

"Where are you going?"

Malone walked out into the clear again. The sun had come up and it threw a long extension of him over the grass. He saw it and thought that's me too.

"Furia? You still behind the door?"

The crack widened. "What do you want?"

"Listen. You and Chief Secco both." I've got to stop shaking, why am I shaking, I feel great. "John? I'm going over to the other side."

"What?" Secco cried.

135

"I'm through. I'm not playing on the team any more."

"What team? What are you talking about?"

"Look at what it's got me."

"Wes," Secco said. "Come back a minute. Let's talk."

"There's nothing to talk about. Not any more."

"But Wes, you can't do a thing like that!"

"Watch me."

"Think of Ellen—"

"Who else am I thinking of? How long do you suppose she'd live with me if I let Bibby die? How long could I live with myself?"

"But this isn't the way to do it—"

Malone took the badge out of his pocket and Secco stopped talking. It said NEW BRADFORD POLICE and the number 7. Lucky seven. He hurled it at the trees. It caught the sun and glittered like a hooked fish. It fell and was lost.

"Furia, you still there?"

"I don't fall for no fuzz trick."

"No trick, Fure. They won't make a deal with you, I will. I know where the payroll money is."

"Where?"

"That's my price. I'll help you get the money back. And get away. You give me back my daughter when you're in the clear. That's the deal. I have no gun and I don't give a damn if you steal a million and live to be a hundred. All I want is my child back and to get her I'm ready to face prison if they arrest me. Deal?"

"And what are your fuzz buddies going to be doing all this time, hold my hand?"

"They'll do what I say. To get you they're going to have to risk shooting me and Barbara, and they won't do that. Will you, John?"

"Won't you think a minute, Wes?" Chief Secco said. "He'll never give you Barbara no matter what you do for him. He'll kill you both after you get him out of New Bradford."

"That's the chance I take."

"If you'll do it my way—"

"I've done it your way. It doesn't work. All I have left is me, myself."

"That's not true."

"It's always been true."

"Than it's always been wrong. Nobody makes it by copping out."

136

"Is that what I'm doing?"

"What would you call it, Wes?"

"All right, then I'm copping out."

"People have to pull together. When we're in the same boat. And we all are."

"Don't preach to me, John."

"Every decent man."

"Every decent man isn't in my spot."

"That's when it's most important! Wes, before it's too late—"

Malone turned his back on the tree. "Furia?"

"Yeah." The spinny voice sounded interested.

"Will you hold off on your five-minute deadline till I can come in and talk to you?"

"What for?"

"You still want that money, don't you? Well, without me you'll never get it. It's in a bank vault."

"In a what?"

"Let me come in and I'll explain the whole thing. You'll never swing the money and a getaway with just Goldie now that you've killed Hinch. You'll need help and I'm your only answer. Do we have a deal?"

"Shut up, Goldie!" The crack widened further. "Okay, you big men out there, I hold off my deadline while your boy tries to sell me. Only I tell you in ABC, if this is some kind of a cop play and you rush the house while we're talking, my first two shots are for Malone and his kid. Put your hands on your head, fuzz, and come on in."

Malone stood loosely in the Thatchers' cold hall while Furia searched him. His eyes were on Barbara. Barbara was sitting on the stairs a few steps up, beside Goldie. Her little fingers were buried in the pile of the stair carpet, clutching. She was staring at her father in disbelief.

"Daddy?"

"Everything's going to be all right, Bibby. You all right?"

"Daddy." She started to get up.

"Keep her there," Furia said, stepping back. "It ain't Old Home Week yet." Goldie pushed her back down without looking away from Malone.

Suffer you bitch.

"It's okay, Bibby, daddy's here, and I'm not leaving you again."

Malone was in a state of excited peace. He had never felt so strong, so secure.

"Never mind with the hearts and flowers, fuzz. Start pitching."

The Colt Trooper was back in Furia's hand, he had reloaded. The Walther was back in his waistband, the rifle was leaning handily against the radiator. The revolver was four feet from Malone's navel.

"We'd better do something about that back door," Malone said. "Just in case. It's broken and eight officers are outside there."

"What do you think I am, some punk? I got a great big freezer and an icebox across it. They start shoving," Furia ripped the Papa Bear mask off and Malone saw his teeth, long and pointed, "bang bang bang. Now what's this crud about a safe deposit box? What kind of a dummy hijacks a heisted payroll and parks it in a bank vault?"

"A smart one," Malone said. "Right, Goldie?"

"Since when did you start bellying up to fuzz?" Goldie wanted to know. "I tell you, Fure, this is a con. I tell you."

"And me with the drop? Relax, doll. I want to hear what's on his fuzz mind. Okay, Malone, it's in a bank vault. How do we get it?"

"Simple," Malone said. "We walk in there and we open the box and we walk out."

"And your buddies let us."

"They'll let us. As long as you have Barbara and me. They'll let us walk out and they won't lift a finger to stop our getaway. Stopping you means Barbara and I die, you've convinced them of that. They won't interfere after I lay it on the line."

Furia looked amused. "And how do we open the box?"

"They'll give us the bank's master key."

The Colt snaked out and bit into Malone's middle.

"You don't have to do that," Malone said. He had not moved. "I'm telling you the truth."

"Yeah? What do you take me for?" His short fuse made Furia's Mickey Mouse ears burn to their points. "You think I don't know how a safe deposit operates? You got to have two keys to open a box, the bank's and yours. So where's the other key? You got it?"

"No."

"Then who?"

"Tell him, Goldie," Malone said.

"Tell him?" Goldie said. "Tell him what? You see what I mean, Fure? He's trying to break us up. That's his con."

138

"Wait a minute," Furia said. "What's she know about it?"

"She knows all about it," Malone said. "She's the one hijacked that payroll from my house and took it that same day to the Taugus National in town. My wife only saw the pants and jacket and thought it was a man. She's the boxholder, Furia. Look at her. Look at her face."

Goldie's face was like the rest of her, in the deepfreeze. The cold breath had turned her cheeks white with frost.

"He's making it up." Her tongue crept over her lips. "Fure, this is Goldie, remember? Would I lie to you? Did I ever?"

"You say," Furia said to Malone. "How about proving it?"

She had to sign when she rented the box. She signed a phony name, but with the same initials. I got hold of a letter she wrote her sister Nanette, went to the bank, and compared handwritings. They're the same."

"Show me."

"I'll show it to you at the bank. They wouldn't let me have it."

"See?" Goldie said. "See, Fure, he's got nothing. Who you going to believe, him or me?"

"You didn't rent a box at the bank, Goldie?"

"No."

"You ain't got a key?"

"No!"

"I think," Furia said, "we'll have ourselves a look. Come down off there."

"Down where?" Goldie chattered. "What are you going to do to me, Fure?"

"See if you got a key. Go into the room."

Goldie rose. "And if you don't find it on me?" she said shrilly. "You'll let me give this sonofabitch what he's got coming?"

"That's my trip. Get in there. You—kid. Go up in the bedroom."

"What are you going to do?" Goldie said again.

"Bibby," Malone said. "Do what the man says. Go upstairs and stay there till I call you."

Barbara scuttled up to the landing and then she was not there. He had not thought she could move so fast. She still had her baby fat.

"Inside," Furia said to Goldie. He took the rifle with his left hand and brandished it. "You, too, fuzz."

They went into the big living room. A tall fire was blazing away. "Is it all right if I stand near the fire?" Malone asked. "I'm cold."

"You stay put. Them fire tools might give you ideas." Furia squinted at Goldie. "Start stripping."

"What?" Goldie said.

"Take it off."

"In front of him?"

"He's pulling a fast one he won't live long enough to enjoy. Get going, Goldie."

Goldie began to fumble with the zipper at the side of her slacks. "You fuzz bastard, you know how many times I saved your brat from getting her head shot off? This is my thanks!" She kicked her shoes away and stepped out of the slacks. She kicked the slacks in Furia's direction.

"I don't think she'd keep it on her," Malone said. "She's hidden it somewhere."

"Oh, you ain't so sure now," Furia said. "Look in her shoes and slacks."

Malone picked up the shoes. He examined the soles, the linings. He tugged at the heels, tried to twist them. Then he picked up the slacks and went through them. He shook his head.

"The shirt," Furia said to Goldie.

She unbuttoned her blouse and shrugged it off, long gold hair swinging. She flung the blouse at Malone's head. He ran his hands over it with special attention to the seams. He shook his head again.

"Bra," Furia said.

She unhooked it, glaring. It fell to the floor. Malone walked over and picked it up. Her flesh was very near his face and he could see through her sheer pink panties. It left him colder.

He was very thorough searching the bra. The stuffing of the cups would make a good hiding place.

"No," he said.

"Drop your panties," Furia said.

"Fure, how could I hide—?"

"Drop 'em."

She dropped them. She stood there looking at Malone. "I'll kill you," she said. "I'm going to kill you after this, you know that?"

"This part I do personal," Furia said. He stepped behind her. "Bend over, Goldie." She began to curse Malone. The last time he had heard a woman use such

140

language was in an offlimits Greek whorehouse, it had somehow not sounded so bad in broken English. He found himself a little shocked. "Turn around."

"Go to hell, goddam you!"

Furia turned her around gently. After a while he stepped to one side and said, "You struck out, fuzz." He raised the Colt. "I told you not to con me."

"And I told you," Malone said. "She's too smart to hide it on herself."

The revolver hesitated. "Then where?"

"She'd hide it where she could get to it fast. It's got to be somewhere in this house."

Furia glanced over at the sofa. Barbara's coat and hat lay there, and two open suitcases. Evidently he had had the woman pack in the early hours for a quick getaway after he began to suspect Hinch's runout. He waved the revolver. "Her bag. The tan one. Go look."

Malone rummaged through the tan one. He was sure the key was not there and he was right. He went through the other bag for luck. It was not there, either.

When he straightened up Goldie was putting her clothes on and Furia was studying her.

"You know something?" Malone said. "She could have been just smart enough to hide it in Barbara's coat or hat."

"She could," Furia said, "if she ever had it. I'm playing along with you so far, fuzz, but don't take advantage of my good nature. You better start getting results." He gestured with the Colt. "Okay, try your kid's things."

Malone handled Bibby's coat and hat as if they were nothing in particular, as if the warm blue wool and her chubby little body had never met.

"No." He deliberately flung the coat and hat aside. He stood studying Goldie, who was zipping up her slacks. He tried to see into her head. "I know," Malone said. "She hid it on you."

"On me?" Furia said.

"Do you carry a wallet?"

"What the hell do I need a wallet for, Diners Club? You're way out, man." Furia looked angry. "Unless you think I'm dumb. Is that what you think?"

"No, no," Malone said. "It has nothing to do with you, only with her. Why not take a look, Furia? What have you got to lose?"

"Plenty," Furia said. "Rolling over to fuzz for one." But

141

then he said, "Hook your fingers at the back of your neck." Malone hooked his fingers at the back of his neck. "One move and you've had it."

"I'm not going to try anything," Malone said.

"Give me that other gun, Fure," Goldie said. Some spit came out. "Let me be the one."

"Why, Goldie. Ain't you the bloodthirsty one."

"I'll cover him, I mean. While you search yourself."

"You'll do what I tell you." Furia began to paw himself with his left hand. When he was finished with his left side he transferred the Colt to his left hand and felt all over his right side. He even got down in a crouch and ran a finger around the insides of his trouser cuffs. "Okay, Malone, nobody makes a monkey out of me."

"I know," Malone said. "I know now."

"You know what now?"

"I thought she was too smart to hide it on herself. I didn't know how smart she is. She figured nobody would think her stupid enough to do that. Neck. Look at the back of her head. Under her hair."

. "Fure, let me kill him!" Goldie screamed.

Furia stood very still.

"Yeah," he said.

He stalked over to her.

She backed off, all the way to the fireplace. She got so close to the fire that Malone was afraid for her hair.

"Fure, I swear to you."

He grabbed her hair and yanked. She yelped and fell against him. He yanked again, downward, and she dropped to her knees.

"I swear, I swear . . ."

Furia took a fistful of the long golden hair at the back of her head and pulled it straight up.

Something was plastered to the back of her skull with adhesive tape.

He ripped it away.

Stuck to the adhesive side, along with some gold and brown hairs, were two flat keys.

"Jesus H. Christ. My own broad." Furia glanced from the safe deposit keys in his left hand to the Colt in his right as if he did not know quite what to do. "You know what I got to do now, Goldie. Don't you?"

Goldie was very fast. "Wait, Fure, wait." Her upturned face schemed with her fear, she was trying to stop him by sheer eye-power. "You kill me and whose going to stay

142

with the kid while you're getting the money back out of the bank? You need me, Fure. You still need me."

"She's right," Malone said. For some reason he was not feeling strong any longer. It was like the tiredness of a week ago, as if none of this had happened.

I'll wake up and Ellen will laugh Loney you're dreaming.

Time came back. "Yeah," Furia said heavily. "What I ought to done, I ought to listened to that yellowbelly Hinch. He always said you were my bag ... Get up, you twotimer bitch. But you ain't my broad no more."

He sounded sad.

"You ain't *nothing*."

Malone stepped out through the front door. The lawn was empty. They had removed Hinch's body.

Behind him Furia spat, "They took the garbage away."

"Don't shoot," Malone called. "It's me." He was wearing the Baby Bear mask. Furia had ordered him to put it on before he delivered his speech. When Malone had balked the little hood said, "It's like you're my boy now, right? Right, Malone?"

"Right," Malone had said.

The sun was well up now. It was going to be a sparkler.

"John?" Malone said. "You can come out from behind the tree. He won't shoot you. No, not the others. Just you."

Chief Secco stepped out from behind his tree.

"You went over," he said. "You really went over."

"There's no time for a sermon, John. I want you to take your men, the whole lot, and clear out of here."

Secco turned away.

"Wait, I'm not through."

Secco turned around.

"We're coming into town—Furia, the woman, Bibby, me—at twelve noon on the dot. There's to be nobody in the bank, John. Nobody, and I mean that. Have Wally Bagshott leave the bank's master key to the boxes on the table outside the vault along with the key to the vault."

"How are you going to open the box without the boxholder's key?" Secco asked almost absently. "You bringing dynamite?"

"I found Goldie's key."

Secco blinked.

"You're to clear the Green, John, the whole area. I don't want anybody or anything on the Green or the side streets, no cars, no trucks, no pedestrians, no shoppers. The stores along Main and along Grange down to Freight Street are to be locked and the salespeople sent home. The offices upstairs in the bank building are to be closed and vacated. You got that?"

"Yes," Secco said.

"Wait, I'm still not through. To make sure there's no interference I want your men and the troopers to line up around the bank, including the parking lot. But without weapons, John. Repeat: unarmed. They're to let us go in, get the money out of the vault, and get out and away. What you choose to do after that is on your own conscience. And John?"

"Yes?"

"You can conceal weapons, you can try throwing tear gas into the bank, there are any number of ways you can stop us. But if that's in your mind I want you to remember: If you don't do just what I said, Barbara and I die first. Furia won't let me carry a weapon, he doesn't trust me. So I'll be helpless. The Vorshek woman will be outside with Barbara waiting and believe me, John, at the first sign of anything wrong she'll kill her, she's worked up a real hate for me because I found the key on her and proved to Furia she was the one stole the payroll from him. They may shoot us anyway after we get clear, like you said. That would be on my head, John. But if you try to queer this, or let the troopers, you'll be as guilty of our deaths as if you pulled the trigger yourself.

"Okay, John, that's it."

Whatever John Secco was thinking—of his responsibilities, of his affections, of victory or defeat as a man and a law officer—the sun on his face did not reflect it.

He raised his arm to the trees.

"You men. We're leaving."

Tuesday

The Payoff

"He's gone off his trolley," Russ Fairhouse said. "There ain't, isn't any precedent for a fool stunt like this, Mrs. Malone. Can't you do something to stop him?"

"What would you suggest?" Ellen said.

They were in the First Selectman's office at a front window diagonally across the Green from the bank. Town hall employees were crowded in other windows peering through the vanes of the venetian blinds. It's like the last scene in that ghastly movie *On The Beach* where there's nothing left on the main street but blowing papers. Ellen had never seen the Green so depopulated, even early Sunday mornings or Saturday nights a half hour after the movies let out. Not a soul but that cordon of state troopers around the bank and they were statues not a muscle moving they didn't look alive. He's got to keep his word, John you've *got* to.

"How would I know?" Selectman Fairhouse said. He was a big man running to lard with beautiful hands, he got a manicure once a week at Dotty's Beauty Salon after hours by special appointment. "All I know is this is not

146

right, Mrs. Malone. It ain't legal or . . . hell, it ain't moral!"

"Neither is a gangster taking a little girl and threatening to kill her."

"But there are other ways—"

"What ways?"

"Then you approve of your husband's action?" Fairhouse asked huffily. "I remind you, Mrs. Malone, he's a paid employee of this town, supposed to be an officer of the law to boot. It makes the whole town look bad!"

"Approve?" Ellen said. "I'll approve of anything that gets my baby back. Thank God for my husband is what I say. And you can take your town and you know what you can do with it."

"He'll go to jail for this!" the selectman said. "If he doesn't get killed by that hood first."

She could almost hear him add and I hope he does.

"Would you please let me alone?"

Fairhouse started to say something, changed his mind, stalked back to his desk, sat down, and viciously ripped the end off a cigar. Who wants this headache anyway. Next election they can wish it on sombody else. A lousy town cop to pull a stunt like this. It will whammy the whole administration. It's all John Secco's fault. The roof falls in about this and over the hill with you my friend.

Ellen was grateful for his retirement. Her brain was as busy as the Green was empty. You can't believe your own eyes sometimes, a person finds that out. Those buildings across the Green looked like falsefronts, the whole thing was taking place on a Hollywood back lot. All it needs are a camera and a director *and there they come to the background music of the noon whistle from the firehouse.*

The black Chrysler sedan went past the town hall at fifteen slow-motion miles an hour.

Ellen got up on her toes and strained.

The blonde woman sat in the rear wearing the Goldilocks mask. There was just the tip of Barbara's blue hat showing she must have my baby down on the seat oh Bibby mama's here. The little monster was in the front seat at the right he had a gun to the head of the driver so the driver must be Loney yes it was she could never mistake the set of his shoulders. Loney was wearing the Baby Bear mask and Furia was wearing the Papa Bear mask. What are they all wearing masks for? It must be that monster's idea of a rib, a thumbnose at the fuzz.

I don't care.
Just let them be safe afterward.
The Chrysler turned left at the corner.

The Chrysler turned left and rolled to a stop on Grange just past the corner of Main, headed the wrong way on the one-way street. Papa Bear got out on the curb side and waved the Colt Trooper, he held the Walther automatic in his left hand and the hunting rifle under his left arm. He was wearing his gloves. The pockets of his Brooks Brothers suit bulged with boxes of ammunition and Malone's belt with its picket fence of cartridges was strapped about his waist over the jacket.

A sigh like an afternoon breeze off the river went through the troopers. Papa Bear glanced at them and raised the Colt to point into the car. Driver's seat. The breeze died.

"Okay, Malone."

Baby Bear opened the driver's door and slid dutifully out from behind the wheel. He came round the hood of the Chrysler and stopped a yard away from Papa Bear, glancing into the car and saying something reassuring to the child. Papa Bear waved the Colt again and Goldilocks got out on the sidewalk, she pushed the child ahead of her without letting go, then she shut the car door and backed against it. Immediately she went into a half squat with her left arm about the little girl. In this way she was protected by the body of the car from a rear attack and by the body of the child from a frontal attack. She gripped Furia's switchblade with the point just touching the child's throat, it made the slightest dent in the white flesh. Not for the perfidious Lady Goldie this time the gun from the royal arsenal. But the knife would serve nicely as a substitute, every trooper eye said.

The child was in shock or they had fed her a sedative. Her lids kept drooping as she tried to keep her father in focus. The mask he was wearing seemed to confuse her.

Papa Bear looked around. He was in no hurry. His camera eye swiveled the full 360° of emptiness like a panoramic shot. It paused briefly one after another at the empty holsters of the troopers.

When he was through with the inspection he said, "Turn around." The angle of his masked head jeered at everything.

148

Baby Bear turned. Papa Bear stepped up to him and touched the muzzle of the revolver to his spine at the third vertebra.

"We go in," Papa Bear decreed. "Hup."

They marched as if a sergeant were chanting cadence up the eight steps of the Taugus National, one behind the other, and went into the bank.

Ellen witnessed the performance through the slats of the town hall window. She saw the Chrysler pull up at the bank the wrong way, she saw Papa Bear get out, she saw her Baby Bear get out, she saw Goldilocks push Barbara onto the walk and grab her and squat with the knife against her throat. Dear Jesus even if she comes away from this alive she'll need a psychiatrist or at least a good psychologist maybe years of therapy oh I don't care just let her stay living.

Ellen saw Papa Bear and Baby Bear make their single-file march into the bank.

That was the beginning of the worst. Because the filming stopped. No, that was wrong, they had already shot the film, it was the projection that stopped, cold dead in the machine. The whole scene was the film including the invisible director and cameraman, they were invisibly part of it along with the visibles. The whole picture froze on the screen outside Fairhouse's window.

Maybe I'm part of it too. And Selectman Fairhouse. And these other people. And the troopers. And the Bears. Maybe we're all part of it, everyone and everything, the Green, the bank, and uneven rooflines of the two-story buildings north south east and west, even the sky and that sun hanging in it like a prop.

It was all frozen on the screen.

Do the images on the frozen screen know about time? Time had simply stopped along with everything else. When she heard the shots and things began moving again she glanced at her wristwatch for the sake of her sanity and saw that thirteen minutes had passed since the two Bears had marched into the bank.

Shots.

Shots?

They had been faint but sharp reports from across the Green, like a sound effect, a drumstick on the rim of a snare drum. Shot shot-shot.

Shots *no*.

Why would Furia be shooting oh he wouldn't shoot Loney why should he shoot Loney Loney went over to him. John Secco told me so . . .

"*Loney.*"

As the wail came from her throat Ellen saw the man in the Brooks Brothers suit and the Papa Bear mask burst out of the bank and race down the steps. He had the revolver in his gloved hand and a bulging canvas bag in his left. He ran bent over, almost double.

It was funny how the troopers remained frozen on the film. Couldn't they see him? He was in front of their noses.

Papa Bear flung the canvas bag in the direction of Goldilocks. She threw up an arm in an instinctive grab but it sailed over her head into the rear seat of the Chrysler and she yanked the door open and scrambled in clutching for it.

Papa Bear scooped up the child as if he meant to break her back.

That was when Ellen Malone heard the casting call.

Wesley Malone in the Baby Bear mask with Furia at his heels in the Papa Bear mask marched into the bank. The pressure on Malone's spine increased while Furia looked the situation over. But the bank was a ghost town, he could see that at a glance, no vice-presidents behind the executive desks, no tellers at the windows, no office girls in the rear, everything put away neatly. Like for Sundays.

"Wide open like a broad," Furia said. "They follow orders good. It's a crime." The muzzle prodded. "Don't you want to know what's a crime?"

"Whatever you say," Malone said.

"A wide-open bank. All that bread laying around. Who needs safe deposit boxes with a sweet setup like this?"

"You won't find any money here," Malone said.

"What are you, on the Board of Directors?"

"I know the big squeeze, Bagshott. And Chief Secco. They're not about to let you walk off with the assets. The cash boxes have been emptied and all the cash is in the big vault, the one with the time-lock."

"Stay right there." Furia edged around and got into the tellers' section. He opened one drawer after another. He banged the last one and came back.

"I can dream, can't I?" Furia shrugged. "Not a plugged subway token. I'll have to make out with that twenty-four grand. Okay, fuzz buddy, where's the safe deposit vault?"

Their steps made lonesome sounds across the floor.

On the desk before the vault lay two keys, one to the steel-barred door, the other to the safe deposit boxes.

"You know something?" Furia said. "I'm going to let you open it." He stepped back a few feet, Colt and Walther at waist level.

Malone picked up the vault key and unlocked the steel-barred door. He swung it in and stepped aside.

"Not on your fuzz life," Furia said. "You open the box, pal."

Malone took the bank's master key from the desk and went into the vault.

"You'll need Goldie's key, too," Furia said. He had the key in his left glove. He holstered the automatic and jiggled the key down into his palm. He tossed the key to Malone and leaned against the entrance to the vault. "Box number 535."

Malone began looking for Box 535.

"I'm getting a charge out of this, you know that?" Furia said. "I mean watching a cop pull a bank job. Never thought you'd be doing a no-no like this, huh, Malone? Makes you like one of the bad guys, know what I mean?"

"Here it is." Malone inserted the bank's key into the left keyhole and turned it. Then he used Goldie's key in the righthand keyhole. He pulled. The narrow door swung open. He drew out the flat black box and turned to Furia.

Furia was watching him with what was surely enjoyment. Behind Furia stood John Secco. John Secco's arm was raised. It held a billy club.

The billy club landed over Furia's ear with a water-logged thunk. Everything fell, the Colt Trooper, the hunting rifle, Furia, his hat. The Colt and the rifle struck the floor first. Secco stepped over Furia's body and picked them up. While Malone was getting his mouth in working order Secco plucked the Walther from the holster. He tossed the three weapons to the desk outside the vault and removed Furia's mask. He took a black cloth out of his pocket, held it by opposite corners, and twirled it several times. He stuffed the fat part in Furia's mouth and tied the ends three times at the back of Furia's neck.

Then he straightened up and they stared at each other.

151

"I thought you could use some help, Wes," the chief said. He sounded quite serious, as at morning report.

Malone tore off the Baby Bear mask. He tried to speak and failed. Finally he made it. "You know what you've just done with your help, John? You've cut Barbara's throat. You had no right, you had no goddamned right. I ought to kill you for this."

"Kill me later," Secco said. "We've got Furia in the bag, now the problem is the woman outside, there's a way it can be pulled off or I'd never have started this. You're not a whole lot bigger than Furia, Wes, especially with these built-up heels he wears. Put on his clothes and mask and hat and the gun belt and the rest. The clothes will be a tight fit but with his mask on and if you run crouched over it'll happen so fast the woman won't have time to realize it isn't him." He stooped over the unconscious gunman. "Take your clothes off while I strip him. Don't stand there, Wes. Get cracking."

Malone stood there.

"You going to stand there till she gets suspicious? Undress."

He found himself undressing at the same fast tempo at which Secco was undressing Furia. At first all he could think of was the process. The way you do it first the jacket then the pants then the shirt. Like at night but you keep your shoes on, both pairs are black, maybe she won't notice, I pray she won't notice. That my feet are bigger. Then the other thoughts started in, like why am I doing this and it's all wrong. Or is it. I made my bed and I was lying in it and along comes John Secco and pulls it out from under me. I'll kill him, I meant it, anything goes wrong. But then why do I feel groovy all of a sudden like I'm swinging for the first time in my life. Like we're socking it to 'em.

Hang on Bibby baby!

"We'll take no chances, Wes," Chief Secco was saying rapidly as he helped Malone into Furia's clothes. "He fired three shots into Tom Howland, he fired three quick shots at Sergeant Lombard this morning and another three into Hinch, three quick shots one and two-three seems to be his style, so I'll do it the same, three quick shots one and two-three in here when you're ready. When this Goldie sees you in Furia's getup running out of the bank after the shots like with the money—I've got a canvas bag for you stuffed with newspaper—she's got to think Furia killed you

152

in here, which he damn well might have. So it'll ring true to her. Throw the fake money bag at her, over her head, she's a greedy one, she'll let go of Barbara and make a grab for it. Then all you have to do is snatch Barbara up and we're home free."

"The troopers, they'll think I'm Furia—"

"No, they won't. They won't interfere till you've got Barbara in your arms. Then they'll jump the woman. The troopers have their orders about this, they know my plan, they're carrying concealed weapons. It'll be rough on Ellen, Wes, she's watching from Fairhouse's office, I did my best but I couldn't keep her away, for a few minutes she's going to think you're shot. I'm sorry, but that's the way it's going to have to be. It's got to look right." He yanked Furia's arms around to his back and snapped handcuffs on the slim wrists. "Just so our hood friend doesn't come to and spoil it. Let me look at you."

Malone adjusted the Papa Bear mask.

"You'll make it. All set?"

He nodded and they left the vault. Malone slapped the Walther into his holster and picked up his Colt Trooper, welcome home. Secco went into a drawer of the desk and dug out a fat canvas bag. Malone took it.

"We go," Malone said in his old voice, and he sprinted for the door.

The man in the Brooks Brothers suit and the Papa Bear mask burst out of the bank and raced down the steps. He had the revolver in his gloved right hand and a bulging canvas bank bag in his left. He ran bent over, almost double.

The troopers did not move.

Papa Bear tossed the canvas bag at Goldilocks. She flung up an arm in an instinctive grab but the bag sailed over her head into the rear seat of the Chrysler and she yanked the door open and scrambled in clutching for it.

Malone scooped up his child and the troopers came unglued. Six of them leaped up the steps of the bank and vanished. The rest swarmed over the car. Each man had materialized a hand gun, Malone did not know from where and he did not care. He was too busy making a fuss over Barbara and wondering why she was shrinking from him, he had forgotten that he was wearing the Papa Bear mask. "It's all right, baby, it's me, daddy, don't you remember?" —a stupid thing to say but it was a time for stupidities like that, at least Barbara seemed to think so.

153

At the familiar voice she stopped staring the unbelieving stare he had come to dread and made a pleased sound and slipped her arms around his neck and laid her head on his shoulder as she always did when he carried her up to bed.

Goldie Vorshek was staring at him just as Barbara had, unbelievingly, but as if she could not trust her ears.

She put up no resistance when they took Furia's switchblade away from her. But when they pulled her out of the Chrysler and reached for the still-closed money bag Goldie hugged it to her breast with both arms like a little girl protecting her dollie and tried to kick and knee every trooper within range. She had two of them writhing on the sidewalk before she was subdued.

Malone watched her capture like the Great Stone Face.

She's the one fed a nine-year-old the booze.

I hope you burn.

That was when the Rams' defensive line hit him.

Ellen tore her child from his grasp as he staggered and transferred Bibby to the other arm and with her small fist dealt him a blow on the chest that landed like a sledge. Before he could yelp uncle she closed in on him again and made a vicious swipe at his mask. The mask ripped and it fell apart.

"Loney?"

She began to cry.

"It's all right for heaven's sake," Malone said peevishly, "I forgot about the mask. Wait till I catch my breath. You hit like Rosey Grier."

"I made you bleed *blood*," Ellen wept, "I've got to cut my nails. Let's go into Sampson's and get it cleaned. Oh, hell, they're closed, aren't they? I left my purse in the town hall like an idiot. Don't you have a hanky? What are you doing in the monster's clothes, you look ridiculous. When I saw you run out like that ... in his mask ... How did you *do* it, Loney? It was wonderful. Was it John's idea? I'll bet it was John's idea. Oh, there's John, it *was*. But you were wonderful too, Loney ..."

"And don't call me Loney!" Malone shouted. "I don't like that goddam name! I never liked it!"

"Why, Loney, I mean—Wes? You never told me."

"I'm telling you now! I hate it."

"Yes, Loney, I mean ... Bibby darling, it's all right. Mama and daddy aren't fighting."

She mothered her child while he stripped off the fragments of Papa Bear mask and threw them away in disgust.

154

He felt around in Furia's pockets until he located a handkerchief. It looked antiseptically clean. For some reason this riled Malone. He applied the handkerchief to his wound still churned up.

After John Secco came the troopers, out of the bank, bringing Furia. Blood was still coming down Furia's face and he was stumbling along like a robot with gasket missing, they had to half carry him. His underwear was too big for him and his hairy shanks and bandylegs were pimpled with cold. A trooper came running up with something that looked like a horse blanket and threw it around him. Furia clutched it to him, shivering. His bugged eyes passed over Malone, Ellen, Barbara without recognition, it was Goldie Vorshek they were hunting. They located her in the grip of three troopers in the Chrysler and in a flash he became Man-Mountain Furia, hero of his dreams, too-big underwear, skinniness, goose pimples and all, in a last struggle for status. He kicked and bit and butted and threw himself from side to side with troopers hanging on to his arms and legs, spinning out an endless line of dirty words, the spin whirled up to a screech, it was laughable and somehow sad, too. A trooper finally ended his nonsense with a well-placed slap and they pushed a cooled-off bad man into a state police car, threw the blanket in after him, and sped off. Another police car pulled up and they transferred a sullen Goldie Vorshek to it and then they were gone, too, along with Chief Secco, who gave the Malones a neighborly wave.

Leaving Mr. and Mrs. Wesley Malone and daughter on the empty corner of the empty street facing the empty Green. It never looked so empty, not even when the film stopped cold.

But then Wallace L. Bagshott creeps through the entrance to the upper floor of the bank building into the lobby, he's been hiding upstairs in Judge Trudeau's law office. He peers out at the Malones, shakes his head, hurries into his bank, and locks the doors. He's headed straight for the bottle of Canadian Club parked in the bottom drawer of his desk that he thinks nobody knows about.

Jerry Sampson opens the doors of his drug store and sticks his head out timidly. He's been hiding behind his prescription counter. He waves over at the Malone family and then wipes his balding head as though it were an August day.

Arthur McArthur Sanford in his Nehru jacket and oriental carpet slippers reopens the stationery and book store, he keeps a running stock of at least three dozen books on display behind an amber translucency, Arthur is a one-man committee to push culture in New Bradford and not getting very far.

Lew Adams with his Theodore Roosevelt mustache preceding him comes out of nowhere and begins taking down the ironwork in front of his jewelry shop. He keeps looking over his shoulder.

On Grange Street running all the way down to Freight stores are reopening, the proprietors were on the premises all the time.

Beyond the Green First Selectman Russ Fairhouse bursts out of the town hall followed by a crowd, they stream over the grass past the bandstand that hasn't heard a tootle in forty years but it's kept in a nice dress of paint for old times' sake, ditto the World War I tank.

Toward the Malone family.

A herd of cars comes running down Main Street from the north alongside the Green to the accompaniment of bawling horns. Cars shoot up to curbs, people pile out even on the Positively No Parking At Any Time side.

Headed for the Malones.

Racing across the bridge from the other side of the Tonekeneke come Young Tru (Hyatt), Edie Golub, old Ave Elwood, and Marie Griggs (she's Ave's night counter girl but she's been filling in today for a day girl who called in sick).

Seems like the whole town's massing, all sizes and shapes and ages (including the Don James family and New Bradford's nine other families of color, *they're* beginning to move in and some people are getting worried). Including Joe Barron of the Army Navy Store who's been trying to organize a Human Relations group, he's pretty new in town, and Marie's boy friend Jimmy Wyckoff, and fat Dotty from the beauty salon, and Father Weil striding along in his cassock and collar (there's really nothing going on at the Romish church this time of day on a Tuesday but the good Father has a flair for drama, it keeps the Church in the public eye, like that's why clergymen in films are always Roman or at least Episcopalian, the Episcoloopians' high church boys wear turned-around collars too, the Prottier ministers are the forgotten clergy) ... the whole town has come out for the tar-and-feathering

156

or the bazaar or the auction or whatever it is that's going on. And they're all bearing down on ex-Officer or is it still Officer Wesley Malone and his girls asking questions, how did they find out so fast, you can't keep anything hushed up in New Bradford but this one breaks all the speed records, while Ellen drinks it up like a thirsty grunt after a dry duty and Malone watches her with wonder, to listen to Ellen chattering away you'd never know what she's just been through.

And Malone is feeling a sneaky glow himself. Like when he took a couple too many belts at the wedding and they spent the first three hours of their honeymoon night in the motel bathroom while Ellen held his head over the toilet bowl. Malone is feeling the sneaky glow that you feel like when you have first dug the Sermon on the Mount or some of that Golden Rule stuff the priests and ministers and rabbis are always spouting on the desert air, or learned about no man being an island or however it was the guy said it, or in other words when you have joined the human race.

It is not late enough in the day for old Sol to be going down over the People which would sort of symbolize Wes Malone's sneaky glow, it is still barely past the halfway mark between sunrise and sunset.

So we just count our blessings and fade out.

THE LAST
WOMAN IN
HIS LIFE

Contents

1.
The
First
Life

And so Ellery stood there, watching the BOAC jet take the Scot away.

He was still standing alone on his island when a hand touched his.

He turned around and it was, of all people, Inspector Queen.

"El," his father said, squeezing his arm. "Come on, I'll buy you a cup of coffee."

The old boy always comes through, Ellery thought over his second cup in the airport restaurant.

"Son, you can't monkey around in this business without once in a while running into the back of your own hand," the Inspector said. "It didn't have to happen this way. You let yourself get involved with the guy. If I allowed myself that kind of foolishness I'd have had to toss my shield in years ago. Human flesh can't stand it."

Ellery raised his hand as if the other were on the Bible. "So help me Hannah, I'll never make that mistake again."

Having said this, he found his glance coming to rest on Benedict and Marsh, in man-to-man conversation at the other side of the dining room.

All men, Shaw said, mean well.

Not excluding Ellery. What was this but the familiar Chance Encounter? Time lines converging for the moment, a brief nostalgia, then everyone on his way and no harm done?

Had he but known.

It began, as such apparently meaningless reunions do, with grips, grins, and manly warmth. The pair immediately accepted Ellery's invitation to move over to the Queen table. They had not laid eyes on him, and vice versa, since Harvard.

To Inspector Queen, Marsh was just a citizen named Marsh. But he had certainly heard of Benedict—Johnny-B to the world of jet, a charter member of Raffles, fixed star of the lady columnists, crony of nobility, habitué of Monaco, Kitz-bühel, and the yachting isles of Greece. January might find Benedict at the winter festival in Málaga; February in

9

Garmisch-Partenkirchen; March in Bloemfontein for the national games; April at the Songkran Festival in Chiangmai; May in Copenhagen for the royal ballet; June at Epsom Downs for the English Oaks and at Newport and Cork for the transatlantic yacht races; July at Henley and Bayreuth; August at Mystic for the Outdoor Art Festival; September in Luxembourg for the wine; October in Turin for the auto show; November at Madison Square Garden for the horse show; and December at Makaha Beach for the surfing championships. These were only typical; Johnny-B had a hundred other entertainments up his sleeve. Ellery had always thought of him as a run-for-your-life man without the pathological stopwatch.

John Levering Benedict III toiled not (toil, he liked to argue, was man's silliest waster of time), neither did he spin except in the social whirl. He was charming without the obvious streak of rot that ran through his set, a fact that never palled on the press assigned to the Beautiful People. He was even handsome, a not common attribute of his class (in whom the vintage tended to sour)—on the slight side, below-average tall, with fine fair hair women adored stroking, and delicate hands and feet. He was, of course, sartorially ideal; year after year he sauntered onto the Ten Best-Dressed list. There was something anciently Grecian about him, a to-the-bone beauty as fine as the texture of his hair.

Johnny-B's paternal grandfather had staked out a stout chunk of the Olympic Peninsula and the timberlands around Lake Chelan to become one of the earliest lumber barons of the Pacific Northwest. His father had invested in shipping, piling Pelion on Ossa—that is to say, according to the gossip, leaving the difficulty of spending the resultant riches to Johnny. In Johnny's set it was often pointed out that with a fortune in the multimillions the feat could not easily be done; that past a certain point great wealth is hard to redistribute. That Johnny tried manfully is a matter of public record. Alimony apparently made mere dents, only enough to bruise; he had just divorced his third wife.

The leash on the runaway tendencies of Johnny Benedict was said to be Al Marsh. Marsh, too, came from a society tree, and he was luxuriously nested in his own right from birth. But he grew up to toil and spin, from choice. With Marsh it was not a question of avarice or anxiety over his wealth; he worked, said those who knew him well, because the life-style of his world bored him. Dilettantism *in vacuo* had no appeal for him. He had taken top honors at Harvard Law, gone on to serve a brilliant apprenticeship to a United States Supreme Court justice, and emerged into the cynical realities of Washington and New York to found a law firm of his own that, with the aid of his family's influence and connections, quietly acquired a sterling clientele and a hallmark reputation. He had offices in both cities.

Experts in such matters nominated Marsh one of the matrimonial catches of any season whatever. He was unfailingly attractive to women, whom he handled with the same tact he brought to his practice of law, and not only because he was elusive. He was a bigger man than Benedict, darkly rugged, with a smashed nose from his college wrestling days, a jaw that looked as if it had been mined in Colorado, and a naturally squinty set to the eyes—"the Marlboro type," Johnny called him affectionately—who seemed born to saddle horses and foreign cars. He had a fondness for both which he indulged when he could find the time, and a passion for flying; he piloted his own plane with a grim devotion that could only be explained by the fact that his father had died in one.

As so often happens in the case of men to whom women respond, other men did not take to Marsh easily. Some called it his aloofness, others his reserve, others his "standoffishness"; whatever it was, it caused Marsh to have a very small circle of friends. Johnny Benedict was one of the few.

Their relationship was not altogether personal. Johnny had inherited from his father the services of an ancient and prestigious law firm which had handled three generations of Benedict investments; but for the management of his personal affairs he relied on Marsh.

"Of course you just flew in from the moon," Ellery said. "It's about the only place, from what I hear, you've never been."

"Matter of fact, I got off the jet from London fifteen minutes ago, and Al here got off with me," Benedict said. "We had some business in London, and th-then there was that auction at S-Sotheby's."

"Which of course you had to attend."

"Please," Marsh said in a pained way. "Amend the auxiliary verb. I know of no law that compels a man to drop what Johnny just dropped for that Monet."

Benedict laughed. "Aren't you always lecturing me about spending my m-money so I've a fighting chance for a profit?" He not only stammered, he had difficulty with his r's, giving his speech a definite charm. It was hard to see a rapacious capitalist in a man who pronounced it "pwofit?"

"Are you the guy who bought that thing?" Inspector Queen exclaimed. "Paid all that loot for a hunk of old canvas and a few francs' worth of paint?"

"Don't tell us what you got it for, Johnny," Ellery said.

"I can't retain figures like that. I suppose you're going to convert it into a dartboard for your game room, or something
equally kicky?"

Marsh signaled for the waiter. "You've been listening to
Johnny's detractors. Another round, please. He really knows
art."

"I really do," Benedict said, pronouncing it "weally." "So
help m-me Ripley. I'd like you to see my c-collection some-
time." He added politely, "You, too, Inspector Queen."

"Thanks, but include me out," the Inspector said. "My
son calls me a cultural barbarian. Behind my back, of course.
He's too well brought up to say it frontwards."

"As for me, Johnny," Ellery said, scowling at pater, "I
don't believe I could bear it. I've never quite adjusted to the
unequal distribution of wealth."

"How about the unequal distribution of brains?" Benedict
retorted. "From what I've read about you and the Glory Guild
case, not to m-mention all those other mental miracles you
bring off, you're a second cousin of Einstein's." Something
in Ellery's face drove the banter from Benedict's voice. "Have
I said s-something?"

"Ellery's fagged," his father said quickly. "The Guild case
was a tough one, and just before that he'd been on a round-
the-world research trip in some far-out places where there's
no charge for the bedbugs or trots, and *that* took the starch
out of his hide. As a matter of fact, I've some vacation time
coming, and we were thinking of taking off for a couple of
weeks of peace and quiet somewhere."

"Ask Johnny," Marsh said. "He knows all the places, especially the ones that aren't listed."

"No, thanks," Ellery said. "Not Johnny's places."

"You've got the w'ong idea about me, Ellery," Benedict
protested. "What's today?"

"Monday."

"No, the date."

"March twenty-third."

"Well, just before I flew to London—on the nineteenth, if
you want to check—I was in Valencia for the Festival of St.
Joseph. W-wild? Before that I attended the Vienna Spring
Fair, and before *that*—the third, I think—I was in Tokyo for
the dollie festival. How's that? C-cultural, wouldn't you say?
Non-wastrel? Al, am I bragging again?"

"Brag on, Johnny," Marsh said. "That kind of self-puff
helps your image. God knows it can use help."

Ellery remarked, "Dad and I were thinking of something
less, ah, elaborate."

"Fresh air, long walks, fishing," Inspector Queen said.

"Ever go fishing, Mr. Benedict? I mean in a mountain stream all by your lone, with a rod that didn't cost three hundred dollars? The simple pleasures of the poor, that's what we're after."

"Then you may call me Doc, Inspector, because I have just the prescription for you both." Benedict glanced at Marsh. "Are you with it, Al?"

"Ahead of you," Marsh chuckled. "A rowboat gets you a cabin cruiser Ellery doesn't know."

"Know?" Ellery said. "Know what?"

"I own a place up in New England," Johnny Benedict said, "that very few people are aware I h-have. Not a bit doggy, plenty of w-woods, an unpolluted stream stocked with you name it—and I've fished it with a spruce pole I cut and trimmed myself, Inspector, and had splendid luck—and a guest cottage about a quarter of a mile from the main h-house that's as private as one of d-dear Ari's deals. It's all terribly *heimisch*, Ellery, and I know you and your f-father would enjoy it. You're welcome to use the cottage for as long as you like. I give you my oath no one will bother you."

"Well," Ellery began, "I don't know what to say. . . ."

"I do," the Inspector said promptly. "Thank you!"

"I mean, where in New England?"

Benedict and Marsh exchanged amused glances again. "Smallish town," Benedict said. "Doubt if you've heard of it, Ellery. Of no c-consequence whatsoever. W'ightsville."

"Wightsville?" Ellery stopped. *"Wrightsville?* You, Johnny? Own property up there?"

"For years and years."

"But I never knew!"

"Told you. I've kept it top-hush. Bought it through a dummy, just so I could have a place to let my hair d-down when I want to get away from it all, which is oftener than you'd think."

"I'm sorry, Johnny," Ellery said, beating his breast. "I've been an absolute stinker."

"It's modest—bourgeois, in fact. Down my great-grandfather's alley. He w-was a carpenter, by the way."

"But why Wrightsville, of all places?"

Benedict grinned. "You've advertised it enough."

"Well, I swan. Wrightsville happens to be my personal prescription for what periodically ails me."

"As if he didn't know," Marsh said. "He's followed your adventures, Ellery, the way Marcus Antonius followed Caesar's. Johnny's especially keen on your Wrightsville yarns. Keeps checking them for mistakes."

"This, gentlemen, is going to be the resumption of a beautiful friendship," Ellery said. "You sure we wouldn't be putting you out, Johnny?"

They went through the time-honored ritual of protest and reassurance, shook hands all around, and that evening a messenger brought an envelope that contained two keys and a scribbled note:

"Dear Sour-Puss: The smaller key is to the guest house. The other unlocks the main house, in case you want to get in there for something—grub, booze, clothing, whatever, it's always stocked. (So is the guest house, by the way, though not so bountifully.) Use anything you need or want from either place. Nobody's up there now (I have no live-in caretaker, though an old character named Morris Hunker comes out from town occasionally to keep an eye on things), and judging from the foul mood you were in today you need all the healing solitude my retreat in Wrightsville can provide. *Bonne chance,* and don't grouch your old man—he looks as if he can use some peace, too.

Fondly,
Johnny

P.S.: I may come up there soon myself. But I won't bother you. Not unless you want to be bothered."

The Queens set down at Wrightsville Airport a few minutes past noon the next day.

The trouble with Wrightsville—and Wrightsville had developed trouble, in Ellery's view—was that it had perfidiously kept step with the twentieth century.

Where his favorite small town was concerned Ellery was a mossback conservative, practically a reactionary. He was all for Thursday night band concerts in Memorial Park, with the peanut and popcorn whistles chirping tweet-tweet like excited birds, the streets lined with gawky boys ogling self-conscious girls and people from the outlying farms in town in their town-meetin' best; and Saturday the marketing day, with the black-red mills of Low Village shut down and High Village commerce swinging.

He felt a special attachment for the Square (which was round), with its periphery of two-story buildings (except for the Hollis Hotel, which towered five stories, and Upham House, a three-and-attic Revolutionary-era inn); in its mathematical center the time-treated memorial to Jezreel Wright, who had founded Wrightsville on an abandoned Indian site in 1701—a bronze statue long since turned to verdigris and festooned with so many bird droppings it looked like a modern sculpture, and at its feet a trough which had watered half a dozen generations of Wrightsville horseflesh. The Square was like a wheel with five spokes leading from its hub: State Street, Lower Main, Washington, Lincoln, Upper Dade; the grandest of these being State with its honor guard of century-old trees, the repository of the gilt-domed red-brick Town Hall and the County Court House building (how many times had he walked up the alley to the side entrance that opened into the Wrightsville police department!), the Carnegie Library across the street (where it was still possible to find books by Henty, Richard Harding Davis, and Joseph Hergesheimer!), the Chamber of Commerce building, the Wrightsville Light & Power Company, and the Northern State Telephone Company; and far from least, at the State Street entrance to Memorial Park, the Our Boys Memorial and the American Legion bandstand. About the Square in those days had been displayed some of the finest fruit of Wrightsville's heritage—the tiny gold *John F. Wright, Pres.* on the dusty windows of the Wrightsville National Bank, the old Bluefield Store, the "Minikin Road" on the street marker visible from the corner window of the Bon Ton, and half a dozen other names passed down from the founding families.

Upper Whistling Avenue, which crossed State Street a block northeast of the Square, led up to Hill Drive, where some of the oldest residential properties had stood (even older ones, great square black-shuttered clapboard affairs, most gone to pot even in Ellery's earliest acquaintance, occupied the farther reaches of State Street). Upper Dade ran northwest up to North Hill Drive, which had been taken over by the estates of Wrightsville's *nouveaux riches* (a *nouveau riche*, in the view of the Wrights, Bluefields, Dades, Granjons, Minikins, Livingstons, *et al.*, being anyone who had made his pile after the administration of Rutherford B. Hayes).

Most of this was gone. The store fronts of the Square were like the façades of the commercial buildings fronting Ventura Boulevard in the San Fernando Valley running out of Hollywood, one of Ellery's favorite abominations—lofty modernisms in glass, stucco, redwood, and neon absurdly dwarfing the mean little stores that cowered behind them. The Hollis, which risked a new marquee just before World War II, had recklessly undertaken a complete face-lift, coming out contemporary and (to his mind) disgusting. The New York Department Store and the High Village Pharmacy had vanished, and the Bon Ton had taken over the entire plinth between Washington and Lincoln Streets and rebuilt from the ground up what to Ellery's sickened eye was a miniature Korvette's. The Atomic War Surplus Outlet Store was of

course no more, and the eastern arc of the Square was almost
all new.

On the high ground to the north, matters were even worse.
Lovely old Hill Drive had fallen before the invading de-
velopers (a few houses had been saved, after a last-ditch
battle by the Landmarks Commission of the Wrightsville
Historical Society, as "historic sites"); the old Hill grandeur
was today a solid rank of high-rise apartment buildings,
frowning down on the town below like concentration camp
guards. Many of the extensive estates on North Hill Drive had
been sold and the section rezoned for one-acre stands of
middle-income private homes. Wrightsville's humbler suburbs
mushroomed to beyond the airport, where whole new communities with regional monickers like New Village and Ma-
hogany Acres had sprouted. At least thirty-five farms Ellery
had known and cherished were extinct. There were new fac-
tories by the dozen, chiefly neat little plants by the wayside
making electronic parts on subcontract to the giants working
for the Department of Defense. Even Twin Hills and Sky
Top Road, to which the well-to-do had inevitably fled, were
beginning to grow tentacles.

And most of the old families had withered away, or the
culls of their descendants had given up, hacked off their roots,
and rerooted elsewhere.

Still, to Ellery it was Wrightsville. The cobbled streets of
Low Village remained, the poor being America's last care-
takers of old things. The Willow River that serviced the mills
ran as yellow and red and turquoise as ever without noticeable
effect on the immortal old willows and alders on its banks
that sucked on its poisonous brew. Al Brown's Ice Cream
Parlor and the refaced Wrightsville Record building on Lower
Main off the Square stood their ground. And the surrounding
hillsides still beamed benign, with the muscular Mahoganies
beyond promising to withstand any onslaught of man except
a saturation attack by hydrogen bombs, which was unlikely,
Wrightsville being too unimportant (the town kept reassuring
itself) in the scheme of things.

So, to Ellery's eye, Wrightsville with all its flaws was a
still-viable Shangri-la.

He hired a Cougar at the car-rental agency in the airport
and the Queens, gladly gulping lungfuls of genuine air, drove
out to Benedict's hideaway.

From the way Benedict had talked Ellery expected a dilet-
tante twenty or thirty acres. They found instead a two-
hundred-acre spread of timber, water, and uncut pasture
halfway between Wrightsville and Shinn Corners, in a farmed-

out section of the valley where it began to creep up into the northwestern hills. The property was barred off by tall steel fencing and posted against hunting, fishing, and trespassing generally, in large and threatening signs bolted to the fence.

"Used to be all dairy farms out this way," Ellery complained as he got out to open the main gate. "The sweetest herds you ever saw."

"Well, don't blame Benedict," his father said. "They were probably given up before he bought them out. Small farms are going out of business all over New England."

"Still," Ellery carped, and he got back into the car with a slam.

The dirt road took them past the main house, which was a few hundred yards in from the entrance, apparently one of the original farmhouses of the property, a spready old two-story clapboard, with half a dozen chimneys, that appeared to house twelve or fifteen rooms. A quarter of a mile farther in they came to the guest house, a five-room Cape Cod-type cottage with a recent look. It lay deep in the woods, in a glade that had been hacked out to let the sun through. As they got out of the Cougar they heard a brook that seemed to be in a hurry and was making a great deal of noise about it.

"Sounds as if we could cast a line right out of the bedroom window," the Inspector said. "Man, what a way to live!"

"If somebody else bakes the bread," Ellery said sourly.

"Ellery, what in hell is the matter with you?" his father cried. "If you think I'm going to put up with a prima donna for two weeks . . . ! We'd better have this out right now. It was plain damn decent of your friend to offer you this place. The least you can do if you feel like bellyaching is keep it to yourself. Or so help me I'll take the next plane back to New York!"

It was a long time since Inspector Queen had talked to him that way, and it so astounded Ellery that he backed off and shut up.

They found the inside of the cottage as *heimisch* as Benedict had advertised. No Park Avenue decorator had been at work here. The furniture—Ellery checked the labels— came from A. A. Gilboon's in High Village, and the household fixtures and hardware had been purchased at Clint Fosdick's or Hunt & Keckley's, or both. "Bon Ton" was written all over the rest. It was a homely, cheerful little place that was long on chintz, "peasant" ware, and rag rugs, and had a fireplace in the living room that made his palms itch for the poker. The shelves held books; there was a stereo and a collection of cartridge tapes; and, tucked away in a corner as if to say there was no law requiring its use, a portable color TV.

The Inspector volunteered to unpack and get them settled while Ellery drove down into town to supplement the larder. They had found plenty of steaks, chops, and poultry in the freezer and a generous supply of canned goods, but they needed perishables—milk, bread, butter, eggs, fresh fruit and vegetables.

"Pick up something, too, son," the Inspector said, "at what's-his-name's, Dunc MacLean's. Rye, Scotch, vodka, anything to warm the bones."

"Unnecessary." Ellery waved. "You missed that retractable bar in the living room, dad. It's stocked with everything from absinthe to Zubrovka."

He passed up Logan's Market on Slocum between Upper Whistling and Washington—he was known there—in favor of the supermarket across the street, where he might expect to go unnoticed. As it was, he had to avert his face to avoid two women he thought he recognized. The trip into town depressed him further; the changes were too numerous and, to his eye, all for the worse. He was glad to get back to the cottage, where he found his father in slacks and an open-neck shirt lolling before a fire with a glass of brown waters in his fist.

"Yes, siree," the Inspector said happily, "this is *the* life."

The old man gave Ellery his head. He neither pushed nor pulled, contenting himself with a suggestion here or there and saying nothing if Ellery begged off. On Wednesday the Inspector spent most of the day fishing (in spite of Benedict's boast about cutting his own spruce pole, the old man found a roomful of sporting equipment that included some superb rods) and hauled in a mess of gorgeous trout for their dinner. Ellery spent that day on his spine's end, listening to Mozart and Bach, with a fillip of Tijuana Brass, and occasionally snoozing off. That night he slept the night through without benefit of sleeping pill or a dream he could recall on awakening—his first unbroken sleep in weeks; he had been living on nightmares. On Thursday the Queens explored the property, tramping over most of Benedict's two hundred acres and coming back ravenous; they devoured a couple of prodigious steaks Ellery charcoal-broiled on the backyard barbecue along with some husky baked potatoes topped with his favorite sour cream and chives. The Inspector pretended not to notice that Ellery polished his plate—the old man had not seen him finish a dinner for weeks.

Ellery had just turned on the dishwasher when he was startled by a jarring buzz. It seemed to come from what looked like an intercom. He snatched the receiver and said, "Who the devil is this?"

"Johnny," Benedict's voice said. "How's the patient?"

"Johnny? I'm just beginning to unlax." Had Benedict followed him up? "Oh, I see, this thing is hooked up to the main house. Two-way?"

"Yes. Ellery, I know I promised not to b-bother you—"

"When did you get in?"

"Late this afternoon. Look, there's s-something I have to tell you. Is it all right if I walk down and palaver for a minute?"

"Don't be a horse's patoot."

Ellery hung up and went to the bedroom the Inspector was using. The old man was just getting into his pajamas.

"Dad, Benedict's here. Wants to talk to us. Or to me. He's coming over from the main house now. Do you want to sit in on this?"

They looked at each other.

"You sound mysterious," Inspector Queen said.

"I'm not looking for trouble, you and God believe you me," Ellery said. "But there's a smell about this."

"All right. But I hope you're wrong, son."

Ten minutes later Ellery admitted a preoccupied Johnny-B —preoccupied, and something more. Worried? Whatever it is, Ellery assured himself, I'm staying out of it with both feet.

"Come in, Johnny."

"Forgive the pajamas and robe, Mr. Benedict," the Inspector said. "I had a strenuous day pacing off your property. I was just going to bed."

"Drink, Johnny?"

"Not just now, thanks." Benedict sank into a chair and looked around. His smile was perfunctory. Something was wrong, all right. The Queens did not glance at each other. "Like it up here?"

"I want to thank you properly, Johnny. I'm really beholden. This is exactly what I needed."

"Ellery and me both," the Inspector said.

Benedict's fine hand fluttered. Here it comes, Ellery thought. "Ellery?"

"Yes, Johnny."

"What I want to tell you. I'm h-having guests this w-weekend."

"Oh?"

"No, no, I'm not booting you out! They'll all stay at the main house. Acres of room there. Al Marsh is due up tomorrow, and Al's secretary—girl named Susan Smith—is coming Saturday evening. Also due tomorrow—" Benedict hesitated, made a face, and shrugged "—my three exes."

"Ex-wives?"

"Ex-wives."

"Excuse me for gawking, Johnny. What is this, Home-coming Week?"

The Inspector decided to improve on the light note. "I've always read what an interesting life you lead, Mr. Benedict, but this is ridiculous!"

They all laughed, Benedict weakly. "I wish it were as funny as that. Well. The point is, I don't want you people to be in any way discombobulated. There's nothing social or nostalgic about this get-together. Strictly b-business, if you know w-what I mean."

"I don't, but that's all right, Johnny. You don't owe us an explanation."

"But I can't have you thinking I'm an Indian giver. You won't be disturbed, I give you my w-word."

It all seemed so unnecessary that Ellery had to fight down his curiosity. They were a long way from the Harvard Yard, and he realized suddenly that he knew very little about Johnny-B that mattered. He had thought the invitation genu-ine. But had Benedict had an ulterior purpose. . . .?

Having given his word, Benedict stopped talking. He seemed hung up on a problem. The silence became de-pressing.

"Something wrong, Johnny?" Ellery asked. And cursed himself for having opened the door.

"Does it sh-show that much? I think I'll take that drink now, Ellery. No, I'll make it myself." Benedict jumped up and activated the bar. It was of the rotating type, swiveling out of the wall. He poured himself a stiff Scotch on the rocks and when he came back he said abruptly, "I have a favor to ask of both of you. I hate asking favors, I don't know why . . . but this one I have to."

"We're under obligation to you, Mr. Benedict," the In-spector said, smiling, "not the other way around."

"There's hardly anything within reason we could refuse you, Johnny," Ellery said. "What's the problem?"

Benedict set his glass down. He pulled a long single sheet of white paper from his breast pocket. It was folded in three. He unfolded it.

"For the record, this is my last w-will and testament." He said this is an oddly chill tone; to Ellery's sensitized ears it sounded like a sentence in a capital crime. Benedict felt his pockets. "I've simply got to start carrying a pen," he said. "May I borrow yours, Ellery?" He stooped over the coffee table. "I'll sign this and date it, and I ask you b-both to w-witness. Will you?"

"Naturally."

"Of course, Mr. Benedict."

They noted how he concealed the holograph text with his forearm as he wrote. When he was finished he flapped the sheet over so that only the bottom lay exposed. He indicated where the Queens were to sign, and they did so. He returned Ellery's pen, produced a long envelope, folded the will, slipped it into the envelope, sealed it, hesitated, and suddenly offered it to Inspector Queen.

"Could I ask you to k-keep this for me, Inspector? For a short w-while?"

"Well . . . sure, Mr. Benedict."

"I don't blame you for looking kind of puzzled," Benedict said in a hearty way. "But there's no big deal about this. Marsh is going to draw up a formal will for me over the weekend—that's why his secretary is coming—but I wanted something down on paper in the meantime." He laughed; it seemed forced. "I'm getting to the age when life looks more and more uncertain. Here today and here tomorrow—m-maybe. Right?"

They laughed dutifully, and when Benedict finished his Scotch he said good night and left. He seemed relieved.

Ellery was not. He shut the front door carefully and said, "Dad, what do you make of all that?"

"A lot of question marks." The Inspector stared at the blank envelope in his hands. "With the money he's got—and lawyers like Marsh—it's a cinch he's had a formal will practically from birth. So this thing he wrote out in longhand that we just witnessed supersedes the previous one."

"Not merely supersedes it, dad," Ellery said. "Changes it, or why a new will at all? The question is, what does it change it from, and what does it change it to?"

"Neither of which is your business," his father pointed out.

"This obviously involves his ex-wives," Ellery murmured; he was back at his pacing, the Inspector noted uneasily. "Business weekend. . . . No, I don't care for the smell of this."

"I can see I'll have to put off that shuteye for a while." The Inspector went to the bar. "I think you can use one, son. What'll it be?"

"Nothing. No, thanks."

"Who are the lucky ladies?"

"What?"

"The women he married. Do you know?"

"Of course I know. The Benedict Saga's always fascinated

me. His first wife came out of a chorus line in Vegas. A bosomy redhead named Marcia Kemp, a sexpot who was thick with some really tough characters until Johnny plucked her out of the state and made an honest woman of her."

"Marcia Kemp." The old man nodded. "I remember now. That one lasted—how long was it? Three months?"

"Closer to four. Mrs. Benedict number two was Audrey Weston, a blonde with acting ambitions who didn't have the talent to make it on Broadway or in Hollywood. She gets a small part now and then, mostly in TV commercials. But Johnny evidently thought she was Oscar or Emmy material— for five or six months, anyway."

"And number three?" the Inspector asked, sipping his Chivas.

"Number three," Ellery said, "I have particular reason to recall." He was still pacing. "Alice Tierney. The reason I paid special attention to Alice Tierney is that I'd read she came from Wrightsville. One of the columnists. Naturally that titillated me, although the name Tierney was unfamiliar to me. Or maybe that's why. Anyway, it seems that this Tierney girl—in her news photos a rather plain-looking brunette—was a trained nurse. Johnny ran his Maserati or whatever he was driving then off a country road—it must have been around Wrightsville somewhere, though the piece didn't say—and was laid up for a long stretch at his 'country home,' the story said, which I realize now must have been the main house here. If Wrightsville ever came into the stories I missed it, which is unlikely; my hunch is that Johnny paid one of his patented *quid pro quos* to keep the Wrightsville hideaway here out of the columns. At any rate, Nurse Tierney was hired on a sleep-in basis to take care of her famous patient, and enforced proximity to a female for several weeks, even a plain one, was apparently more than Johnny could resist. After the usual Benedict-type courtship he married the Tierney girl. That lasted the longest—nine and a half months. He was legally unhitched only a month or so ago."

"A redheaded Vegas mob girl, a New York no-talent blond actress, a brunette plain-Jane small-town nurse," the Inspector mused. "Doesn't sound as if they have much in common."

"They do, though. They're all huge women. Amazons."

"Oh, one of those. The little guy who keeps shooting for Mount Everest. Must give fellows like Benedict a sense of power, like when they get behind the wheel of a souped-up car."

"My innocent old man," Ellery said with a grin. "I'll have to give you a couple of sex-and-psychiatry books appropri-

ately marked. . . . And he's asked all three up for the weekend, along with his lawyer, for a change of will—or at least
he says so—and he's kind of nervous about it all. You know
something, dad?"

"What now?"

"I don't like it. One bit."

The Inspector brandished his glass. "And you know what,
sonny? You're going to quit this racing up and down like that
road runner in the commercials and you're going to sit down
here and watch the Thursday night movie—*right now*—and
this weekend you'll keep your schnozz strictly out of your
friend Benedict's affairs—*whatever* they are!"

Ellery did his best, which faltered only once. On Friday
evening after dinner he felt the healthful need to walk.
Making an instant diagnosis, the Inspector said, "I'll join you."
When they got outdoors Ellery turned in the direction of the
hunted like a yellow hound dog. His father seized the quivering paw. *"This* way," he said firmly. "We'll go listen to the
music of the brook." "Poetry really doesn't become you, dad.
If I'd wanted to communicate with Euterpe I'd have used
the stereo." "Ellery, you're not going down to that house!"
"Now come on, dad. I'm not going to barge in on them or
anything like that." "Damn it all to hell!" shouted the old
man, and he stamped back into the cottage.

When Ellery got back his father said anxiously, "Well?"

"Well what, dad?"

"What's going on down there?"

"I thought you weren't interested."

"I didn't say I wasn't interested. I said we oughtn't to get
involved."

"House is lit up like Times Square. No sounds of girlish
laughter, however. It can't be much of a party."

The Inspector grunted. "At least you had the sense to turn
around and come back."

But they were not to remain uninvolved. A few minutes
past noon on Saturday—the old man was about to lie down
for a nap—there was a knock on the door and Ellery opened
it to a very tall blond girl with the bony structure and
empty face of a fashion model.

"I'm Mrs. Johnny Benedict the Two," she said in a drawl
that sounded Method-Southern to Ellery's ears.

"Of course. You're Audrey Weston," Ellery said.

"That's my professional name. May I come in?"

Ellery glanced at his father and stood aside. The Inspector
came forward quickly. "I'm Richard Queen," he said. He
had always had an eye for pretty girls, and this one was

prettier than most, although in a blank sort of way. Her face looked as if it had been stamped out of a mold, like a doll's.

"Inspector Queen, isn't it? Johnny's told us you two were staying at the guest cottage—practically threatened to knock our heads together if we didn't leave you alone. So, of course, here I am." She turned her gray, almost colorless, eyes on Ellery. "Aren't you going to offer me a drink, dahling?"

She used her eyes and hands a great deal. Someone had evidently told her that she was the Tallulah Bankhead type, and she had never got over it.

Ellery gave her a Jack Daniel and a chair, and she leaned back with her long legs crossed and a long cigaret smoldering in the long fingers with the long fingernails that held the glass. She was dressed in a floppy silk blouse in fashionably wild colors and a calfskin skirt that was more mini than most, to her cost, for it revealed shanks rather than thighs. A matching leather jacket was draped over her shoulders. "And aren't you wondering why I disobeyed Johnny?" she drawled.

"I was sure you'd get around to it, Miss Weston," Ellery said, smiling. "I ought to tell you right off that I'm here with my father at Johnny's kind invitation to get away from problems. This is a problem, isn't it?"

"If it is—" the Inspector began.

"My evening gown is missing," Audrey Weston said.

"Missing?" the Inspector said. "A dress?"

"What do you mean missing?" Ellery said, leaning into the wind. "Mislaid?"

"Gone."

"Stolen?"

"You want to hear about it, dahling?"

"Oh. Well. As long as you're here. . . ."

"That gown set me back a bundle. It's all black sequins, an Ohrbach copy of a Givenchy original, with an absolutely illegal back and a V-front open to the bel—navel. And man, I want it back! Sure it was stolen. You don't just mislay a gown like that. At least I don't."

Her speech had been accompanied by so many vehement gestures and poses that Ellery felt tired for her.

"It probably has the simplest explanation, Miss Weston. When did you see it last?"

"I wore it to dinner last night—Johnny likes formality with women around, and when in Rome, y'know. . . . Even if the Roman is your ex."

So she expected to get something out of Johnny-B this weekend. Probably all three of them . . . Ellery tucked the surmise away. As if he were on the case. Case? Which case? There was no case. Or was there?

"I hung it in my closet when I went to bed last night, and I noticed it hanging there this morning when I dressed. But when I came up from brunch to change my outfit the evening gown wasn't hanging there any more. I ransacked the room, but it was gone."

"Who else is staying at the house?"

"Al Marsh, Johnny, of course, and the two other exes, that Kemp tramp and Miss Yokel from Wrightsville here, Alice Tierney, and what he ever saw in her—! Oh, and two characters from town who make like a maid and a butler, but they went home last night after they cleaned up. They were back this morning and I asked both of them about my gown. They looked at me as if I were out of my everloving mind."

If one of them is Morris Hunker, baby, Ellery chuckled to himself, *you ain't seen nothin' yet.*

"Did you ask any of the others?"

"Where do you think I'm from, Dumbsville? What good would that have done, dahling? The one who lifted it would only deny it, and the others . . . oh, it's just too embarrassing! Do you suppose I could impose on you to, well, find it for me without raising a fuss? I'd go poking around Marcia's and Alice's bedrooms, but I'd be sure to get caught, and I don't want Johnny getting, I mean thinking, well, you know what I mean, Mr. Queen."

For the sake of the amenities he was willing to concede that he did, although in truth he did not. As for the Inspector, he was watching Ellery like a psychiatrist observing if the patient would curl up in fetal position or spring to the attack.

"Nothing else of yours was taken?"

"No, that was it. Just the gown."

"Seems to me," Inspector Queen said, "either Miss Kemp or Miss Tierney borrowed it for some reason, and if you'd just ask them—"

"I can see you don't know anything about Paris-type gowns, Inspector," the model-actress drawled. "They're like Rembrandts or something. They couldn't wear it without giving themselves away. So why take it? Y'know? That's why it's such a mystery."

"How about the maid?" Ellery asked.

"That tub? She's five-foot-two and must weigh two hundred."

"I'll see what I can do, Miss Weston," he said.

She played her exit scene seductively and with much emotion, sweeping out at last after half a dozen more "dahlings" and a long trailing goodbye arm, and leaving him with the scent of Madame Rochas Perfume for Ladies. The moment she was gone the Inspector barked, "Ellery, you're not going to start poking around for some stupid evening gown and spoil your vacation—and mine!"

"But I just promised—"

"So you're unreliable," the Inspector snorted, settling down with the Wrightsville *Record* Ellery had picked up in High Village.

"I thought you were going to take a nap."

"Who could sleep now? That phony knocked it all out of me. Now that's that, Ellery. Understand?"

But that was not that. At thirteen minutes past one the door called again, and Ellery opened to a vision in flesh, curves, and genuine red hair—a rather large vision, to be sure. She was almost as tall as Ellery, with the build of a back-row showgirl: long-muscled legs, long dancer's thighs, and a bust of Mansfieldian proportions. She was dressed for the greatest effect, in briefs and a halter, with a coat loosely open over all; it showed a great deal of her. Her flaming hair was modestly bound in a scarf.

"Marcia Kemp," Ellery said.

"Now how in Christ's name did you know that?" The redhead had a deep, coarse, New York voice—from the heart of the Bronx, Ellery guessed. Her green eyes were glittery with anger.

"I've had an advance description, Miss Kemp," Ellery said with a grin. "Come in. Meet my father, Inspector Queen of the New York City police department."

"Grandpa, fuzz is just what I need," the Kemp woman exclaimed. "You'll never guess what's happened to me. In Johnny-B's own house, mind you!"

"What was that?" Ellery asked, ignoring his father's look.

"Some creep heisted my wig."

"Your *wig?*" the Inspector repeated involuntarily.

"My green one! That piece of shrubbery set me back a whole hundred and fifty bucks. I go down to breakfast this morning, or lunch, or whatever the hell it was, and when I got back . . . *no wig!* Can you tie that? It left me so goddam uptight . . . I need a shot. Straight bourbon, Queenie baby, and lean on it."

He poured her enough bourbon to make a Kentucky colonel stagger. She tossed it down as if it were a milk shake and held the glass out for more. He refilled it. This one she nursed in her powerful hands.

"You last saw this wig of yours when, Miss Kemp?"

"I wore it last night to dinner along with my green lamé evening gown. Johnny likes his women to do the dress-up bit. It was still on my dressing table when I went downstairs this morning. When I come back it's gone with the wind. If I didn't know how Johnny hates a rumble I'd tear those bitches' luggage limb from limb! Could you find it for me, Ellery? Hush-hush, like? Without Johnny knowing?"

"There's no chance you mislaid it?" The Inspector asked, hopefully.

"Gramps, I ask you. How do you mislay a green wig?"

"A dress and a wig," Ellery yapped after he got rid of the redhead. "Something missing from each of the first two ex-wives. Is it possible that the third—?"

"Son, son," his father said in not entirely convincing reproof. "You promised."

"Yes, dad, but you'll have to admit . . . ."

And indeed Ellery was looking more like his old self, with a near-jaunty bounce to his step and at least a half sparkle in his eye that for some time had been missing altogether. The Inspector consoled himself with the thought that it was likely one of those pesky little problems, with the simplest of explanations, that would keep Ellery harmlessly occupied while time and river washed away the stains left by the Glory Guild case.

So, when at midafternoon Ellery suddenly said, "Look, dad, if there's any logic in all this, the third one ought to be missing something, too. I think I'll stroll over . . . ," the Inspector said simply, "I'll be down at the brook with a rod, son."

Benedict had had a sixty-foot swimming pool built behind the main house. It was still covered by a winter tarpaulin; but summer furniture had been set out on the flagstoned terrace at the rear of the old farmhouse that he had had laid down in the reconstruction, and there Ellery found Alice Tierney stretched out in a lounging chair, sunning herself. The spring afternoon was warm, with a gusty little breeze, and her cheeks were reddened as if she had been lying there for some time.

The moment he laid eyes on her Ellery recognized her. During one of his trips to Wrightsville he had had to visit the hospital. On that occasion, attending the object of his visit, she had been in a nurse's cap and uniform—a large girl with a healthy butt, a torso of noble dimensions, and features as plain as Low Village's cobbles and as agreeable to the eye.

"Miss Tierney. I don't suppose you remember me."

"Don't I just!" she cried, sitting up. "You're the great Ellery Queen, God's gift to Wrightsville."

"You don't have to be nasty about it," Ellery said, slipping into a wrought-iron chair.

"Oh, but I mean it."

"You do? Who calls me that?"

"Lots of people around here." Her cool blue eyes shim-mered in the sun. "Of course, I've heard some say the gift comes from the devil, but you'll find sour-pusses everywhere."

"That's probably because of the rise in the crime rate since I began coming here. Smoke, Miss Tierney?"

"Certainly not. And you oughtn't to, either. Oh, futz! There I go again. I can never forget my training."

She was in mousy slacks and jacket that did nothing for her, and he thought her long straight hair style was exactly wrong for her face and size. But it all tended to dwindle away against her general air of niceness, which he suspected she cultivated with great care. He could understand what Johnny Benedict, with his superficial view of women, had found so appealing about her.

"I'm so glad you decided to come out of your shell," Alice Tierney went on animatedly. "Johnny threatened us with all sorts of punishment if we didn't let you strictly alone."

"I'm still not diving back into the drink. As a matter of fact, I came here for only one reason: to ask what may strike you as a peculiar question."

"Oh?" She did seem puzzled. "What's that, Mr. Queen?"

Ellery leaned toward her. "Have you missed anything today?"

"Missed? Like what?"

"Something personal. Say an article of clothing."

"No. . . ."

"You sure?"

"Well, I suppose something could be . . . I mean I haven't taken inventory." Alice Tierney laughed, but when he did not laugh back she stopped. "You really mean it, Mr. Queen!"

"I do. Would you mind going to your room right now—quietly, Miss Tierney—and checking over your things? I'd rather no one in the house knows what you're about."

She rose, drew a breath, smoothed her jacket, then launched herself toward the house rather like an oversized missile.

Ellery waited with the patience of a thousand such inter-ludes, when a puzzle loomed which gave off no immediate meaning, only a promise for the future.

She was back in ten minutes. "That is queer," she said, plumping back into the lounge chair. "A pair of my gloves."

"Gloves?" Ellery looked at her hands. They were big and capable-looking. "What kind of gloves, Miss Tierney?"

"Long evening gloves. White. The only such pair I had with me."

"You're sure you had them."

"I wore them to dinner last night." The red in her cheeks

deepened. "Johnny prefers his women to look, oh, untouchable, I suppose it's what it is at bottom. He hates slobbygobs."

"White evening gloves. Is anything else of yours missing?"

"Not that I know of."

"You checked?"

"I looked through everything. Why in the world should someone steal a pair of gloves? There's not much use for evening gloves in Wrightsville. Among the class of people who'd steal, I mean."

"That, of course, is the problem. Miss Tierney, I'm going to ask you to keep this to yourself. About the theft, and about the fac⁺ that I've been asking questions."

"If you say so, of course."

"By the way, where is everybody?"

"They're getting ready to drive over to the airport to pick up Al Marsh's secretary, a Miss Smith. She's due in at the field at five thirty. Annie and Morris are starting dinner in the kitchen."

"Morris Hunker?"

"Is there more than one?" Alice Tierney grinned. "You know Morris, I take it."

"Oh, yes. But who's Annie?"

"Annie Findlay."

"Findlay . . . ?"

"Her brother Homer used to run the garage down on Plum Street. You know, where High and Low sort of meet."

"Homer Findlay and his Drive Urself! For heaven's sake. How is Homer?"

"Peaceful," Miss Tierney said. "Cardiac arrest. I closed his eyes in the Emergency Room at WGH six years ago."

Ellery left, shaking his head at Old Mortality. And other things.

Inspector Queen had taken the Cougar down into town and came back chortling over a find. He had stumbled on a store, new to Ellery, which sold fresh fish and shellfish—"not frozen, mind you, son, you freeze fish, shellfish especially, and you wind up losing half the flavor. Wait till you see what I've got planned for the menu tonight."

"What, dad?"

"I said wait, didn't I? Don't be so nosy."

What his father served that evening was, he said, an "Irish bouillabaisse," which Ellery found indistinguishable from the Mediterranean variety except that it had been made by an Irishman who left out the saffron—"can't abide that yellow stuff," the chef declared. It was delicious, and Ellery

gave it its due. But after dinner, when the Inspector suggested they go into town to see "one of those naked movies"
(Wrightsville had acquired an art cinema), Ellery grew less
communicative.

"Why don't you go see it, dad? I don't feel much like a
movie tonight, even a naked one."

"Sometimes I wonder! What'll you do?"

"Oh listen to some music. Maybe get potted on Johnny's
slivovitz or akvavit or something."

"May I live to see the day," his father grumbled; and, surprisingly, he took off.

There's libido in the old boy yet, Ellery thought, and
blessed it.

He had no intention of communing with Mozart or the
three Bs, or the international contents of Benedict's bar. As
soon as the sound of the Cougar died, Ellery slipped a dark
jacket over his white turtleneck, rousted a flash from the tool
room, left several lights burning in the cottage and a stereo
cartridge playing, and stole outside.

There was a new moon, and the darkness was as dark
only as dark can be in Wrightsville's woods. He kept his hand
over the light as he walked up the path toward the main
house. There was a rawness to the night; he would have
welcomed a symphony of peepers, but apparently the season
was too early or the weather discouraged them, even though
spring was officially a week old. If the Inspector had been
present to ask him what he was doing, Ellery could not
honestly have answered. He had no idea what he was about,
except that he could not get the three thefts out of his head.
And since they had taken place in Benedict's house, he was
drawn there like a flower child to a pot party.

There was something maddeningly logical about the thefts.
An evening gown, a wig *à la mode,* and evening gloves. They
went together like pieces of a jigsaw. The difficulty was, when
they were assembled they represented nothing. The three
articles had some value, of course; and, value being relative,
theft for a material reason could not be dismissed as a possibility, although the monitor who sat deep in Ellery's brain
kept shaking its infallible little head. The obvious reason, that
they had been stolen to be worn, was even less appealing: if
the thief had been one of the ex-wives, it meant that she had
included one of her own things in order to spread the guilty
area, an absurd complexity considering the peculiar nature of
the thefts; and if the thief had not been one of the ex-wives
but some woman from Wrightsville, where could she wear the
stolen finery without becoming suspect?

Morris Hunker he eliminated without a doubt; the old

Yankee would not have taken a crust from a sparrow if he were dying of hunger. Annie Findlay, of course, was an unknown quantity to him, and the simple answer might be that the roly-poly sleep-out "maid" had been unable to resist the glittery gown, the fantastic wig, and the—to her—unusual gloves. But Ellery had understood that, like Hunker, Annie hired out for her livelihood to special employers like John Benedict; in a small town like this she could hardly have indulged a regular weakness for other people's belongings without long since being found out. Besides, lightfingered hired help were practically unknown in Wrightsville. No, Annie as the culprit just didn't scan.

Then who? If it had been a prowler, surely he could have found far more valuable and negotiable pickings in the Benedict house than a second-hand gown, a green wig, and a pair of women's evening gloves (undoubtedly soiled). Yet the three women had reported nothing else missing. And certainly if Benedict or Marsh had suffered a loss, he would have heard by this time.

It was the kind of trivial-seeming puzzle that always drove Ellery to distraction.

He circled the house, choosing his path with stealth. The front and the side where the kitchen and pantry must lie showed no lights; evidently Hunker and the Findlay woman had cleaned up after dinner and gone home. But lights blazed onto the terrace through the French doors Benedict had had installed in the living room's rear wall during his reconstruction of the farmhouse.

Ellery edged onto the patio, keeping to the shadows beyond the lighted area. He chose a position under the branches of a forty-year-old pink dogwood tree very near the house, from where he could see into the living room without being seen. The room must be warm: one of the French doors was ajar. He heard their voices clearly.

They were all there: Benedict, his ex-wives, Marsh, and a girl who could only be Marsh's secretary, Miss Smith. The secretary was seated at the edge of a sofa, to one side, legs crossed, with a pad on her knee and a pencil poised; she wore a no-nonsense navy blue skirt of medium length, a tailored white blouse, and a white cardigan thrown about her shoulders and buttoned at the neck. There was nothing youthful or even womanly about her; her mechanical makeup gave her horsy face a circus precision; she was, in fact, quite masculine-looking aside from her legs, which were shaped well and surprisingly feminine. She told Ellery something about Marsh. A man who would select a Miss Smith for private secretarial chores could be relied on to reserve his office hours for business purposes exclusively.

Two of the ex-wives seemed dressed for a race, in evening getups that evoked the yachtman's starting gun.

Audrey Weston's blond beauty was offset by black evening pajamas and a black crepe tunic, with a broad red satin sash tied high above the waist that underscored her breasts, and needle-heeled red satin shoes that added inches to her main-mast height; she wore a bracelet of gold links that looked heavy enough to secure an anchor, and gold coil earrings.

The generally flappy, full-canvas effect of Audrey's outfit, exciting as it was, barely held its own with Marcia Kemp's. The redheaded expatriate from Las Vegas had trimmed down to the bare poles; her turquoise evening sheath was so painted to her body that Ellery wondered how she was able to sit down without cracking her hull . . . and, as a corollary, whether Benedict's wives numbers two and one had put their heads together in planning their racing strategy. Was the contest fixed?

By contrast, Alice Tierney's coloring showed darker against the whiteness of her gown and accessories; she looked pure and chaste in it, and very nearly striking. It was as if she realized that she could not by natural endowment outshine her predecessors and so had shrewdly employed a tactic of simplicity.

But if Audrey's and Marcia's calculated art and Alice's calculated artlessness were designed to stir old passions in Benedict's libido, the effects were not visible to the Queen eye. Outwardly, at least, he was as unmoved by their bountiful charms as a eunuch. If proof of his general contempt for the trio were needed, Ellery found it in Benedict's attire. The millionaire being so finical about his women, one would expect consistency, or at least *noblesse oblige,* in the form of a dinner jacket; but while Marsh was suitably in black tie, Benedict was wearing an ordinary brown suit—as if, being Johnny-B, he could afford to flout the conventions he expected of his ex-wives. It made Ellery see his old friend in a newish light.

Ellery felt no qualms at eavesdropping; he never did when his curiosity was engaged. He had long since had this out with himself. (He did not recommend it as a general practise; only—as in the practise of bugging—when performed by experts for lawful purposes, in which category he felt entitled to place himself.)

What they had been talking about before his arrival, Ellery gathered, was "the new will" Benedict was having Marsh draw up for him "tomorrow." (So he had not told the ex-Mrs.

Benedicts of the holograph document he had signed in the Queens' presence Thursday night, and which lay in the Inspector's pocket at this moment.)

"But that's nothing but fraud," Audrey Weston snarled.

"Fraud?" The redhead from Vegas uttered a four-letter word with great sincerity. "It's murder!"

Alice Tierney looked pained.

"You know, Marcia, your vulgarity is so lacking in originality," Marsh said from the bar, where he was replenishing his drink. "I'll give you this, though: people know just where they stand with you at all times."

"You want me to give you a personal reading right now, Al?"

"Heaven forbid, dear heart!" He enveloped his drink hastily.

Ellery found himself bound to his dogwood. Fraud? Murder? But then he decided it had been hyperbole.

"Leeches!" Benedict's sang-froid was gone. "You know damn w-well what our marriages were. Strictly business. Contracts with a m-mattress thrown in." He stabbed at them with his arms. "Well, I'm finished with that kind of stupidity!"

"Down, boy," Marsh said.

"You know our d-deal! The same in each c-case, a thousand a week, payable till your remarriages or my death; then, on my death, each of you under my will, if still not m-married"—*which will?*—"gets a settlement in a lump sum of one m-million dollars."

"Yes, but look what we signed away," Alice Tierney said in a soft and reasonable voice. "You made us sign prenuptial agreements in which we had to renounce all dower and other claims to your estate."

"Under the threat, if I recall correctly—and, brother, do I!—" Audrey Weston said caustically, "that if we didn't sign, the marriage was off."

"Sweetie," Marcia Kemp said, "that's the great Johnny-B's style."

Marsh laughed. "Still, girls, not a bad deal for leasing Johnny the use of your bodies, impressive as they are, for a few months." He had made too many trips to the bar; there was the slightest slur to his speech and a stiffness to his smile.

"Impressive is as impressive does—right, Al?" Benedict brandished a hand graceful as a dagger. "The p-point is, pets, I've been thinking a great many things over, and I've decided that with you three specimens I didn't get my m-money's worth. So I've changed my mind about the whole bit. Besides, there's a new element in the plot I'll get to in a m-minute. I'm having Al write my new w-will tomorrow, as I told you, and you can be n-nice about it or not, it's all the s-same to me."

"Hold on, dahling!" Tallu was back. "You can't change a settlement just like that, you know. A girl scorned has some rights in Uncle Sam country!"

"I do believe you didn't read the f-fine print, Audrey," Benedict said. "The agreements in no case made your renunciation of dower rights and other claims against my estate c-contingent on what I chose to leave you in my will. Read it again, Audrey, will you? You'll save yourself an attorney's fee. Right, Al?"

"Right," Marsh said. "Also, the agreements and the will they're attached to were in no way affected by the decrees."

"And if I want to change my mind about those three millions, there's not a b-bloody thing you can do about it." Benedict displayed his teeth. "I assure you that what we're planning is p-perfectly legal. Anything that might be iffy—well, I'll match my beagle against yours on any track in the land."

"Wuff," Marsh said.

"In other words, buster," and the redhead showed *her* teeth, "you're going to the muscle."

"If I must."

"But you promised," the ex-nurse said. "Johnny, you gave me your word. . . ."

"Nonsense."

Marcia had been thinking. She lit a cigaret. "All right, Johnny, what's the new deal?"

"I'll continue to p-pay each of you a thousand per week until you remarry or I d-die, but the million-apiece lump-sum payoff on my death, that's out."

Marcia spat one word: "Why?"

"Well, it's really none of your b-business," Benedict said, "but I'm getting married again."

"You've got to be kidding," Audrey cried. "You catch a case of marriage every spring, Johnny, like a cold. What's getting remarried got to do with anything?"

"You couldn't be that mean," Alice wailed. "A million dollars is no joking matter."

"So you'll be hitched to this broad for a few months," Marcia growled, "and then—"

"This time it's d-different," Benedict said, smiling. "This time," and he stopped smiling, "I'm in love."

It was Audrey, the blonde, who shrieked, *"Love? You?"* but the incredulity might have been sounded by any of them. Then they all burst into laughter.

"Al, get him to a shrink presto," the redhead said, "before he drops what's left of his marbles. Listen, bubby, the last thing you were in love with was your mama's titty. What do you know about love?"

Benedict shrugged. "Whatever it's called, I've c-caught it. I want to settle down—go ahead and snicker!—breed a flock of kids, lead a normal l-life. No more chick-chasing or marriage quickies. My next wife is going to be the last woman in my life." They were roosting there like three birds on a perch, bills gaping. "That's the m-main reason behind this move. If I'm going to be the f-father of children, I want to secure their future. And their mother's. I'm n-not going to change my mind about that."

"I still say it's fraud," the blonde snapped. "Or was that will you showed me prior to the divorce proceeding, leaving me a million dollars—was that another con?"

"If it was, he conned me, too," Marcia barked. "And I say it again. It's plain murder to cut us off after we've given you—"

"I know, Marcia—the b-best months of your life." Benedict grinned. "You three never would let me finish a sentence. I was about to announce that this isn't going to be a total l-loss to you. What's m-more, you'll have till tomorrow noon to decide. How f-fair can a fairy god-husband get? Al, d'ye mind? A Black Russian."

It was a new one to Ellery, and he watched Marsh busy himself at the bar. Marsh blended what appeared to be vodka and some coffee liqueur over ice.

"Decide what, Johnny?" Alice asked in a defeated voice.

"Tell you in a minute. The point is, if you three do agree, Al makes out my new w-will and that will be that."

"What—is—the—deal?" Audrey as Audrey. No stagey nonsense now.

"A thousand a week as at p-present, with the usual hedge in case of remarriage, and on my death each of you receives one hundred thousand dollars. And that's the end of the g-game as far as our foursome is concerned. Granted a hundred th-thousand isn't a million—thank you, Al—but it's not exactly b-birdseed, either. Even for three rare birds like you.

"So think it over, ladies. If you decide to make a court fight of it, I tell you now before w-witnesses: the new w-will tomorrow won't leave you a red c-cent! I might even change my mind about the thousand a week. Nighty night."

And John Levering Benedict III drained his Black Russian, waved it in their general direction, set the empty glass down, and went upstairs to bed as if he had had an active but rewarding day.

Benedict left behind him an atmosphere of anger, frustration, and curiosity, with curiosity dominant on a field of gold.

"Who is this babe Johnny's going to marry?"

"Do you know? You know, goddam it!"

"Tell us, Al! Come on. . . ."

The Amazons surrounded Marsh, pushing their soft pleni-tude at him.

"Please, girls, not before Miss Smith. We run a proper ship in the home waters, don't we, Miss Smith? That's it for to-night, by the way. You're on your own. Perfectly free to raid the kitchen if you want a snack."

"I'm on a diet," Miss Smith said unexpectedly, and the lawyer looked surprised. Ellery gathered that the personal re-mark was not characteristic of Miss Smith's professional be-havior. She shut her stenographic book over the pencil with a little snap. "Good night, Mr. Marsh," she said emphati-cally, and marched upstairs as if the ex-wives had gone back into a bottle. She had taken down every word uttered in the room during Ellery's surveillance.

"I know you know who she is, Al," Audrey said, shaking him playfully.

"Is it that hatcheck broad they say he's been giving the treatment to lately?" big Marcia wanted to know.

"He wouldn't dream of making a mistake like *that* again, dear," Alice said sincerely.

"At least I never sucked blood like you did when he picked you up in this outhouse they call a town," the redhead re-torted. "Bat Girl! Is there anything lower than a blood-sucker?"

"Look who's talking!"

"Come on, Al," the blonde whinnied, "stop hogging the sauce. I want a drink, dahling. And shovel us the dirt."

Marsh shook them off and walked back to the bar with his glass. "Mine not to shovel, mine but to do as I'm told. My advice to you, offered absolutely free, is to accept John-ny's offer and be damned to him. Turn it down and you'll wind up like the call girl in the gay bar—I mean to say, girls, with a handful of nothing. That hundred thousand per ex is the most you'll ever get out of Johnny, and you've got about twelve hours to grab for it. Think it over. You can verbalize your pretty little decisions to me in the morning."

"You go to hell, dahling," Audrey said. "What about my drink?"

"Why don't you go to bed?"

"I'm not desperate enough. Oh, all right, I'll get it myself." The blond actress got up and sauntered to the bar.

"You know what you are?" Marcia said to the lawyer in

an even voice. "You're a lousy brown-nose. Mix me a Gibson, will you, Audrey?"

"Mix it yourself."

"You're a charmer. Don't think I won't." The redhead joined the blonde at the bar.

"Al . . . ," the brunette from Wrightsville began.

"You won't get any more out of me than they did, Alice. Good night."

"You can't dismiss me as if I were Miss Smith! Or a child." Alice gave him a cold and thoughtful look on her way to the bar.

Ellery was more intent on observing Marsh. Marsh had evidently had enough alcohol for the moment; the glass he set down was more than half full. But he was continuing to smoke full blast. He had been chainsmoking menthol cigarets ever since Ellery began to eavesdrop, and he was chainsmoking them still. Well, Ellery thought, being legal eagle as well as companion and confidant to a man like Johnny-B did not exactly make for an untroubled existence. The Marlboro man sitting his faithful steed might well develop, along with calluses, a neurosis or two. Even agoraphobia.

Ellery studied the heavy male features and the big and sensitive hands, and he wondered if Marsh had any notion of the can of peas his friend and client had so blithely opened. Marsh's intelligence had been systematized by his legal training; surely he must be able to analyze the possibilities. Well, perhaps not surely. He hasn't had my conditioning in murder, Ellery thought. It takes experience and a soiled mind to think of a thing like that.

He slid off the terrace, and on his way back to the cottage —using the flashlight sparingly—Ellery let conditioning take charge. His thoughts did not provoke, amuse, or engross him. The exercise, as usual, was futile. The trouble with foreseeing homicide on the sole ground of past performances was that there was no profit in it. The victim was never convinced before it was too late for convincing, and warning off the potential murderers either spurred them to a more cunning crime or planted an unsocial thought where none had been. The victim, like all mortals, assumed that he was immortal, and the murderer, like most murderers, that he was infallible. Against these diseases there was no specific.

It was all very sad and discouraging; and Ellery was grumbling away in his sleep before Inspector Queen got back from his movie.

It came off on schedule, almost as if Ellery had planned it. He groped for the light-chain at the eruption of the telephone, found it, dragged it, blinked at his watch and noted the time as 3:03 A.M., fumbled about for the phone and found that—all before he was really awake. But the gasp and heave in his ear were like a wash of seawater.

"Who is this?"

"J-J-J. . . ."

"Johnny? Is this Johnny?"

"Yes." He was hauling the breath from his lungs as if it had weights attached. "El . . . ?"

"Yes, yes, what's wrong?"

"Dying."

"You? Wait! I mean, I'll be right over."

"No . . . time."

"Hang on—"

"M-m-m. . . ." He stopped. There was a gurgly sob. Then Benedict said, "Murder," in a quite ordinary way.

Ellery said swiftly, "Who, Johnny? Tell me. Who did it?"

This time the dragged-out breath, interminable.

And Johnny Benedict said distinctly, "Home," and stopped again.

Ellery found himself irritated. Why does he want me to know where he is? I know where he is. Or must be. At the main house. Using the extension. It made no sense. He was making no sense. If he could call me, he could be lucid. He had no right to be out of his head—to go this far only to tell me he was calling from home.

"I mean, who attacked you?"

He heard some meaningless sounds. It was exasperating.

"Hold on, Johnny, hold on! Who did it?" It was like trying to coax a recalcitrant child. "Try to tell me." He almost said "daddy" instead of the pronoun.

Johnny tried, according to his lights. He was on the "home" kick again. He said it three times, each time less distinctly, less assertively, with more of a stammer. Finally he stopped trying and there was nothing but a defeated *thunk!* at the other end, the phone hitting something, as if Johnny-B had flung it away or, what was less pleasantly probable, had dropped it.

"What is it, son?"

Ellery hung up. To his surprise, he found himself yawning. It was his father, in the doorway. The Inspector did not sleep well any more. The least interruption in the rhythm of his environment disturbed him.

"Ellery?"

He told the Inspector what Johnny had said.

"Then what are you standing here for?" the old man yelled, and dived for his bedroom.

There's no hurry, Ellery thought as he hurriedly pulled on his pants. Johnny's gone with the wind he sowed.

Wrightsville strikes again.

The Cougar covered the quarter mile in nothing flat. The main house was dark except for two windows upstairs which they took to be in Benedict's room, the master bedroom. Ellery jumped out, and the Inspector cried, "Did you remember to bring that key Benedict gave you?" to which Ellery replied, "Hell, no, I forgot it. Who ever used a key in Wrightsville?" and was immediately vindicated, because the front door, while it was closed, was not locked.

They ran upstairs. The master bedroom door stood open.

Benedict was in puce-colored silk pajamas, a milk-chocolate-striped silk kimono, and Japanese slippers. He lay in a heap on the floor beside the bed and he looked like a cake just out of the oven, decorated, and set aside to cool. The cradle of the telephone was on the nightstand; the receiver dangled to the floor. There was amazingly little blood, considering the wounds in Benedict's head.

The weapon lay on the floor six feet from the body, between the bed and the doorway. It was an oversized, heavy-looking Three Monkeys sculpture in a modern elongated style, cast in iron. Both the material and the stylistic distortion gave its familiar "see no evil, hear no evil, speak no evil" homily an irony terribly grotesque. Neither man touched it.

"He's dead, of course," Ellery said.

"What do you think?"

"For the record." Ellery's lips were tight, "We'd better verify."

The Inspector squatted and felt Benedict's carotid.

"He's dead. What I can't understand is where he found the strength to pick up a phone."

"He obviously found it," Ellery said coldly. "The point is: having found it, what did he do with it? Not a damned thing!"

And in an aggrieved way he wrapped a handkerchief around his right hand, picked up the receiver, punched the button on the cradle for an outside line, and from too, too solid memory dialed the number of Wrightsville police headquarters.

"It's going to be some time before Newby gets here," Ellery remarked to his father, replacing the phone. "Which is prob-like the dead. Maybe we'd better check their carotids, too."

"Let 'em be," the Inspector growled. "Their time is com-ably just as well. By the way, these guests of Johnny's sleep-ing. What do you mean 'just as well'?"

"The night desk man, a fellow named Peague—I'm betting he's related to Millard Peague, who used to have the locksmith shop on Crosstown and Foaming—says the chief went to a Red Man blast tonight and just got into the sack, so he won't appreciate having to get up and come out here. The three radio cars on the graveyard tour are all over at Fyfield Gunnery School—some students got high on speed or something and they're wrecking the administration building. It's developed into a full-scale engagement—state police, patrol cars from Slocum as well as Wrightsville—the locals won't be able to get here for hours, Peague says. While we're waiting for Newby we may as well make ourselves useful."

The Inspector looked doubtful. "I hate cutting in on another cop's turf."

"Newby won't mind. The Lord of battles knows we've charged shoulder to shoulder often enough. Let's see if we can find any writing materials."

"What for?"

"Superman or not, Johnny'd have written something in preference to phoning—if he could. My hunch is we'll find nothing."

They found nothing. It gave Ellery a small satisfaction.

One mystery was solved. On the opposite side of the room from the windows, helter-skelter on the floor as if thrown there, they found the three articles of clothing Benedict's ex-wives had reported missing: Audrey Weston's black sequined gown, Marcia Kemp's green wig, and Alice Tierney's white evening gloves.

Ellery examined them eagerly. The evening gown was long enough to trail on the floor; the wig was not only absurdly green but distended—it looked like an excited hedgehog; the gloves were of high-quality kid. None of the three showed even a pinpoint of bloodstain.

"So they weren't being used at the time of the assault," the Inspector mused. "A plant?"

"Three plants," Ellery said, squinting. "Otherwise why leave all three? If Johnny's assailant had wanted to implicate Marcia, he'd have left just the wig. Or Audrey, just the gown. Or Alice, just the gloves. By leaving all three he implicates all three."

"But why?"

"That is the question."

"But I don't get it, Ellery."

"I wish I could enlighten you. I don't, either."

"Something tells me we should have stood in Manhattan," the Inspector said gloomily.

The bed had been slept in; the spread had been neatly

folded at the foot, the bottom sheet was wrinkled, and the pillow still showed the depression made by Benedict's head.

"He certainly didn't go to bed with his robe on," Ellery said. "That means something woke him up, and he jumped out of bed and slipped into his robe and slippers. So the next question is: what disturbed him?"

"No sign of a struggle," the Inspector nodded. "It's as if the killer didn't want to spoil the neatness of the room."

"You're getting whimsical, dad."

"No, I mean it. No clothes thrown about, chair as naked as a jaybird, and I'll bet if you look in that hamper you'll find. . . ." Inspector Queen darted into the bathroom and yanked up the cover of the laundry hamper, which was just visible from the foot of Benedict's bed. He exclaimed in triumph, "What did I tell you? Shirt, socks, underwear—neatly deposited before he went to bed."

The Inspector came out and looked about. "He must have been left for dead, Ellery—on the bed or floor—and when the killer was gone, Benedict somehow found the moxie to crawl to the phone and call you."

"Agreed," Ellery said. "Also, from the absence of a struggle I'm tempted to conclude that Johnny knew his assailant. Although, of course, it could have been a housebreaker or other stranger who jumped him and got in an incapacitating blow just after Johnny got out of bed and put his robe and slippers on. That's one of those alternatives you never quite eliminate."

"But what did he kill him for?" The Inspector was going through the elephant-ear wallet lying on the nightstand. The wallet was fat, like the craw of a Strasbourg goose. The Rolex watch with the matching bracelet beside the wallet was an 18-carat gold, 30-jewel affair that must have set Benedict back over a thousand dollars.

"For money, that's what for," Ellery said. "But not the kind of goose feed you tote around. I went to bed worrying about exactly that. What's this?"

"This" was a walk-in wardrobe closet. The Queens walked in and routinely took inventory. Hanging on racks, with the neatness of a tailor's shop, were a dozen or so custom-made suits in fabulous fabrics and numerous shades of blue and gray; two summer dinner jackets, one white, the other burgundy; a variety of pastel-hued slacks and sports jackets; a white yachting uniform, hound's-tooth golf togs, a brown plaid hunting and fishing outfit; four topcoats, in charcoal gray, light gray, garbardine tan, and chocolate; three overcoats, one black with a velvet collar, another navy blue double-breasted, the third a casual tan cashmere. The shoe racks held dozens of pairs of shoes—conventionals, cordovans, alligators, suèdes, two-tones; an assortment of boots and athletic shoes; blacks and browns and grays and tans and oxbloods. On an upper shelf lay ten hats and caps, from a black homburg to a severe dark brown fedora, through the well-dressed man's Alpine, woodsman, and other sporty styles. An enormous revolving rack offered a selection of four-in-hand neckties, ascots, bow ties, and scarves in all the basic solid colors, in combinations, and in a range of materials and designs that would not have disgraced Sulka's.

The Inspector marveled. "Why in God's name did he need all these duds? In Wrightsville, of all places?"

"And this is just a hideaway," Ellery pointed out, "where he apparently did little entertaining and no visiting. Imagine what the closets in his New York, Paris, and other apartments must look like."

The bureau was a built-in affair with haberdasher's drawers stacked with custom-made shirts of every description: broadcloths, Pimas, silks, synthetics; in whites, blues, browns, tans, grays, greens, pinks, even lavenders, in solids and in pinstripes; with button cuffs and French cuffs; with dress collars and buttoned-down collars; including a collection of plaids and flannels and other outdoorsy items, and another of frilled and lacy as well as conventional summer dress shirts. Several drawers turned up a selection of knitwear. Others held T-shirts and shorts by the dozens, chiefly of silk, and handkerchiefs functional and ornamental. And in one lay a shop-sized stock of hose, in woolens, lisles, nylons, silks; in blacks, browns, grays, blues; in solids and in combinations. And, of course, a jewelry drawer for a collection of tie clasps, tackpins, cufflinks, and other essentials of the bureau.

The Inspector kept shaking his head. Ellery's remained at rest, all but his eyes, which reflected a puzzle of some sort.

It was as if he had mislaid something, but could remember neither what it was nor where he had mislaid it.

Waiting for Chief Newby, the Queens went about rousing Benedict's guests. The reason for the undisturbed sleep of the ex-wives and Marsh was detectable at once by anyone with less than a severe cold. The air in the bedrooms was sour with alcohol; evidently the three divorcees and the lawyer had done some serious extracurricular drinking after Ellery's departure from his eavesdropping post on the terrace. They were a little stubborn about waking up.

As for Miss Smith, Marsh's secretary, she had locked her bedroom door, and Ellery had to pound for several minutes before she responded. There were no fumes in her room. "I sleep like the dead," Miss Smith said—a figure of speech she clearly regretted a moment later when he told her why he had roused her. From the noises immediately emanating from her bathroom, Miss Smith was paying the price the three other women should have paid but had not. Ellery left her to fortify her rebellious stomach.

As far as he and his father could make out, Marcia Kemp, Audrey Weston, and Alice Tierney greeted the news of Benedict's violent death with stupefaction. They seemed too stunned to grasp the implications; there were no hysterics and very few questions. As for Marsh, he gaped at the Queens from a graying face, his big hands trembling. "Are the police here yet?" he asked; and Ellery said, "On their way, Al," whereupon the lawyer sat down on the bed mumbling, "Poor old Johnny, what a stinking deal," and asked if he might have a drink. Ellery brought him a bottle and a glass; Inspector Queen warned the quintet to remain where they were, each in his own room, and took up a sentry post at the door of Benedict's bedroom; and that was all.

Ellery was downstairs waiting for Newby when the chief— tieless, a topcoat thrown over his uniform—stalked into the house.

Anselm Newby had succeeded Chief Dakin, who personified law and order in Wrightsville for so long that only the thinning ranks of oldtimers remembered his predecessor, a fat, spittoon-targeting ex-farmer named Horace Swayne. Dakin, who always reminded Ellery of Abe Lincoln, had been the old-fashioned small-town incorruptible policeman; Anse Newby was of the new breed, young, aggressive, and scientifically trained on a city-sized police force. He was a ball of fire where Dakin had been a plodder, yet he had had to prove himself a dozen times over before the town would grudgingly grant that he might be able to fill part of old Dakin's size-13 shoes. Newby's fate it was to be a small, delicate-appearing man in a community where any suspicion of effeminacy was hated rather than despised, and in a police chief was considered a crime in itself. He soon disabused the town on this score. When the rumors reached his ears he tracked them to their source, shucked his uniform jacket, and administered a scientific beating to the offender—who had a six-inch height and thirty-five-pound weight advantage—that was the talk of Wrightsville's bars for many years. With this demonstration of his masculinity Newby had no further trouble with rumormongers. And with his stinging voice and eyes of inorganic blue, unwinking as mineral, he tended to grow on people, not always pleasantly.

"Sorry about this, Chief—" Ellery began, not altogether humorously.

"You're always sorry about this," Newby snapped. "I'm suggesting to the First Selectman that he haul arse on up to the capital and see if he can't talk our assemblyman into pushing a bill through the legislature putting Wrightsville off limits to anybody named Queen. Can't you set foot in this town without causing a homicide? I didn't know you were visiting, or I'd have put out an A.P.B. on you! How are you, Ellery?"

"I feel as rotten about it as you, Anse," Ellery said, pumping the delicate hand. "Rottener. I purposely kept our visit quiet—"

"Our? Who'd you come up with?"

"My dad. He's upstairs keeping an eye on Benedict's room and the body. We're here on a rest cure. On Johnny Benedict's invitation."

"Father or not, he probably doesn't know your Wrightsville record as well as I do, or he'd never have come. For a cop to take a vacation with you is a busman's holiday for sure. And look what Benedict's invite got *him*. Well, tell me about this one, you hoodoo."

"Let's go up."

Upstairs, the Inspector and Newby shook hands like adversaries; they had never met. But when the old man said, "I hope you don't mind our poking around while we waited for you, Chief. I don't care much myself for police officers who stick their noses into other men's territory." Newby warmed perceptibly. "Mighty lucky for me you were here, Inspector," he said, and Ellery let his breath go.

It took the best part of forty-five minutes to brief the Wrightsville chief on the marital and testamentary situations that had presumably led to Benedict's murder, while Newby examined the body and the premises.

"I left orders to get my tech men out of bed," Newby said. "Where the hell are they? Ellery, d'ye mind? Fetch those five people down here while I notify the coroner's doc to climb out of his sack and bring his tail over here. We just don't have the kind of setup and manpower you're used to, Inspector," he said in what sounded like an apology, and he made for the telephone in the foyer.

"He seems to think he has to put a show on for me," the Inspector remarked to Ellery.

Ellery grinned, "I didn't realize Anse was that human," and hurried upstairs.

The five trooped into the living room in a symbiosis of reluctance and relief. None of them had been told more than the unembellished fact of Benedict's murder; each having been isolated from the others, they had had no opportunity to ex-change speculations or recriminations or to compare stories; they were all, in the flamboyant word of the times, uptight. Even more interesting, the ex-wives tended to cluster together where before Benedict's death they had staked out inde-pendent territories in the living room.

As for Miss Smith, not unexpectedly after her exhibition of secretarial aloofness, she showed signs of strain. The bout with her stomach had left her pale and ill. She mewed for a brandy, at which Marsh, even in his preoccupation, looked astonished. And she kept babbling away in a complaining voice, principally to Marsh, as if the predicament in which she found herself was all her employer's fault. At least four times she whined, "I've never had anything to do with a murder before," as if he had dragged her into something very common in his set; until Marcia Kemp tossed her red locks and said grimly, "Oh, for chrissake, shut *up*," at which Miss Smith looked frightened, clutched her brandy, and subsided.

"Now look, folks," Newby said when the Inspector had identified the five. "I know darned little about this setup, though I guarantee you I'll know a lot more about it before I'm through. But as of this minute I have no notion who killed Mr. Benedict. So that's our first order of business. Anybody here got anything to tell me that's going to cut our work down?"

No one seemed able or prepared to do so. Until finally Marsh said in a voice as gray as his face, "Surely, Chief, you can't believe anyone here had anything to do with Johnny's death?"

"All right, that formality's out of the way. Anybody hear anything after getting to bed? An argument, a fight? Or even just footsteps?"

No one had. Deep sleep had been the order of the night during the period of the murder (they claimed at first), in the main induced by bourbon and vodka. Except, again, in Miss Smith's case. (Miss Smith did not "drink"—she placed audible quotation marks around the word. The brandy in her clutch was for restorative purposes.)

The ex-Mrs. Benedicts, it seemed, had originally found sleep elusive. Freshly bedded, they said, they had been wakeful.

"I tossed and tossed," Audrey Weston said. "So I thought if maybe I did some reading. You know." (Ellery waited for her to add "dahling," but the blonde seemed to realize that Chief Newby would not take kindly to the endearment.) "I came downstairs and got a book."

"Where downstairs, Miss Weston?" Newby asked.

"This room. From those bookshelves there."

"Was anybody down here while you were?"

"No."

"How long did you stay?"

"Just long enough to pick out a book."

"Then you went back upstairs?"

"That's right."

"How long did you read, Miss Weston, before you tried to get to sleep again?"

"I found I couldn't. The type began swimming before my eyes."

"Which book was it?" Ellery asked.

"I don't recall the title," the blonde said haughtily. "Something—the latest—by that Roth person."

"Philip Roth?"

"I think that's his Christian name."

"Harry Golden will be delighted to hear it. The title wasn't *Portnoy's Complaint*, was it?"

Miss Weston grew haughtier. "I'd forgotten."

"Miss Weston, if you'd begun *Portnoy's Complaint,* I don't believe the type would have swum before your eyes. The fact is you read for some time, didn't you?"

"The fact is, *dahling*," Audrey Weston spat, "I was so absolutely *revolted* I threw the disgusting thing across the room! Then I went downstairs for another book, and I got one, and started to read *that*, but that was when the sauce hit me and I got very sleepy all of a sudden, so I put out the light and the next thing I knew I was out of this world. And don't ask me what the other book was, Mr. Queen, because I haven't *any* recollection. It's still in my room if you think it's important."

"So you made two trips downstairs during the night."

"If you don't believe me, that's your problem."

"It may well be yours," Ellery said thoughtfully, and stepped back with a wave to Newby. "Didn't mean to monopolize, Anse. Go ahead."

"What time was it, Miss Weston, when all this happened?"

"I haven't the foggiest."

"No idea at all?"

"I wasn't watching clocks."

"Not even your wristwatch when you undressed?"

"I just didn't."

"Can't you make a guess what time it was? One? Two? Three?"

"I don't know, I tell you. Marcia, what time did I go up to bed?"

"You answer your questions, dearie," Marcia Kemp said, "and I'll answer mine."

"I'll tell you what time it was when you went up to bed," Alice Tierney said suddenly. "It was just about two."

"It couldn't have been that late!" Audrey cried.

"Well, it was."

"You tossed and tossed," Newby said, "then you went downstairs for *Portnoy's Complaint,* which you read for how long?"

"Really," the blonde said. "I wasn't counting. A short while."

"Fifteen minutes? A half hour?"

"Maybe. I don't know."

"Or an hour?" Ellery murmured.

"No! Closer to a half hour."

"In other words, Mr. Roth's opus revolted but held you for a half hour or more. I got the impression from what you said before that you'd hardly begun reading when you flung the book aside in disgust. You're really not making very responsive answers."

"Why are you after me, Mr. Queen?" the blonde cried. "What are you, out to get me or something? All right, I read that foul book a good long time, and the second one I hardly glanced at. But it all comes out the same at the end, because I was fast asleep *long* before whoever killed Johnny killed him."

Newby pounced. "How do you know when Benedict was killed, Miss Weston? No one here mentioned it."

She was stricken. "Didn't . . . ? Well . . . I mean, I just assumed. . . ."

He let it go. "Did you happen to see anyone on your trip downstairs or on your way back up? Either time?"

"Nobody. The bedroom doors were all shut, by the way, as far as I could see. I naturally thought everyone but me was asleep."

Newby said suddenly, "How about you, Miss Kemp?"

But she was ready for him. "How about me?"

"Did you fall right asleep when you went up to bed?"

"I wish I could say I did," the redhead answered, "but something tells me when you've got nothing to hide in a case like this it's better to tell the truth, the whole truth, and nothing but the truth. I'd had a real snootful down here and I didn't think I'd make it to the hay, I was so rocky. But I no sooner hit the bed than I was wide awake—"

"Hold it. What time was it when you left to go to bed?"

"I was in no condition to tell time, Chief. All I know is it was after Audrey went upstairs."

"How long after?"

Marcia Kemp shrugged.

"I can tell you," Alice Tierney said. "It was close to two thirty."

"You li'l ol' timekeeper, you," the redhead growled. "Anyway, my head was spinning, and I thought food might settle my stomach down, so I went downstairs to the kitchen and made myself a dry chicken sandwich and a cup of warm milk and brought them back up to my room. Grandpa there spotted the plate with the crumbs on it and the dirty glass when he woke me up a while back. Tell 'em, Grandpa."

"I saw the plate and the glass, yes," Inspector Queen said. He had been standing by the French doors overlooking the terrace, keeping himself out of the way.

"See?" Marcia said. She was wearing a shortie nightgown under her negligee, and the negligee kept coming apart. Ellery found himself wishing she would fasten it so that he could keep his mind on the testimony. Under the translucent stuffs she appeared like a giant flower about to burst into blossom. "The warm milk must have done it because after a while I corked off. I didn't know a blessed other thing until old fuzz there woke me up."

"Did you happen to see anyone during your trip to the kitchen and back?"

"No."

"I suppose you didn't hear anything around the time of the murder, either?"

"You're not catching me, buster. I don't know when the time of the murder was. Anyway, I didn't hear anything *any* time."

Alice Tierney's difficulty had been the alcohol, too. "I'm not much of a drinker," the Wrightsville ex-nurse said, "and I'd had a few too many last night. I went up to my room after Marcia, and when I couldn't fall asleep I crawled to the bathroom for something for my head. I couldn't find aspirin or anything in the medicine chest, so I went to the downstairs lavatory where I'd noticed some Bufferin during the day. I swallowed a couple and went back to my room. The Bufferin didn't help much, so I tried cold compresses. Finally out of desperation I took a sleeping pill from a bottle I found in the medicine chest—I hate sleeping pills, I've had too much experience with them—and that did it. I went out cold." Like Audrey and Marcia, Alice had seen no one and heard nothing.

"Funny," Chief Newby remarked. "With all that cross traffic up and down the stairs last night, you'd think somebody would have run into somebody. How about you, Mr. Marsh? What did you go traipsing downstairs for?"

"I didn't. Once I got to my room I stayed there. I had more than my quota last night, too, especially after Johnny went up to bed. I don't think I was conscious for two minutes after my head hit the pillow. The next thing I knew Ellery was shaking me."

"What time did you go up to bed?"

"I don't know exactly. My impression is it was right after Alice Tierney, but I'm fuzzy about it."

"No, that's right," the Wrightsville girl said.

"And you, Miss Smith?"

Challenged by name Miss Smith started, slopping what was left in her snifter. "I can't imagine why you should question me at all! I don't think I ever said more than a hello to Mr. Benedict when he visited Mr. Marsh's office."

"Did you leave your room last night after you went to bed?"

"I did not!"

"Did you hear anything that might help us, Miss Smith? Try to remember."

"I told Mr. Queen before you got here, Chief Newby, I sleep very soundly." ("Like the dead," Ellery reminded her silently.) "I thought I might have a busy day Sunday and I need my sleep if I'm to function efficiently. After all, I wasn't invited to this house as a guest. I'm here only because I'm Mr. Marsh's secretary."

"Miss Smith can't have anything to do with this," Marsh said. He said it rather harshly, Ellery thought. "I don't mean to tell you your business, Chief, but isn't all this a waste of time? Johnny must have been killed by some housebreaker who got in during the night to steal something and lost his head when Johnny woke up and surprised him."

"I wish it were that simple, Mr. Marsh." Newby glanced at Ellery. Ellery promptly went out and came back with the sequined gown, the wig, and the evening gloves.

"Since you're all Mrs. Benedicts," Ellery said to the ex-wives, "from here on in I'm going to make it easier on us by addressing you by your given names. Audrey, you came to me yesterday afternoon to report the theft of a gown from your room. Is this the one?"

He offered the black dress to the blonde. She examined it suspiciously. Then she got up slowly and fitted it to herself. "It looks like it . . . I suppose it is . . . yes. Where did you find it?"

Ellery took it from her.

"Marcia, is this the wig you told me yesterday somebody stole from your room?"

"You know it. If there's another green wig in this town I'll eat it." The redhead slipped it over her boyish crop. "This is it, all right."

"Alice, these evening gloves?"

"There was a slight nick in the forefinger of the left hand," the brunette said. "Yes, here it is. These are mine, Mr. Queen. But who had them?"

"We don't know who had them," Newby said, "but we know where they wound up. We found them in Benedict's bedroom, near his body."

This remark produced an almost weighable silence.

"But what does it mean?" Alice exclaimed. "Why should somebody steal my gloves and then leave them practically on Johnny's corpse?"

"Or my evening gown?"

"Or my kook wig?"

"I don't understand any part of this." Marsh was back at the bar, but he was paying no attention to the glass in his hand. "This sort of thing is your dish of blood, Ellery. What's it all about? Or don't you agree a burglar, or maybe a tramp—?"

"I'm afraid I don't," Ellery said. "There is a bit of sense to be made out of it, though, Al, and that's where you come in."

"Me?"

"Anse, do you mind?"

Newby shook his head. "You know more about this setup than I do, Ellery. Forget the protocol."

"Then let me shortcut this," Ellery said. "I was out on the terrace listening when Johnny made that speech last night about his intention to write a new will. I assume, Al, that since you were the lawyer who drafted Johnny's original will —the one extant when he came up here the other day—and the purpose of the weekend was to write a new will, you brought a copy of the old one along with you?"

"Yes." Marsh's tough jaw was belligerent. "You were eavesdropping, Ellery? Why?"

"Because I was uneasy about Johnny's situation, and events have borne it out. I'd like to see the will in your possession."

Marsh set his glass down on the bar. His jaw had not declared a truce. "Technically, I can refuse—"

"We know what you can do, Mr. Marsh," the chief said with a twitch of the whiplash. "But up here we aren't so formal in murder investigations. In my territory, Mr. Marsh, murder opens up a lot of doors. Let's see Benedict's will, please."

The lawyer hesitated. Finally he shrugged. "It's in my attaché case. In my room. Miss Smith—"

"Never mind," Inspector Queen said. "I'll get it."

They had forgotten he was there. He was out and back

in the same unobtrusive way. "For the record, Mr. Marsh, I didn't open it."

Marsh gave him a queer look. He opened the case and drew out a thick folded document in a parchment slipcase. This he handed to Newby, who drew out the will, riffled through its numerous pages, and passed it to Ellery, who spent rather more time on it.

"I see that the basic will was drawn up a long time ago, Al, with supplementary sections added after each marriage and divorce."

"That's right."

"And according to the additions, the weekly payments to each divorced wife of a thousand dollars stop on Johnny's death but the will leaves her, if unmarried at such time, a principal sum of a million dollars as a final settlement."

"Yes."

"Then each ex-wife," Ellery said, "had a million dollars' worth of vested interest in seeing that this will remained in force until Johnny died."

"That's a rather funny way to put it, but I suppose so, yes. What's the point?"

"Oh, come, Al, I know a lawyer of your standing and background doesn't like to be mixed up in a nastiness like this, but you're in it and you'd better face up to the fact. What I overheard from the terrace last night, in the light of what subsequently happened, confirms every fear I've had. If Johnny'd survived the night, he intended to write a new will today. The new will, he said, while it would continue these ladies' thousand a week till their remarriage, at his death would cut their settlements from a million to a hundred thousand—a mere ten percent of what they could figure on collecting if he didn't or wasn't able to write the new will. And if they contested, he warned them, he wouldn't leave them a cent. I ask you, Al: From Audrey's, Marcia's, and Alice's standpoints, wasn't it a lucky break that Johnny failed to live through the night?"

Marsh gulped his drink. And the subjects of Ellery's soliloquy sat so very still they scarcely disturbed the flight of the molecules in their vicinity.

"So the way it looks," Chief Newby announced in the hush, "you used-to-be-wives of Benedict's had motive and opportunity—equal motive and opportunity. And, I might add, equal access to the murder weapon."

"I don't even know what the weapon was!" Audrey Weston, leaping. "You didn't tell us. For God's sake, I couldn't commit murder. Maybe Alice Tierney could—nurses get used to blood. But it makes me *sick*. . . ."

"I'll remember that, Audrey," Alice said in a hypodermic voice.

"For nine hundred thousand dollars, Miss Weston," the chief remarked, "most anybody could commit most anything. And oh, yes. Your evening gown was found on the scene of the crime."

"But I told Mr. Queen yesterday that it was stolen from me!" she wailed. "You found Alice's gloves and Marcia's wig up there, too, didn't he say? Why pick on me?"

"I'm not, Miss Weston. Whatever applies in this case applies to all three of you. So far. I grant you, finding all those articles in Benedict's room doesn't add up. But there they were, and juries tend to go not by fancy figuring but by plain facts."

"There's a fact in this case none of you knows," Ellery said. "Dad?"

Inspector Queen stepped forward. "On Thursday night— that was before any of you people came up here—Benedict dropped in on Ellery and me at the guest house. He told us that Marsh was going to write a new will for him over the weekend, but that, wanting to protect himself in the meantime, he'd drawn up the substance of it in his own hand and he wanted us to witness it."

The old man produced the long envelope Benedict had consigned to his care.

"My son and I watched Benedict sign and date this holograph will, we signed as witnesses, he slipped it into this envelope, and he asked me to keep it for him temporarily."

"We don't know what's in the holograph," Ellery said "—he didn't let us read it, or read it to us—but we assume it sets forth the same provisions as the one he intended Al Marsh to put in more formal language today. Under the circumstances, Anse, I believe you have every right to open it here and now."

The Inspector handed the envelope to Newby, who glanced at Marsh. Marsh shrugged and said, "You've made it clear where the local law stands, Chief," and stepped over to the bar to refill his glass.

"Did Benedict say anything to you about writing out the new will himself in advance of the weekend, Mr. Marsh?" Newby asked.

"Not a word." Marsh took a he-man swallow and flourished the glass. "Come to think of it, though, he did ask me some questions about phraseology and form in the case of a holograph will. It didn't occur to me he was seriously asking for himself."

Newby slit the envelope with his penknife and withdrew

the handwritten will. The Queens rubbernecked. As they read, the three men looked increasingly surprised and puzzled.

The chief said abruptly, "You'd best take a look at this, Mr. Marsh."

Newby waved the crowding ex-wives back and offered the document to Marsh, who handled the paper, his glass, and a smoldering cigaret like a boy learning to juggle. Finally he set glass and cigaret down, and read.

He, too, looked puzzled.

"Read it aloud, Al." Ellery was watching Audrey, Marcia, and Alice. The trio were craning like giraffes. "Just that pertinent paragraph."

Marsh frowned. "He revokes all previous wills—the usual thing—and leaves his residuary estate quote 'to Laura and any children' unquote. He goes on: 'If for any reason I am not married to Laura at the time of my death, I bequeath my residuary estate to my only living kin, my first cousin Leslie.' That's the gist of it." The lawyer shrugged. "It's sloppily drawn, but in my judgment this is a legal will." He returned it to Newby and retrieved his glass and cigaret.

"Laura," Marcia muttered. "Who the hell is Laura?"

"It couldn't be that hatcheck number he's been seen with lately," Audrey said. "From what the columns have been spilling, her name is Vincentine Astor."

Alice said, "He's never mentioned a Laura to me."

"Or me," Audrey complained. "Is it possible that two-legged rat got married secretly before he came up here?"

"No," Ellery said. "Because in that event he'd probably have written that he was leaving his estate to 'my wife Laura,' the common form, rather than simply 'to Laura.' If he died before he married her, the phrase 'my wife Laura' on a will predating the marriage might well invalidate the document and toss a will case involving millions into the surrogate's court for years. No, Johnny was anticipating his marriage to Laura—'if for any reason I am not married to Laura,' etcetera, tells us that. Al, do you know who Laura is, or might be?"

"He never mentioned a woman of that name to me."

"I agree with you, Ellery," Chief Newby said. "He meant to marry this Laura right off and figured he'd jump the gun by writing her into his interim will beforehand. He protected himself by that 'if for any reason' clause. He must have been awfully sure of her."

"It's a tough, tough world for poor old Laura," Marcia said with a laugh that was more of a bray. "Whoever knocked Johnny off did her out of a load of rice, Russian sable, square-cut emeralds, and Paris originals."

"Absolutely correct," Ellery said. "She won't inherit now, whoever she is. The estate goes to Johnny's cousin. Who is Leslie, Al, do you know?"

"Leslie Carpenter. Everyone else in both the Benedict and Carpenter families is gone. I'll have to notify Leslie about this right away."

"Read the part about our hundred thousand dollars, Mr. Newby," Alice said.

Newby glanced at the will in his hand. "I can't."

"What do you mean?"

"This will doesn't mention you or Miss Kemp or Miss Weston. There's nothing in it about leaving you a hundred thousand dollars apiece. Or ten dollars." After the shrieks died the chief said, "It figures. He wasn't going to commit himself on paper to you ladies for one red cent beforehand."

"That was smart of Johnny," Marsh said with a laugh.

"Shrewd would be the word," Ellery said. "He meant to propose a deal, as he subsequently did, and he saw no reason to settle his part of the bargain before you had a chance to settle yours. Also, at the time he wrote this will out I imagine his only concern was the protection of Laura or Leslie."

"In other words," said the Inspector's dry voice, "if one of you ladies knocked Benedict off, all you're going to get out of it is a choice of your last meal."

Newby's tech men and the coroner's physician drove up then, with the lightening sky, and the chief sent the ex-Mrs. Benedicts, Miss Smith, and Marsh back to their rooms and sought the phone to notify the Wright County prosecutor and the sheriff's office. The Queens left for a few hours' sleep.

Driving slowly back to the cottage in the damp dawn, Ellery said with a scowl, "I wonder how right Marsh is about that holograph will standing up."

"You told me he knows his business," the Inspector said, "so his opinion ought to be worth something. But you know how these multimillion will cases go, Ellery. Those three are sure to find hungry lawyers who for a big contingency fee will tie the case up for years."

Ellery shrugged. "Marsh and that other law firm Benedict had wished on him wield an awful lot of clout. Well, we have to assume the holograph knocks out the earlier will and, as you said back there, whoever pulled the homicide committed a murder for nothing. This Leslie Carpenter fellow picks up all the marbles."

"You can imagine how those vultures are feeling right now. Especially the one who beat Benedict to death. . . . Something wrong, son?"

Ellery looked vague.

"You're all of a sudden a hundred miles away."

"Oh. Something's been bugging me ever since we left Johnny's bedroom."

"What's that?"

"I don't know. A feeling. That we've overlooked something."

"Overlooked what?"

Ellery braked the Cougar in the carport and switched off the ignition.

"If I could answer that, dad, I wouldn't be bugged. Out. Sack time."

Benedict's cousin Leslie drove in during the early afternoon of Monday.

To the surprise of everyone but Marsh, it was a woman who got out of the airport taxi. "It never occurred to me you'd assume the name Leslie meant a man," Marsh said to the Queens. "I've known her through Johnny since she was in deep orthodontia. How are you, Les?"

She turned a glad smile on Marsh. She was years younger than Johnny-B, and the Queens soon perceived that she was not only of a different sex from her late cousin, she was of a different species. Where Benedict had been the child of fortune, Leslie had had to scrimp all her life.

"My mother, who was Johnny's aunt—Johnny's father's sister—got the heave from my grandfather. In the good old Victorian-novel style, he disinherited her. It seems that mother was too much of a rebel and didn't have the proper reverence for capital. And worst of all she insisted on falling in love with a man who had no money and no social standing." Leslie smiled mischievously. "Poor grandfather, he couldn't understand mother, and he accused daddy to his face of being —oh, dear—a 'fortune hunter.' Dad a fortune hunter! He thought less of money than even mother did."

"You paint a filial picture," Ellery smiled.

"Thank you, sir. Dad was the typical absent-minded professor who taught in a country school at a starvation salary, tyrannized by a school board who thought anybody who had read more than two books was a dues-paying Communist. He died at the age of forty-one of cancer. Mother was sickly, had a rheumatic heart . . . if this sounds like soap opera, don't blame me, it actually happened . . . and I had to go to work to support us. That meant leaving school. It was only when mother died that I was able to go back and get my degree. In sociology. I've been working in the fields of welfare and education ever since.

"Johnny evidently nursed a guilt feeling because mother

had been kicked out, so that his father inherited everything and passed it along to him. Poor old John. He kept looking us up and pressing money on us. Mother and dad would never take any. Me, I wasn't the least bit proud. I gratefully accepted John's financial help after mother passed away, or I'd never have been able to go back to college at all, I had too many debts to pay off. The way I saw it," Leslie said thoughtfully, "Johnny's making it possible for someone like me to complete her education was encouraging him to do something useful with his money instead of throwing it away on a lot of gimme girls. And if that's a rationalization, so be it." And Leslie's little chin grew half an inch.

Inspector Queen (*concealing a smile*): "Miss Carpenter, did your cousin John ever indicate to you that he was going to make you the principal beneficiary of his estate under certain circumstances?"

"Under no circumstances, never! I didn't dream he'd leave me so much as grandfather's watch. We used to argue our social and political differences—remember, Al? Al will tell you I never pulled my punches with John."

"She certainly did not," Marsh said. "Johnny took a great deal from you, Les, more than from anybody. He was crazy about you. Maybe in love with you."

"Oh, come, Al. I don't think he ever even liked me. I was the bone in his throat—I kept telling him I was the voice of his superego. As far as I was concerned, John Levering Benedict the Three was a nonproductive, useless, all-wrapped-up-in-his-own-pleasures parasite, and I was the only one with the nerve to tell him so. There's so much he could have done with his money!"

"Aren't you overlooking something?" Marsh asked dryly. "He has done it, Les. Now."

Leslie Carpenter looked amazed. "Do you know, I'd forgotten! That's true, isn't it? Now I can do all the wonderful things. . . ."

There was something about the capsule autobiographer that tickled Ellery, and he surveyed her with an interest not altogether professional. On the outside she was a porcelain bit of femininity, looking as if you could see through her if you held her up to the light, but experience in reading character told him she was made of tough materials. There was a tilt to her little head, a glint in her eyes, that signified *Sturm und Drang* for anyone she disapproved of.

But what he perceived in her, or thought he did, went deeper than a strength developed through the exercise of poverty and the need to fight back in a world that crushed pacifists. There was a womanliness in her, a sweet underlying honesty, a lack of guile, that drew him. (And she possessed that paradox of nature, blue eyes that were warm.)

He thought it wonderful, then, that Leslie turned to Marsh and asked abruptly, "How much am I inheriting, Al?"

"The answer to that goes back to Johnny's father. Under Benedict Senior's will, on Johnny's death his heir or heirs would receive the entire income from the Benedict holdings. Mind you, Leslie, I said income, not principal. Mr. Benedict didn't believe in distributing principal, even after he was dead. The principal remains in trust and intact."

"Oh," Leslie said. "That sounds like a letdown. How much will the income come to?"

"Well, you'll be able to do a few good works with it, Les, and maybe have a few dollars left over for yourself. Let me see . . . oh, you should be collecting an income of some three million dollars a year."

"My God!" Leslie Carpenter whispered; and she fell, weeping, into Marsh's arms.

The press and the networks had descended in clouds late on Sunday, when the news of Johnny-B's murder got out of Wrightsville. The invasion brought with it the usual orgy of sensationalism and slush. Newby and his small department, groggy from coping with the riotous student mass-trip at Fyfield Gunnery, had their hands overfull; in the end, the chief had to call on the state police for assistance, and a number of importunate newsmen and slop sisters were escorted from the grounds. Order was restored when a news pool was agreed upon, consisting of one representative each of the wire services, the TV networks, and the radio people. A single round-robin conference with the ex-wives and Leslie Carpenter was authorized to take place in the living room of the main house, a brouhaha that the Queens and Newby observed out of range of the cameras, watching and listening for some slip or lapse, no matter how tiny or remote. But if their quarry was one of the disinherited women, she was too guarded to give herself away. The women merely contended for camera exposure and had nothing but kind and grieving words for the passing of their Lord Bountiful. (The trio had evidently made a pact not to malign Benedict in public for tactical reasons, at least until they could consult counsel about the will trick and the prestidigitation of their millions.) Leslie Carpenter limited herself to an expression of surprise at her windfall and the statement that she had "plans for the money" which she would disclose "at the proper time."

At this juncture Marcia Kemp was heard to say, "Which is going to be never, baby!"—not by the press, fortunately for her, only by the Queens and Chief Newby. They questioned the redhead about the remark later, when the news people were gone. She explained quickly that she had been referring to the coming contest over the holograph will, which she was "sure" she, Alice, and Audrey would win; she had certainly not intended the remark as a threat to Miss Carpenter. (Newby thereupon assigned an officer to keep an eye on Miss Carpenter.)

But that was the only note of discord.

There followed the surprising episode of the little hill and what stood upon it.

During the idyllic (pre-homicide) part of their stay, while exploring Benedict's property, the Queens had come across what looked like a Greek antiquity in miniature, a sort of ancient temple for dolls, with a little pediment and some more than creditable frieze-figures of a bucolic nature, little Doric columns, and for fillip two heavily stained-glass little windows. The tiny structure stood on the crest of a hillock surrounded by meadow, a pleasant if incongruous sight in the New England countryside.

The Queens, *père et fils,* walked around the diminutive construction wondering what it was. It did not look old, yet it did not look new, either. Ellery tried the adult-sized bronze door and found it as immovable as the entrance to SAC headquarters.

"A playhouse for some rich man's little girl?" the Inspector ventured at last.

If so, it was an expensive one. This is genuine marble."

It did not occur to either man that it might have been built by John Levering Benedict III to shelter his moldering mortality.

But that was what it proved to be, a mausoleum. "Johnny left a covering letter about it," Al Marsh told them Monday night. "He wanted to be laid away in it. He had a horror of being planted in the elaborate family vaults—there's one in Seattle and one in Rhinebeck, New York. I don't really know why—in fact, I doubt Johnny did himself. At heart he was a rebel like his Aunt Olivia—Leslie's mother—only he had too much of his father in him, who in turn was dominated all his life by the grandfather. Or, as Johnny put it, 'I inherited my father's disease—no guts.' It's my opinion Johnny hated everything that had gone into creating the Benedict fortune.

"Anyway, shortly after he purchased this property he designed the mausoleum—rather, had an architect blueprint it to his specifications—and hired a couple of oldtimers, country masons, practically an extinct breed, I understand, from around here to build it on that rise above the meadow. He brought in a sculptor from Boston to do the figures in the pediment; and the only reason he went to Boston for one is that he couldn't find a local sculptor. Johnny loved this town and the surrounding country. The marble comes from the Mahoganies up there, native stuff. He left a special maintenance fund in perpetuity, by the way. He said, 'I expect to lie here for a long time.' "

"But how did he finagle a cemetery permit?" Inspector Queen asked curiously. "Doesn't this state have a law against burial in private ground?"

"I had something to do with that, Inspector. I rooted around and found that the section of land where that hill and meadow lie has been in dispute between Wrightsville and Wright County for over a hundred and seventy-five years, the result of a surveying error in the eighteenth century. Wrightsville's always claimed that the meadow is within the town limits, with Wright County just as stubbornly maintaining that it's outside the disputed line. The claims have never been satisfactorily adjudicated; it's one of those Biblical problems these old communities run into sometimes, with no Solomon around to settle them. I worked through a local law firm, Danzig and Danzig, and we just stepped into the legal No Man's Land and presented the contending parties with the accomplished fact. The thing is in such a tangle that I could assure Johnny he might count on resting in peace in that miniature temple till the day after Armageddon. So he went ahead with his plans."

On Wednesday, Benedict's body was officially released by the coroner's office (the jury, having little of evidential substance to go on but the meager autopsy report, found that the deceased had come to his death "by a homicide caused by a blunt instrument hereunder described at the hand of person or persons unknown"); and on Friday, which was the third of April, Benedict was laid to rest in his meadow.

There had been a fierce if hushed competition for the business. Wrightsville's mortuary needs were served by three establishments: Duncan Funeral Parlors (the oldest in town), the Eternal Rest Mortuary, and Twin Hill Eternity Estates, Inc. They cuddled together on the east side of Upper Whistling Avenue (across from The Nutte Shop and Miss Sally's Tea Room) like three cotyledons in a seed. The notoriety of the case, which in an earlier day would have caused the conservative gentry of the embalming fluid to shudder and shy, only spurred their descendants to the chase; it was not every day that a local undertaking parlor was called on to bury a Benedict, and a murdered Benedict at that.

The determinant in the selection of the Duncan establishment was free enterprise. The incumbent, Philbert Duncan, had absorbed his art at the knees of the old master, his father, whom envious detractors had called "the slickest people-planter east of L.A." Johnny Benedict's letter of instructions on the subject of his interment had directed that his remains be encased in a stainless-steel inner container of a solid bronze casket of specified quality and design. No such magnificent box being available at any of the Wrightsville parlors, there was talk of postponing the funeral until the appropriate one could be shipped up from Boston. But Philbert Duncan drove over to Connhaven in the middle of the night of Wednesday-Thursday (presumably after moonset by the light of a dark lantern) and returned in triumph at dawn carting the specified coffin; it turned out that he had a cousin, one Duncan Duncan, who was in the business in Connhaven, a good-sized city in which demands for $5000 caskets, while uncommon, were not unknown.

Benedict's instructions had also called for an Episcopal funeral service, since he had been baptized and confirmed in the Anglican communion; and old Father Highmount was pressed into service for the occasion, having to come out of retirement because his successor, young Reverend Boyjian (he was, to Ernest Highmount's horror, not only Low Church but of *Armenian* descent!) was in the Bahamas with his wife on a vacation financed by the vestry in lieu of a much-needed rise in salary.

As the one and only next of kin, Leslie Carpenter decided to bypass a formal service in the church because of the rowdy press and the great curiosity of the public. A delegation of Benedict's closest friends, selected by Leslie on Marsh's advice, came by invitation from south, east, and west. It was calculatedly not large, so that the company assembled on the meadow before the little Greek temple at two o'clock Friday afternoon, even with the pool from the news media included, was handled without difficulty by Chief Newby's officers, with the state police relegated to the boundaries of the property to balk crank crashers and just plain nosy noonans from town.

It could not be said that Father Highmount produced a snappy service. He had always been a mumbler, a failing that had hardly improved with age; he was also suffering from a sloppy spring cold and he was having trouble with his dentures, so that most of what he said before the mausoleum came out a mumbo jumbo of mutters, squeaks, snuffles, and spit. About all the Queens heard with any clarity were "resurrection and the life," "*Dominus illuminatio* The Lord is my light," "My soul fleeth," "St. John fourteen one," and a final mighty "one God, world without end Amen!" which was miraculously free of sludge.

But the day was lovely, the breeze ruffled the old man's few fine silvery hairs in benediction, and no one seemed to mind the unintelligibility of his message to the dead man. For there was a quality of sincerity in his performance, a devotion to what he was saying over the invisible stranger in the casket (Leslie had wisely decided, in view of her cousin's wounds, not to put Philbert Duncan's cosmetic artistry to the test by having an open-coffin service), even though no one understood the old man but himself—there was in this quality a something that raised the flesh and brought a meaning out of the mystery. In spite of himself, Ellery was impressed.

He found himself reflecting that the whole bit—Benedict's valueless life, his dearth of accomplishment in spite of unlimited means, his uncompensated guilts, his failure to contribute anything but money to sad and greedy women who promptly threw it away, and finally a brutal death on the eve of what might have turned out to be his reformation—the whole bit was out of the theater of the absurd. Or, for that matter (thinking of the mausoleum), of Sophocles.

Still, he had redeemed part of his worthlessness. Aside from the mysterious Laura, Benedict had thought to provide for the far-out contingency—an act of incredible foresight, when one thought about it—that he might not survive the weekend. In which case, he had decided, everything went to little Leslie Carpenter, who had a very positive idea—as she had apparently told him so often to his face—of what could be done with three million a year.

So his life had not been all wasteland.

Ellery half expected the hapless Laura to put in an appearance at the funeral—in a dramatic black veil surely—weeping for sympathetic cameras and perhaps angling for a paid interview with LIFE or LOOK, or the slushier newspapers. But no mystery woman showed up in Wrightsville or sent a telegram or a letter to Leslie or Marsh or the police; and no unidentified funeral wreath arrived to pique the press, Newby, or the Queens.

Only Leslie, Marsh, a trapped Miss Smith, the three ex-wives, Chief Newby, and the Queens remained while Duncan's assistants carried the bronze casket into the mausoleum, set it precisely on the catafalque, arranged the many wreaths and floral baskets artistically, and emerged to lock the door and hand the key to Chief Newby. Who turned it over to Marsh, as the attorney of record, for safekeeping until the estate should be settled.

There was no conversation on the tramp back through

the fields to the house. Glancing over his shoulder, Ellery saw the stained glass in the little building glow in the sunlight, and he hoped that Johnny Benedict was comforted, although—his unorthodox views being what they were—he doubted it.

The fleet of taxis and private cars had all driven off; only two state policemen were left guarding the road; in spite of the sun and the breeze, there was a clammy feel to the air, and not only the women shivered.

Waiting for them inside was young Lew Chalanski, an assistant prosecutor of Wright County, the son of a popular former prosecutor, Judson Chalanski. Young Chalanski conferred with Chief Newby aside, smiled his father's famous vote-getting smile, and left.

Newby's poet's face was preoccupied.

"I understand everyone here except Alice Tierney, who's local, lives in New York City. You're all free to go home."

"Meaning you haven't got a damned thing on us," Marcia Kemp said, tossing her red head like a flamenco dancer. "Or you'd never let us out of your state."

"Correction. What it means, Miss Kemp," the chief said, "is that we haven't enough evidence against any individual to bring before a grand jury at the present time. But I want to emphasize: this is an open case, under active investigation, and you three ladies are the hot suspects. Do any of you have plans to leave New York State in the immediate future?" They said they did not. "That's fine. If the situation should change, however, get in touch first with Inspector Queen at his office in Centre Street. The Inspector's agreed to act as liaison man for us up here."

"How cosy," Audrey Weston sniffed.

"We cops stick together—sometimes," Newby said. "Well, ladies and gentlemen, that's it for now. This house, as the scene of a homicide, is going to be under seal, so I'd appreciate it if you left as soon as possible."

On the plane out of Boston the Inspector said, "Why so close-mouthed, Ellery?"

"I can't decide whether to admire the cleverness or marvel at the stupidity."

"Of whom? What are you talking about?"

"Of whoever left those three things in Johnny's bedroom along with his body. Each one points to a different ex-Mrs. Benedict."

"We've been all through that. It's a cinch somebody planted them."

"It certainly looks that way."

"The thing is, though—what would the point be of framing three different women for the murder? And aside from that. A frameup has to make sense on the face of it—it has to look legitimate if it's to fool the cops. What investigating officer in his right mind would believe that three women visited that bedroom, presumably at different times, and each one dropped an article of her clothing on the scene, presumably in her excitement or by accident, and so implicated herself? Anyone who'd expect a 'frameup' like that to work would have to be AWOL from the cuckoo house."

Ellery stared out the window at the flooring of cloud they were gliding over, and he nodded. "It's much likelier we're dealing with Miss Smarty Pants. Who lifted something belonging to the other two and deliberately left all the articles—her own included—on the scene in order to spread the inevitable suspicion and so, so to speak, distribute her guilt. She knew that she and the other two ex-wives were the natural —in fact, the only viable—suspects. Since all three had identical motive, opportunity, and access to the weapon—in effect, making herself one-third of a suspect instead of a standout individual."

"Unless it was a conspiracy," Inspector Queen mused. "The three of them, recognizing they were all in the same boat, ganging up on Benedict."

"That's the one situation in which they wouldn't have left clues to themselves at all," Ellery retorted. "No, it was just one of them."

"But you aren't satisfied."

"Well, no," Ellery said, "I'm not."

"What's bugging you?"

"The whole thing."

The plane hummed along.

"And another thing," the Inspector said. "Why did I let you con me into promising Newby I'd follow through on this Laura woman? God knows I carry a heavy enough case load as it is! And suppose we find her—so what? I can't see how she could possibly be implicated."

"Unless Johnny told her something."

"Like what? Spell it out for an old illiterate."

"You also weren't cut out to be a comedian! She has to be found, dad, you know that, long shot or not. It shouldn't be too hard. He must certainly have been seen with her in public. Marsh can tell you Johnny's favorite haunts."

"Newby also asked me to check out the three exes," his father grumbled.

"*Noblesse oblige.* Some day Anse may be able to help you out on a tough Manhattan homicide."

"And you're the lousy comic's son," the Inspector said tartly; after which they flew in silence.

But not all the way. Because ten minutes out of Kennedy Ellery suddenly said, as if they had never stopped talking, "Of course, this is all on the assumption that Johnny was slugged by Marcia, or Audrey, or Alice. Suppose he wasn't."

"You suppose," his father retorted. "My supposer is all tired out. Who else could it have been?"

"Al Marsh."

The Inspector swerved in his seat. "Why in hell should Marsh have knocked Benedict off?"

"I don't know."

"He's independently wealthy, or if he's in financial trouble he certainly didn't stand to gain anything under Benedict's wills. He was also Benedict's personal attorney, confidant, closest friend—what earthly reason would Marsh have to splash Benedict's brains all over the place?"

"I told you, I don't know. But we do know he had the same opportunity and access to the weapon that the three women had. So all he lacks is motive to be as suspect as they are. If you're going to lend Newby a hand, dad, I suggest you dig into Marsh and see if you can come up with a possible motive. My offhand guess would be women."

"Laura?" the Inspector said instantly.

Ellery looked out the window.

"I love the way you assign the work," his father said, sinking back. "Any other little thing?"

"Yes." Ellery's nose wrinkled. "And this one makes me feel like a heel."

"No kidding. Let me in on it."

"Leslie Carpenter. It's a thousand-to-one shot, but . . . check out her alibi for last Saturday night."

And so, with the jet touching down on a runway in the Borough of—by coincidence—Queens, their vacation came to an end and one of Ellery's queerest cases began.

2.
The
Second
Life

WRIGHTSVILLE, April 9 (API)—
The nationwide search for "Laura
Doe" has turned up 48 Laura Does
who claim to be the mysteriously
missing fiancèe of the late John Levering Benedict III, millionaire playboy murdered on the night of March
28-29 on his hideaway estate in New
England.

Anselm Newby, chief of police of
Wrightsville, ——————————,
where the crime took place, believes
that there has been a misunderstand-
ing on the part of the public. "Doe is
a name given by the law to people
whose last names are not known,"
Chief Newby said in a statement is-
sued today. "We do not know the
missing Laura's family name. It is almost certainly not Doe. That would
have to be a miracle."

Excerpt from Transcript, N.Y.P.D.:

Sergeant Thomas Velie: Your name is?
Claimant: Laura-Lou Loverly.
Sgt. V.: Beg pardon?
Cl.: It used to be Podolsky. But it's Loverly now.
Sgt. V.: Address?
Cl.: It's that big apartment house on West 73rd and Amsterdam. I can never remember the number.
Sgt. V.: New York City.
Cl.: Where else?
Sgt. V.: Your letter claims you're the Laura that John Levering Benedict the Three promised to marry. Tell me the circumstances, Miss Podolsky.
Cl.: Loverly. Notice how close it is to Levering?
Sgt. V.: How long you been calling yourself Loverly?
Cl.: Since way before, don't worry.
Sgt. V.: Since way before when?
Cl.: Before I met this john.
Sgt. V.: Okay. The circumstances of your meeting.
Cl.: Well, this particular evening he was up in my apartment, see?
Sgt. V.: Doing what?
Cl.: What do johns usually do in a girl's apartment?
Sgt. V.: You tell me, lady.
Cl.: I don't believe I care for your tone of voice, Officer. You can't talk to me like I'm some ten-dollar trick.
Sgt. V.: How did he happen to be in your apartment?
Cl.: A girl can have relationships with people, can't she? Johnny phoned me. For like an appointment.
Sgt. V.: Did he identify himself as John Levering Benedict Three?
Cl.: Are you kidding? Who listens to names in my set?
Sgt. V.: Where did he get your phone number?
Cl.: We had mutual friends.
Sgt. V.: Like for instance.
Cl.: Oh, no. You ain't got—haven't some pigeon here. I don't drag my friends into fuzzyland.
Sgt. V.: All right. Describe this Johnny.
Cl.: Dressed?
Sgt. V.: I'm not interested in his wardrobe. I mean color of eyes, hair, height, weight, build, scars, birthmarks, and etcetera.
Cl.: To tell the truth, it's kind of hazy. With all the menfriends I got. I mean, but it was the same john, believe you me. I recognized him right off from the news photos. Look, Sarge, he was sloshed to the eyebrows that night. So he wants to know—like they do—how I got into the life. You know. So I give him the usual sob story and, so help me, he starts crying on my bozoom. "You poor, poor kid," he says, "what a

lousy bitch of a break. You deserve better. Every girl does. So you know what, Laura-Lou? I'm going to marry you." Just like that, so help me. Of course, I didn't take him serious, you understand. Not until I read—

Sgt. V.: Date.

Cl.: What?

Sgt. V.: What date did this proposal of marriage happen on?

Cl.: I jotted it down in my little book somewhere. Here. See? March 22nd.

Sgt. V.: No, I can't touch it. Refer to it if you have to. Was that March 22nd of this year, Miss Podolsky—I mean, Loverly?

Cl.: Sure this year.

Sgt. V.: Thank you. Don't call us, we'll call you.

Cl.: You giving me the brush? Just like that? What are you, a fuzz wisenheimer?

Sgt. V.: One more lying peep out of you, sister, and I'll book you for wasting a city employe's time. On March twenty-two Mr. Benedict was in London, England. That way out.

Vincentine Astor? She don't work here no more. Just didn't show one night, and not even a postal card since. That's the way most of these broads are, you can't depend on them worth a damn. The best ones are the marrieds who are supporting some bum and a couple kids, they can't afford to walk out on the management. Why she quit? How do I know why? Who knows why they do anything? Maybe she didn't like the color of the hatcheck room. No, I don't remember him. Not from his photo, anyways. Sure I've seen other pictures of him in the papers, TV, you don't have to get sore. I know they say he came into my club a few times, I'm not saying he didn't. I'm only saying I don't remember seeing him. Kickbacks to the what? Oh, the mob. What are you talking about? I don't know what you're talking about. Oh, you mean Vincentine might have been kicking back some of her pay to some hoods or something and fell behind and got in dutch? Look, I run a clean club here, Officer, I don't know nothing about no mob. What? When didn't she show up? You mean when did Vincentine rat on me? Wait a minute while I look it up. Yeah, here. She quit me it was Sunday, March twenty-ninth. Yeah, yeah, her home address. Here. Say, Officer, you wouldn't happen to know of a stacked broad wants a job? Reliable? You know?

No, Miss Astor moved out the end of the month, let's see now, yeah, as of the thirty-first it was. Yes, sir, paid up right to the day she left. No, these are furnished, so she didn't have to call a mover or anything, just packed her bags and called a cab. No, I don't know a thing about her private life. I don't stick my nose in my roomers' keyholes like some land-

ladies around here I could mention. As long as they're quiet,
I always say. And don't give my house a bad name. What
man? Oh. No, sir, can't say I ever did. I mean, I never saw
him in this house. Though his picture does look sort of familiar, you might say. Say, isn't this the playboy who—? Well, I
never. I'll be. No, she didn't leave no forwarding address; I
asked her for one but she said it's not necessary, I won't be
getting any mail. Was that girl mixed up with *him?*

Excerpt Interview, N.Y.P.D.:

Detective Piggott: Name, Madam?
Claimant: Miss.
Det. P.: Miss what?
Cl.: Laura De Puyster Van Der Kuyper.
Det. P.: Hold it. Are they like one word, or—?
Cl.: De—Puyster—Van—Der—Kuyper. P-u-y. K-u-y.
Det. P.: Yes, ma'am. Address?
Cl.: Definitely not.
Det. P.: Pardon?
Cl.: I do not have to tell you my place of residence. I never
give that information to anyone. A girl never knows.
Det. P.: Miss Kuyper—
Cl.: Miss Van Der Kuyper
Det. P.: Miss Van Der Kuyper. I have to put your address
down on this report. It's regulations.
Cl.: Not my regulations. You claim you're a police officer—
Det. P.: What else would I be? Sitting here at this table in
police headquarters asking you questions?
Cl.: I've heard of that kind of smooth talk before. It's the way
they get into your apartment and attack you.
Det. P.: If you were attacked, Miss Van Der Kuyper, that's
a different department.
Cl.: I'm not going to tell you about it. Or anyone. You'd like
me to, wouldn't you? Splash me all over the filthy news-
papers.
Det. P.: Age?
Cl.: You may put down I am over twenty-one.
Det. P. (begins to speak, changes his mind, writes, "Over 50"):
Look, Miss Van Der Kuyper, we have this confidential com-
munication from you claiming you know or rather knew John
L. Benedict Third and you are the Laura he allegedly proposed
marriage to. Is that correct?
Cl.: That is precisely correct.
Det. P.: Now. How long were you acquainted with this John
L. Benedict Third?
Cl.: For ages and eons. Veritably.
Det. P.: Could you be like more exact, Miss Van Der Kuyper?
Cl.: Exact about what?
Det. P.: About the time you made his acquaintance.

Cl.: Is there time in Paradise? Our marriage plans were murmured in Heaven. I am not ashamed to proclaim our affection to the universe. We met in a secret Persian garden.

Det. P.: Where, where?

Cl.: It is so crystal in my memory. That soft, immoral—immortal evening. The moon great as with child. The drunken scent of frangipani sweet in our quivering nostrils, and of divine cinnamon, and anise, and thyme.

Det. P.: Yes, ma'am. This secret garden was in Persia, you say? Just where in Persia?

Cl.: Persia?

Det. P.: I should think that does it, Miss Van Der Kuyper. Fine, fine, it's okay. You'll hear from us in due course. No, ma'am, that's our job. If you'll kindly follow the matron. . . .

Trip sheets for when did you say? Tuesday, March thirty-first. Wait a minute. Hey, Schlockie, I got to talk to you; look Officer, if you'll give me a few seconds. We got nothing but kooks roll out of this shop.

Oh, say, you still checking the air pollution in here? I'm sorry, Officer, you can't take this life if you don't make a funny once in a while, excuse me. These hackies are going to be my death, to listen to them they got beefs not even the Mayor heard of. Yeah, certainly. Tuesday, March three-one. Here it is, Joseph Levine. You want his license number? Picked up the fare at that address as of ten thirty-four A.M., discharged passenger at Grand Central. No, Joe won't be pulling in till four forty-five, five this afternoon. Think nothing of it. Always glad to do the P.D. a favor. Yeah.

> Finally, there's the story out of Washington, where rumors grow thicker than cherry blossoms at Japanese festival time, that a subcommittee of Congress may launch an investigation into the search for the mysterious Laura in the John Benedict murder case, on the alleged ground that there is no Laura and never has been, that it's all been some sort of press agent's plot to promote something or other, a movie or a new TV series or something, as such constituting a fraud on the public innocence, and therefore being the legitimate concern of the nation's lawmakers, who clearly have nothing more important to do. Good night, Chuck.

My dear fellow, I knew Johnny-B as well as any man alive—even though Al Marsh didn't have the elemental good manners to invite me to the obsequies—and I swear to you on my honor, and you may print this, that when Johnny wrote that clause in his will about some "Laura" or other and how he was going to marry her, he was simply pulling the leg of the whole mother-frugging world. He told me in absolute confidence that he was through with the marriage bit. It was just after his final decree from that country R.N. from—what's it called? Titusville? Dwightsville? something rare and wonderful like that. "Muzzie," Johnny said to me, "just between you, me, and the nearest pub I've had it. Up to here. No more wedding marches for Johnny-B. From now on I'm strictly tone-deaf, fancy-free, and staying away from aisles." His exact words. And you may quote me. No, not Mussie. Muzzie, with a double z.

> The jet set continues in a busy-buzzy-tiz over the Johnny Benedict tragedy. There has been hardly any other topic of conversation among the B.P. for weeks and weeks, or at least it seems weeks and weeks. Everyone wants to know who Laura is—Laura, now known among Johnny-B's cronies as "the last woman in his life." Compounding the mystery is the fact that no one can recall anyone named Laura in or out of Johnny's circle. . . . This column can now reveal that Jackie and Ari. . . .

Yeah, I'm Levine. Joseph W. What fare? Now, how the hell do you expect me to remember some dame I picked up God knows how far back? I know, I know, I can read the date on the trip sheet. Okay, so she was a big platinum-type broad with a built. You got any idea how many dames like that a New York hackie picks up in a day? Look, Mac, I'd like to help you out but I just ain't with it on a hooha like this. I hack I figure three out of every ten fares to some terminal, and what I do at Grand Central is I dump them at the bottom of the ramp, pick up another fare, and away I go. If they start telling me the story of their lives and why they're leaving New York and where they're going I blow my ears out like a whale or something and I let it go right on through—I should worry why they're leaving and where they're off to? Sorry, Officer, I'm such a drip-dry on this. Let me tell you in confidence, though, I don't think there's *enough* police brutality. Some of the creeps I run into in my line of work you couldn't beat their brains out with a stainless-steel jack handle, they ain't got any. Thanks? For what? Did I tell you something?

Look, Sidney, we're supposed to be keeping our mouths shut about the Benedict case—orders straight from Inspector Queen. I know I owe you. Okay, but for chrissake protect your source. We just put out a flyer on this Vincentine Astor. No, we haven't got a thing on her. Except what's likely a coincidence that she quit her job at the Boy-Girl Club March twenty-ninth. No, I'm telling you, Vincentine isn't wanted except for routine questioning. We have no hard evidence that Benedict ever knew her except to check his hat with. Yeah, we know he visited the Boy-Girl Club a number of times within the past few months. If Vincentine was the hat-check girl Benedict was giving the rush to lately, he sure changed his M.O., because he must have met her strictly on the q.t. away from his regular hangouts. The general feeling around here is that the reason she quit at the club and left town two days later had not a damn thing to do with Benedict. I'll give you a little bonus, Sidney, and then I got to go. The word is that the brass upstairs are sore as hell at Inspector Queen for getting New York mixed up in this Benedict brawl, I mean to the extent of carrying the ball for this jerk-town police chief. As if we haven't got enough headaches around here. Who? No, I haven't seen Ellery for days. I guess he heard the rumor, too, and doesn't want to get his old man in worse dutch than he is already.

MEMORANDUM

TO: Inspector Richard Queen, N.Y.P.D.
FROM: Anselm Newby, Chief, Wrightsville

I wish I could report progress of some sort. I can't. The only fingerprints we found in Benedict's bedroom were his, Morris Hunker's, and Annie Findlay's, and Morris's and Annie's had perfectly good reasons to be there. The stains on Benedict's robe and pajamas and in the room generally are all of the same blood-type as his. The iron of the weapon is a rough welding job and would normally take poor prints, our tech man says, but he has reason to believe that it was also wiped clean with something just in case. He was not able to bring out so much as a partial latent. We have not been able to come up with a lead to any suspicious person or persons in the vicinity of the Benedict property on the night of the murder. The detailed p.m. reports no additions to the prelim report. Death was definitely caused by the blows to the head, and there was no sign of toxic or other foreign substances in the internal organs except traces of alcohol accounted for by the drinks Benedict is reported to have drunk during the evening before he went to bed. And that's about it. I hope you're having better luck at your end.

Anselm Newby,
Chief of Police

P.S.: Have you had any success tracing Laura? What does Ellery say? I haven't heard a word from him since you both left Wrightsville.

A.N.

Enc.: Photocopies of fingerprint, bloodstain analysis, and autopsy reports.

MEMORANDUM

TO: Chief A. Newby, Wrightsville
FROM: R. Queen, Inspector, N.Y.P.D.

I am sorry to report that the Laura investigation is at a standstill.

We will keep at it, but of course you understand that we carry a very heavy load of our own these days which of course has to take priority over courtesy cases such as our current assistance with the Wrightsville murder.

Ellery has said very little to me about the case. My feeling is he is as hung up on it as the rest of us.

R. Queen,
Inspector, N.Y.P.D.

MEMORANDUM

TO: Inspector Richard Queen, N.Y.P.D.
FROM: Anselm Newby, Chief of Police, Wrightsville,——

I understand your position about the Benedict case, and I am sorry that your vacation in Wrightsville got you and your son involved in it. In all fairness that was none of my doing, and if my recollection is correct the original suggestion that the N.Y.P.D. help us out on the case came from Ellery.

If your case load is too heavy to enable you to assist a fellow police officer in the investigation of a prominent Manhattan multimillionaire international playboy, let me know by return mail and I will personally write to your immediate superior and take you and the N.Y.P.D. off the hook.

In the above case I should appreciate your sending me all reports you have accumulated thus far, the originals if possible, photocopies if not, especially reports concerning Audrey Weston, Marcia Kemp, and Al Marsh.

I am very grateful for your assistance.

A. Newby,
Chief, Wrightsville P.D.

TO: Chief Anselm Newby, Wrightsville Police Department
FROM: R. Queen, Inspector, N.Y.P.D.

I did not intend anything in my last note to give you the impression that I was trying to go back on my promise. I was merely pointing out that we could not afford to put as much time, effort, and man-hours into an out-of-city (and state) case as if the homicide was within the N.Y.P.D.'s direct jurisdiction.

I have shown your memorandum to my superiors and they have agreed to allow me and my staff to continue assisting you in the Benedict investigation, especially since—as I pointed out in a conference just concluded with certain high officers of the Department—ramifications of the case lead directly into New York City and two of the three prime suspects are residents of Manhattan.

As a routine matter we have checked out Leslie Carpenter's whereabouts on the night of Saturday-Sunday, March 28–29. She has an airtight alibi for the general time-period of the crime. She was in Washington, D.C., from late afternoon of Friday, March 27, to the evening of Sunday, March 29, attending a two-day Urban Corps conference. Every hour of Miss Carpenter's time during those two days is accounted for.

There is nothing further to report on Audrey Weston and Marcia Kemp. Both are keeping pretty much to their Manhattan apartments. If they have seen an attorney about the will situation we do not have any information. I assume there is similarly nothing from your end on Alice Tierney.

I will soon be sending you a background report on Al Marsh, per your request. Best personal regards.

Richard Queen,
Inspector, N.Y.P.D.

"On Marsh?" Ellery said, reaching across the Inspector's desk.

Inspector Queen ignored the hand. "You can look at it later. There's nothing in it you don't know about him except you never mentioned that Al isn't his real name."

"I never mentioned it because, if you were a friend of Al's in our Harvard days, you were quickly conditioned not to. I suppose the report notes that he was christened Aubrey, as in C. Aubrey Smith, rest his stiff-upper soul. Anyone who called Al Aubrey like as not wound up with a shiner or a bloody nose."

"According to one source," the Inspector said, " 'Aubrey' was an inspiration of his mama's. I can't say I blame him. It's a hell of a tag for a grown man to have to tote around."

"Al once told me that when he was in grammar and prep school—private, of course, about which he was suprisingly bitter—he had to lick every kid in his grade before he made the 'Al' stick. 'Al' doesn't stand for Albert, or Alfred, or Aloysius, by the way—for just Al, period."

"His fancy ancestors must be swinging in their graves."

"By the time he got to Harvard he was too big to tackle even in fun. He was a varsity back and he won the Ivy League wrestling title in his weight class. I doubt if anybody in the Yard knew his name was Aubrey except his most intimate pals, and we had more sense than to bring it up. But I never did learn much about his family background. Al didn't talk about it."

The Inspector scanned the report. "His father came from a line of international bankers and high society. His mother, it says here, was a Rushington, whatever that is. Marsh Senior was killed in the crash of his private plane just after Al was born."

"That might explain something," Ellery said. "He used to talk about his mother all the time. Never about his father."

"Mrs. Marsh never remarried, even though she was a young woman when her husband died. She devoted the rest of her active life to Aubrey, and when she became an invalid he returned the service—looked after her like a nurse. The feeling among his friends is that that's why he never got married. And by the time his mother kicked off he was a confirmed bachelor."

"His mother left everything to him, of course."

"What else?"

"How much?"

"Loads. Marsh isn't as rich as Benedict was, but after the first few millions is there any difference?"

"Then Al is rock-solid financially."

"Like the Chase National Bank."

"No trouble? Gambling, bad investments, anything like that?"

"No. He's pretty much a conservative where money is concerned. He doesn't gamble at all."

"So there's no motive."

"Not a whimper. He doesn't gain from any of Benedict's wills, he wouldn't need it if he did, and every source we've tapped indicates that he's a topflight attorney with a reputation for absolute personal honesty as well as professional competence."

But Ellery persisited. "That kind of conclusion depends on the reliability of the source. Have you been able to investigate his handling of Johnny's affairs?"

"Yes, and as far as we can tell it's all legal and aboveboard. Granted we couldn't be sure without a plant inside, what could Marsh hope to accomplish by diddling with Benedict's funds? It could only be for a financial reason, and we're absolutely positive Marsh has no money worries whatsoever. Anyway, most of Benedict's capital is under the management of Brown, Brown, Mattawan, Brown, and Loring, that old-line law firm, and not under Marsh's at all."

"How about women?"

"How about them?"

"I mean a possible romantic rivalry."

"Nothing. What we've dug out indicates that Marsh has never been involved with any number on Benedict's hit parade except, on occasion, in his legal capacity, when Benedict wanted to pay some girl off or make some sort of settlement on her to close the book when he'd got tired of her."

"And the ex-wives?"

Inspector Queen shook his head. "Nothing there, either. Marsh got to know them through Benedict, except the Kemp girl, and his contacts with them were strictly as Benedict's friend and, in the course of time, as Benedict's attorney. Anyway, Marsh's preference in women is the opposite of Benedict's. Marsh goes for small, feminine-type females."

Ellery grinned. "Al once showed me a photo of his mother. She was a small, feminine-type female."

His father frowned. "Will you clear out of my office and let me do some of my own work?" The Inspector had an old-fashioned sense of propriety, and cracks about possibly unhealthy mother-son relationships did not amuse him. As Ellery was opening the door the old man asked, "Where you off to now?"

"I thought of something I want to ask Al about Johnny. I'll tell you about it later."

Mr. Marsh, Miss Smith said, was tied up with a client and could not under any circumstances be disturbed. Anyway, Mr. Marsh never saw anyone except by appointment. Unless, her hostile glance suggested, it was the kind of snoop business that experience had taught her to associate with the presence of one Ellery Queen? Miss Smith's tone and demeanor were such that, had she been barefoot, love-beaded, and unkempt, she would have spat the word "pig" at him, with an appropriate modifying obscenity; as it was, being a lady and the product of a no doubt Victorian mother, she could only resort to the subtleties of eye- and vocal cord-play to express her loathing.

Mr. Queen, ever the gentleman in the presence of a lady, scribbled a few words and asked with utter *politesse* that Miss Smith in her secretarial capacity convey the note to Mr. Marsh, client notwithstanding.

Miss Smith: I can't do that.

Mr. Queen: You astonish me, Miss Smith. It may be that you will not do that, or that you may not do that, but that you cannot do it—since you seem normally ambulatory and otherwise in unimpaired possession of your physical faculties —I do not for an instant believe.

Miss Smith: How you do go on. You think you're smart. You're the kind who makes fun of people.

Mr. Queen: I'm emphatically nothing of the sort. I simply feel it my duty to the cause of semantic hygiene never to allow a grammatical slovenliness to go uncleansed.

Miss Smith: You must have a real dandy time all by yourself listening to the radio and TV commercials pollute the English language.

Mr. Queen: Miss Smith, how marvelous! You have a sense of humor! Now will you take that note in to Al, like I asked you?

Miss Smith: You made a booboo! You said 'like' instead of 'as'!

Mr. Queen: Alas, so I did. Demonstrating the fallibility of even the purest purist. The note, Miss Smith?

Miss Smith: You made that mistake purposely. You're pulling my leg.

Mr. Queen: No, but is it permitted? I might add that I have admired your limbs, Miss Smith, from the moment I laid eyes on them. Ah, you're smiling. We advance. The note?

Al Marsh came out for a moment, glancing at Miss Smith in a puzzled way.

"Miss Smith seems all of a flutter, Ellery. Charm, or an emergency?"

"Hardly the first, and no to the second. It's just that I wanted to ask you something about Johnny. It won't take a minute—"

"I don't have a minute. The old gent in my office takes a dim enough view of me as it is. His point is that keeping a man of his age waiting—he's ninety—constitutes a felonious act. How about meeting me at my place? Sevenish? Dinner, if you've no other plans. Louis used to cook at Le Pavillon. Miss Smith will give you my address if you don't know it."

It proved to be a duplex penthouse high over Sutton Place. Above the dismal city—in spite of calendars, not quite out of winter, not fully into spring—Ellery found himself luxuriating. A houseman named Estéban ushered him into a man's huge habitat of feudal oak, Spanish iron, velvets, brass, copper; a place of lofty ceilings, hunter's trophies, and weapons. While he waited for Marsh to appear Ellery strolled about taking his peculiar inventory, totting up the stock that declared the man.

There was not a trace of modernism about the apartment, such of it as he could see; it might have come out of an exclusive men's club of the Nineties. The small private gymnasium off the living room (the door was open) displayed weights, barbells, exercycles, parallel bars, a punching bag setup, and other paraphernalia of the aging ex-athlete; that was to be expected of Marlboro Man. But there were surprises.

Half a short wall was taken up with stereophonic equipment for the high fidelity reproduction of a large collection of LPs and cassettes. There was a great deal of Tchaikovsky and Beethoven, he noted, struck by the romanticism he had not associated with Marsh. The hi-fi was playing "Prince Gremin's Air" from *Eugen Onegin*; Ellery recognized the Russian-singing basso as Chaliapin, whose great masculine voice he often sought for his own reassurance.

A leaded-glass bookstack enchanted him. It contained rare American, French, and British editions of Melville, Rimbaud, Verlaine, Henry James, Proust, Wilde, Walt Whitman, Gide, and Christopher Marlowe, among many others—rank on rank of literary giants, many in first editions the sight of which made Ellery's wallet itch. There were rare art books of enormous size illustrated with the paintings and sculptures chiefly of da Vinci and Michelangelo. A row of niches in the oak walls held busts of historical figures whom Marsh evidently admired—Socrates, Plato, Alexander, Julius Caesar, Virgil, Horace, Catullus, Frederick the Great, Lord Kitchener, Lawrence of Arabia, and Wilhelm von Humboldt.

"I see you're casing my treasury," Marsh said, turning off the stereo. "Sorry to keep you waiting, but that old fellow has had me hopping all afternoon. Drink?" He had changed to a lounge suit with an open silk shirt; he wore huaraches.

"Anything but bourbon."

"You don't go for our native elixir?"

"I once got myself beastly drunk on it. Why do I malign the beasts? Humanly. I haven't been able to sniff it since."

Marsh went behind his taproom-sized bar and began with energy to make like a bartender. "You? Got drunk?"

"You make it sound like a capital crime. I'd just been extinguished by the then light of my life."

"*You?* Had an affair with a girl?"

"It certainly wasn't with a man. What do you take me for, Al?"

"Well, I don't know. Here's your gin on the rocks. That's as far from bourbon and branch as you can get." Marsh sank into a chair that dwarfed him, nuzzling a concoction of un-guessable ingredients. "I've never thought of you as really human, Ellery. I must say I'm relieved."

"Thank you," Ellery said. "I envy you those first editions. I'm beginning to grasp the full advantages of wealth."

"Amen," Marsh said. "But you didn't drop into my office this afternoon, or here tonight, to admire my etchings. What's on your mind?"

"Do you recall that Saturday night in Wrightsville, Al?"

"It's written in acid."

"As you know, I was eavesdropping from the terrace while Johnny was delivering that spiel about his new-will intentions."

"Yes?"

"Something I overheard him say that night has been bother-ing me. I'm not clear about what he meant. He remarked that his three marriages had been 'strictly business.' Just what did he mean by that?"

Marsh settled back with his glass and a menthol cigaret. "By the terms of his father's will, contrary to popular belief, the Benedict fortune was left in trust and all Johnny received was three hundred thousand dollars per annum out of the income from the estate. Well, I don't have to tell you that to a lad of Johnny's tastes, upbringing, and habits three hundred thousand a year didn't begin to provide for his standard of living."

"He broke his father's will?"

"Unbreakable. But not unshakable." Marsh shrugged. "Johnny asked me what, if anything, could be done to raise the ante. I studied Benedict Senior's will and found what looked like a possible loophole. More in jest than anything else I pointed it out to Johnny—a looseness of expression in one of the provisions that might yield an interpretation Mr. Benedict had never intended."

"Sounds fascinating. What was it?"

"One clause in the will gave Johnny the sum of five million dollars out of the principal estate quote 'when my son John marries' unquote."

Ellery laughed.

"Of course you'd see it. Johnny certainly did. 'When my son John marries' could reasonably be construed to mean 'whenever my son John marries'— in other words, every time he married he was entitled to collect another five million from the estate. I actually wasn't serious when I called the wording of the clause to Johnny's attention, and I didn't dream he would rearrange his life to revolve around it. But that's just what he did. He insisted on going into court with out argu-ment about construing the 'when' as 'whenever,' and it was typical Johnny-B luck that the court upheld our interpretation. So then he launched his series of marriages, divorces, and re-marriages."

Ellery was shaking his head. " 'Strictly business' is right. His marriages were keys to the strongbox. Another key, another haul."

"Exactly. There was no misrepresentation to the women. They understood just why he was marrying them and just what they could expect to get out of it. I might add, Ellery, that I was completely against Johnny's change of heart about those million-dollar settlements." Marsh's big hand tightened about his glass. "I suppose it's silly of me to admit this, but the fact is I had a considerable row with Johnny about that intention of his to change from the million to the hundred-thousand-dollar settlements. I told him it would be an act of bad faith, a cop-out, really, certainly unethical, and I wanted no part in it. In the end we left it unresolved—I mean my participation in it."

"When did this row take place?"

"On the jet coming back from England, when he first broached his plan."

"You sounded pretty much on Johnny's side that night, Al. Are you sure you aren't trying to snow me?"

"I'm not snowing you. Johnny made it clear to me that last weekend in Wrightsville that, friends or no friends, if I didn't do it for him he'd get some other lawyer to. It forced me to do some weighing and balancing. I'd known Johnny since we were teenagers—hell, I loved the guy. And I could hardly defend the ethical conduct of three girls who'd walked into a cold-blooded money deal under the guise of romance with their eyes wide open. In the end I picked Johnny, as of course he knew I would. Although I confess I've had qualms since."

Ellery sipped his gin. Marsh rose to freshen his drink, whatever it was.

"All right," Ellery said at last. "I suppose it's easy to make value judgments in a vacuum. About this Laura everybody's looking for, Al. You really have no notion who she might be?"

"No. I've begun to think—along with a great many others, I understand—that Laura existed only in Johnny's fertile mind. Although what motive he could have had for writing an imaginary beneficiary into a will is beyond me."

"She exists, Al. One other thing. What was the state of Johnny's financial health around the time of his death?"

"He was ailing again. You know, Johnny was the world's softest touch. He was a lifelong victim of his guilt for having come into so much money. He especially couldn't turn down a friend. One of his last exploits—which is typical—was to build a catsup factory in Maryland somewhere to produce a new kind of goo for an old pal, so-called, whose wife came up with the recipe one night—you won't believe this—in a dream. Johnny tasted it, pronounced it divine, and before he —and it—were through he sank eight hundred thousand in it, an almost total loss. Do you want a few hundred cases? We couldn't sell any, and the last I heard Johnny was giving it away, with few takers."

"I meant, Al, was he due for another five-million-dollar marriage deal? Could that have been his reason for intending to make this Laura number four?"

"Well, according to his own words he was going to re-marry," Marsh said dryly, "and he certainly could use the five million. Draw your own conclusion."

"Then you believe that all that talk of his about the Laura romance being the real thing at last was a lot of self-deluding nonsense?"

Marsh shrugged again. "I wish I knew. It's conceivable that he may have thought he was in love for the first time in his life—for all his knocking about Johnny in some ways was still an adolescent. Yes, Estéban?"

"Louis say you and guest come now," Estéban said in considerable agitation. "Louis say you and guest no come now, he quit."

"My God." Marsh jumped to his feet, looking stricken. "Ellery, *vite, vite!*"

Louis's dinner warranted Marsh's haste. It opened with an Icre Negre caviar from Romania and a Stolichnaya vodka; the soup was a *petite marmite*, served with an 1868 Malmsey Madeira. Then Estéban brought a heavenly *quenelles* with *sauce Nantua* accompanied by an estate-bottled Montrachet, Marquis de Laguiche 1966; for the *pièce* Louis had prepared a delectable *noisettes de veau sautées*, each serving crowned with a blackish, toothsome *cèpe* which could only have come from a French boletus bed (the small round veal steaks, Ellery learned, had been flown in from Paris; the proper cut, according to the word as transmitted from Louis, was un-obtainable in the United States and, even assuming it could be procured locally somewhere, Louis turned his culinary thumb down in advance. "He has nothing but contempt for the chefs in *les Etats-Unis*," Marsh explained, "who substitute loin or kidney veal chops for the *noisettes véritables* and call them the real thing. In fact, Louis has nothing but contempt for practically everything not French." "Forgive him, Al," Ellery pleaded, "for at least at the range your paragon of *les pots et pans* knoweth precisely what he doeth"); with the *noisettes* came, in magnificent simplicity, garnished new potatoes, a Château Haut Brion of the 1949 vintage, and a braised Romaine salad; followed by a delicate *fromage de Brie* (air-mailed by Fauchon) and a Château Cheval Blanc St. Emilion 1949; a Dobos Torta which decided Ellery to make Bucharest his next continental port of call; a champagne sherbet; and finally an espresso with a thirty-year-old private-stock Monnet cognac.

"This has been one of Louis's lighter dinners, whipped up more or less on the spur," Marsh said slyly. "Nevertheless, *agréable au goût, non?*"

Ellery whispered, *"Vive la France!"*

"It's a question of professional pride, I guess," Chief Newby grumbled, leaning back in his swivel chair and tonguing a fresh cigar. "Have one?"

"I'm not smoking this week," Ellery said. "What is?"

"I've never had a homicide this important. I'd hate to flub it."

"I know what you mean."

"You don't know what I mean, Ellery. You've got too blame good a statistical record. But I'm a back-country cop who all of a sudden gets hit with a big-time case, and it's got me uptight, like the kids say. You know, I've been thinking."

"You have company, Anse. What exactly about in your case?"

"We've been going on the assumption that the motive for Benedict's killing ties in to the will situation and the three ex-wives."

"Yes?"

"Maybe no."

"Anse," Ellery said severely, "I don't appreciate anyone's cryptic remarks except my own."

"I mean, suppose the motive had nothing to do with Benedict's wills?"

"All right. For instance?"

"I don't know."

"Thank you, Chief Newby. You have now joined a very select group."

"No kid, there could be something."

"Of course, but what?"

"You haven't struck anything in New York?"

"We haven't struck anything anywhere. Dad's people have failed to turn up anything or anyone in Johnny's life that provides a possible reason for someone to break into his

Wrightsville house and kill him. And by the way, Anse, did your tech men find any trace—any at all—of a B. and E.?"

"No. It was either an inside job, like we've been figuring, or an outsider who got in and out without leaving a trace. Go on, Ellery."

"Go on where? I've just completed my statement. Nobody. Not even a theory about anyone. For a while we fumbled around with a Vegas contract theory, possibly tied in somehow to Marcia Kemp—those boys hit on contract with no respect for caste or class, true democracy in action. Although the whole trend in their set these days is away from violence. But we drew a blank. No evidence that Johnny-B ever welshed on a betting loss, in Vegas or anywhere else for that matter, according to—believe me, Anse—highly reliable sources. We've turned up no involvement with the Corporation, or the Combine, or whatever the Mafia's calling itself this month. Anyway, the pro touch is missing in this murder. Contract killers come equipped with their own working tools; they certainly don't depend on picking up a Three Monkeys on the scene to beat their victim's brains out."

"Then it could have been an amateur job for a personal reason, like somebody had a grudge against him for something."

"I told you, Anse. Nothing like that has turned up."

"That doesn't mean it couldn't be."

Ellery shrugged. "I have long had a convenient murderer for cases that stall. I call him, as I pull him out of my hat, The Man From Missing Forks, Iowa. Sure it could be, Anse. Anything *could* be. But you know and I know that most homicides are committed not out of the blue for obscure or bizarre reasons by the pop-up gent from Missing Forks, but by someone connected directly or obliquely to the victim for a reason that, to the killer at least, seems perfectly sensible, if not inevitable. The problem is to put your finger on him and/or it. So far we've been surveying the terrain for all the possibles, with no luck. What you do is, you keep plugging away with the hope that sooner or later, preferably sooner, your luck is going to change."

"So it still may come down to those three women and the will," Newby grunted, emerging from his cloud.

"You don't sound satisfied."

"With that theory? It's too—now don't laugh, Ellery!—too damned easy."

"Who's laughing?"

"You sure you didn't run up here on something you're keeping back from me?"

"Anse," Ellery said, and rose. "May I have the key now?"

"Then why do you want to go back to Benedict's place?"

"You're not the only one with uneasy feelings. The key, Anse?"

"If you don't mind," the chief said, rising also, "I think I'll keep you company."

Newby drove Ellery over to the Benedict property in his 1967 unmarked Dodge (to avoid notice, he claimed); he unlocked the front door and waved Ellery in before him, following on the visitor's heels. Ellery galloped upstairs and into Johnny-B's bedroom as if he expected to be greeted there by a miracle, or the answer, which his whole air announced would have been the same thing.

"You act like you forgot something, Ellery," the Wrightsville police chief said. "What?"

"I wish I could tell you." He was looking about the room as if he had never laid eyes on it.

"You mean you won't tell me?" Newby cried.

"I mean I don't know."

"Damn it, stop answering me in riddles!" the exasperated man said. "You remind me of that Sam Lloyd puzzle book my mama used to keep in her parlor."

"I'm not being coy, Anse. I really don't know. It's simply a feeling, like yours, that the three women and the will as an answer is too easy."

"But what kind of a feeling is it?"

"I've had it before," Ellery said slowly, touring the room. "Often on a case, in fact." He avoided the chalked outline of Benedict's body on the floor. "A feeling that I've missed something."

"Missed something?" Newby swung about suddenly as if he had heard a door creak open. "What?"

"That," Ellery intoned, "is the question. What? I've keelhauled my brain, couldn't come up with it, and decided that a return to the scene might be what the doctor ordered." He paused at the bed. "Here?" Glanced at the nightstand. "There?" Into the clothes closet. "There?" At the windows. Into the bathroom.

"You're putting me on," Newby muttered. "By God, you've got me creepier than a kid in a haunted house!"

"I wish it were that ordinary," Ellery said with a sigh. "No, Anse, it's not a put-on, it's a hangup. There's something here, something I saw—something I'm seeing, damn it all!—and for the life of me I can't latch onto it." He addressed the chalk outline on the floor. "Well, it was a long shot, Johnny, and like most long shots it didn't come in." He nodded disgustedly at Newby. "I'm through here, Anse, if you are."

The first break in the case came, as breaks usually do, out of the drudgery of plodding police work.

The concentration of effort on the part of Inspector Queen's staff had been on the three ex-wives, notwithstanding Chief Newby's failure of enthusiasm. Several interesting reports on the women noted that, with the cutoff on Benedict's death of their $1000 weekly incomes, and with their cash settlements held up if not gone forever by the holograph will, two of them at least were in financial difficulties. Audrey Weston and Marcia Kemp had been living up to their alimony incomes. (Alice Tierney, Newby reported, had on the contrary been living frugally in frugal Wrightsville and had saved a considerable sum, although the settlement outlook had turned her sullen and uncommunicative.) In fact, both the blonde and the redhead had been compelled to go back to work, if any. The Weston girl was making the rounds off-Broadway, so far without success; the ex-Vegas chorine was hawking the Manhattan nightclubs through her agent for a "starring" turn somewhere. But no one was snapping up the Kemp girl, either. Apparently times had changed. The notoriety they had been enjoying as a result of the Wrightsville murder was no longer the kind of open-sesame that used to break down golden doors in the days of the New York *Mirror*.

The discovery about Marcia Kemp turned up during the routine investigation of her present and past, and the development appeared significant.

Ellery learned about it on Sunday, April 19. On arising that morning he had found himself alone in the Queen apartment, and a note from his father saying that the Inspector had had to go down to Centre Street and suggesting that Ellery follow. Which he did so precipitously that he did not even stop for his cherished Sunday breakfast of Nova Scotia salmon, sweet butter and cream cheese, *cum* generous slice of sweet Spanish onion, all on toasted bagel and accompanied by freshly brewed coffee in copious quantity.

He found Sergeant Velie with the Inspector.

"Tell him, Velie," the Inspector said.

"I think we got something, Maestro," the very large sergeant said. "Ever hear of Bernie Faulks?"

"No."

"He's a punk in the rackets, a small wheel the pigeons call the Fox, or Foxy, because he's got a genius for beating the rap. He's been collared I don't know how many times on charges that didn't stick—armed robbery, B. and E., A.D.W., burglary, you name it; his one big rap, a charge of murder during an attempted felony—armed holdup—he beat when he was acquitted through the failure of a key witness to come through for the D.A. This *shtunk* Faulks is a miracle man. He's never served a day behind bars."

"What's the point, Velie?" Ellery asked. "I passed up my lox and bagel for this."

"The point is," Sergeant Velie said, "we been digging into Marcia Kemp like we had advance information, which we didn't, and by God we struck oil. You know what, Maestro?"

"Stop milking it, Velie," the Inspector said; he looked tired.

"No," Ellery said, "what?"

"The Kemp babe and Foxy Faulks—they're married."

"I see," Ellery said, and he sat down in the cracked black leather armchair he had forbidden his father to throw out. "Since when?"

"I'm way ahead of you," his father said. "I'd like nothing better than to be able to hold her on a charge of bigamy, but the fact is she didn't marry Faulks till after the divorce from Benedict."

"How accurate is your information, Velie?"

"We got a copy of the marriage license."

"Well," Ellery pulled his nose, by which the Inspector knew he was cerebrating furiously. "That does put a new light on Miss Kemp. And raises all sort of interesting questions about Mr. Faulks. When can the happy couple be interrogated?"

"I wanted them here today," the Inspector said, "but Foxy is out of town. He'll be back late tonight, you sure, Velie?"

"That's what my source says," the sergeant said, adding less grandly, "My prize pidge."

"Well, I want Mr. and Mrs. Foxy Faulks here in my office at nine on the nose tomorrow morning."

At nine-five Monday morning Ellery strolled into his father's office to find the Inspector, Sergeant Velie (looking vindicated), Marsh (in his capacity of executor for the Benedict estate), an edgy Marcia Kemp (in a purple minidress and mod hat that emphasized her Amazonian proportions), and a man Ellery naturally took to be Bernie the Fox Faulks. Faulks was younger than Ellery had expected him to be, or he had the knack of looking younger; his was the sort of baby face that maintains its bloom into the fifties, then sags into old age overnight. He was undeniably handsome; Ellery thought it quite reasonable that a girl of Marcia's background and outlook should have fallen for him. The petty hood reminded him of a young Rock Hudson—tall, lean, and on the boyish-faced side. He was just the least bit overdressed.

"You know everybody here but Faulks," Inspector Queen said. "Foxy, this is my son Ellery. In case you're interested."

"Oh, yes, it's a great pleasure, I'm sure, Mr. Queen." Foxy

clearly decided not to offer his hand for fear of a rebuff. He had a dark, intimate voice suitable for a sex movie. For the next few minutes he kept sneaking glances at the civilian Queen.

"We were just discussing Miss Kemp's marriage to Mr. Faulks," the Inspector said, settling back in his aged swivel chair. "You notice, Ellery, I use her maiden name. She prefers it that way. Don't you, Mrs. Faulks—I mean, Miss Kemp?"

"It's usual in show business," the redhead said. The flush on her face seemed too deep for street makeup. "But I still don't get . . . Bern, why don't you say something?"

"Yeah, sweetie." Her husband shifted his feet; he had refused a chair, as if to be better prepared for flight. "Yeah, Inspector. We don't understand—"

"Why I asked you two down here?" The Inspector showed his dentures like the Big Bad Wolf. "For one thing, Mrs. Faulks, how come you didn't tell Chief Newby when he was questioning you up in Wrightsville that you were married again? You'd have saved us the trouble of digging the information out for ourselves."

"I didn't think it had anything to do with . . . well, Johnny and all," the big showgirl burbled.

"No? Mr. Marsh," the Inspector said, turning his smile on the attorney, "has Mrs. Faulks—as Marcia Kemp—been receiving a thousand dollars a week from Mr. Benedict since their divorce, and if so has she been cashing or depositing the checks, according to your records?"

"She certainly has." Marsh raised his attaché case. "I have every canceled voucher that went through Miss Kemp's bank right here—each made out to 'Marcia Kemp' and endorsed 'Marcia Kemp' in her verifiable handwriting."

"These canceled vouchers cover the whole period since the date of her undisclosed marriage to Faulks?"

"Yes. Up to and including the week of Johnny's death."

"Did she ever notify Benedict, or you as Benedict's lawyer, that she was remarrying or had remarried and that therefore under the terms of her agreement with Benedict the thousand-dollar weekly checks should stop, since she was no longer legally entitled to them?"

"She did not."

"How about that, Mrs. Faulks? That constitutes fraudulent acceptance in my book. I think the District Attorney's office is going to see it the same way, if Mr. Marsh decides to press charges on behalf of the Benedict estate."

"If I may put in a word?" Faulks said elegantly, and as if he were a mere bystander. Marcia sent him a long, green, dangerous look. "I never saw that agreement, so of course I had no way of knowing that Marcia's accepting the grand per week was illegal—"

Marcia made the very lightest choking noise.

"—but you got to understand, Inspector, my wife doesn't know about such things, she can't hope to cope—hope to cope! I'm a poet and don't know it!—with a bigshot mouthpiece, I mean lawyer, like Mr. Marsh; she's got no head for the smart stuff at all, she'd probably forgotten all about that clause, like you do when Mr. Right comes along—hey, baby?" He fondled her neck, smiling down. She nodded, and his hand found itself fondling the atmosphere.

"You've got an understanding husband, Mrs. Faulks," the Inspector said approvingly. "But I think it would be easier on you if you talked for yourself. You'll notice there's no stenographer present, none of this is being taped, and you haven't been charged formally with any crime. Our main interest is the Benedict murder; and while I'm not making promises, if it turns out this marriage of yours had nothing to do with the homicide you'll probably be able to work something out about that money. What's your feeling, Mr. Marsh?"

"Of course I can't promise anything, either. I certainly can't commit the estate to overlooking Mrs. Faulks's having collected money from my late client under circumstances that look dangerously like fraud. But it's true, Inspector, that my chief concern is the murder, too. Cooperation on Mrs. Faulks's part will naturally influence my attitude."

"Look, bud, who's bulling who?" Marcia demanded bitterly. "What are you going to do, Al, take it out of me in blood a pint at a time? I'm dead busted and I haven't got a job. My husband's broke, too. So I couldn't pay that money back if I wanted to. Sure, you can haul me up on criminal charges, Inspector, and the way things have been going for me you know what? I wouldn't give a hairy hoot in hell if you did. It's also a rap your D.A. might find it tough to make stick in court. Bern here knows some real sharpie lawyers."

"Speaking of Bern here," Ellery said from the wall he was supporting at the rear of the office, "where did you happen to be, Bern, on the night of Saturday–Sunday, March twenty-eight–twenty-nine?"

"It's a funny thing you should ask that," Marcia's husband said in his sexy voice. "It so happens I can answer that quick like a bunny, which ain't—isn't such an easy shmear, as I don't have to tell you gentlemen. On the night of Saturday–Sunday, March twenty-eight–twenty-nine, it so happens I was one of six fellas picked up in a raid on a little private game we were engaging in in a hotel room off Times Square. I

don't know what those meathead cops were thinking of, making a big deal out of a friendly poker session, just passing the
time, you understand, like the boys do on Saturday night,
have a few beers, a couple pastrami sandwiches—"

"I'm not interested in the menu," Inspector Queen snarled;
he was glaring at Sergeant Velie, who was attempting the
difficult feat of making himself look like a dwarf for having
failed to check out the Fox's alibi beforehand. "What precinct
did you wind up in?"

"I don't know the number. It's the one in the West
Forties."

"You don't know the number. Faulks, you know the numbers of the Manhattan precincts better than I do—you've
spent half your life in them! Velie, what are you waiting
for?" Sergeant Velie nodded hastily and jumped out of the
office. "Sergeant Velie's gone to do a little checking. You
don't mind waiting?"

Dad, dad, Ellery said in his head, as an ironist you're still
pounding a beat. It was a lost cause, he saw, and saw that
the Inspector saw it, too. Mr. Faulks was breathing without
strain, as confident of the outcome of the sergeant's telephone
call as a roulette dealer presiding over a fixed wheel. True,
there was a trace of anxiety on his wife's face; Faulks even
patted her hand, which was larger than his; but this could be
accounted for by a certain lack of communication between
the recently marrieds. Once, when Marcia said something to
him in a low voice, he made a fist and tapped her affectionately on the chin.

When the sergeant returned to whisper into the Inspector's
ear, Ellery detected the twitch in his father's mustache and
saw his fears confirmed: the mustache twitch was an unfailing
sign of inspectorial disappointment.

"Okay, Foxy, you can take off with the missus." Their
speedy crossing to the Inspector's door was a thing of antelope
grace. "Oh, just one thing," the Inspector said to the ante-
lopes. "I don't want either of you even going over to Brook-
lyn without checking with my office first."

"He was picked up that night as he claims?" Ellery asked
when the pair fled.

"Well, yes," Sergeant Velie said, trying to pass the episode
off as immaterial. "There'd been a lot of heat from upstairs
about Times Square gambling when that Congressman who's
always kicking up a storm sounded off for the TV—seems one
of his campaign contributors got rooked in a crooked crap
game and yelled for mamma—so the word came while you
were on vacation, Inspector, to crack down, which the Gambling Squad did. That's how come Foxy got caught in that

hotel. A stool gave the tip-off, but by the time the Squad got there the lookout had flashed the signal and the boys broke in to find Foxy and his lodge brothers playing a hot game of penny ante. The lookout must have been their bagman, too, because the detectives didn't find any big bills on the players or the premises. Anyway, the six were held for a couple hours at the station house and let go. That included Foxy Faulks. He was at the precinct between midnight about and two A.M. He couldn't have gone to Wrightsville by three-o-three without a spaceship."

"So there goes our break," Inspector Queen said glumly. "Another blasted nothing. Just the same, Velie, assign two men to keep their eyes on Faulks especially. I don't like the smell of him—he's dangerous. Ellery, where you going?"

"For a walk," Ellery said. "I'll get more action in the street than I'm getting here."

"Who conned who into this, and whose friend got popped?" his father groused. "Go take your walk, and if you're mugged in some alley don't come crying to me!"

"You sure about this, Barl?" Newby asked, tapping the report with a skeptical forefinger.

"You know old Hunker," Officer Barlowe said. "I do believe he's been sneaking out there, Chief. Keeping an eye on the place. You hire Morris, you've bought yourself Old Faithful. If he says he seen lights in the house late at night, I buy it."

"Anything missing?"

"Not that I could tell."

"Then why would anyone pussyfoot around in there in the middle of the night?"

Officer Barlowe, who was new to the Wrightsville force, decided that this was a rhetorical question and consequently kept his mouth shut.

"I'd better take a run out there myself," Newby decided. "Meantime, Barl, you keep an eye peeled on that place, and pass the word along."

The next day the chief wrote to Inspector Queen: "Morris Hunker reported seeing lights on in the Benedict main house Monday night, April 20, past midnight. The old man claims he investigated—he would!—but by the time he got into the house the lights had been turned off and he could not find anyone there. I then went over the premises personally and found no evidence that anything had been taken or even disturbed. Whoever it was either being extra-careful or old Hunker imagined the whole thing; he is not as quick-minded

as he used to be. I thought, though, I had better let you and
Ellery know about this."

"She wants to see me," Al Marsh said over the telephone.
"Naturally, I'm not going to see her alone. Can you be present, Inspector Queen?"

"Hold on a minute," the Inspector said. "Ellery, Audrey
Weston has called Marsh for an oppointment. Says she has
something important to tell him concerning the Benedict
estate. Do you want to sit in?"

"Tallulah Revisited?" Ellery exclaimed. "I certainly do."

"Ellery will come, too," the Inspector said into his phone.
"You figuring on anyone else, Mr. Marsh?"

"Leslie Carpenter. If it concerns the estate it concerns her."

"When's this for?"

"Wednesday at two thirty, my office."

"Tomorrow?"

"Yes."

"We'll be there." The Inspector hung up. "I wonder what
the blonde's got up her sleeve."

"I'm glad somebody has something up something," Ellery
said. "It's been a most unsatisfactory case."

Marsh's office was off Park Row, in an old set of buildings
that reeked of musty estates and quill pens.

On his original visit, Ellery had nearly expected to see old
gentlemen in Prince Alberts stalking along the corridors, and
bewhiskered clerks in leather cuff protectors, and green eye-
shades toiling away on high stools in Marsh's office. Instead,
he had found sharp-looking young mods in a stainless-steel
interior, the latest indirect lighting, and a strictly functional
office. Miss Smith, of course, was for all seasons.

"They're in Mr. Marsh's office waiting for you, Mr. Queen,"
she said, sniffing twice in the course of the sentence.

Mr. Queen's only reference to Manhattan's constipated traffic
was by indirection. "How did they get here on time," he
asked, "by B-52?", and allowed himself to be ushered into
Al Marsh's private office. Miss Smith immediately sat down in
a corner of the room, crossed her formidable legs, and opened
a notebook.

Ellery found one stranger in the assemblage, a man in his
forties with eyes like steak knives and a complexion resem-
bling barbecued beef, in the general getup of an habitué
of the Playboy Club. This man glanced accusingly at his
wristwatch as Ellery entered, by which Ellery knew that he
was present in the interests of Audrey Weston, at whose taut
side he stood.

"I believe the only one you don't know is this gentleman,

Ellery," Marsh said. "Ellery Queen, Sanford Effing, representing Miss Weston."

Ellery was about to offer his hand when Audrey's attorney said, *staccato,* "Can we get down to it?"

Marsh waved Ellery to a chair and reseated himself, to light one of his menthol cigarets. "All right, Mr. Effing. You do that."

Ellery began to pay the strictest attention after a smile at little Leslie Carpenter and a nod to his father.

"From what Miss Weston's told me about John Benedict's will," the lawyer said, "there's a rather queer phrasing of a key clause. I'd like you to quote me the exact language, Mr. Marsh, of the clause that refers to this Laura."

Marsh opened the top drawer of his steel desk and withdrew a Xerox copy of the Benedict holograph will. He handed it to Effing.

"Your recollection was correct, Miss Weston," Effing said with satisfaction. "Benedict left his residuary estate quote 'to Laura and any children' unquote. Mr. Marsh, the phrase 'and any children'—what exactly do you take that to mean?"

"Any children by Laura," Marsh said.

"Ah, but it doesn't say that, does it?"

"What do you mean?" Marsh said, startled.

"I mean it doesn't say that, period. If Benedict had meant 'any children by Laura' it's our perfectly reasonable contention that he would have written 'any children by Laura.'"

"But that's nonsense," Marsh protested. "What other children could Johnny have been referring to but children presumably resulting from his contemplated marriage to this Laura?"

"To any children," and Effing bared his large and shiny teeth, "that Benedict may have fathered by any mother whatsoever."

"We know of no such children," Marsh said firmly, but beginning to look doubtful.

"You're going to find out about one of them, Mr. Marsh, in three seconds. Miss Weston, tell these people what you told me."

"I have a child," the blond girl said, speaking for the first time. The stagey voice quivered a little. "Johnny's child." She had been sitting with hands clasped and head lowered, but at this statement she made fists and looked up defiantly, her colorless eyes taking on a gray sparkle, like jellyfish suddenly touched by the sun. "And you don't have to look at me, Al, as if I were a monster from outer space! It's the truth."

"Your unsupported statement to that effect means less than

nothing to me as a lawyer, as Effing will tell you," Marsh said sharply. "For a claim as important as this, the surrogate is going to demand indisputable proof. And even if you can prove your allegation, in view of the rest of that paragraph in the will I'm not at all sure your interpretation would stand up in court. As far as my considerable knowledge goes—speaking not only as John Benedict's attorney but as his close friend as well—he never so much as hinted to me that he was the father of a child by you."

"He didn't know about it," Audrey said. "He died not knowing. Besides, Davy was born after the divorce."

"Johnny didn't notice you were pregnant?"

"We separated before it showed."

"You never notified him you were carrying his child?"

"Davy was conceived the last time Johnny and I were intimate," Audrey said. "Right after that we separated and he divorced me. I had my pride, Al, and—okay—I wanted revenge, too. I was goddam mad at the way he treated me, tossing me out of his life like I was—like I was a pair of old shoes! I wanted to be able to tell him later in his life—when he wasn't a cocky stud any more—tell him that all these years he'd had a son he didn't know a thing about . . . *and wasn't going to.*"

"Indeed, Mr. Congreve, Heav'n has no rage, and so forth," Ellery muttered; but nobody heard him.

"Now, of course," Effing said smoothly, "with the father dead, the situation is quite different. Why should the son of the father be denied his birthright, and all that jazz? I don't have to go through the routine, Marsh. You know how surrogates feel about the rights of infants. Regular old mammy-tigers, they are. I'd say Miss Carpenter's got something to worry about."

Ellery glanced at Leslie, but aside from a certain pallor she seemed serene.

"Tell us more about this child," Inspector Queen said abruptly. "What's his full name? When and where was he born? Do you have custody of him? If not, where and with whom is he living? That's for openers."

"Hold it, Miss Weston," Effing said, making like a traffic cop. "I don't think I'm going to let my client answer those questions right now, Inspector. I'll merely state for the record that the boy is known as Davy Wilkinson, Wilkinson being my client's legal maiden name, Arlene Wilkinson—she took 'Audrey Weston' as her stage name—"

"Johnny didn't know that, either," Marsh said. "How come, Audrey?"

"He never asked me." Her hands were back in her lap and her blond head was lowered again.

Marsh pursed his lips.

"Miss Weston felt she couldn't adequately bring up her child and at the same time pursue a theatrical career, too," Effing went on. "So she gave the baby out for adoption immediately—in fact, the arrangements were settled before the birth—but she knows where Davy is and she can produce him on reasonable notice when necessary. The people who adopted him are certainly as interested in securing his legal rights and insuring his future as the natural mother is."

"The fact that she can produce the child," Marsh said, "is a far cry from proving Benedict was its father."

"Then you're going to fight this?" Effing asked with an unpleasant smile.

"Fight? You have a peculiar idea of an attorney's responsibilities. I have an estate to protect. Anyway, in the long run it's the surrogate you're going to have to satisfy. So worry about impressing him, Effing, not me. I'll have my secretary send you a transcript of this meeting."

"Don't bother." Sanford Effing unbuttoned the three buttons of his sharp suit coat. A little black box hung there. "I've recorded the entire conversation."

When Audrey and her lawyer were gone, Marsh relaxed. "Don't worry about this, Leslie. I don't see how they can prove the boy is Johnny's especially now that she's admitted before witnesses that she never told Johnny about this Davy. That's why I was careful to pinpoint that part of her testimony. The will is perfectly clear about Johnny's intentions: if he was not married to Laura at the time of his death, his estate was to go to you, Leslie, period. Unless this Laura comes forward with proof of a marriage to Johnny, which seems very unlikely now, it's my opinion you're in the clear."

"That's one of the difficulties a mere layman runs into," Leslie said, "dealing with lawyers."

"What is?"

"Trying to get a meeting of minds that isn't all fouled up in quidnuncs and quiddities, or whatever your jabberwocky is. I'm not the least bit interested in the law of this, Al. If I'm convinced the Weston woman had a child by Johnny, as far as I'm concerned that's it. In my lawbook the boy would be entitled to his father's estate, not me. It's true I've been making plans for the money—a certain project in East Harlem I had my heart specially set on—but I'm not going to break down and boohoo about it. I've been churchmouse poor and largely disappointed all my life, so I can put all this down to a dream and go back to washing out my nylons and hanging them up to dry on the shower rail. Nice seeing you again, Inspector, Mr. Queen. And Miss Smith. Just let me know how it all comes out, Al."

And with a smile Leslie left.

"Now there is a gal," Inspector Queen said "—if I were, say, thirty years younger—"

"Almost too good to be true," Ellery fretted. When his father said, "What did you say, son?", he shook his head, said, "Nothing of importance," and began to fumble with his pipe and the tobacco discovery he had just made by mail in a Vermont country store. Everybody knew there was no particular harm in smoking a mild pipe tobacco if you didn't inhale. He got the briar fired up and drew a deep lungful of the aromatic smoke.

"That's all, Miss Smith, thank you," Marsh was saying; and Miss Smith stalked past the Queens to the office door. Ellery thought he detected a certain twitch of her hip as she passed him. "You know, there's an irony in this development. Benedict Senior's will, as I told you, contained an ambiguity that allowed Johnny to draw another five million every time he contracted a new marriage. Now Johnny's will—I wish people would take lawyers' advice about not trying to write their own wills!—also contains an ambiguity *he* didn't intend . . . I wonder about this Davy."

"We can be all-fired certain Audrey Weston has a kid farmed out somewhere," the Inspector said in the quaint slang of his youth. "She'd have to be an idiot to try to pull a stunt like this based on nothing but hot air. And Effing doesn't strike me as the kind of lawyer to take on a tough case that could drag along in the courts for years without something good and solid behind it. If Effing's in on it, there's a child, all right. But that the child was Benedict's, that Audrey never told him about it . . . ." The old man shook his head. "I don't know how this claim ties in, Mr. Marsh, if it ties in at all, but one thing's for sure: we have to start with the fact. How do you plan to establish that the boy is or isn't Benedict's son?"

"I don't have to establish either," Marsh said. "Proving the child is Johnny's is Effing's problem."

"Effing," Ellery repeated with distaste. He unfolded from the chair. "*Un type,* definitely. What—or who—next? Coming, dad?"

In these days of universal holdups, muggings, assaults, rapes, homicides, and other public indecencies it is a seldom-noticed fact of urban life that there is one class of citizen for whom late-night strolls in little-frequented places of the city hold no terrors; to the contrary, he positively looks forward to his midnight meander in the park.

And who is this hero, this paragon of courage? Some holder of the black belt? A just-returned Congressional Medal of Honor winner, schooled to the wiliest tricks of Charlie? Alas, no. He is the robber, mugger, assailant, rapist, or man-slaughterer himself, who, like the vampire bat hanging in its cave, finds warmth and security where simpler creatures feel a shivering fear.

Which explains why, in an early hour of Friday, April 24—"estimated as on or about 2:00 A.M.," was the way a detective noted it later in his report—Bernie Faulks walked into Central Park (East) by the Fifth Avenue entrance immediately south of the Museum of Art, and made his way with confidence to a certain clump of bushes behind the building, where he settled himself in the tallest one and at once merged with the shrubbery and the night.

If Marcia Kemp's husband felt any fears, they were certainly not of the dark or of nightmarish things like switchblades at his throat; that side of the street had been thoroughly explored territory to him since his boyhood.

Still, there was tension in the way he stood and waited.

The moon was well down in the overcast sky; there was little light in the shadow of the museum; the air insinuated a sneaky chill.

Faulks wore no topcoat. He began to shiver.

And wait.

He shivered and waited for what seemed to him an hour. It was really ten minutes later that he saw something take shape on the lamplit walk he was watching. It held its form for a moment, then glided into the shadow of the museum and headed his way. Faulks stood quite still now.

"You there?" its voice whispered.

The tension left him at once. "You bring the bread?"

"Yes. Where are you? It's so dark—"

Faulks stepped unhesitatingly out of his bush. "Give it to me."

He extended his hand.

There are soundless shrieks in the darkness of such moments, a dread implosion of more than mortal swiftness, that inform and alarm. Faulks experienced these even as the newcomer did indeed give it to him—a bulbous envelope, and immediately something else. For the Fox made as if to turn and run.

But he was too late, the knife had already sunk into his belly, blade up.

Faulks groaned, his knees collapsed.

The knifer held the weapon steady as the dying man fell. The weight of his body helped it slice down on the blade.

With the other hand Faulks's assailant took back the envelope.

The knife landed almost carelessly on the body.

The murderer of Marcia's husband stripped off rubber gloves, thrust gloves and envelope deeply away, then fled in a stroll northward toward an exit different from the place of entry . . . to a hurrisome eye just another foolhardy New Yorker defying the statistics of Central Park's nighttime crime.

"Ellery? I'm over here."

Ellery went through the police line, blinking in the spotlights, to where his father was talking to a uniformed man. The man saluted and left to join the group of technicians, scooter men, and other officers around the body.

"That was the Park patrolman who found the body," the Inspector said. "You took your time getting here."

"I'm not exactly full of zap at four o'clock in the morning. Anything?"

"Not yet." And the Inspector went into a song and dance —a song of profanity and a dance of rage—and it was as if he had been saving it all up for his son's arrival, preferring the thickness of blood to the thin edge of bureaucratic protocol. "Somebody's going to catch it for this! I gave orders Bernie Faulks was to be staked out around the clock!"

"How did he get away from his tail, and when?"

"Who knows when if we don't know how? Probably over the roofs of next-door apartment buildings. Velie had men posted back and front. Roof—nobody. I'll have his hide!"

"Aren't you the one who's always beefing about the manpower shortage in your department?" Ellery said. "Velie's too old a hand to slip up on a routine thing like that unless he simply had no one to assign to the roof."

The Inspector confided in his mustache. So all right. That was the case. Helping that cow-pasture chief out. And at half-rations personnelwise. The truth was—he almost said it in audible accusation—it was all Ellery's fault. For dragging him up to Wrightsville in the first place.

"What?" the Inspector said.

"I said," Ellery repeated, "that this could be a coincidence."

"How's that again?"

"Faulks was one of the bad guys from puberty. Who knows what enemies he's made? I'm betting you'll find them crawling back under every second rock. My point is, dad, his murder tonight could have nothing to do with the Benedict case."

"That's right."

"But you don't buy it."

"That's right," the Inspector said again. "Any more than you."

There was a flurry of sorts just beyond the lighted area. The bulk of Sergeant Velie emerged suddenly into the glare with his right hand decorously anchored on Marcia Kemp Fauks's left elbow. She made the sergeant look like a normal-sized man.

The Inspector hurried over, followed at a 4 A.M. pace by Ellery.

"Has Sergeant Velie told you what's happened, Mrs. Faulks?"

"Just that Bern is dead." She was inner-directed rather than shattered by grief, Ellery thought; or she was in shock. He did not think she was in shock. She had got into wide-bottomed slacks and a nautical shirt and thrown a short leather coat over her shoulders. She had not stopped to make up. There were traces of cream on her cheeks and a towel was wrapped turban-fashion about her head. She was trying not to look over toward the group of officers. "How did it happen, Inspector Queen?"

"He was knifed."

"Knifed." The redhead blinked. "Murdered? . . . Murdered."

"It could be hara-kiri," the Inspector said flatly. "If he was Japanese, that is. Yes, Mrs. Faulks, murdered, with a switchblade his killer had the nerve to drop on the body, it's so common and untraceable. And you can bet without fingerprints. Are you up to identifying your husband?"

"Yes." It was almost as if Marcia had said, Of course, what a silly question.

They walked over to the group—detectives from Homicide, Manhattan North, the Park precinct—the officers stepped back, and the widow looked down at her late spouse without hesitation or fear or anguish or revulsion or anything else visibly human, so far as Ellery and his father could determine. Perhaps it was because she was emotionally disciplined, or the victim was not gruesome. The doctor from the Medical Examiner's office, who was off to one side packing up, had covered everything but the head, and he had closed the eyes and mouth after the photographer took his pictures.

"That's Bern, that's my husband," Marcia said, and did not turn immediately away, which was odd, because they almost always did—one look and let me out—but not Marcia Kemp, apparently she was made of crushed rock; she looked down at him for a full thirty seconds more, almost with curiosity, then turned abruptly and finally away. "Do I go now, Inspector Queen?"

"Are you up to answering a couple of questions, Mrs. Faulks?" he asked, very kindly.

"Not really. I'm pooped, if you don't mind."

"Just a couple."

She shrugged.

"When did you see your husband last?"

"We had dinner around seven thirty, eight o'clock. At home. I wasn't feeling well, so I went right to bed—"

"Oh? Didn't have to call a doctor?"

"It isn't that kind of unwell, Inspector. I get clobbered once a month."

"So you didn't see him again?"

"That's right. I dropped off to sleep. I'd taken a pill."

"Did you happen to hear him leave your apartment?"

"No."

"So you have no idea what time he left?"

"No. Please, Inspector. That's more than a couple, and I've got cramps."

"Just a couple more, and you're through. Did Bern say anything to you last night about having to meet somebody, or having to go out, anything like that?"

"No."

"Was he in trouble of some kind?"

"I don't know. Bern was pretty uptight about his affairs."

"Even with you?"

"Especially with me. He says to me—he used to say to me —the less you know the less you'll worry."

Ellery said, "Who wanted to kill him, Marcia?"

She had forgotten he was there, or perhaps she had not known. It was he rather than his question that startled her. "Ellery. I don't know of anybody. I really don't."

"Could it be he welshed on a gambling debt?" the Inspector suggested. "Or got in bad some other way with one or another of his playmates?"

She shook her head. "I really don't."

"Do you have any idea why he was knifed? Any at all?"

"None at all."

"Okay, Mrs. Faulks. Velie, take her home—just a minute. Doc?" He took Dr. Prouty's brisk young staff doctor aside. Ellery strolled along. "What's the verdict?"

"I set the time of death on a prelim estimate as around two A.M., give or take a half hour."

"Any reason to suspect the knifing might not have been the cause of death?"

"Didn't you see that belly of his?" the young man from

the M.E.'s office said. "Though of course we'll find out for sure on the P.M."

"Nothing else?"

"Not a thing. Anything here?"

"Not so far. If you ask me, Doc, we won't find so much as a bruised blade of grass. An operator cool enough to leave the sticker on the body for us isn't going to lose his monogrammed cigaret case on his way out."

"Okay, Inspector?" asked Sergent Velie.

The Inspector nodded, and Velie marched the big widow away. The young doctor waved and trudged off.

Ellery said, "She lied in her capped teeth."

"Your manly intuition?" his father inquired.

"I'm the son of my old man. You didn't believe her, either."

"You said it, I didn't. She knows something, Ellery."

"We're communicating again after a gap in the generations. What led you to your conclusion, Inspector Queen?"

"Marcia's not the type gal to know so little about her hubby's affairs. She worked Vegas a long time. She knows these bums, and she'd make mighty sure she kept tabs on Foxy."

"Exactly my reasoning. The only puzzle about Marcia is why she married him in the first place." Ellery looked after the departed couple. "Could love possibly go so far?"

"I wouldn't know. Or if I ever did I've forgotten."

"I'd keep her on a short leash, dad."

"Velie will. We'll know everything she does and everybody she says hello to."

"How about Audrey? Alice? Marsh?"

"They'll be checked right off." The Inspector shivered. "I'm cold and tired, son. Getting old."

"He had two hours' sleep and he's cold and tired," Ellery proclaimed to Central Park. "How decrepit can you get? Come on, grandpa, I'll take you home and tuck you into bed."

"With a toddy," his father said, hopefully.

"With a toddy."

By Friday morning the autopsy report was in from the Medical Examiner's office, and by Friday evening the little standing army of suspects had been checked off. Audrey Weston had landed a part in an off-Broadway production the previous week—it was tentatively called *A, B, C, D, E, F orGy*—and she had been home alone Thursday night, she said, hard at work studying her five sides. No confirmation. Alice Tierney, it turned out, had been in New York, not Wrightsville. She had driven down on Thursday and registered at a

midtown hotel; she was in Manhattan, she said, to see Al
Marsh on a matter connected with Johnny-B, an estate matter.
"It's a long drive and I was tuckered out," the report quoted
Miss Tierney. "So I went to bed very early." She had attempted to reach Marsh by telephone before turning in, she
stated, but had been unsuccessful. (There was a record of her
call at the hotel, and it was also confirmed by Estéban.)
Marsh had gone out Thursday evening for a big night on the
town, he said (he was in bad shape, the report said); his date
was a stunning showgirl whose career had been launched in
the centerfold of *Playboy* and who had zoomed from there
into millionaire dates; however, in the course of their rounds
she had ditched him for a certain Italian movie director who
had muscled in on Marsh at a notorious disco—the details
were in the Friday morning newspapers, featuring the director
with his ample bottom esconced in a bass drum, throwing up
from a right to the solar plexus—after which Marsh had pro-
ceeded to go solo pub-crawling. Subsequent details were
vague in his memory. Estéban had poured him into bed
about 3:30 A.M. An attempt to log his course through the
bars of after-midnight Manhattan proved spotty and unsatisfactory.

"It's just like in one of your books," Inspector Queen
grumbled. "You'd think *once* one of the suspects would have
an alibi that could be proved and eliminate her. Or him,
damn it. But no, Foxy Fauks was knifed between one thirty
and two thirty, and not one of the three can prove where
they were—"

"He was," Ellery corrected automatically.

"—so we're back where we started from. Maybe you were
right, Ellery."

"I was? About what? I can't think of anything recently."

"About Faulks's murder having nothing to do with the
Benedict case."

"Nonsense."

"You brought it up yourself!"

"One has to cover everything," Ellery said stiffly, and
he went back to pulling his nose. He was actually engaged
in his favorite exercise in futility these days, trying to solve
the mystery of the clothing thefts from Audrey Weston,
Marcia Kemp, and Alice Tierney. It all seemed like ancient
history by now, and he was beginning to feel like an in-
adequately funded archeologist; but the dig went on, secretly,
in his head, where no one else could trespass.

"You know," Ellery said to little Leslie Carpenter, "if I
hadn't met you in a case I'd ask you for a date."

"What a horrid thing to say."

"Horrid?"

"You imply that I'm a suspect in Johnny's death."

"I was only stating a principle," Ellery said, bathing sybaritically in the blue warm pools of her extraordinary eyes. "It's bad policy to enter into a personal relationship with someone you've met in the course of a continuing investigation. Muddies the thinking. Makes waves where dead calm is called for. By the way, do you consider yourself a suspect in Johnny's death?"

"Certainly not! I was talking about you."

"Let's talk about you. You know, I never thought I could go for a halfpint, speaking femalewise."

"You are *not* a groove, Ellery Queen!"

They were in Al Marsh's outer office, waiting for Audrey Weston. Marsh was trying to get rid of a client who was overstaying his appointment. Inspector Queen sat restively nearby, munching Indian nuts in lieu of lunch.

Ellery was about to launch himself splash into the pools when the client reluctantly departed. Marsh beckoned Leslie and the Queens into his private office.

"What's this one all about, Mr. Marsh?" the Inspector demanded. "Seems to me I spend more time in your office than in mine."

"It's Audrey, as I told Ellery over the phone." Marsh swung a tier of law books out and it became a bar. "Proving that the law isn't always as dry as it sometimes seems. Drink, anyone? Don't usually indulge during office hours—Miss Smith doesn't approve—but I think I'll make an exception this afternoon. I'm still not over that hairy night last Thursday, and I have a feeling I'm going to need it." He poured a long one. "I can recommend the Irish, Inspector."

"I'm working," the Inspector said bitterly.

"I'm not," Ellery said.

"Les?"

"No, thanks," Benedict's heir said with a shudder.

"I mean," Ellery went on, "there are no regulations on my job. Sorry, dad. Irish and soda, Al. Did you know that the Irish invented whiskey? The English didn't find out about it till the twelfth century, when Henry the Second's boys invaded the sod and came back with a few stolen hogsheads. Thank you, sir. To Henry the Second's boys." When he had drunk a healthful draught Ellery said, "What does Tallulah want?"

"If you mean Audrey, she didn't call this meeting, I did." Marsh lit a menthol cigaret. "I've dug out some information on this paternity claim of hers. While we're waiting—did you know that Alice Tierney's in town?"

"We know," the Inspector said, sourly this time. "Is it a fact that she's visiting New York to see you?"

"Let's see, this is Monday . . . I saw her Friday, Inspector," the lawyer said. "I didn't tell you people about it because I knew I'd be seeing you today."

"I hope you aren't going to pull one of those 'this is a lawyer-client confidence' things," Ellery said.

"Not at all. Miss Tierney has come up with what the Little Flower used to call a 'beaut.' She had the gall to claim—get this—that Johnny promised her the Wrightsville property, the buildings and the land, as a gift."

"Oh, dear," Leslie said. "She sounds desperate."

"No proof, I take it."

"You're so right, Ellery. She has no evidence of any kind to back up her story. It isn't plausible on the face of it—did she expect me to swallow it? Anyway, I told her as politely as I could to stop wasting my time and hers. Yes, Miss Smith?"

Miss Weston and Sanford Effing had arrived, the blonde nervous, Effing narrow-eyed and sniffy, searching for clues like a bloodhound. When they were seated and everyone had got over the strain of being polite, Marsh (who had restored his wall before their entrance to its lawbook look) said, "Take this all down, Miss Smith. Is your tape recorder on, Effing? Good. I've done some poking into your client's allegation that she had a child by John Levering Benedict the Third whom she placed for adoption."

"And found that her allegation is true," Audrey's lawyer said severely.

"And found that her allegation—as it legally affects the disposition of the Benedict estate—is false," Marsh said. "There was and is a child, a male child named Davy Wilkinson—I have his adoptive surname as well, but in the child's protection I am keeping it confidential—but Davy is not John Benedict's son."

"He is, he is!" Audrey cried.

"Miss Weston, may I handle this?" Effing asked in a pained way. "My client says that he is, Marsh, and she ought to know."

"She ought to, but in this case Miss Weston seems confused. I have the date of birth from the records of the hospital where Davy was born. That date is eleven months and three days *after* the date of the divorce. Manifestly we have a marital impossibility. I think, Mr. Effing, you'll have to agree that there's no point to pursuing this further. Unless Inspector Queen wishes to do so?"

"If you're implying that there's attempted fraud here, Counselor," Sanford Effing stated icily, "I not only resent the implication on Miss Weston's behalf, but on my own as an attorney. I wouldn't have taken this case if I didn't have every reason to believe my client's claim to be the substantive truth. I do think she's been unwise to insist—"

"Ah, we get down to the old bippy," Marsh said, smiling. "To insist what, Effing?"

"About the dates. Please clear up that date situation, Miss Weston, here and now. You have no choice."

Audrey went into an elaborate hand-twisting routine. "I didn't want anyone to know . . . I mean, it was like—like stripping myself naked in public. . . ."

"Come on, Miss Weston," Effing said sternly, "it's too late for modesty."

"I said we were intimate for the last time before the divorce because I was ashamed to admit that Johnny and I had sex on a number of occasions after the—after the decree." The North Sea-water eyes began to look stormy. "But that's the truth, Al, so help me Almighty God. We did. It happened mostly at my apartment, but once in his car . . . oh, it's too embarrassing! Anyway, on one of those *intime* occasions little Davy was conceived. My poor, poor. . . ." And the seas heaved and sloshed, drowning Ellery's hopes that the blonde would insert before the noun "baby" the traditional adjective "fatherless."

A general cloud of discomposure moved in to overhang the office. Even Miss Smith, whose mouth had been imitating a fish while she stenographed the proceedings, shut it and kept it shut with considerable compression.

Marsh permitted the nor'easter to blow itself out.

"Audrey. If your attorney won't tell you this I'll have to, for old times' sake if for no other reason. Even if you can show that you and Johnny engaged in sexual intercourse after your divorce, that would not in itself prove that he was the father of your child. You know that; or, if you don't, Mr. Effing certainly does.

"It's my belief that you've made up the whole story, postmarital coitus and all. I'm reasonably sure I'd have known from Johnny if you and he were sleeping together after the divorce. From some things he confided in me—which I won't divulge publicly unless you force me to—your story is highly suspect. It simply doesn't tally with his feelings about you—do I have to say it?—especially sexually."

"You have no right to make a judgment before all the facts are in!" her lawyer shouted.

"I have every right to my personal opinion, Effing. At any time. However, I see no point in denying it: that's going to be my professional opinion as well, unless you come up with legal proof of your client's claim that Mr. Benedict was the father of her child."

Audrey howled, "You haven't heard the end of this, you shyster!" She was all the way off-stage now, being Arlene Wilkinson.

Effing rushed her out.

"Bad," Ellery said. "Very bad."

"I thought it turned out very well myself," Marsh said. "Certainly for old Les here."

"I'm speaking of Audrey's performance."

"Oh, I can't help feeling sorry for the poor thing," Leslie said. "Call me a square, but she is a mother—"

"A mother," Marsh said dryly, "who's trying a con game."

"You don't know that, Al. Johnny might have—"

"Not a chance, dear heart. See here, do you want this estate or don't you? I thought you had all sorts of socially progressive plans for the money."

"I do!" And the pools blazed from their depths. "What I want to do first—"

"Excuse me, Miss Carpenter," Inspector Queen said, jumping up. "The New York City police department has all sorts of progressive plans for my services. Mr. Marsh, from now on how about you don't call me, I'll call you? Okay? Ellery, you coming?"

"You go on ahead, dad," Ellery said. "I have all sorts of socially progressive plans myself. May I see you home, Leslie? Or wherever you're bound?"

But Inspector Queen's anxiety to get the Benedict case off his back was not yet to be relieved. Nothing was going anywhere—his staff was bogged down in the Faulks investigation, weltering in leads to enemies of Marcia Kemp's late husband whose names (as predicted) proved to be legion—and the old sleuth had hopes that there it would exhaust itself, so that he could get back to earning his salary for legitimate services rendered the City of New York.

Besides, it was impossible to live with Ellery these days. He went about with a fixed, almost wild, look, something like an acid head on a bad trip, frequently making noises that conveyed little but confusion. When his father asked him what was upsetting him, he would shake his head and become mute. Once he delivered himself of an intelligible reply; or at least a reply composed of intelligible components: "It's the women's clothes, and something else. Why can't I remember that something else? How do you remember what you've forgotten? Or did I forget it? You saw it, too, dad. Why can't you remember?"

But the Inspector had stopped listening. "And why don't you take that Carpenter girl out again?" the Inspector said. "She seems like good medicine for you."

"That's one hell of a reason to take a girl out," Ellery said, glaring. "As if she were a prescription!"

There matters stood when the call came into Centre Street from Chief of Police Newby. Inspector Queen immediately dialed his home number.

"Ellery? We have to run up to Wrightsville."

"What for? What's happened?" Ellery asked, yawning. He had spent a rousing night with Leslie at a series of seminars on the subject of "Economic Solutions to the Problems of Urban Obsolescence."

"Newby just phoned from up there. He says he's solved the mystery of those lights old Hunker saw in the Benedict house."

"Yes? What's the answer? Mice in the wiring?"

The Inspector snorted. "He wouldn't say. Sounds miffed by what's going on down here. Or rather what isn't. He seems to feel that we're neglecting him. He just said if we wanted to find out what he's turned up, we know where he is."

"Doesn't sound like Anse," Ellery said; but perhaps it did. What did he know about Anselm Newby, or anyone else, for that matter? Life was but a dream, and so forth.

They got off the plane at a late evening hour of Sunday, May 3, and no Wrightsville police car awaited them.

"Didn't you notify Newby's office what plane we'd be on?" Inspector Queen demanded.

"I thought you did."

"At least Newby didn't ignore us deliberately. Cab!"

The chief was off duty; the desk man buzzed him at home, and the Inspector thought—aloud—that he took his sweet time getting to headquarters. The chief's greeting was correct, but unmistakably on the cool side.

"I haven't made up my mind yet what to do about her," Newby said. "On the one hand, I can't see the advantage in charging her—"

"Do about who?" Inspector Queen asked. "Charge who?"

"Didn't I tell you?" Newby asked calmly. "It's Alice Tierney my man Barlowe caught in the Benedict house late last night. She's the one who's been making with the midnight lights. It's a cockamamie story she tells, just wild enough to make me wonder if it mightn't be true. Frankly, I don't know whether she's gone off her rocker, or what."

"What story, Anse?" Ellery asked. "You're being damned enigmatic."

"Didn't mean to be," the chief said, Yankee-style. "Maybe you better hear it from her direct. Joe, buzz Miss Tierney's place and if she's home ask her to come down to HQ right off, the Queens want to talk to her. If she's out, try and find out where we can reach her."

"Why don't we go to her?" Ellery suggested. "It might be better tactics."

"She'll come," Newby said grimly. "After that yarn of hers, she owes me."

Alice stalked in fifteen minutes later.

"When the Queens command, little old commoner Alice obeys," she said coldly. It seemed to Ellery that she had been drinking. "It's all right, Chief, you don't have to stand up with the royalty and be polite. Not after last night."

"Miss Tierney, you were caught trespassing on private property. What did you expect Officer Barlowe to do, kiss your hand? I could have charged you with breaking and entering. I still can!"

Of the two, Newby was the more obviously agitated. (Ellery guessed why in a moment. Alice Tierney was a nice Wrightsville girl from a nice Wrightsville family. Nice Wrightsville girls from nice Wrightsville famlies were not caught prowling about other people's empty houses in the middle of the night. Like most small-town police chiefs, Newby was a defender of the middleclass faith.) Not that Alice was serene. Her normally unheated eyes had acquired a glow not far from ignition. She radiated hostility.

"Sit down, Alice," Ellery said. "No reason why we can't talk this over without fireworks. Why have you been going through Johnny's house when you thought you wouldn't be seen? What have you been looking for?"

"Didn't Chief Newby tell you?"

"We just got here. Sit down, Alice. Please?"

She sniffed, then tossed her head and took the chair he offered. "You know by this time, I suppose, that I told Al Marsh about Johnny's solemn promise to me? That he wanted me to have the Wrightsville property?"

"Marsh told us," the Inspector said.

"Did he tell you that he laughed in my face, practically?"

"Miss Tierney," the Inspector said. "Did you expect the attorney in charge of an estate to take a claim like that seriously, backed up by nothing but your unsupported word?"

"I won't argue with you, Inspector Queen. With anybody. I'm convinced there's proof!"

"What kind?"

"A note, some paper or other signed by Johnny leaving the property to me. We got along beautifully during our marriage—lots better, he told me, than he got along with Audrey and Marcia. I really don't understand why he divorced me! He'd keep telling me how much he appreciated the nursing care I gave him after his automobile accident, how —entirely aside from our original agreement—he was going to leave the Wrightsville real estate to me. I naturally expected he would do it in his will. But he didn't, so I'm convinced he must have done it in some other paper, something he tucked away in the main house somewhere. I knew nobody would believe me—I appealed to Al Marsh against my better judgment. That's why I said nothing about it at the will session, and why I've been looking for the paper by myself late at night."

For the first time her voice rose.

"*I want it.* My weekly income is stopped, I haven't inherited that lump sum from Johnny—I'm entitled to salvage *something!* He meant that property for me, it's mine, and I'm going to have it!"

In a blink it occurred to Ellery—in the way a film shifts from scene to scene—that Alice Tierney was not the starched and stable angel of mercy of his comfortable characterization. The people who held feelings in as a matter of training and even nature were the ones who had most, under stress, to let out; and Alice was not far from the bursting point.

"My men and I went all through that house," Chief Newby said wearily. "You're not going to find what we couldn't, Miss Tierney."

"How about the guest cottage?" Ellery suggested. "Any chance that Johnny left something there, Anse?"

Newby shook his head. "Barl—Barlowe—and I searched the cottage today. Nothing doing."

"And if Marsh had found anything like that in Benedict's papers," Inspector Queen remarked, "he'd have to have mentioned it."

"I suppose I ought to check with him . . . maybe you ought to do it, Inspector." Newby added, not without a gleam in his eye, "New York, y'know," as if Manhattan Island were Richard Queen's personal property.

The Inspector found Marsh at home entertaining, from the background sounds of revelry. Ellery gathered from his father's end of the conversation that Marsh was not exactly overjoyed at the interruption. The Inspector hung up scowling.

"He says no such paper exists anywhere in Benedict's effects or he'd have let us know right away. He's sore that I even questioned him about it. Awfully touchy all of a sudden."

"That doesn't sound like the Al Marsh I knew," Ellery said. "Could he have fallen in love?"

"Then some girl is lucky," Alice said bitterly. "Outside of his damned sense of professional ethics Al is a pretty wonderful guy. *He'd* never promise a girl something and then forget."

"Forget is the word, Miss Tierney," Newby said. "That's what I'm going to do. Why don't you do likewise and run along? I'm not charging you with anything, so you're in the clear." He rose. "Do you have your own car, or do you want one of my boys to run you home?"

"I'll manage, *thank* you."

When she was gone Inspector Queen remarked, "That was a big nothing."

"Well," the chief said, "I'm sorry I dragged you gentlemen up here."

"I didn't mean it that way! Look, Newby, we seem to have got off on the wrong four feet—"

"It just seemed to me you ought to talk to her yourselves, Inspector, that's all."

"You were perfectly right. If police work was a success a hundred percent of the time, what fun would it be?"

"Plenty!" Newby said; and he grinned and they shook hands all around.

It was too late to book a flight back to Boston and New York, so the Queens plodded across the Sunday-night-deserted Square (which was round) and checked into the Hollis for the night. They bought toothbrushes and toothpaste at the cigar counter, washed up, and went down to the main dining room. It was late, the restaurant held about six other people, the Chef's Special (which from experience Ellery maintained was the only dish on the menu that was ever edible) was all gone, and they had to settle for two almost snorting steaks, which the Inspector's dentures could not negotiate. They got back to their room scarcely on speaking terms.

They were just taking their shoes off in the silence when the phone rang. Ellery said, "Big deduction coming up: Newby. Who else knows where we are?" and answered it.

It was Newby.

"If you're undressed, dress. If you're still dressed, stay

that way. I'll pick you up in front of the Hollis in two and a half minutes."

"What now, Anse?"

"Tierney Rides Again. Barlowe just spotted her sneaking into the Benedict grounds. He radiophoned in."

"You know what that kook is doing?" the young officer exclaimed when they pulled up at the Benedict house; he had been waiting for them in a rhododendron bush. "She's trying to break into the whozis—that little stone house where Benedict is buried. I'd have stopped her, Chief, but you said not to do anything till you got here—"

"The *mausoleum?*" Ellery said; and they all ran, led by Barlowe with his oversized flashlight.

It was like something out of *Wuthering Heights* in the cloudy night.

She had pried the heavy mausoleum door open with a crowbar, and she was inside, in the light of a kerosene lantern, among the withered flowers, struggling with the lid of the bronze casket. It took Barlowe and Ellery to wrench her away, and Newby had to jump in to help hold her.

"Alice, please, you mustn't do anything like this," Ellery panted. "Why don't you be a good girl and calm down? We can go outside and talk this over—"

"Let—go—of me!" she screeched. "I know my rights! He promised me! The note has *got* to be in the coffin. It's the only other place it could be. . . ."

Her face was rigid, a mask of flesh, the eyes hardly human.

Officer Barlowe stripped off his blue coat and they wrapped it about her as a makeshift restraining sheet, lashing the sleeves at her back.

The four men carried her from the mausoleum on the top of the hill, across the meadow in the dappled dark, to the radio car. The chief relayed a call for an ambulance from Wrightsville General through the headquarters switchboard; and they held her down and waited.

There was little conversation. Her screams were too demanding.

May dragged by, going nowhere.

The hunt for the elusive Laura limped, hesitated, and finally came to a halt. Whoever the mysterious woman named in Johnny Benedict's will was, she had either taken refuge in a mountaintop cave or decided she wanted no truck with a murder case.

"In which event," Ellery said, "Johnny never married her, as we've maintained all along. So she gets nothing out of revealing herself except publicity, which she evidently wants none of."

"Unless . . . ," and Inspector Queen stopped.

"Unless what, dad?"

"Nothing. What thoughts I get these days are pretty wild."

"You mean unless Laura killed Johnny for a motive we have no lead to yet?"

"I told you it was wild."

"Maybe not so wild. It would explain why she hasn't turned up . . . I wish I *knew*," Ellery groaned. "Then I could get some work done." His novel-in-being felt like the cliffhanger of the old movie-serial days; it was tied helplessly to the track while his deadline came hurtling down on it like Old 77.

A, B, C, D, E, F orGy opened in a converted pizzeria on Bleecker Street to a scathing review in the *Post*, a series of witticisms in the *News*, silence from the *Times*, and a rave notice in the *Village Voice*. All went into detail about the third-act nude scene (the *Voice*'s description was matter-of-factly explicit about Miss Audrey Weston's blond charms, which apparently overshadowed those of the rest of the ladies of the cast out of sheer volume). The play began to do an SRO business. Miss Weston, interviewed by one of the East Village papers, said: "Until now I have as a matter of professional as well as personal integrity rejected any role that called on me to appear in the nude. But Ali-Bababa's production is a different kettle of fish, dahling. (*Sure*, the interviewer interjected, *it stinks*.) It positively shines in this dull theatrical season. (*That's what stinking fish do, all right*, the interviewer interpolated.) I'm proud to be a part of it, clothes or no clothes." (*Stay in your pad and have your chick do a striptease*, the interviewer advised. *It's cheaper*.)

Marsh heard nothing more from Miss Weston, nee Arlene Wilkinson, or from her attorney, Sanford Effing, about the alleged paternity of Johnny-B *in re* Davy Wilkinson, infant, adoptive surname unrevealed. The consensus of Marsh, the Queens, and an assistant from the District Attorney's office was that said Attorney Effing must have advised his client either, (1) that she had no case that stood a chance in the hell of the courts; or, (2) regardless of the juridical odds, that she did not have the scratch to finance what could only be a long-drawn-out litigation (meaning chiefly the attorney's fee). For Miss Weston's sole source of income these days, it appeared, was her salary from *A, B, C, D, E, F orGy*.

The case of Alice Tierney took an unexpected turn for the better. From her action and appearance that Sunday night at Benedict's mausoleum, Ellery would have sworn that she had gone off the deep end beyond rescue; he had seen psychotics in the "dilapidated" cells of mental hospitals with the same liverish lips and wild-animal glare. But she made a remarkable recovery in the psychiatric ward of the Wrightsville General Hospital. She was a patient there, behind bars, for two weeks under the care of Dr. P. Langston Minikin, chief of the hospital's psychiatric service, after which he had her transferred to a nursing home in Connhaven, where she remained for another two weeks and was then discharged in the custody of her parents and elder sister Margaret, who was also a registered nurse. Dr. Minikin diagnosed Alice as a schizophrenic personality, but the episode itself, he said, was a hysteric seizure, probably isolated, and not likely to be repeated except under very extreme pressure.

Dr. Minikin told Chief Newby, "She seems resigned now to the fact that Benedict either forgot his promise or changed his mind—at any rate, that he left no written authorization or other record for the transfer of the property at his death. She's a bit withdrawn over what she considers the raw deal he gave her, but in my opinion she's already managed a good adjustment, and in amazingly fast time. I don't believe Alice will do any more prowling, Anse." He hedged his bet. "She may do other things, but not that." It was not conducive to Newby's peace of mind.

But the really astonishing development of the month was the announcement that Marcia Kemp Benedict Faulks was taking unto herself a fourth surname.

It was not so much the fact iself that was to be marveled at in this age of multiple marriages as the identity of the lucky man. Ellery hardly believed the evidence of his eyes as he read the daily reports of his father's detectives and their confirmation in the gossip and society columns.

A romance was burgeoning between the ex-Vegas redhead and Al Marsh.

"Not that it's any of my affair," Ellery said at a three-way dinner in a hideaway East Side restaurant one night toward the end of May, "but how in Cupid's name did it happen? I never caught even a glimpse between you and Marcia of any romantic interest. On the contrary, I thought you disliked each other."

Marcia's hand groped, and Marsh engulfed it.

"You learn to hide things," the lawyer smiled. "Especially when you're the attorney in the triangle, and more especially when what you have to cover up is the McCoy."

"Triangle?" Ellery said. "You and Marcia—behind Johnny's back?"

Marsh's smile widened.

"Hardly," Marcia said. "I found out that Al ought to be

carrying an Equity card. I thought he detested me. That's why I always tried to give him a hard time. You know how broads are."

"Look," Marsh said. "I couldn't cut in on Johnny either for personal or professional reasons. I had to suppress my feelings. I shoved them so deep I was hardly aware I had them, or I'd have married Marcia soon after Johnny divorced her. He met her through me, you know. I was in love with her when to Johnny all she was was a marriage of convenience."

The redhead squeezed his hand. "I know it's only a few weeks since Bernie died, but that marriage was from hunger —I was on the rebound from Johnny, I'd known Bernie Faulks in the Vegas crowd, and you've got to admit Bern was loaded with S.A. . . ."

"You don't have to apologize, dear heart," Marsh said. "It was a mistake, Ellery, and Marcia and I see no reason to waste any more of our lives. Dessert, baby?" he asked her as the waiter hovered.

"Gawd, no! A bride has to think of her architecture, especially when she's built like the George Washington Bridge to start with."

Further prying was obviously futile. Ellery gave up.

It was to be a private wedding in Marsh's Sutton Place duplex; even the date was kept from the press. The few friends Marsh invited—Marcia said she had none she could trust—were pledged to secrecy and asked to come quietly to the apartment at two o'clock on the afternoon of Sunday, June 7. At the last moment Marcia decided to ask Audrey Weston and Alice Tierney—"I know it's bitchy of me," Marcia said, "but I do want to see their faces when Al and I are hitched!" (To her chagrin Alice declined on the excuse of her recent illness; Audrey did not bother even to respond.) The only other wedding guests were Leslie Carpenter, Miss Smith, and the Queens.

The knot was tied by Mr. Justice Marascogni of the State Supreme Court, an old friend of the Marsh family. (Ellery felt an extraordinary relief on being introduced to the judge; he had been half expecting—when he heard that a judge was to perform the ceremony—the appearance of old Judge McCue, whose similar role in the nuptials that climaxed his last investigation had concluded on such a cataclysmic note.) But this time the marriage-maker came, performed, and left with no cataclysm at all.

Until, of course, about forty-five minutes later.

It was curious how it happened, the accumulating clichés of all such affairs—"Isn't it June today? She's a June bride!"

—the June bride's hilarity when someone exclaimed over the first champagne toast after the man-and-wife pronouncement, "Why, now your name is Marcia Marsh. How quaint!"—and the acting out of the small roles: Judge Marascogni's unfortunate lisp, through which "Marcia" sounded uncomfortably like "Martha," as if the groom were marrying another woman entirely, and the sibilants in the marriage service seemed increased a hundredfold, making everyone nervous anticipating the next one; the peaceful, almost imperceptible, way in which Miss Smith got smashed on her boss's champagne and eventually salted her glass over the death of her hopes (was there ever a homely secretary to a man as Marlboro-handsome as Al Marsh who did not secretly cherish such hopes?)— collapsing in Ellery's arms weeping her lost love, having to be laid on the groom's bed (by the bride) making Ellery wonder just how smashed she really was; the merriment over the wedding cake (not a creation of the great Louis, who was not a baker but a chef; an ex-colleague of his, who *was* a baker, had created it at Louis's command), the traditional awkwardness of the first bride-and-groom two-handed slice, and the bride's quite expert subsequent solo performance with the cake knife . . . until, as it has been noted, some forty-five minutes later, when the cake was one-third gone and Ellery found himself, through no conscious design he could recall, alone with it. Alone with it, the others having eaten their fill and scattered throughout the duplex.

The slices had all been taken from the two lowest tiers of the cake, leaving the upper tiers intact.

Highest of all, on the eminence, like triumphant mountain-climbers, stood the stiff little plastic figures of the bride and groom in their sugar-frosted canopy.

The little couple stared up at him crookedly. In slicing the cake Marcia had accidentally touched them and the canopy had slipped; they stood a bit askew.

Something popped in Ellery's head.

Like a tiny smoke-bomb.

The smoke drifted about, brushing his thoughts, dissipating, vanishing—the same elusive thing he had failed to grasp in Benedict's Wrightsville bedroom and elsewhere, later, in annoying retrospect. The something he had seen but failed to notice. The something he had not been able to grasp.

But this time he grasped it.

He grasped it when, in an act not really of volition, Ellery reached out in an absent way to straighten the surrogate bride and groom in their canopy. Perhaps he was thinking too hard, or not thinking at all, or alternating between desperation and despair. In any event, the plastic couple jiggled out of their base and the little groom fell to the rug.

Leaving the bride alone in the canopy.

Ellery frowned his displeasure.

This is wrong, he thought. He hoped, for Al Marsh's sake, that the fall was not symbolic. There had been marriage failures enough in this case.

That was Ellery's first thought.

His second was to bring the couple together again. Naturally. Was there ever a more sinful moment for separation and disruption? The little bride stood so bravely forlorn in her canopy. And the little groom looked so doleful and deserted lying on the floor, so out of things, so robbed of the spirit of nuptial joy.

Therefore Ellery stooped to pick up the groom and restore him to his rightful place.

That was when the lightning struck; the lightning that—as on past occasions, if he was lucky—ripped through the overcast of the long dry spell and shattered the air clear.

"We've got to go up to Wrightsville right away," he said to Inspector Queen. "Or I've got to go if you can't."

He had drawn the Inspector onto Marsh's terrace, away from the others. New York sparkled in the sun. It was one of the city's rarely beautiful days. Marsh—or Marcia—had picked a good one, all right.

"I'll go, too," Inspector Queen said.

"No questions?"

His father shrugged.

"Am I that transparent?"

"I'm your old man."

"It's a wise father. What did Johnny call her?"

"What did Johnny call who?"

His failure to correct the Inspector's grammar was significant. "Laura. The last woman in his life, wasn't that how he put it? No, you didn't hear him. Poor Johnny."

"I suppose you'll tell me what you're talking about," the Inspector said, "in your own sweet time, as usual."

"I think I can suggest a lead," Ellery said.

The old man's ears twitched. "To Laura?"

"At least I can tell you what her last name is. Or may be."

"Ellery, don't play games! How could you possibly know her last name? All of a sudden like this?"

"Try Mann—M-a-n-n. It might be a longer name, dad—Manning, Manners, Mannheim, Mandeville, Mannix. Something like that."

The Inspector squinted at him in absolute disbelief. Then, shaking his head, he went off to find a phone.

Ellery became conscious of his hand. There was something in it. He looked down. It was the little plastic groom. He stepped off the terrace and made for the wedding cake. Estéban was alone there, collecting used champagne glasses.

"Where are Mr. and Mrs. Marsh going on their honeymoon, Estéban?" Ellery asked. "Do you know?"

"They no go, Mr. Queen." The houseman looked around conspiratorially. "Till next week, I think. Mrs. Marsh she's got to close up her apartment. She do much other thing, I think. You no tell nobody?"

"Not a breathing soul," Ellery said, and very carefully he restored the little groom to its lawful place beside its bride.

3.
The
Third
Life

They dropped into Wrightsville with the setting sun. Inspector Queen telephoned Newby from the tiny airport lounge.

"Meet us at the Benedict house," the Inspector told him. "Don't bother with a police car—I mean for us. We'll take a cab."

Chief Newby was waiting for them at the door. He had it unlocked and waiting.

"What's up, Inspector?"

"Ask *him*. Maybe you'll have better luck than I've had. I couldn't get a word out of him, and I still can't."

The chief looked at Ellery reproachfully.

"I'm not being coy," Ellery grumbled. "I've had considerable to think through. Shall we go in?"

They went in. The house was musty-smelling, and Newby went about throwing windows open. "Anybody want a drink?" Ellery asked. When the older men refused he said, "Well, I do," and he took an Irish neat, and another, then set the bottle down and said, "Let's go upstairs."

He vaulted up to Benedict's bedroom, and waited impatiently in the doorway.

"The answer was here from the start," he said. "That Saturday night. March twenty-eight, wasn't it? Almost two and a half months ago. I could have saved us a lot of wear and tear. And Faulks his miserable life . . . well, it's all slops under the bridge. Come in, gents, and be seated. Don't worry about disturbing the evidence. It isn't the kind you can disturb."

"What?" Newby said, vague as a fish.

"Don't try to make anything out of it," Inspector Queen advised him. "Not just yet, anyway. He always starts this way. You sit down and you listen. That's what I'm going to do, Newby. I've had to do it a hundred times." And the Inspector seated himself on the bedroom's only chair, leaving the edge of the dead man's bed to the chief, who perched himself on it gingerly with an uneasy eye on the door, as if to orient himself to the nearest exit.

"You weren't there, Anse," Ellery said. "I mean in Marsh's apartment today, when he and Marcia were married. After the ceremony I found myself with the wedding cake, just the three of us—"

"The three of you?"

"The little plastic bride and groom and me."

"Oh. Oh?"

"They were, as usual, under a canopy at the top of the cake. And the groom fell off. Do you see?"

"No."

"It left the bride alone up there"

"Well, sure. So what?"

"So that was wrong, wasn't it?"

"Wrong?" Chief Newby repeated. "What was?"

"I mean, you look at the bride standing up there by herself, and it's obvious there's a missing element."

"Oh. Well, naturally. The groom. Anybody would know that. Is that what you flew up from New York to tell me?"

"That is correct," Ellery said. "To tell you that there was something missing.

"From the beginning I've felt that there was a crucial clue in this room, a vital element of the murder, only I couldn't get my finger on it. Of course, when you think you can't remember something you take it for granted that it's something you saw, something that was there but slipped your mind. That lone little bride today told me my mistake. The clue in Johnny's bedroom here wasn't something I'd seen and forgotten, it was something I had not seen—*something that should have been here but wasn't.* Something which my mind unconsciously groped for, failed to find, and whose omission it registered.

"Dad."

"Yes, son?"

Ellery was at the clothes closet. "The room is exactly as it was on the night of the murder except that Johnny's body, the contents of the nightstand, and the three women's stolen articles of clothing aren't here now. Correct?"

"No," the Inspector said. "The weapon."

"And the Three Monkeys, yes. Everything else in the bedroom is as it was. That would include this wardrobe closet of Johnny's and its contents, wouldn't it?"

"Yes?" His father was intent.

"So what's in the wardrobe closet now is what we inspected on the night of the murder. Very thoroughly, I might add. Garment by garment. Remember? Even Johnny's hats, shoes —everything."

"Yes?" the old man said again. In the same way. Newby was still imitating a fish.

"Let's do a repeat. Go through the closet and call out whatever you see. As you did that night. Listen hard, Anse. See if you catch it. It isn't easy."

Inspector Queen began with the accessory items, enumerating: neckties, four-in-hands, ascots, bow ties, scarves, in all basic colors and combinations—

"Including browns?" Ellery interrupted.

"Sure including browns. Didn't I say 'all'?"

"Go on."

"Ten hats and caps—"

"Is any of them brown?"

"This brown fedora."

"Shoes?"

"Cordovans, alligators, suèdes—"

"Never mind the leather. How about the colors?"

"Blacks, browns, grays, tans—"

"Browns and tans noted. Overcoats?"

"Navy blue double-breasted, black with a velvet collar, cashmere—"

"Which color cashmere?"

"Tan."

"Brown family. Topcoats?"

"Charcoal, tan, chocolate—"

"Brown family again. That's enough to make my point. Step out of the closet, dad, and go through the drawers of the bureau there, as we did on the night of the murder. Take the shirt drawers first. Do you find any shirts in shades of brown?"

"Sure—"

"How about the hose drawer? That one. Any brown socks?"

"Plenty."

"You left out his suits." Newby was fascinated—puzzled, but fascinated.

"We did, didn't we?" Ellery said. As usual at such times, there was something of the actor about him, enjoying his performance. "All right, dad, start with Johnny's conventional suits. Which colors are they?"

The Inspector said sharply, "They're all in shades of blue and gray. Period!"

"Yes," Ellery said. "No browns or tans. That's what kept bugging me, Anse, even though I couldn't identify it: the basic fashion color brown that wasn't represented in Johnny's suits, in spite of the fact that practically everything else in his wardrobe included articles in brown and/or tan."

"Maybe he just didn't bring a brown suit up here."

"Unthinkable. Johnny regularly made the Ten Best-Dressed

Men's list. He wouldn't have worn brown shoes, or a brown hat, or a brown topcoat, or certainly a brown or tan shirt, with anything but a suit in some shade of brown. If he had brown accessories here, they had to be intended for at least one brown or tan suit.

"But I didn't have to make a deduction about it," Ellery continued. "Johnny did have a brown suit on the premises. I saw it with my own eyes. *On* him. The night he was murdered. He was wearing it when I was skulking on the terrace doing my Peeping Tom act while he held forth to his ex-wives about his plans for a new will. He was wearing the brown suit when he left them for the night and went upstairs to go to bed. That means he took the brown suit off up here, in this room, when he undressed and got into his pajamas. But when he phoned us at the guest cottage and we dashed over here and found him dead—*no brown suit*. No brown suit in his closet, as we've noted; no brown suit thrown over a chair or deposited anywhere else in the bedroom as you would expect after he'd undressed to go to bed—dad, you actually remarked on the neatness of the room, how no clothes were strewn about. You even specified what Johnny had deposited in the laundry hamper of the clothing he'd been wearing: socks, you said, underwear, shirt."

Newby muttered. "Then what happened to his brown suit?"

"That, Anse, is the question. To answer it you obviously must ask yourself first: who do we know was in this room later that night besides Johnny?"

"Who? His killer."

"Answer: Johnny's killer took away Johnny's brown suit. Q.E.D."

Newby threw an irritated glance at the Inspector. But Richard Queen was peering into the past. Or perhaps it was the future.

"Q.E.D. my Aunt Martha's hind leg," Newby said crossly. "It doesn't Q.E.D. a damned thing to me. *Why?* Why would his killer take Benedict's suit away?"

"You've just hit pay dirt, Anse. Let's go back. What do we know the murderer did after he entered the bedroom? He did three things we're now sure of: He killed Johnny. He left Audrey's gown, Marcia's wig, and Alice's gloves on the floor. And he made his escape with the suit Johnny had taken off in undressing for bed.

"Let's concentrate on number three—your question, Anse: why did Murderer, in escaping after his crime, take Johnny's suit with him?

"Was it because the suit contained something he wanted?

No, because if that were the case he had only to take it from the suit and leave the suit behind.

"Or was the theft of the man's suit meant to symbolize 'a man'? That is, to point suspicion to the only other male in the house that night, Al Marsh? All the others were women —Audrey, Marcia, Alice, Miss Smith."

"Then why would the killer also leave the three articles of women's clothing?" the Inspector objected. "Those seemed to point to women."

"Disposing of that theory—right, dad. And there's another objection to that: we didn't even realize a man's suit was missing. If that had been Murderer's intention, he would have managed to call the fact of the missing suit to our attention. But he didn't."

"Can either of you think of still another reason?"

After a barren interlude Newby said, "You'd think there'd be a dozen possible reasons for a thing like that. But I can't think of one."

Inspector Queen confessed, "Neither can I, Ellery."

"That's because it's obvious."

"Obvious?"

"What was it," Ellery asked, "that the murderer took away?"

"Benedict's brown suit."

"A man's suit. What are men's suits used for?"

"What are they *used* for? What do you mean, son? To wear. But—"

"To wear," Ellery said. "As clothing. The common, every-day reason. But why should Murderer need clothing in leaving Johnny's room after the murder? Surely he came there wearing something. Had he been splashed with blood—was that the reason he had to have a change of clothes? But Johnny's head bled remarkably little—we noted that on the scene, dad. Or even if some blood had got on Murderer's original clothing, that would hardly have necessitated an entire change—pants as well as jacket—in the middle of the night, in a darkened house. No, it must have been something else about what Murderer was wearing when he came to Johnny's room that compelled him to discard it and dress in Johnny's suit as a substitute. Do you see it now?"

Chief Newby looked helpless.

Inspector Queen exploded, "Hell, no!"

"But it's so clear," Ellery cried. "What was Murderer wearing when he came into Johnny's room that he might have felt he could not wear in leaving after the crime? You still don't see it? Well, what clothing definitely not Johnny's did we find on the floor—dropped there?"

"Those women's things." The Inspector was gaping.

"That is right. If Murderer came to Johnny's bedroom wearing Audrey's evening gown, Marcia's wig, and Alice's gloves, and for some reason decided to leave them behind, then Murderer would have required other clothes to leave in."

Chief Newby exclaimed, "One of those three gals, wearing the gown, the wig, and the gloves, came to Benedict's room, stripped, left them as clues to spread the guilt, and put on the suit Benedict'd been wearing to get back to her own room in." His face darkened. "That makes no sense at all. She'd have come in a dress or a kimono or something and just carried the three clues in her hand."

The Inspector asked slowly, "Are you saying it wasn't one of his ex-wives, Ellery?"

"You've answered your own question, dad. Audrey, Marcia, Alice—none of them would have planned to go to Johnny's room to kill him under such circumstances as to leave herself without clothes for her getaway."

"But Ellery, they were the only women there!" Newby said.

"No, Chief, wait a minute," the Inspector said. "There was a fourth woman on the premises. Marsh's secretary, Miss Smith." But when he looked at Ellery he said, "Not her, son?"

Ellery was shaking his head. "You're forgetting, dad, that we've postulated Murderer's going to Johnny's room wearing the stolen women's clothing. That means Murderer was the one who stole them in the first place. But when were they stolen? Audrey reported to us that her gown was missing as early as noon that Saturday. Marcia told us that her wig was gone not an hour later. And when I talked to Alice and she couldn't find her gloves, it was only midafternoon. In fact, it was during that conversation that Alice told me the others were preparing to drive over to the airport to meet Miss Smith's plane, which was due in, Alice said, at five thirty.

"So Miss Smith couldn't have been the one who stole the gown, wig, and gloves. Therefore she wasn't the one who went to Johnny's room that night wearing them."

"But there was no other woman in the house," the Inspector protested.

"Exactly."

Pauses have shades, like colors. This pause was unrelieved black.

The Inspector fumbled for some light. "But Ellery, there was only one other person there."

"Exactly."

"Al Marsh. . . ."

"Exactly."

And there was the pause again, less dark, more like a lightning-struck sky.

"Do you mean to say," Inspector Queen yipped, "do you mean to say it was Marsh—*Al Marsh*—who went to Benedict's bedroom that night all rigged out in a woman's evening gown, wearing a woman's wig and a woman's gloves. . . ?"

"It's where the argument led us."

"But that would mean," Newby fretted, "that would mean—"

"—that we're investigating a case," Ellery said in a somber voice, "the real nature of which we didn't suspect until now.

"Al Marsh went to Johnny's bedroom that night in full drag, and what happened there forced him to leave the feminine clothing behind. He put on Johnny's suit to get safely back to his own room. Johnny's brown suit . . . when we find it, we'll have him."

"Find it?" the Inspector mumbled. "Fat chance. He'll have got rid of it long ago."

"I don't think so," Ellery said. "No, there's a good chance he may not have. Shall we go see?"

There was no flight out at that hour, and Ellery would not wait. Newby said grimly, "Take my car. I wish I could go with you."

The Queens drove all night, alternating at the wheel. They had breakfast in an all-night cafeteria on 1st Avenue and were at the door of Marsh's duplex a few minutes past eight o'clock in the morning.

"Mr. Marsh he's asleep, Mr. Queen," the houseman said, blinking in the entrance hall. "No can wake him up—"

"Is Mrs. Marsh with him?"

"She no move in here yet."

"Then you go on about your business, Estéban," Ellery said. "I'll take the responsibility of waking Mr. Marsh."

They barged into Marsh's bedroom without knocking. It was a spacious place of massive woods, hand-hewn and masculine. An eight-foot reproduction in marble of Michelangelo's *David* graced the room.

The lawyer turned over in bed suddenly and opened his eyes.

"Easy, Marsh," Inspector Queen said.

Marsh remained that way, in a half twisted posture, arrested in mid-movement. He looked formidable. His torso was naked and full of muscles and, surprisingly, hairless, as if he used a depilatory.

"What do you want?"

He sat up then. But he made no move to get out of bed. He drew his legs up under the red silk sheet and folded his heavy forearms over them, as if to hold them in check.

"What do you want?" he asked again.

"Johnny's suit," Ellery said gently. "You know, Al. The brown one he was wearing the night he was schlogged."

"You must be insane."

"Is it what *I* am, Al? Or what *you* are?"

Marsh shut his eyes for the briefest moment, like a child. When he opened them Ellery saw that they were old, bitter, and retreating.

"I don't know what you're talking about," he said in a mechanical way. "I have nothing of Johnny's here. Go ahead and look. And be damned to you."

His wardrobe closet was a roomy walk-in, like Benedict's in Wrightsville. Among the many garments on the racks they found two suits that, to Ellery's recollection, were approximately the same shade of brown as the missing Benedict suit.

"What size do you wear, Marsh?" Inspector Queen asked. "Never mind. According to the labels these are forty-four longs, Ellery. Benedict couldn't have worn more than a thirty-eight regular—maybe even a thirty-six. So these are Marsh's." None of the other suits was the color of Benedict's. "Any other suits in the apartment, Marsh?"

"This is your party." Marsh's throat sounded dry. He licked his lips. "I don't have to tell you, incidentally, Inspector, that I've seen no sign of a search warrant."

"There's one on the way," the Inspector said. "Sorry we jumped the gun a bit, Marsh. Would you rather we held up till the warrant gets here?"

The lawyer shrugged his heavy shoulders.

"I won't make an issue of it. I've got nothing to hide."

The Inspector looked the least bit worried. He glanced at Ellery. But if Ellery felt misgivings he did not betray them. He was going through the suitcases that were piled up in a corner of the wardrobe room. The cases were empty.

Ellery straightened up suddenly and stepped out of the closet. "I'm still partly in shock," he said, and drew his father aside, out of earshot of Marsh. "Of course it wouldn't be out in the open. He's hidden it in his clothes-hiding place."

"His what?"

"Marsh leads a secret life, doesn't he? That follows from what we've found out about him. During the day he acts the part of a normal man. But nights—some nights—and weekends—some weekends—he lives his other life. That means he has to have a hiding place for the clothes he wears when he's on the prowl."

The Inspector sprang back into the closet. He found the nearly invisible seam in the panel and the concealed spring in less than three minutes. Half the rear wall of the closet slid open.

Marsh had got out of bed and joined them in the closet. His pajama pants were shocking pink. His eyes were wild.

"Don't do that," he said. "Please don't go in there. I beg of you."

"Sorry, Al."

They were all there—street dresses, smart women's suits, cocktail gowns, evening gowns, high-heeled shoes, nylon stockings, hip huggers, an assortment of panty hose, panty girdles, silk panties, brassieres, slips. And at least a dozen wigs, in various styles and colors. And a vanity table loaded with a full freight of makeup materials. And a pile of gaudy magazines featuring handsome and muscular young male nudes.

And, among the gowns, the lone intruder, a man's suit, a brown suit, the brown suit John Levering Benedict III had worn on the last night of his life.

Under the law I have to warn you, *Inspector Queen began.* Never mind, I know my rights, but I want to explain, it's important, *Marsh said. Moved by an abscure emotion, Ellery had tossed him a robe from the closet; he was very Marlboro striding about the bedroom, and it deepened Ellery's somberness. His father had died in an accident when he was very little, he explained; his mother, who never remarried, had been his evil genius.*

She ruined me. I was her only child and she had had her heart set on a daughter. So she rejected my sex—not consciously, I'm sure; she was a Victorian throwback. Believe it or not she kept me in dresses, long hair, and dolls almost until I reached school age. And she'd had me christened Aubrey. I hated the name. You can imagine what boys made of it. At school I fought and licked every boy who made fun of me. I was big and strong enough to do it. I kept at them till they called me Al. Al it's been ever since.

But the damage was done. With no male figure to counterbalance my mother's influence—ours was a completely female household—whatever causes these things took hold and dominated me. I found out the truth about myself in my freshman year at Harvard. I'd long since wondered why I felt no particular yen for girls, like my friends, and had to fake interest; now I came to the realization that what I was feeling for Johnny couldn't be palmed off as ordinary man-to-man friendship . . . I never let Johnny know. The concealment, the need to watch myself, to pretend, cost me dear. It had to find an outlet somewhere. Inevitably there was an episode in a bar, well away from the Yard . . . then another, and another. It became an addiction, like heroin. I fought it with all my strength, feeling such shame and guilt afterward that I threw myself into college sports, especially wrestling. Until I realized why I had gone into contact sports. And gave them up.

Marsh went to the wall beside his bed and pressed something. A section of the wall slid away to disclose a fully stocked bar. He seized a bottle of bourbon and filled a water glass. He downed half its contents without lowering his head.

It wasn't only Johnny who never suspected. You didn't, Ellery—no one did. I was ludicrously careful. I never cruised anyone connected with the college, even the ones I knew would be approachable. All my pickups were made far off campus, like the first one, mostly in downtown Boston. My great fear was that I'd be found out. I suffered more than I can describe . . . from the agony of alienation . . . the effort to disguise my real wants . . . the need, the craving, to be in the life.

Oh, God, *Marsh said,* you can't imagine what it's like, the nervous tension, the inner turmoil, the loneliness—particularly the loneliness when I was putting on my act in the straight world. And the persistent overdrinking—it's a wonder I didn't become an alcoholic, but I suppose my fear of self-betrayal acted as a brake . . . I never considered for a moment going to a psychiatrist . . . I know I should have adjusted, as other people have; accepted what I was. But I couldn't, I just couldn't. For every hour of peace—why do I call it peace? it was merely a truce—I fought an eternity of all-out war.

When my mother died and I came into the family fortune, I was even worse off. I now had the independence and the means to widen the area of my secret life, but the dangers of discovery were also multiplied, therefore the fears and shames and guilts. Also, no matter how much I engaged in the life, I felt incomplete—what someone has termed "unfulfilled and unfulfillable." It's like compulsive eating, or any other sympton of something wrong . . . the disgust I felt cruising for a trick, the demeaning deals with hustlers, the sordid hanging around public washrooms in hotels, railroad stations, airport terminals, bus depots, angling for a pickup . . . a marine, a drunken sailor, offering money for an hour in some cheap hotel . . . and the greatest dread of all, that while I was cruising at a gay bar or beach or in some park—wherever people in the life congregated—someone I knew in the straight world would run into me and spread the word . . . most hideous thought of all, some reporter who'd recognize me. . . . . Do you know what the first commandment in the gay life is? "Thou shalt not be found out." You've got to understand that. I mustn't be found out. I could bear almost anything but exposure . . . I said a reporter would be the worst. That's not true. The worst would be a detective from the Vice Squad, playing the role of pickup. . . .

Marsh's delivery, which had begun in halting fashion, began to pick up smoothness and speed, like a partially clogged drain that had cleared. The purge of confession reddened and convulsed his face; his fists flailed away almost joyously at the pain of cleansing himself.

Forgive me for going into such detail, *he said, and downed the rest of his drink.* I'll get right to what you want to hear. *He set the glass down on the bar quietly and turned to face them.*

From the moment Johnny and I flew to that art auction in London, I had the exciting feeling that he'd suddenly guessed my secret. It wasn't for any reason I could put my finger on. Now that I have some perspective on it, it was an illusion brought on by the intensity of my desire for him. I talked myself into believing that all these years, while I'd been hiding what I was from him, Johnny had been hiding from me that he was secretly in the life, too.

Is sounds absurd to me now, when I say it; there was really no basis for it. But, so powerful was the need, that's what I convinced myself of. I convinced myself that Johnny was giving me suggestive looks . . . inviting me to make advances . . . cruising me to come to his bedroom that weekend in Wrightsville after everyone else was asleep so that we could make love.

From the start of the weekend I felt a kind of crisis in identity that turned physiological with great rapidity. It sapped my usual control. That Friday night, when Audrey, Marcia, and Alice came downstairs all dressed up, something happened to me. Audrey's stunning evening gown with the sequins, Marcia's silly "fun" wig, Alice's elbow-length gloves . . . all of a sudden I was madly attracted to them. I had to have them . . . put them on . . . parade around in them. If we'd been in the city I could have used one of my own drag outfits, but we were in that damned backwoods town. . . . And there was my beloved Johnny—the satisfied passion of my life—practically in my arms . . . signaling to me, as I thought, giving me the come-on. . . .

I slept hardly a wink that night.

By Saturday morning I was beyond reason or caution. While the women were out of the house or downstairs somewhere, I stole the gown, the wig, the gloves from their bed-rooms.

I hid the gown and the gloves under the mattress of my bed, and the wig in the bottom of my wastebasket under a camouflage of crumpled tissues.

Marsh seemed scarcely conscious of them now, and the Queens settled themselves with great caution for the next few crucial minutes.

By late Saturday night I had no defenses left. My will power was gone. All I could think of was Johnny and how much I wanted him. I don't know how I got through that endless evening, Johnny's dreary spiel to those three. It was especially bad after he went to bed. I thought the women would never go up to their rooms. Finally, the last one did.

You have to realize I'd had a great deal to drink. I'd tried to hold the drinking down, but it had got to me. Maybe it was because of the excitement building up.

Marsh began striding again. Hands clasped, at one time wringing, another knuckle-cracking. Head lowered; rushing toward his denouement like a lemming.

I waited till I thought everyone must be asleep. Then I got the gown and gloves out from under my mattress, and the wig from the wastebasket. I opened the secret pocket in my two-suiter bag—I'd had it specially made—and took out the supply of makeup I keep handy there—a liquid powder base, rouge, face and body powder, false eyelashes, lipstick, mascara. The works. And I . . . changed.

His voice faltered before the last word. After he uttered it he was silent for so long that the Queens disciplined their breathing. Finally, he shook himself like a dog.

It wasn't a bad fit—you know how big they are, with Johnny's yen for women twice his size. Though I had to pass up shoes. Their shoes wouldn't have gone on my feet, and of course I couldn't put on my men's shoes, I'd have looked ridiculous. . . .

Marsh paused again, and Ellery thought how bright Einstein had been to insist on relativity. Marsh said he would have looked ridiculous in men's shoes. True, but how did he think he looked in a woman's dress? For the first time, as a result of Marsh's comment, Ellery truly saw him as not the Marlboro man but the transvestite.

I opened my door and listened. *Marsh said it liturgically, as if he were in communion with some deep, ineffable force.* The house was so still it sang—you know how they are sometimes in the middle of the night. I can remember my throat, how there was a gong pounding at the base of it. It was almost pleasant. I could even see pretty well; there was a good nightlight burning in the upper hall.

Nobody I could see.

Nothing.

I felt wonderful.

So alive.

I walked up the hall to Johnny's bedroom. I half expected the door to open for me as I came up and Johnny to be standing there waiting.

But it didn't, and he wasn't. I tried the knob and it turned and the door swung with a creak like a haunted house, and I went in and shut it and it creaked again, and Johnny's voice said, "Who's that? Who's there?" in a mumble, and I felt around on the wall for the switch and then the room lit up and there was my darling sitting up in bed all sleepy and blinky, not naked as I had imagined he'd be, but in his pajamas.

Marsh's rhapsodic monotone, which had had the devotional quality, fell so low it became a mutter. They had to strain to hear him.

I think at first he thought I was Audrey, or Marcia, because he rolled out of bed and snatched his robe and put it on.

But then his pupils must have adjusted, because he recognized me. You could see his eyes do it.

They scarcely heard him at all now. He was clenching air with his fists and, feeling nothing, opening his big hands in a curiously supplicating way.

Could you speak a little louder? *Inspector Queen asked softly. Marsh looked at him, frowning.*

I've seen his eyes many times since, *he said with more volume.* At night. Even daytimes. I could read them like a neon sign. Recognition. Comprehension. And then shock.

They stayed shocked just long enough for me to compound my mistake. That stupid mistake. I wasn't thinking at all at that moment. It was sheer feeling.

The flowering, you might say. The bursting point.

I stripped off the gloves and wig. I tore the gown off. Stood there naked. And I took a step toward him and held out my arms, and that was when I saw the shock in his eyes turn to revulsion, absolute revulsion.

He said to me, "You filthy, filthy pig. Get out of my house."

Marsh turned his back to them and made little throat-clearing noises. When he spoke again it was to unoccupied space, as if he had wished them away and they had obediently disappeared.

I found myself saying some things to him then . . . I remember . . . about my love . . . my years of fighting to hide it from him. . . .

I knew it was worse than useless—his eyes told me that—but I couldn't stop myself, it all came out, everything, and all the time I knew it was a fatal mistake . . . that he wasn't capable of understanding . . . any more than you . . although I hope . . . I hoped . . . .

He never raised his voice. It was brutal. He was cruel, viciously so. The things he called me . . . unforgivable things from an intelligent, civilized man . . . even if he couldn't share my feelings, he'd known me so long, we'd been such friends. If I'd been a leper and deliberately infected him out of malice he couldn't have shown more hate, as if I were his enemy . . . . All the time he was cutting me to bits, the shame, the guilt, the fear—the panic—grew. All my years of being careful—successfully—thrown away in one uncontrollable act. In one night.

He was threatening to expose me.

I don't know why Johnny reacted so violently to what he'd found out about me. I hadn't really done anything to him except reveal myself for what I was. He couldn't handle the revelation. Maybe he had a deep-seated hangup about inversion. A lot of men do . . . as if they're afraid the same thing is buried in *them*, and by attacking it in others . . . I don't know.

I had no time to analyze Johnny then. I was too busy panicking.

He was threatening to expose me; and that would be the end of me. At that moment that was all I could think of—that, and shutting his mouth. The cast-iron Three Monkeys thing was on his bureau and the next thing I knew I found myself smashing him over the head with it. It was like a reflex. No rational thought behind it. He mustn't tell. I must keep him from talking.

That's all I knew.

Marsh turned around and they saw the surprise in his eyes at the sight of them, and then the distaste, almost the contempt, as if he had caught them eavesdropping. But even that drained rapidly out of his eyes, leaving them empty.

It never occurred to me that Johnny wasn't dead. I simply took it for granted. He looked dead . . . sprawled there . . . his pale, almost green, face . . . the blood . . . .

I opened the door a crack and looked out and my heart jumped. There was a tall girl on the landing in a dressing gown, about to go downstairs. She turned her head a bit, and I saw it was Andrey Weston.

Paralyzed, I watched her go down.

She was down there only a couple of minutes. She came back up with a book and went to her room.

I looked down at myself. I was naked. I'd forgotten. I began to shake. Suppose she'd seen me?

I'd hardly had time to feel relieved when Marcia came out of her bedroom—I knew instantly it was Marcia, because I saw her red hair as she passed under the nightlight—and she headed for downstairs, too.

I suppose desperation calmed me down. I hadn't dreamed that people would be wandering about the house in the middle of the night.

All I could think of now was getting safely back to my room. Marcia was downstairs—she might come back at any moment, as Audrey had. I didn't dare go the way I was, without a stitch on—that would be a dead giveaway if I were seen . . . and the thought of getting back into drag, the way I had come, was even worse. Suppose one of the women saw me in women's clothes? In *their* clothes?

Yet I had to get out of Johnny's bedroom.

There was only one thing I could think of, and that was to put on something of Johnny's. The brown suit he'd been wearing was lying on the chair. I managed to squeeze into it. . . .

Ellery nodded. Both shoulder seams of Benedict's suit were split open, a fact the District Attorney was going to appreciate.

At the last moment it came to me—fingerprints. My brain was working independently; it wasn't mine. No panic now. I felt nothing. I used the handkerchief I found in Johnny's pocket—it's still there—and wiped off everything I'd touched . . . the Three Monkeys where I'd held it, the door-knob, whatever I'd come in contact with.

I ran back to my own room.

I locked the door, took off the suit and packed it at the bottom of my suitcase. And washed. . . .

Marsh shut his eyes again.

He said in an exhausted, final way, There was Johnny's blood on me.

That was the body of it.

There were appendages. Why had he hung onto Benedict's suit?

"Was it because it had belonged to Johnny?" Ellery asked.

"Yes."

Queen *fils* regarded Queen *père*. The Inspector could only shake his head.

"You realize, Al, there's blood inside the jacket? Undoubtedly Johnny's, which got on your bare hide when you struck him and then smeared the lining when you put the jacket on for your escape. Didn't it occur to you that, with the blood types matching—Johnny's and the stains'—and the suit found in your possession, it was the most damaging kind of evidence against you?"

"I didn't think it would be found. Nobody, not even Estéban, knew about the hidden closet. Anyway, I couldn't bring myself to part with the suit. It was Johnny's."

Ellery found himself turning away.

Inspector Queen wanted to know about the marriage. "It doesn't add up, Marsh. Not in view of what you've just told us about yourself."

But it did.

On the night of the murder Marcia, who was occupying the room next to Marsh's, heard his door open and peeped out. He was in the full flight of his obsession and he neither heard nor saw her. As Marsh passed under the nightlight in the hall, bound for Benedict's room, Marcia got a full view of his face and, in spite of the woman's outfit and makeup he was wearing, she recognized him.

"Marcia's the only one I know of who for a long time had had suspicions about me," the lawyer said. "She's very shrewd and perceptive about such things, with her show business background and the years she's knocked about places like Las Vegas. At any rate, what she saw in the hall that night, she told me later, confirmed what she'd always suspected. If she had testified what she'd seen when Chief Newby and you people were questioning us, she'd have blown the case sky high the night of the murder."

But Marcia had foreseen an advantage in silence, and events soon repaid her perspicacity. The death of Benedict cut off her weekly income, and his failure to specify the expected lump-sum settlement in his holograph will left her without a penny. She confided Marsh's secret to the petty hood she had married after her divorce from Benedict, and Foxy Faulks grabbed the opportunity.

"Sweet setup for blackmail," Inspector Queen said, nodding. "She'd spotted you in drag, she certainly guessed that you were the one who had murdered Benedict, and you're a rich man. No wonder you killed Faulks. You did, didn't you?"

"What else could I do?" Marsh said, and he shrugged. "I don't have to tell you people how blackmailers operate. They'd have bled me white, and I'd never have been out of danger of exposure." He had arranged to meet Faulks behind the Museum of Art in Central Park late at night, presumably for a payoff, and instead had given Marcia's husband a knife in the abdomen.

"I figured that would scare Marcia off my back," Marsh went on, "out of just plain self-preservation. She'd have to realize that if I was willing to kill Faulks, I wouldn't shrink from killing her as well. Therefore she'd fade out of the picture.

"But Marcia came up with a very smart counter-ploy. She proposed that we get married. She pleaded a persuasive case. Our marriage would give her the financial security she wanted, and it would give me the smokescreen I needed to hide what I was. A lot of us, by the way, marry for precisely that reason. And she didn't have to remind me that a wife can't be made to testify against her husband, if it ever came to that. Well, we never got really started, thanks to you, Ellery. She's still preparing to move in here."

Ellery said nothing.

To which Marsh said a curious thing. "I wonder what you're thinking."

"Not what you think I'm thinking, Al," Ellery said.

"Then you're an exception. If only people stopped regarding us as some sort of monsters . . . let us live our lives out as we're constituted, in decent privacy and without prejudice, I don't believe this would have happened. It would have been possible for me to propose, and Johnny to reject, without disgust and vitriol on his part or panic on mine. He wouldn't have castigated or threatened me. I wouldn't have lost my head. We might even have remained friends. Certainly he'd still be alive."

"Poor Johnny," Marsh said, and was silent.

The Queens were quiet, too. A great change had come over Marsh in the past few minutes. He looked juiceless, squeezed dry of his vital constituents; he looked old.

Finally Inspector Queen cleared his throat.

"You'd better get dressed, Marsh. You'll have to come downtown with us."

The lawyer nodded, almost agreeably.

"I'll wash up."

He went into the bathroom.

They had to break through the door.

Marsh was lying on the tiled floor.

He had swallowed cyanide.

In the middle of the night after Marsh's suicide Ellery popped up out of sleep like a smoking piece of toast, groped for the nightlight, kicked the sheet, and ran to his father's bedroom.

"Dad!"

The Inspector stopped snoring to open one eye. "Unnh?"

"Vincentine Astor!"

"Wha'?"

"Vincentine Astor!"

"Unnh."

"Nobody would have a name like that legitimately. It's got to be a take-on, a phony—somebody's idea of class. I'm betting she's Laura! Laura Man-something!"

"Go back to sleep, son." The old man took his own advice.

But Laura Man-something the vanished hatcheck girl of Manhattan's Boy-Girl Club turned out to be. They found Miss Manzoni in her native Chillicothe, Ohio, in the shadow of Mt. Logan among the mysterious mounds, putting books back in the stacks of the Carnegie Library. She was living with her father, stepmother, and a mixed brood of original and acquired Manzonis in a pleasant frame house on a street of dying elms. Her father, Burton Stevenson Manzoni, had been employed in one of Chillicothe's paper mills for twenty-seven years.

Laura Manzoni was a surprise. She was not the bold, platinum-and-enamel gum-chewer they had expected. Pretty and stacked she was; but otherwise Laura was softly chestnut-haired, soft-eyed, soft-spoken, and a gentleman's lady. She had majored in drama at Oberlin, and she had gone off to New York for the predictable reason, with the predictable result.

For eating and sleeping money, when her grubstake ran out, she had dyed her hair, bought a mini-miniskirt and peekaboo stockings, applied a thick coat of theatrical makeup to her fresh Midwestern face, and bluffed her way into the hatcheck job at the nightclub. There she had met Johnny Benedict.

He claimed, Laura said, to have seen through her masquerade "to the essential me" immediately. She resisted his invitations for three weeks. Then they began to meet after hours, discreetly; this was as much, she said, at Benedict's insistence as at hers.

"Finally he told me he was serious about me," Laura said, "and then that he loved me. Of course I didn't believe him; I knew his reputation. But Johnny was such a charmer. He really was. He knew how to make a woman feel she was the center of everything. And the most he ever tried to do was kiss me. Still, something about him held me back. . . .

"I suppose I wanted very much to be convinced, but I kept putting him off. It's hard for a girl like me to believe what a man like Johnny tells her—a young and handsome multimillionaire—even, or maybe especially, if he doesn't make passes or propositions. What made it harder . . . he kept talking about our getting married. As if it were all settled. Johnny couldn't believe any girl he was rushing would turn him down. I kept telling him I wasn't sure, I needed time, and he kept saying that time was for clock punchers, that we were going to be married right away, that he'd made all his plans, and that sort of thing."

"Did Mr. Benedict ask you to sign any sort of agreement?" asked the plainclothesman whom Chief Newby had sent to Chillicothe to question her.

"Agreement?" Laura shook her head. "I wouldn't even if he had, regardless of what it was. As I say, I just wasn't sure of myself. Or, for that matter, of Johnny. In fact, when he told me he had to go up to Wrightsville—"

"Then you knew about Mr. Benedict's get-together with his ex-wives the weekend of March twenty-eighth?"

"He didn't say why he was going especially, or who'd be there. Just that he had some unfinished business, as he called it, to clean up. That was the trouble."

"Trouble, Miss Manzoni? What trouble?"

It then came out. Laura's uncertainty about Benedict's sincerity and motives trapped her into an act that had preyed on her conscience ever since. His vagueness about the purpose of his Wrightsville weekend had fed her misgivings; with Laura's middleclass, Midwestern upbringing—in spite of what she had always considered her emancipation from it—all she could think of was a "love nest" and "another woman." Hating her suspicious, but telling herself that it was a test that would decide the issue of Johnny Benedict for her one way or the other, she had rented a car that Saturday and driven up to Wrightsville.

"I don't believe I'd even thought through what I was going to do when I got there," the girl said. "Maybe some grandiose visions of finding him there with a chick, telling him off in a curtain speech, and making a glorious exit. When I did get there—I was actually turning into Johnny's driveway—I was suddenly overwhelmed with shame. I saw how wrong the whole thing was in a kind of reverse rush of feeling, the way you do sometimes. I hadn't trusted Johnny, I didn't trust him then, and I knew I never would or could. So I turned the car around and drove right back to New York. And that Sunday morning—I was too upset to go to bed—I heard over the radio that Johnny'd been murdered during the night."

Fear—that she might have been seen outside the house or in Wrightsville or the vicinity and at once involved in the murder—sent Laura fleeing to Chillicothe and home. She had never told her family about her link to the young society man whose name and photograph were in the newspapers and newscasts. When the story broke about the mysterious Laura named as Benedict's beneficiary in his holograph will in the event of their marriage, she had needed no attorney to tell her that she had no claim on the Benedict estate, since the event had never taken place.

She would have fought identification as the missing Laura, Laura said, with tooth and nail if Benedict's murder had not been solved.

"I've had a boy friend here in Chillicothe—on the next block, in fact—since childhood," Laura Manzoni said to Newby's emissary, "who's wanted to marry me since we graduated from high school. We're on the verge of setting the date. But his folks are real hardshell Baptists and, while Buell would stick by me if I were dragged through the papers and TV, they'd make things very unpleasant for us. Can you keep my name out of this? *Please?*"

They kept her name out of it . . . "the last woman in Benedict's life," Inspector Queen repeated. "Isn't that what he called her that Saturday night?"

"He was wrong," Ellery said dourly. "Laura Manzoni wasn't the last woman in Johnny's life."

"She wasn't?"

"She wasn't."

"But then who was?"

Ellery held his drink up to the light and squinted at it. It was straight sour-mash bourbon. He made a face and tossed it down like medicine.

"Al Marsh."

"Marsh," Inspector Queen said, dropping the news magazine. He had been reading about Marsh's funeral, and the recapitulation of the events that had let up to it. In the new freedom of expression enjoyed by the press, the story was explicit, too much so to the Inspector's old-fashioned taste. "I still can't get a feeling of reality about it."

"Why not?" Ellery demanded. "In your time you've investigated whole botanical gardens of men like Marsh, dad. Every police officer has. You know that."

"But it's the first time I was involved in a case with one on a personal basis. Marsh looked and acted like such a *man* of a man, if you know what I mean. Maybe if he'd been the obvious kind—"

"In his own way he was."

The old man stared.

"His apartment," Ellery said. "He practically threw his secret in your face."

"If so, I didn't get it."

"There's an excuse for you. You weren't entertained there."

"You mean all that manly type furniture, and the athletic equipment and so forth? Coverups?"

Ellery smiled faintly. "They were coverups in Marsh's case, certainly, but hardly clues, or society would really have a problem! No, it was a clue like a sequoia—so tall and broad I missed it entirely. His music library—more Tchaikovsky and Beethoven than anyone else. His rare and first editions—Proust, Melville, Chris Marlowe, Gide, Verlaine, Henry James, Wilde, Rimbaud, Walt Whitman. His art books—chiefly da Vinci and Michelangelo. The busts he had on display—Alexander the Great, Plato, Socrates, Lawrence of Arabia, Virgil, Julius Caesar, Catullus, Horace, Frederick the Great, von Humboldt, Lord Kitchener."

"So what?" his father said, bewildered.

"You Victorian innocent!" All those historic gentlemen had, or are reputed to have had, one thing in common . . . along with Aubrey alias Al Marsh."

The Inspector was silent. Then he said feebly, "Julius Caesar? I didn't know it about *him*."

"We don't know it about most. An Englishman named Bryan Magee wrote a book a few years ago that he called *One in Twenty*. In it he makes the statement that the idea that deviates can necessarily be recognized as such is a myth. The overwhelming majority of them, of both sexes, Magee says—and he did a vast job of research in preparation for two TV documentaries he presented on the subject—are outwardly indistinguishable from normally sexed people. It can be anybody—the brawny fellow working beside you in the office, your bartender, the guy next door, the friend you play bridge with every Thursday night, the cop on your beat, or your mousy Cousin Horace. One in twenty, dad—that's the current statistic. And that figure may be far too conservative. Kinsey claimed it was one in ten. . . . Anyway, there it was, the clue in Marsh's living room. Staring me in the mandibles. Like the figleafless *David* he enshrined in his bedroom, eight feet tall and naked as the day Michelangelo lovingly made the original . . . I can't say I'm proud of my role in this caper, dad. And not only for that reason."

"You mean there was another clue, too?"

"Clue is hardly the word. It was—excuse the pun—almost a dead giveaway. Johnny *told* me who'd done it."

"Told you?" Inspector Queen scratched his mustache angrily. "Told you, Ellery? How? When?"

"As he was dying. When he came to from the beating, after Marsh left him for dead, Johnny realized he had only a short time to live. In those last few moments preceding death he experienced one of those infinities of clarity, when time stretches beyond its ordinary limits and the dying brain performs prodigies of thought in what we three-dimensional air-breathers call seconds.

"He knew there were no writing materials handy—you'll recall you and I searched when we got there and failed to find any. Yet he wanted desperately to let us know who had attacked him, and why. So he managed somehow to use the extension phone to the cottage."

Ellery frowned into the past. "Johnny knew my first question—anyone's first question under the circumstances—would be: who did it? But in that timeless flash of brilliance, as he was groping for the phone, he found himself in a fantastic situation."

"Fantastic situation?" The Inspector frowned into the present. "What do you mean?"

"What I mean is," Ellery said, "how could he tell me who had murdered him?"

"How could he tell you? What are you talking about, Ellery? All he had to do was say the killer's name."

"All right," Ellery said. "Say it."

"Al."

"Oh, but that could have been an uncompleted attempt to say 'Alice.' How would we have known it wasn't?"

"Oh," the Inspector said. "Well, then Marsh."

"Could have been the unfinished start of 'Marcia.' "

The old man began to look interested. "I see what you mean! . . . Then Marsh's christening name, Aubrey. You'd have understood that."

"Would I, dad? In light of Johnny's speech impediment? How could I ever have been sure he hadn't meant to say 'Audrey'?"

"Huh." The Inspector thought deeply. "Huh!" he said. "Funny problem, at that. . . . How about the word 'lawyer'? No possible mixup there. Marsh was the only lawyer Benedict could have meant."

"Johnny was probably thinking in terms of names only. But assuming he thought of 'lawyer,' see what a bind he found himself in. He was intending to marry Laura, a girl he loved; her name was in the will he'd given you to put in your pocket. If he said 'lawyer,' we might have mistaken the word for the name—'lawyer' for 'Laura'! Remember, he had great difficulty pronouncing the letter *r*. Between the impediment and his dying diction, it was too great a risk to take."

"Then the word 'attorney'!"

"Might have sounded like 'Tierney,' " Ellery said, "because of the same difficulty with his *r*'s." He shook his head. "An extraordinary situation that wouldn't occur once in a million cases. But it did in this one."

"Wait—a—minute," the Inspector articulated. "Hold your horses, Professor! There's one thing Benedict could have said that you wouldn't—you couldn't—have misunderstood. Same as if he'd put his finger on Marsh in front of witnesses! Marsh was the only *man* besides himself in the house—all the rest were women. Why didn't Benedict simply say the word 'man' and take the chance you'd understand he meant Marsh?"

"Just what I asked myself, dad. But he didn't, and naturally I wondered why. Of course, he might not have thought of it. But suppose he had? The possibility raised a fascinating line of speculation. If he thought of saying 'man' and rejected it in those endless few seconds, then—as in the case of the names—there must have been a basis for similar confusion—"

"But no name in the case sounded like 'man,' " the Inspector objected.

"Yes, but did we know all the names in the case? We did not. There was one conspicuous omission. We didn't know Laura's last name! That what suggested to me that Laura's surname might be M-a-n-n or might begin with M-a-n or M-a-double n—Manners, Mannheimer, something like that. It turned out to be Manzoni. That must have been, then, why Johnny didn't say it. He was afraid that, if he could get out only the first syllable before he died or became unconscious, we'd believe—when we discovered Laura's family name—that he'd been accusing her of killing him."

The old man was shaking his head. "I never heard anything like this in my whole life! But Ellery, you said Benedict did identify his killer to you. The old dying-message thing you're so crazy about."

"Could it be premature senility?" Ellery made a face. "At the time I didn't even realize it was a dying message! And then I dismissed it from my alleged mind. Dad, what was it Johnny said to me over the phone when I asked him who had attacked him?"

"He said some stupid thing like he was home, or something like that."

"It wasn't stupid, and he didn't say *he was* home. He uttered the one word, 'home.' In fact, he repeated it three times. I thought he meant he was calling from home, that is, from the main house, in his muddled dying condition answering a "who' question with a 'where' answer. I should have taken into account at least the possibility that when I asked 'who' he'd answered 'who.' "

"Who—'Home'? 'Home' isn't a who, Ellery. Unless it was somebody's name. But there wasn't anybody named—" The Inspector looked startled. "He didn't finish," he said slowly. "It was a longer word—*beginning* with 'home.' "

"Yes," Ellery said, muffled, out of a well of self-disgust. "If Johnny had finished the word, or I'd had the mother wit I was presumably born with—we'd have solved the mystery of this case actually before the victim drew his last breath."

"Then, Ellery, what Benedict meant to say was the word—"

"Homosexual."

⊘

SIGNET Thrillers by Mickey Spillane

☐	**THE BIG KILL**	(#AJ1441—$1.95)
☐	**BLOODY SUNRISE**	(#AJ1403—$1.95)
☐	**THE BODY LOVERS**	(#J9698—$1.95)
☐	**THE BY-PASS CONTROL**	(#E9226—$1.75)
☐	**THE DAY OF THE GUNS**	(#J9653—$1.95)
☐	**THE DEATH DEALERS**	(#J9650—$1.95)
☐	**THE DEEP**	(#AJ1402—$1.95)
☐	**THE DELTA FACTOR**	(#AJ1041—$1.95)
☐	**THE ERECTION SET**	(#E9944—$2.50)
☐	**THE GIRL HUNTERS**	(#J9558—$1.95)
☐	**I, THE JURY**	(#AE1396—$2.95)
☐	**KILLER MINE**	(#W8788—$1.50)
☐	**KISS ME DEADLY**	(#Q6492—95¢)
☐	**THE LAST COP OUT**	(#J9592—$1.95)
☐	**THE LONG WAIT**	(#J9651—$1.95)
☐	**ME, HOOD**	(#AJ1679—$1.95)
☐	**MY GUN IS QUICK**	(#J9791—$1.95)
☐	**ONE LONELY NIGHT**	(#J9697—$1.95)
☐	**THE SNAKE**	(#AJ1404—$1.95)
☐	**SURVIVAL . . . ZERO**	(#E9281—$1.75)
☐	**THE TOUGH GUYS**	(#E9225—$1.75)
☐	**THE TWISTED THING**	(#Y7309—$1.25)
☐	**VENGEANCE IS MINE**	(#J9649—$1.95)